The Metal of the Dead

Concha Espina in 1922.

The Metal of the Dead

Concha Espina

Translated by Anna-Marie Aldaz

Lewisburg
Bucknell University Press
London: Associated University Presses

Associated University Presses
2010 Eastpark Boulevard

Associated University Presses
16 Barter Street
London WC1A 2AH, England

Associated University Presses
P.O. Box 338, Port Credit
Mississauga, Ontario
Canada L5G 4L8

The paper used in this publication meets the requirements of the American National Standard for Permanence of Paper for Printed Library Materials Z39.48-1984.

Library of Congress Cataloging-in-Publication Data

Espina, Concha, 1869–1955.
    [Metal de los muertos. English]
    The metal of the dead / Concha Espina ; translated by Anna-Marie Aldaz.
       p. cm.
    Includes bibliographical references.
    ISBN 0-8387-5545-3 (alk. paper)
    I. Aldaz, Anna-Marie, 1944– II. Title.
PQ6609.S5 M413 2003
823'.64—dc21   2002014346

Contents

Translator's Preface

CONCHA ESPINA (1869–1955) WAS A PROLIFIC WRITER, AND SHE IS generally regarded as the first Spanish woman author to rely primarily on her publications as a source of income. Though she cultivated all literary genres, she is considered first and foremost a novelist. The majority of her novels, especially the early ones, reflect a deep emotional attachment to her birthplace, the port city of Santander, and the surrounding Cantabrian region in northern Spain.

After Concha Espina's marriage to Ramón de la Serna at the age of twenty-three, the couple moved to Valparaíso, Chile, where the first two of their five children, Ramón and Victor, were born. When they returned to Spain almost four years later, they settled in the house that Concha Espina's family owned in Mazcuerras, and it is in this small Cantabrian village that their son José and their daughter Josefina were born. Concha Espina uses Mazcuerras, which she calls Luzmela, as the setting of her first novel, *La niña de Luzmela* [The Girl from Luzmela, 1909], and the town changed its name to Luzmela in her honor.

A year after the birth of their son Luis in 1907, Concha Espina, who was growing increasingly unhappy in her marriage, arranged for a separation from her husband. From then on, she supported herself and her children mostly from her writings. In her excellent study of Concha Espina, one of the very few available in English, Mary Lee Bretz points out that the author was a true pioneer in this endeavor, because "Although Rosalía de Castro and Emilia Pardo Bazán had already broken many barriers, neither had attempted to earn a livelihood from writing."[1]

Concha Espina's works earned her popular success and also critical acclaim, as evidenced by the literary honors she received. The Real Academia Española de la Lengua [Spanish Royal Academy of Language] bestowed its prestigious Fastenrath Prize on one of her best novels, *La esfinge maragata* (1914) (*Mariflor*, 1924); for her play, *El jayón* [The Foundling, 1918], she received the Academy's Espinosa Cortina Prize; her collection of short stories and essays, *Tierras del aquilón* [Lands of the North Wind, 1924], was the winner of the Academy's Castillo de Chirel prize; and *Altar mayor* [High Altar, 1926] won the Cervantes National Prize for Literature, though recent critical opinion no longer holds that novel in the same high esteem. Concha Espina was also nominated twice for the Nobel Prize for Literature, the first time in 1923, a few years after *El metal de los muertos* (1920) was published, and the second time in 1932, when she would have needed only one more vote to win.

As Mary Lee Bretz remarks, *El metal de los muertos* "represents a significant contribution to the modern Spanish novel,"[2] and shortly after its publication, the book appeared in German, Russian, and Swedish, but not in English. Prior to the present translation, the only three of Concha Espina's novels available in English were *La esfinge maragata* (1914), translated as *Mariflor* (1924) by Frances Douglas, who was also the translator of *Dulce nombre* (1921), titled *Red Beacon* (1924), and Terrell Louise Tatum's translation of *Agua de nieve* (1911) as *The Woman and the Sea* (1934).

Widely regarded as one of Concha Espina's best novels, *The Metal of the Dead* is set apart from the author's other works by its pronounced populist sympathies and emphatic denunciations of injustices. Based on historical facts and on the author's own observations, it describes some of the events that led up to the 1917 strike organized by the miners of Río Tinto, Spain's oldest copper mine. As the author tells us in her essay "Autobiografía" [Autobiography], she spent several weeks in Nerva—the nearest town to the mine where she could find lodging—and even went down into the tunnels to gather firsthand information for her book, which she hoped would be, "una obra de justicia y de arte" [a work of justice and of art].[3]

The Metal of the Dead, which has the distinction of being one of Spain's earliest fictional work of social protest, is reminiscent of Emile Zola's well-known masterpiece *Germinal* (1885), in its critcism of the miners' labor conditions and in its detailed description of the events leading up to the strike. As Pablo Gil Casado points out in his comprehensive analysis of the social novel in Spain, despite occasional stylistic flaws, the book continues to be of interest today as a valuable testimonial.[4]

The mine is the novel's focal point, and Concha Espina draws upon a rich and highly specialized vocabulary to describe its geological structures and to explain the different mining operations. The narrative also pays much attention to the nearby Tinto River (at times referred to as the Saquia or the Odiel), pointing out that it gives its name to the mine, while in turn deriving its name "tinto" [dark] from the high copper content that blackens its water. Though there are numerous references to the history of the mine and its earliest excavations during Phoenician and Roman times, the book's focus is on the years 1916–17, when the mine was being exploited by the Río Tinto Company Ltd., a British company that had bought the mine, along with more than four thousand acres of surrounding land, from the Spanish Government in 1873.[5]

Aside from a few chapters that summarize past events, the incidents in The Metal of the Dead develop in chronological order. Interestingly, the approximately hundred pages that make up part 1 of the novel give an almost minute-by-minute account of the thoughts and actions of the six principal characters during the short time span of a day and a half, in late August of 1916; part 2 jumps ahead to June of 1917, and chronicles the events that lead up to the strike in August of the same year.

The novel's opening chapters take place in Cantabria, but the setting soon shifts to the Andalusian province of Huelva, the location of the Río Tinto mine. In her abundant and detailed landscape descriptions, Concha Espina retains many of the actual place names, although she fictionalizes the most significant ones. Thus, the name of the province's capital is changed from Huelva to Estuaria and the town of Río Tinto is given the symbolic name of Dite (one of the names for Pluto, god of death and the underground); the owners of the Río Tinto Company are called "nordetanos" [Northlanders], or inhabitants of "Nordetania" [Northland]; and Bella Vista, the exclusive residential area built for the families of Río Tinto's British manager and administrative staff, is altered slightly to the synonymous "Vista Hermosa."

Readers familiar with Samuel Butler's *Erewhon* (intended to be the reversed spelling of "nowhere") will notice that Rehtron, Concha Espina's name for the Río Tinto Company Limited, is "norther" spelled backward. In the case of the novel's British protagonists, a backward reading of their fictional surnames also reveals one of their essential personality traits: the ruthless general manager is called Martín Leurc (cruel); the fawning but hypocritical administrator in charge of labor relations is named Jacobo Pmip (pimp), and the engineer who sympathizes with the miners' plight is called Leonardo Erecnis (sincere).[6]

In their informative introduction to the most recent edition of *El metal de los muertos* (1996), Antonio Garnica Silva and Antonio Rioja Bolaños observe that Concha Espina also alters the names of those Spanish characters who are modeled after real-life figures, though she maintains a phonetic similarity between their true and fictional names. Thus, the novelistic counterpart of Eladio Fernández Egocheaga, the principal organizer of the miners' labor movement, is called Aurelio Echea; among the minor characters, the name of Cristóbal Roncero, the noble-spirited doctor who attends and supports the miners (and whom Concha Espina met in Nerva and accompanied on his rounds), is changed to Alejandro Romero; and Romero's helper, Félix Lunar appears as Félix Garcés.[7]

Among the protagonists who must be singled out in the novel's epic cast of characters are Aurora and Gabriel. These two young people from Cantabria fall in love but are separated when the rebellious and idealistic Gabriel antagonizes the representative of the powerful canning and salting factories. Barred from earning a living from fishing, Gabriel is forced to work as a miner, first in Cantabria and later in Huelva. Aurora's nightmarish descent into the mines to look for Gabriel—reminiscent of Orpheus's attempt to bring Eurydice back from hell—is described in minute and lyrical detail.

In most of Concha Espina's works, the principal protagonists are women and *The Metal of the Dead* is no exception. Although the novel includes important male figures, particularly those of Gabriel Suárez and Aurelio Echea, the author paints a careful portrait of three women who have rather different personalities. Aurora is a young, working-class woman with great inner fortitude and determination who fights valiantly against her adverse social conditions. In contrast, her rival, Casilda, a miner's daughter, is driven to criminal acts by her uncontrollable passion for Gabriel. The author has given her third heroine, Rosario, some autobiographical traits, depicting her as a modern, well-educated young woman of the middle class, and as a dedicated reporter for a socialist newspaper who exercises her journalistic calling with religious fervor. After Rosario and her brother José travel to Dite to write an investigative report on the miners, they both become ardent champions of the miners' cause.

The author also deplores man's avaricious exploitation of minerals and writes about the ravages caused by the excavations in animistic terms, comparing the hollowed mountain to a patient suffering from cancer and other ailments. The novel is particularly critical of the Rehtron Company, which it blames not only for destroying the environment, but also for doing little to diminish the danger the miners have to face and for failing to improve their squalid living conditions. At times the criticisms are editorial, and at other times the author uses Aurelio Echea as her mouthpiece, but in both cases the accusations are usually based on historical fact, as for instance when Echea mentions that the miners do not have access to electricity, even though it is available to the inhabitants of Vista Hermosa.[8]

Much emphasis is also placed on a further aggravating circumstance, namely that the company, which rules over the miners' bodies and souls like a feudal lord, is a foreign entity on Spanish soil. Yet even though the Rehtron Company is the novel's principal target, Concha Espina had the courage to also criticize both the Spanish government and the Catholic Church for siding with the company rather than with the miners. Consequently, when the novel first appeared in Spain, it was applauded by some, while others—including some of the author's closest friends—reacted with shock and displeasure.[9]

The Metal of the Dead has been faulted for not offering a more definite political doctrine and for ending somewhat abruptly and without a resolution. Undoubtedly, as the author recognized herself, Echea's Christian Socialism is vague and utopian: he envisages a society where human justice and equality reign supreme. In the end, the strike he organizes does succeed in disrupting the company's mining operations, but it also imposes immense hardship on the miners, without visibly improving their conditions. Yet any depiction of the strike of 1917 (like the preceding ones of 1888 and 1913) as anything more than another step in the struggle for social reform would have been a distortion of historical events.[10]

With the years, Concha Espina's political views became increasingly more conservative, and during the Spanish Civil War (1936–1939) she was placed under house arrest by the Republicans for overtly sympathizing with the Falangists. Her rightist leanings in later life may have played a part in the diminished interest in her work during the decades following her death. Recently, however, Concha Espina is again the subject of articles and dissertations, as scholars rediscover that her best works deserve study for their literary merits.

Notes

1. Mary Lee Bretz, *Concha Espina* (Boston: Twayne Publishers, 1980), 17.

2. Bretz, 71.

3. Concha Espina, "Autobiografía," in *Concha Espina. De su vida. De su obra literaria al través de la crítica universal.* (Madrid: Renacimiento, 1928), 16.

4. Pablo Gil Casado, *La novela social española, 1920–1971* (Barcelona: Seix Barral, 1973), 90.

5. Charles E. Harvey, *The Rio Tinto Company: An Economic History of a Leading International Mining Concern (1873–1954)* (Cornwall: Alison Hodge, 1981), 175.

6. Concha Espina's penchant for anagrams is evident in the pseudonym Ana Coe Schnip with which she signed her first published poem, "Azul."

7. Antonio Garnica Silva and Antonio Rioja Bolaños, "Presentación," in Concha Espina, *El metal de los muertos* (Huelva: Fundación Río Tinto y Universidad de Huelva, 1996), 20–26. In his admirable study of the writer's life and works, Gérard Lavergne mentions that when Eladio Fernández Egocheaga (in political exile in Mexico at the time) heard about Concha Espina's death, he sent his condolences in a telegram signed, "Aurelio Echea," in *Vida y obra de Concha Espina*, translated by Irene Gambra (Madrid: Fundación Universitaria Española, 1986), 360.

8. Leonard Unthank Salkield, *A Technical History of the Río Tinto Mines: Some Notes on Exploitation from pre-Phoenician times to the 1950s* (London: The Institution of Mining and Metallurgy, 1987), 18.

9. Carlos Fernández Cuenca, "El metal de los muertos fue la más difícil . . . de las novelas de Concha Espina." *Correo Literario* (15 July, 1952), 10.

10. Although Concha Espina could not know this at the time she was writing her novel, the strike of 1917 turned out to be a prelude to the more prolonged one of 1920. Harvey, 177.

Acknowledgments

I WOULD LIKE TO EXPRESS MY GRATITUDE AND APPRECIATION TO Don Alfonso de la Serna for sending me a picture of Concha Espina, his grandmother, and for his kind words of encouragement. I am indebted to the Fundación Río Tinto for granting me permission to use photographs from their archives, and to my colleague Pete Self, who processed the pictures. My most sincere thanks to Louella Holter for her expert editorial assistance. Finally, I would like to thank Northern Arizona University for an Organized Research grant in support of the present translation.

The Metal of the Dead

Part I

1

The Red Path

Voices from the Sea

Darkness was setting in and the young man began to walk faster, hoping to reach his destination before nightfall. A sickly old dog followed him, panting. The air was hot; the Northeast, slumbering under the wings of twilight, released the August heat. The highway climbed inland along the valley, fleeing from the sea toward the mountains. Like a sigh piercing the air, the eternal murmur of the waves pounding the shores impetuously was still afloat over the landscape. That sound, which grew louder with distance, touched the very core of the traveler's heart. He stopped and heaved a sigh as well and, turning back, he stared mournfully at the shoreline whose boundaries were blurred mysteriously by the mantle of mist that enveloped the sea.

The dying light encircled him and revealed the characteristic traits of a sailor: an above-average height, broad chest, tanned complexion, an inquisitive and firm gaze, callous hands, and the deep and thoughtful expression of someone who has explored the depths of the abyss. He was probably around thirty years old; his intelligent, masculine face betrayed a certain bitterness, and a slight squint gave his dark, infatuated eyes a sad and stubborn look. His appearance—bareheaded, disheveled, dressed in a blue cotton suit and soft hemp-soled sandals—confirmed that he was a humble but noble sailor from northern Spain.

As he gazed intently at the distant Cantabrian landscape, he thought he could see some protruding points that moved swiftly like wings. These gliding white drops were probably sails puffed up by the wind, but they could be mistaken for pale hands waving, "Goodbye . . . goodbye!"

The red orb, expiring in the blood cast by its own light, was also bidding farewell as it tinged the entire western landscape with its crimson hue, while on the eastern side, land and sea were falling asleep in the darkness of the night.

MOUNTAIN ROADS

The traveler tore himself away from his intense contemplation with a gesture that was at once haughty, abrupt, and sorrowful. He wiped away some tears with the back of his hand and mumbled a few painful and bitter words, while his dog, howling plaintively, struggled to retrace his steps, as if impelled by exhaustion or longing to return to the abandoned home near the sea. But submissive and faithful, the dog continued to climb, his tongue lolling. His master did not take his eyes off the road, which on the other side of the highway turned into a narrow, red path leading to the mountain pockmarked by mining operations.

The path's blood-red color deepened, and the shadow of the mountain grew darker in the solemn loneliness of the surroundings and in the silence of the hour. Suddenly, in a curve, other footsteps were about to cross with those of the sailor. A man wearing a corduroy suit and a cap came walking along the path. He studied the young man carefully, and when he was standing practically next to him, he asked:

"Do you work at the mine?"

"No, but I want to sign up."

"You've come from the harbor, right?"

"Yes."

"Well, I've been authorized by the foreman to sign you up and I can do it right here. What's your name?"

"Charol."

"That's not a name," mumbled the list keeper, taking a notebook from his pocket.

"Oh, yes it is!" replied the young man, embarrassed. "My other name is Gabriel Suárez."

"Well, you're on the list now. Show up tomorrow at eight o'clock at the entrance to El Bosque so you can start working in the mine with your companions. Is that clear?"

"Yes, it is."

"Goodbye."

The list keeper set off without another word, leaving the young man lost in thought. He turned around and took another look at the seashore, while his dog stretched his neck in a raspy yawn. A feeling of anxiety overcame Charol as he considered his new life. There, at the edge of the red boundary marker overgrown with mountain greenery, he was leaving behing an occupation that since his earliest days had enveloped him in briny aromas, daring impulses, wild independence. Now he was forced to give up even his capricious and rebellious nickname, obligated by the discipline of an unknown captivity that seemed dreadful and menacing ... This was what fate had decreed.

He resigned himself with inconsolable sadness.

Pale and remote, the moon began to rise with a gentle invitation to silence; in the wide-open spaces of the landscape, the whiteness of the night weighed softly on the sea.

2

Two Lives

SHE AWAKENS WITH A SIGH BUT HER SPIRIT REMAINS LULLED BY faraway childhood memories that make her forget her present misfortunes. Suddenly Aurora opens her delicate eyelids and sits up anxiously; she feels that sleep had pierced her dark mood, but now she is being tossed back into reality again. Propped up against the pillow, she shakes off her sleepy thoughts, flooding her consciousness with a shower of memories. All the past years parade vividly before her up to the present moment of her dreaded awakening.

She sees herself as a little girl, without a father, brought up amidst wasteful extravagance, under lowly social conditions. Her cold and violent home was full of cheap and scandalous luxury, laced with a sordid intimacy. She grew up without the solace of tender care and played by herself because, in school and in the street, the other children of her age turned away from her; she was constantly troubled by their harsh looks and disdainful gestures.

One day, revelations and discoveries lifted the veil of ignorance slightly and she learned that her mother was an immoral woman of easy virtue. Little by little, Aurora became melancholy and moody, and even before having outgrown her childhood days, she began to feel ashamed of eating white bread and sleeping in a fluffy bed. At the same time, she worried about not being able to elude the towering shadow of her inevitable destiny.

Whether out of charity or calculation, some relatives took her to America and the little girl's crystal-clear eyes shone with delight at seeing the unfurling of the sea by whose shores she had been born. She loved the sea with such fervent devotion that, according to some people, her blue eyes had turned to green from looking at the water so much.

In the New World, where Aurora landed like a little migratory bird, she enjoyed some untroubled years and became more light-hearted and trusting. She believed that fate had taken a different direction, just as the birds, flowers, and stars seemed different to her in America. The woman who had brought her over was not a model of scrupulousness, but in the end she was captivated by the girl's virtuous nobility, which flourished amidst corrupt surroundings like a plant surviving without sunlight. And the girl maintained her unspoiled and sunny disposition, while her contact with different people and places, as well as her stormy childhood, gave her a certain bold brawniness by the time she reached the bloom of her eighteenth birthday.

Her beauty attracted much envy, and many temptations presented themselves in the guise of more or less honest offers. But Aurora was waiting for a signal from her heart and she calmly ignored all amorous entreaties.

Her guardians began to grow impatient. It was all good and fine for the young girl to be high minded and proper, but not to the point of refusing a marriage that could have benefited them. It began to dawn on them that they were not going to reap any reward for having sheltered the abandoned girl and brought her up with fondness and dedication to be a lady.

In the midst of these deliberations, they were surprised to receive a letter from Aurora's mother, who wanted her daughter to come back to her home by the northern coast. The request was repeated so authoritatively that Aurora agreed with a heavy heart to return to Traspeña and leave behind her hospitable asylum, where she had hoped to redeem herself from her wretched fate.

A Meeting

The homecoming was the darkest moment in Aurora's life. She returned in the full splendor of her charms, heaped with useless trifles, exotic skills, and strange customs that were a mixture of modern tastes and the excesses of an improvised gentility. Thus, Aurora's natural elegance was hidden under a

layer of artificial varnish, and her loveliness was like a customs seal on some merchandise destined for the brothel. It
was rumored that she had been exploited by her cunning relatives in America and that her mother planned on continuing
that shameful commerce for her own benefit.

A crass curiosity gave the newcomer notoriety in the neighborhood, and she was treated with the most insolent effron-
tery. Her mother, who should have been protecting her, did
not beat around the bush and told her bluntly: use your beauty
to earn a living before your youth fades all too swiftly. This is
when the doomed girl began to fight a cruel battle in which
she only followed the dictates of her heart. Ill and impover-
ished, her mother despaired over not being able to earn
money and over Aurora's rebelliousness. Summoning all her
perverted skills, she tried to break Aurora's haughty spirit by
forcing her to do the most menial tasks.

But the girl suffered valiantly, bearing the yoke of slavery
with proud tenacity. She, who had been brought up like a
young lady and who was accustomed to the corresponding
amenities and refinements, had to climb the mountains to
gather gorse and peat or take a heavy basket of corn to the
water mill. She earned her wages by working as a washer
woman by the river and by doing farm work in the grain fields.
When there were no other chores left to be done, she carried
a hamper with fish on her head, trying to keep up with the fast
pace of the other women sardine vendors along the path.
Bruised and battered, she felt the briny sea water flowing
down her lovely, soft skin to mingle with the bitterness of her
sweat and tears.

The first day she went to the docks to sell fish, a sailor
helped her adjust the overflowing tray on her head. When she
rose up again from kneeling on the floor, she found herself
face-to-face with Charol. They exchanged a few insignificant
and trivial words, but at the same time they gazed deeply into
each other's eyes. From that moment on they were friends.

Aurora, who only admitted the sufferings of her lonely cal-
vary to herself, felt she had met someone special in the sailor,
and he believed that he recognized in her the embodiment of
an image glimpsed in a confused dream a long time ago. They
looked for each other with eagerness and uncertainty until
they became convinced that they had known each other in

earlier lives, maybe on a star that no longer existed and whose empty shell still whirled around in a vacuum. And together they saw life as something brittle and strong, beautiful and sad.

Their two stories had indelible similarities: they were both being pulled into the same fatal orbit; the stigma of their family background had cast an insurmountable shadow on their childhood and continued to cloak them in shame and neglect. To make matters worse, their intelligence and emotions were imbued with a strong spirituality, flashes of boldness, and moments of restless impulses. Both had acquired scattered notions of high-minded culture, random drops of light that illuminated their ignorance and kindled their spirits, thirsting for ideals.

They had inklings of a doctrine they believed to be new, a humanitarian and regenerative creed to which they paid tribute in their innocent hearts, without realizing that, amidst the millennial rocks of heresy, these pure waters of eternal spring flowed directly from Jesus' generous and divine heart to today's men of good will. Touched by the violent spark of sublime love, they looked for loftiness and pride amidst the awful realities so they could fulfill their hope for a superior concept of life.

During their first meetings, they confided their secrets to each other and they both had a blind faith in each other's sad voice as they told their tale of sorrows. Charol never doubted the courageous young girl's purity and her iron will to resist the entanglement of vice. She listened with gentle pity to the story of his life, which was rough and wretched in the early years until a poor, sad, and kindly woman took him in. After her death, he was left alone again by the sea, with a strong yearning for tenderness, and alienated from his companions because of his radically different views.

As the young man told his new friend about his past, he delighted in giving many details when describing the happy moments, especially those that opened up the world for him. He had basked in the love of that charitable woman who cared for him as she would have for the son she lost and who softened his hard life with incredible sweetness. Out of gratitude for her saintly mercy, he began studying the basics of seafaring and crossed the sea in a transatlantic ship. He reached new lands, settled by their enticing shores, and learned about life and desire.

In the year Charol began his wanderings, Aurora was being born to a woman who was just as despicable as his mother, and it was not much later that as a small infant playing on the beaches of Cantabria she was so beguiled by the turbulence of the waves that her eyes turned green like the sea. Then, just as the sailor was on his way back to Traspeña, Aurora immigrated to America. Perhaps their ships exchanged greetings silently as they sailed past each other out on the open sea, headed in opposite directions and separating two lives that were destined to be reunited.

When Charol returned to the home near the shore that had sheltered him, he found it deserted. His benefactress had died and, as a final proof of her devotion, she left him her humble possessions: some modest household goods, a few coins she had saved, and a wretched and churlish dog who was the epitome of loyalty. This dog, crouched near the entrance, moaning and starving, ended up being his only companion.

Charol's spirits had sunk and he had lost his drive to tackle challenging tasks. He bought a fishing boat, La Josefita, and hired some of his companions who were even poorer than he was. As a fervent believer in the laws of brotherhood, he drew up a contract that was unheard of in the coasting-trade: every haul was to be distributed equally among the crew members of La Josefita and Charol would forfeit the owner's allotted share, which was usually more than half the catch. This noble gesture earned the sailor great popularity among the hirelings and a definite resentment among the employers. Among the latter, the owners of the steamboats showed the greatest hostility because they interpreted his unusual behavior as insolence.

The two companies that owned the steamboats, one a cannery, the other a salting factory, were overseen by the same inspector of weights and measures, a man who made up in boisterousness what he lacked in efficiency. Between them, these companies monopolized the fishing industry that had been established near the docks of the modest village of Traspeña by a wealthy philanthropist. Feeling sorry for the sailors, the generous founder had wanted to improve the sailors' miserable wages by guaranteeing them a sale after every haul.

But in the hands of unscrupulous administrators, the great man's noble intention ended up harming those it was designed to benefit.

The administrators succeeded in convincing the trusting absentee owner to buy steamboats, and then they hired sailors at measly wages to operate them. No other vessel could compete with these new boats, which were speedier and yielded more than the valorous efforts of sailboats and rowboats. The steamboats guaranteed the delivery of fresh seafood, and the companies, under the pretense of selflessness, made an exorbitant profit and exerted a shameless domination over the hapless trade unions.

Delirium

When Charol was still the owner of his boat and equipment, he wanted to run his small enterprise like a true brotherhood. The administrators in the canneries considered him a fool and a madman and predicted his imminent ruin. Their opinion was prophetic. Using contemptible excuses, the buyers paid the lowest possible price for *La Josefita's* catch, and the port official, a navy sergeant who always sided with the most powerful in any litigation, started to plague the boat with fines. The winter storms, which forced the boats to remain anchored at the docks, further contributed to the impoverishment of the idealistic employer.

This was around the time that Charol and Aurora began confiding in each other. The young girl had boldly shaken off the label of corrupt with which she had been branded upon her arrival back home. Her heroic attitude shielded her from sin and evil with such honorable resolution that it silenced the cruelest murmurs and forced even her shameless mother to give up her odious schemes. Charol's harsh and self-sacrificing life encouraged Aurora to follow virtue's austere path. In the rough and terrible hours of work, she felt realized as a woman and, emboldened by her victory, she savored the taste of battle that reminded her of other worthy causes she had defended in the past.

Looking back at that time, she regretted not having taken better advantage of it. The finery, trinkets, and the elegant way of life had vanished abruptly, and Aurora was forced to suppress her genteel and refined tendencies with an iron will. But even when she had to earn a living by carrying fish to the market, the one reminder of her ladylike days was her undiminished beauty, which grew more spiritual and reserved every day. Tall and willowy, with warm, pale-green eyes, abundant blond curls, sunburnt cheeks, and a soft smile on her gentle lips, she had a wistful and suggestive charm that was full of mysterious allure.

Charol looked at her in awe, amazed by her strength, and anxious to foster her hopeful illusions with every passing day. Their meeting seemed providential to them, and, in their innocence, they made an intimate and dangerous pact in which they promised to help each other by setting an example, bestowing tenderness, and having a deep and radiant faith in something uncertain and nebulous.

In the village these two courageous dreamers were seen as delirious creatures, victims of an unknown and harmful ambition, but their close friendship did not raise any suspicions. It was believed that they were steeped in bizarre ideas and estranged from life by an unusual illusion that no one quite understood. Meanwhile, the two poor idealists, valiant knights of spiritual adventures, swirled and tumbled amidst the dust of humanity, enveloped in the fantastic delirium of Love . . .

For a few months, the lovers lived absorbed in their secret adventure, tipsy with their daring. For him, this unexpected glory was a bewitching spell; she saw her fall as irrefutable proof of her fate, but she looked at herself without blushing and without remorse, only with a humble sadness, tinged with pride at being loved by a good man.

Charol wanted to get married, but Aurora did not.

"What for?" she asked.

"So I can give you a name that I have made honorable," objected the sailor. "My behavior has whitewashed the name my mother gave me. We are the products of our deeds."

"Well, that's good enough for us," the young girl asserted so seriously and firmly that they did not talk about the matter again.

SLAVES OF THE SEA

Charol had been forced to sell his boat, and it was as one of its crew members that he braved the winter rains toward the end of the sea bream fishing season. One stormy February evening, *La Josefita* went out to sea to fish for sturgeon, around forty miles from Traspeña. The cold northerly wind was blowing harshly and the sea was rough. After nine hours of hauling, the fishermen released a long fishing line and retrieved the previous one that had only a modest catch because the fish were not biting in these freezing temperatures.

The return trip to shore was extremely difficult. The wind, more violent than ever, shredded the clouds, and sleet battered the exhausted crew. The main mast had to be lowered because the boat could not sustain it; after the smaller bowsprit mast was hoisted, it too had to be replaced by the smallest sail raised in times of a squall. But even that tiny piece of cloth, which fluttered anxiously like a soul's last prayers, was too much for the foundering boat.

The ten crewmen, pelted by the fury of hail and hurricane winds, grabbed the oars. In this maneuver, the skipper slipped, and, still holding on to the sailcloth, he inadvertently dropped the main rudder. A young sailor, not much older than a child, jumped up from the bow, trying to catch the rudder so he could keep the boat wind-aft. Flushed from his anxious exertion, he was able to steer the rudder for a moment, but suddenly he released it with an anguished cry as he was tossed overboard by a rough and tempestuous blast. When after wrestling furiously with the waves they managed to fish him out, both his arms were broken.

Wrapped in wet clothes, the hero rested on the deck, while his companions fought bravely to save their sad lives. Black from the cold, drenched in water, their hands callused from the oars, they rowed desperately. Rising up like a sign of hope, the coast came into view on the horizon, and the slaves of the sea intensified their effort. The veins in their chests and hands throbbed with ambitions, and human desires roared rebelliously in their entrails.

At the end of a frightful journey, *La Josefita* reached the port and while the wounded man was taken to the hospital, Charol went to sell the fish they had caught after battling for twenty hours, always within reach of death's pale mantle. All the drama of a fisherman's life was reflected in the depths of his dark eyes. Bareheaded, humbled by exhaustion and discouragement, he stood in front of the company representative, who sneered at him disdainfully and said:

"So you've brought three bushels? Well, I'll pay you five pe-setas for each."

Unable to compete with the powerful canneries, most buy-ers stayed away from the docks, which meant that Charol had no hope of getting a better price in a bidding. Inevitably forced to accept the offer, he bravely refrained from protesting against its unfairness.

"That's fifteen pesetas!" he mumbled plaintively. "Half of that goes to the owner and there are nine men. We'll get less than one peseta each."

"That's your problem."

"No, sir! It's too little. We'll wait for the weather to clear and we'll sell them in Villanoble."

"You're not allowed to keep fish aboard for more than twenty-four hours. If you can't leave before then and try to sell it to me again, I'll give you fifteen cents."

This threat cut the air like a razor's edge, and suddenly the sailor jumped on top of him, slapping and insulting him:

"Thief!"

The outspoken youth ended up in jail. Every day during the two months that her grim and bitter friend languished behind a window with affronting bars, Aurora visited him, consoling him during their exchange of tender and faithful words. She was always accompanied by Bolina, Charol's decrepit dog, whose cloudy eyes seemed tired from crying, and who moved with increasing difficulty and whimpered more. At every visit, Aurora brought the sailor a simple cold snack to make his prison fare more palatable. There was always a morsel left for the dog, crouched near the bars, who did not expect anything more than a caress.

Dawn

By the time the prison gates opened for Charol, the doors of his house had been boarded up and his possessions confis-cated by the authorities. The fishermen, afraid of the boss's insatiable thirst for vengeance, invented excuses for not let-ting Charol join their crew. Thus, the sailor had to live as he had as a child, hiding in nooks and crannies along the shore. Though he hated to be too far from Aurora, he was reluctant to drag her along with him as long as he had no peace of mind and was aimlessly adrift to God knows where.

Now that Charol was hunted and persecuted, Aurora loved him more than ever. She followed him into the murky caves, cheering him with sunny words in his harshest and most bitter hours, and her generous love rekindled the young man's spirit. He succeeded in having someone recommend him to an engineer at a nearby mine, and one afternoon he fled from the coast, hoping the land would offer him the help the sea had denied him.

Aurora was to wait under a sheltering roof for the happy moment when the two of them could be reunited again. But very soon she received a troubling letter from her friend. Accused of being a malicious anarchist, he had been given a week's notice. He didn't know where to go; maybe he would sign up on a cargo boat leaving from Torremar and in need of additional crewmen. He closed those sad and confused lines affectionately with, "Never lose your faith in me."

The letter reached Aurora at nightfall and she decided that she would look for her friend the very next day. She had to tell him a sweet and tremulous secret that might change his decision to embark on that uncertain and aimless voyage.

"I'll start out bright and early," thought the girl. "By noon I'll be back and no one will have even noticed my absence." She sighed, longing for the moment when she could lift the sacred burden from her heart.

This morning, as she awakes and opens her eyes in the dark, she emerges abruptly from the fog of her dreams and remembers clearly her sadness and suffering. And yet despite destiny's treacheries, her veins throb strongly with the joy of life. Merciful hope illuminates Aurora's terrible memories burning in the depths of her sea-green eyes, and she is able to dispel the harmful ghosts with a smile. Light-footed, she walks over to the window through which a sliver of light enters. She opens the shutters and stands there for a minute in a daze, hiding her bulging waistline with a bashful gesture, while the sun sinks a dagger into her naked, sunburnt flesh.

3

Rocks and Flames

GRAZED BY A SECRET

SHE SETS OUT, AVERTING HER EYES FROM THE ROAD, ACCOMPANIED by the sea breeze, the aroma of hot fruit, and the gentle rustling of the leaves. It seems to her that the world's soul beats in her heart and that her footsteps echo in the sands of time. From the depths of the cornfields, she can see the solitary and austere mountain, rising above the shore, undulating like a wave and wounded by red tunnels that have drained all blood from its heart.

The enamored young girl is headed in the direction of that mountain, and her eyes, filled with the fields' luminosity, are able to discern the poetry in the flowers and shrubs. She is careful not to disturb the dark line of ants, which like a quivering thread leads from the roadside ferns to the adventures of the path.

The morning air is hot. On one side of the road, far from the shade of the poplars, a crimson footpath winds along the side of the fields and climbs up to the mountain, whose scraped face, under the sky's blue canopy, is as red as flesh being tortured by terrible, bloodstained hands. Looking at this new route, Aurora feels pangs of anxiety. Her deep, green eyes, which see and absorb everything, search the horizon longingly for the seashore and finally settle humbly on the unknown path.

A chirping lark passes by on its skyward flight; between two fragrant bushes, a pale spider stretches her web on top of the grass. The young girl admires the gossamer thread with which the weaver spins her nest, and she avoids stepping on the yellow tendrils that the penny-royals extend along the plowed ground.

The deafening roar of the excavations reaches her from the mine; though shaded by the mountain peak, the air becomes inflamed and the footpath twists in its red solitude. Growing increasingly calmer and more resolute, the young girl from the coast advances, feeling in her heart the light graze of wings and guarding the anxious murmurs of a secret in her conscience.

THE BLOOD OF THE MINE

At the edge of a precipice, the footpath widens considerably and is invaded by the sounds of manufacturing as it winds around the mountain where the industrial buildings—sheds for mining tools, sentry boxes, mining products, and railroad tracks—are located. Aurora crosses the platform amidst a group of girls who are arriving at the workshops and along with them she enters a noisy, zinc-plated shed with a protruding roof and an interior flight of stairs leading down to the bottom of the fissure.

The shed houses the buddle—a whirling apparatus used for washing the crushed ore—which turns and turns, collides, roars, and clamors ceaselessly. Its iron jaws devour the calamine and spit it out into monstrous strainers, which in turn pass it through a finer sieve. From there it flows into turbulent channels and finally into a quivering mold for casting.

The continuous moving about of the sieves, the constant rotation of the tremel that evens out the material, the vibrations of the tables as they turn, the crackle of the springs and axles, and the motion of the drums and metal plates produce an overwhelming effect. The rhythm, gestures, and curves of metal straps and rollers, cables and torrent flumes, together with the air, dust, water, and rocks, create a delirious sound of power and pride, the tremendous harmony of a torrential flow.

On the second floor, young women are lined up along both sides of the endless ribbon of wet and tremulous calamine, and they purify the ore as it runs between their skillful fingers. Everything corrodes and hums around the docile figures of these workers, who smile, steeped in the blood of the mine and caught in industry's haughty grip.

Aurora descends the steps of the building, pushed by the racket and commotion, but she is unsure about what to do when she reaches a platform as deep and as hot as the one above. She is reluctant to ask for Charol, and, hoping to find him on her own, she approaches the furnaces that are lined up in a row. Tall and mute, the vaulted furnaces burn with closed mouths, without revealing a spark or flame. In contrast, trakes and pokers are used to help the calcination process and to push the ore along the bottom of the reverberatory furnaces. At every opening, a worker prods the burning belly and pokes around in the red-hot coal to extract the purified earth. The stirring with an incandescent pole releases a river of embers, and a pitchfork is used to remove the gleaming dross from it.

The skin of these workers who are glued to the furnaces is aflame; they breathe with difficulty and have a sickly look. Seeing them, Aurora is worried that the man she is searching for will look the same. In an atmosphere filled with dust and acidity and against the light of their volcanic task, the young men painfully straighten out their torsos and flash a malicious smile.

Aurora continues to make her way amidst the nude torsos of the workmen, who pause in their task to say something flattering to her. But impatient and confused, she decides to leave this terrible area of calcination and take the road back up along the shore, past the place where the metal is being washed, to reach the bulwark of the mountain. Negotiating the uneven terrain, the piles of material, and the rails of a small railroad system, she walks along, again deafened by the machinery's horrendous noise. The cold trembling of the Linkenbach tables, the eternal lament of the red waters, the diabolic tumble of the yellow rocks and of the earth leaden with zinc penetrate her flesh. Covered by dust and smoke, she is out of breath from the trek and the heat.

When she arrives upstairs, she is caught up once more in the feverish activities, and she suddenly finds herself in a big, open shed where the women workers beat the excavated rocks with hammers to remove the gangue. Persecuted and tormented by the hammering as if she were receiving the blows herself, Aurora walks from one end of the premises to the other without seeing a single familiar face. She is tormented by the exposure to the noisy, hot hustle and bustle, and her affliction oppresses her like a nightmare.

THE TUNNEL

Aurora is about to leave the workshop, uncertain where to go, when she hears someone ask:

"Listen, who are you looking for?"

She stops in surprise and does not know what to answer. "I'm looking for a miner," she finally tells the cheerful and rustic young girl who is observing her curiously.

"What's his name?"

"Charol."

"I don't know him. Is he your husband?"

"Yes . . ."

"Where does he work?"

"I don't know."

"That's going to make it difficult to find him. The keeper of the list could give you some information."

"I'm a stranger around here and I'm afraid to ask."

Aurora's voice sounds as helpless as that of a child, and the other girl counsels her with sudden kindness:

"Go up a little farther, following the railroad tracks. When you reach a sign that says 'Lamp-shop,' ask for your man there and maybe they can help you."

Aurora thanks her for the advice and heads for the mountaintop, feeling more hopeful. In the distance, she can see the sign, close to the mine's entrance. When she arrives there, she enters the barrack to ask her question. An old man answers her:

"My son is the one in charge of the lamps and he isn't here right now."

"Does he know the men who are down there?" asks the girl, glancing fearfully at the dark entrance.

"Sure. Each man who receives a lamp from him has to give his name and number."

"Will he be back soon?"

"Maybe."

"I can't wait for him."

This sentence is filled with inconsolable grief. The old man looks into the young girl's pure eyes and sees them flutter with tremors from her heart. Talking to her a little longer, he finds out that Charol is Gabriel Suárez, the worker who is accused of being an anarchist, and he tells her that Gabriel works on the bottom floor of the mine.

"I'm going to look for him," declares Aurora firmly.

"You need permission and an oil lamp."

"Where can I get that?"

"Well, look," the old man tells her, touched by her sweet and serious worry. "Just now the foreman is over there with a visitor. Do you see the fellow in the corduroy suit?"

"Yes, sir."

"The one walking behind him with the lamps is my son. If you can catch up with them and if they let you go down, you're in luck."

The girl does not hesitate a minute. Without losing sight of the group, she hurries along the uneven steps of the ridge leading up to the tunnel. There is an eruption of abundant bloom that bursts forth from every mountain fold and each gap in the rocks: mallow, elder, chamomile, plantain, violets mingle their fragrance with the lush vegetation. The earth's blood flows with a miraculous green vigor that pushes upward to the top, rising up into the blue sky.

4

The Ravished Earth

Looking into the Abyss

Aurora finds herself bathed by a wave of healthy freshness, enveloped in a peaceful blanket of silence, protected by a soothing solitude. As she walks along the soft and dark ground covered by rails, she can see the fading of some flickering lights. Trying to catch up with them, she lifts her lamp, instinctively hoping it would illuminate the horizon. But the lamp only casts a glimmering halo that reveals parts of the reinforced walls, the propped-up roof, and an oozing humidity that pours out of all the corners with the gentle sound of tears.

The young girl is filled with subliminal joy by these fresh and profound sounds of quiet weeping that seem to stream like fertile irrigation from the depths of an overflowing heart. Suddenly the sound of a sharp whistle reaches her from the gallery, and a noise that grows louder and louder reverberates and shakes the ground, causing the flapping of dark wings in the air. Frightened, Aurora throws herself to one side and the cowardly candlewick flutters in the lamp as a small train speeds by, leaving behind a burst of smoke and muffled tremors. But now she can no longer see the lights that preceded her. Again she hears the crying of the cold rock and the harmonious enchantment created by the awakening of previously silent voices.

She stops at a tunnel gate where the turntable for the railroad controls are located and from where the train tracks branch out. Uncertain about which direction to take, she turns toward the right, trusting in fate, but she confuses her own footsteps with those of the visitors she had hoped to overtake. The terrain dips sharply and the crossway, which is far nar-

rower than the gallery, resounds and resonates, as if filled
with the rhythm of loud breathing.

The violent descent that plunges her deeper into the frightening labyrinth becomes broken up into steep steps. As Aurora carefully places her foot within the gaunt circle of light,
she leans down over the abrupt decline and takes a fearful
look into what seems to her the abyss of life.

The roots of the mountains perspire, and there are sounds
of the earth's ceaseless shudder, the profound heartbeat of the
seeds, and the rock's painful labor: a legion of souls mumbling
revelations about the eternal miracle of creation. The young
girl advances, listening to nature's efforts to speak, hearing in
amazement mute creatures suddenly raise their voices, and
she forgets in a bright daydream that she had been lost in the
confusion of nebulous darkness. All she can feel with unusual
delight is the mystery that lies beneath the ground, and she
yields to the strong life force, paying close attention to the incomprehensible dialogues and the hallucinatory visions.

She brushes up against the slope of a lode that protrudes
like a huge scar, wrapped in soft clay and buried in the rocky
arms of the gallery's wall. A forest of props supports the weak
layers of terrain. Tiny pieces of earth, like sweat beads or
crystal grains, keep falling through the large splits of wood.

Wide openings and hollow areas, bends and crossroads sub-
divide the enormous lode into clusters. Noticing some murky
shapes in the far distance of one of the numerous bends, Aurora is prompted to lift her lamp again. The tenuous light of
the raised lamp does not fall on the twisted brass of the props
any more, but loses itself in a dark tower of silence. Below, a
valley of shadows opens up at the feet of the young girl, who
is bewildered by the frightful surprise of finding herself at the
edge of a precipice. Suddenly, she sees some candlelights like
hers emerge from the darkness. These lamps look like the
ones that preceded her in the first tunnel and they flicker er-
ratically just like the flames on tombs or at the bottom of slimy
pools. Undecided about whether to proceed or to turn back,
she risks a few more hesitant steps forward, then stops, surprised to see other lights from deep within that are almost
swallowed up by the cavern.

A burst of sounds rises up from the dark depths: human
voices, the creaking of props, clanking of tools, sliding of ava-

lanches—all the nervous racket of activity, sounding like the
mine's laughter or delirium.

THE TORCH

Suddenly, on top of the distant mountain peak, a shining
beacon is lit, which illuminates a monstrous cave: it is the hollow made by the excavations in the side of the mountain. The
zones that are left behind are sterile, stripped of the trunks
that form the supporting columns in the lode, and the earth's
bones are exposed, twisted in absurd contortions and tormented by painful fragmentation. Its flesh surgically removed,
the mountain supports its skeleton with dolomite braces and
fills the void with reefs, palaces, altars, and tombs. It raises
monuments, chisels balconies, traces roads, and decorates its
heights with surprisingly abundant vegetation.

In this dizzying factory full of dens and dungeons, each pro-
trusion threatens to tumble, each profile opens up, sharpens,
and shines with beautiful iridescence and cries with eternal
tears. Nothing can stop the growth of the splendidly fragile
arches and porticos, and in their incredible audacity they dare
reach the very cupola of the peak, even though the tremors in
the sand and gravel put them at risk of tumbling.

Halfway up this incredible cave, a strange console juts out,
and Aurora opens her eyes in amazement to see the light of
the supreme orb scintillate like a hanging lamp, endowing the
surroundings with fantastic splendor. From up above comes
the sound of some loud words that reach her with varying
clarity. They echo in the air three times like the cries of the
goshawks when they migrate on moonlit nights, piercing the
clouds and filling the valley with three rounds of their song.
The voices belong to a miner who scolds Aurora while his
lamp illuminates the lacerated mountain.

"Who are you looking for? Get out of there! Women are not
allowed down into the mines!"

At first she does not understand, but then she sees the visitors for whose benefit the mine is being illuminated in all of its
terrible magnificence, and in the pit to the left she catches a
glimpse of miners with their spades attacking the metal merci-
lessly. Her impulse is to flee but her lamp is losing color, turn-

ing from blue to a tragically pale yellow. Stirred by a dark breath, the colorless plants tremble, and a pearly drop of cold water hangs from the tip of every shoot. A pale rainbow touches the cavernous profiles and dissolves gradually . . . The cavity in the mountain darkens again except for scattered red-hot embers that undulate above the excavation's roar.

THE BLIND PATH

Aurora turns back, leaning for support on the granite wall, and her sea-green eyes remember the terrible vision of the ravished earth and the naked mine. She treads bravely on the dusty and crumbling soil, intending not to return to the top by climbing back up the steep, eroded path that brought her down here, but rather to continue downward to the source of the fire that she saw flickering in the deep cave: she wants to descend to the earth's entrails to search for the companion of her life.

She climbs down the first steps she can find in the darkness, and once more she is beneath a ceiling supported by numerous props amidst which rocks emerge creaking, complaining, and threatening. Laments rise up from the soil mistreated by mineral sparks that are as hard as brilliant particles. Gripped in fascination by this extraordinary spectacle, Aurora suffers in her own flesh the martyrdom of the oppressed, dislodged, prodded, and desecrated terrain. She treads the blind path with respectful compassion, listening religiously to the endless murmur of inanimate objects. She has lost her fear of being alone and wants only to continue descending to the very depths of the excavation without having anyone stop her with threats or prohibitions. There, at the bottom of that indefinable clamor, where implements furiously devour the kidneys of the mine, she will rescue her beloved and together they will climb back up into the sunlight.

The ground becomes steeper and craggier, and in the depth of silence every sound resonates like a sonorous drop; the exhalation of embers heats the air as if a gigantic fire were waiting in hiding at the end of the brutal road. Squeezed in by the supports and exhausted from the rough descent, oppressed by the heat and the cramped conditions, Aurora suddenly

glimpses a strange, inert brightness that gradually reveals itself to be a pale sliver of sun.

A Celestial Gaze

An enormous fault permits the sunlight to reach the buried
folds of the mountain, and the sudden luminosity turns the
polished side of the lode into a mirror. The quarry rises up
conspicuously at the edge of the crevice, and everything here
acquires an accent, an expression, a look. Rocks of diverse or-
igins and stratified deposits from various eras form the downward slope, which changes in material and color, imbued with
an amazing beauty and vital grace. All of life is contained
here; human greed stopped before reaching this magnificent
wedge through which the celestial gaze penetrates into the
earth's muffled depths to let the sun awaken the sleeping
rocks and to rouse the stones. And in the final pages of its
book, Nature's manifold soul records Time's labors and the
history of a world filled with supernatural art.

5

The River of Oblivion

REVELATIONS

AFTER A MOMENT OF HALLUCINATORY SURPRISE, AURORA SITS down on an unsullied base, and, leaning against the silky wall, she looks with clairvoyant eyes at the slippery surface, where the centuries have turned mountain filaments, fluvial slime, mud from lakes, and plant and animal remains into petrified characters that resemble a mysterious alphabet and give the strata their unusual hues.

Every terrestrial formation left its face and footprint on the mineral layers. The veins of Triassic rocks have kept clay traces of vanished creatures; monstrous reptiles, tridactyl birds, primitive fish and dinosaurs, imprints of rain and glaciers were buried in the shallow silt of granular limestone and carved into the mountain. Every palpitation was recorded by Time in its petrified weaving; with infinite patience, it preserved the shadow of a wing, the mold of a rose, the print of a finger, the rest of a nail from the oldest species. In the depths of the waters, life never completely disappeared, because the marine sediments and the estuaries' tender sea moss humbly suffered the torture that hardens and the pain that transforms, and, changed into marble, jasper, rock, and metal, they rose up to the clouds. And here, preserved in a block of enduring beauty, the remote beings that had often tumbled into the abyss survived, because nothing in God's hands is ever lost.

The blood-colored veins look human, and some of their luminous areas glisten like eternal souls; they wait and suffer, meekly obeying the laws of an inscrutable eternity, and they question Aurora with obstinate pupils made of crystal. She listens with fervor to the iridescent questions of a hundred

42

strange eyes that seem to shimmer with tears. And now she feels burdened with the weight of the other life she carries inside her, and suddenly she realizes with clear certainty that nothing can bloom and grow in Nature without pain.

Anxiously, she looks for shelter under the wall's natural vault, which covers her golden hair with a fine gauze of bluish powder, and she remains there, absorbed, smitten by the sun's terrible hatchet blow, detached from a reality that buries her in the craggy earth.

The dividing line in the crack descends clearly and sharply along the mysterious dark mouth like a dagger cleft between two huge masses: above, ethereal wings, opening up to light; below, the frightening confines of nameless things. And along the lode's high and shiny surface, the region's geological vestiges are arranged neatly and horizontally, as legibly as on a map.

In the same deposit there are brittle rocks that in their transmutation have produced the purest china clay, porphyritic sandstone, kidney-shaped flint, rosy crystals covered with vegetation. The macle, which steals its coloration from shale, shines in black prisms, wrapped in clear glass; the translucent calamine masses glisten in fibrous clusters with the luminosity of a mother-of-pearl mixed with gray. The columns of mica-covered feldspar stand out with their ever-changing colors, radiant veins, and carbonous ribbons in the form of a cross; the star-shaped white lead glows with a blue, diamond-like brilliance.

Once more Aurora hears the miraculous mumble of rocks, flames, shades, and sounds that gesticulate and sob; they ascend until they feel the chill of the open space and then descend to surprise the voices that speak beneath the earth. To the young girl the mountain's barely perceptible creakings sound like urgent revelations, as if suddenly the lode's dynamic force formed a single cry destined to pierce her sensibility.

She notices her thoughts floating up, tied with radiant threads, igniting her with unknown fires. Her burning heart moans like green kindling, consumed by a new-found tenderness, and Aurora stands up with an involuntary impulse of anxious restlessness.

THE MIRACLE

The road she follows along the crevice's edge is blocked by a boulder that became dislodged during the painful excavations carried out on the walls of the mount. The treasures of the mountain are torn up and fragmented, but their magnificence is generously preserved in each scattered piece. And the bedazzled young girl kneels down in order to pick up, one by one, the prisms and lozenges; the talismanlike stones with signs and crosses; the fossils, persistent like life itself, where numerous solid skeletons have left their mark, but that yearn nostalgically for the firm and round imprint of slithering invertebrates.

Aurora's hands take on the efflorescent colors of the various rocks: snow white, peach red, Prussian blue, a confused mixture of hues, perhaps distilled from the purple mollusk's liqueur, the cuttlefish's ink, the serpent's venom, the branchiopod's transparent cloak. Bounteous marvels glide through her inquisitive fingers: unusual incrustations, crystal arrows, empty molds; residues of joints, valves, vibratile cilia, feathers and leaves; the dust of thousands of exotic creatures that were believed to have come from the stars or been begotten by the deluge.

In the warmth of a certain cranny, Aurora finds a large, empty, crescent-shaped Venus shell with sharp edges. She picks it up and looks at it in fascination, without knowing its origin; she drops it gently amidst the white clumps of gypsum and the yellow ribbons of sulfur. The spell of her fervent but whimsical search breaks, and she walks around the obstacle on the road to continue her descent on the ever steeper and rougher slope.

The sun continues to infiltrate the fissure with trembling rays and magic brilliance.

THE COLD VEIN

A crystalline murmur and humid exhalation rise up from the deep darkness, and, as if pushed by the jaggedness of the terrain, the young girl enters an enormous grotto that is illuminated by a light above, like a forest at dusk. The ground slopes gently, and in the part that is plunged in darkness there is a ghostly and forsaken river, reminiscent of Lethe. The river must have entered through a crack in the mountain, and it flows between two silent cavities, sleepy in the whirlpool and swift in the current of water that never stops. A sad and fertile moss grows along its discolored shore, and here the transformation takes place of all the organisms destined to become metal: the fish with red and blue crests, the porcelain marine snails, the vegetable roots, the three-layered shells.

Underneath the dislocated walls and the winding vault, the stones acquire human forms, as in a sculptor's studio; lively like animated souls, they transmit a fearful secret in every crystal fraction. The twilight's pale splendor increases the enigma contained in the metallic clots, the rocky seams, and the sullen-looking supports.

The river throbs like a frightened heart as it widens into a pond. Aurora follows its course with a strange fear, and, looking at her reflection in the depths of the sleepy waters, she is surprised to see that she has been transformed by her surroundings: her pupils have the waxy shine of turquoise; her hair is aflame with sunflowers; her lips are pursed in a sphinx-like smile; her dress glitters as if bedecked by jewels. She does not recognize herself, and for the first time during this strange journey she experiences the astonishment and apprehension that are natural in such a risky adventure. She is frightened by the murmur of the cold vein and the mute palpitations of blind fish swimming toward a horizon that seems to signify the end of hope.

As she grows more accustomed to the twilight, she can see a boat with an open brim, rocking gently, its cable moored to the shore: it seems ready for a voyage to a place where all that lives ceases to exist. Looking at the boat apprehensively, Aurora turns away from this spot to which a strong yearning had attracted her like an evil spell. With a nimble mind and an open heart, she returns to reality, clinging to life despite all its anxieties.

A single word forms itself eagerly on her lips: it is the new name of the sailor who had changed his destiny at the end of the red path, "Gabriel! Gabriel!" The echoes of the archangel's name reverberate with the same unusual novelty in the sinister, gloomy cave as in Aurora's painful love. She cries out for the protection she seeks and buries her own griefs, tossing them into the waters of oblivion.

Then she flees nervously through the labyrinths of the mine, leaving the lamp on the ground, with no intention of descending any further, certain as she is of having reached the bowels of the earth.

The Necklace of Lamps

After a last look at herself in the watery mirror, Aurora retraces her steps with anxious rapidity, intent on returning to the fissure. She takes a random path, and when the light begins to fade, she regrets not having her lamp; she thinks of turning back but she is overcome by fear. Her forces abandon her as she advances mechanically, groping in the dark. Beside herself, she shouts, "Gabriel! Gabriel!" and then runs after her own voice. Rushing around aimlessly, she stumbles and falls headlong, hurting her hands.

The passageway hums like a snail and she hears someone approaching with swift steps. Anticipating another peril, Aurora tries to hide herself by curling up against the wall. The lamp that comes closer and stops belongs to a young boy, dirty and panting, who is loaded down with pickaxes and small picks. Not much older than a child, the picket carrier has smooth cheeks, a strong brow, and gentle eyes that look at the young girl in astonishment, mistaking her for a fantastic vision. Since she looks so timid and bashful, he thinks she is younger than she is, and he wonders:

"Are you the one who shouted?"

"Yes, I was calling Gabriel, Gabriel Suárez, a miner . . ."

"The one who squints, has that sad look, and is accused of being an anarchist?"

"That's the one."

"Is he a brother of yours?"

"Yes, he's my brother," answers Aurora with spiritual fervor.

"He's not here any more."

"What do you mean?"

"He left yesterday."

"Where did he go?"

"To join the navy so he could go far away," the boy tells her wistfully, harboring a childish dream, while Aurora mumbles some incomprehensible words that trail off, smothered by a sob.

"Don't get upset," adds the picket carrier, sorry about the pain his words have caused, "maybe he hasn't left yet. All I know for sure is that he wanted to enlist on a freighter that sails from Torremar today."

"What time is it?" the girl manages to ask, having lost all sense of time and distance, and hoping she could still overtake the fatal boat on shore.

"It's time to leave," answers the boy, realizing that he is late. And still in a state of amazement, he asks:

"But how did you get down here?"

"Without permission and by taking the path into a very dark entrance."

"And without light?"

"With a lamp like yours that I forgot near a river."

"You've been by the river?"

"Yes."

They whisper as if they were in church, bewildered by the strangeness of this moment that seems unreal. "Now you'd better come with me," says the boy with sudden decisiveness, "we have to run because they're going to do some blasting."

He takes her hand and they escape at full speed, in anxious silence; Aurora holds the lamp so her companion can carry the utensils. The air grows thinner because the path they take is only walled on one side and exposed to the open-pit excavations on the other. Suddenly, the entire mine, black like a spider, seems to echo their nervousness. The constellation of lamps accompanying the sounds of a muffled trot gives the scene the air of an Egyptian festival of lights: it is the miners fleeing from the dust, scattering fireflies along the mineral fields. The lights wrap around the mountain's dark brown pit like strands of a necklace, while inside a stampede pounds the galleries furiously and makes the stones tumble ominously in the opaque distance.

The roar of the explosions and the spurt of landslides extinguish the red stars. One by one they disappear into the mine's terrible night, while the fugitives escape through cuts and cracks to reach the main tunnel, whose entrance is illuminated by the sun's glare. Aurora and the young boy also emerge into the sunlight amidst a group of workers. Having been introduced to the list keeper, she asks him with a last glimmer of hope about Gabriel Suárez.

"He left last night," he tells her, "and his plan was to embark on an English freighter this morning in Torremar."

She overhears some crude jokes, risqué compliments, and insolent laughter from the men who spout vulgarities with undisguised zest: it is time for freedom, frolic, fun, and a chance to approach a woman.

The noonday sun is hot and there is not a single cloud in the sky. The sizzling landscape grows hazy in the vivid brightness, and on the other side of the mountain the sea murmurs its gentle prayers. Intimidated by the calm sky, stretched on the torture rack of the wheel of life, Aurora must face her tragic destiny alone . . .

6

The *Hardy*

The Farewell

Dawn is about to see the birth of a new day. The morning star, an early riser, descends to bathe its face in the sea as the light blazes a trail across the horizon.

Near the crane on the dock, the *Hardy* loosens its cables and anchor and begins to maneuver. Without worrying about the strong current, the ship lurches forward amidst the siren's hoarse blast and the crew's picturesque hustle and bustle. The British freighter, which does honor to its name, left Cardiff with half of its cargo and picked up the other half in Torremar. It is on its way to the Andalusian port of Estuaria, where it will exchange the coal for copper before returning home. The ship's hull is tall and dark, its keel is painted ochre, and its deck is defended by cannons that are manned by an officer of the British Royal Marine.

Out of obligation or as a courtesy, the *Hardy* carries a pair of travelers aboard, who at this time are standing on the upper deck, carefully observing the ship's activities, the landscape, and the coast. They are young and look like brother and sister. Her curly dark hair, which she wears short like a schoolgirl, surrounds an interesting face, and her eyes shine with a wondrous sadness. A similar enchantment glistens in his lighter-colored and more adventurous pupils, lending his manly face a spiritual grace. Both are dressed simply but with a certain elegance that is surprising on that ship's poop deck.

Gabriel Suárez's skin and clothes are blackened from working as a stevedore in the ship's hold; the red-faced man from the mine has turned black at sea. As he suffers and struggles, he looks with envy at the ship's mast, which is made from the

49

wood of a giant tree that once conversed with winds aloft and now soars above the waters like a bird.

When the ship's bow begins to plunge and rise, the young man leaves his work to say goodbye to the shore, which beckons to him imperiously. Standing in the shed above the hatchway, he lets his eyes wander longingly over the land covered with fields and gardens, atuned to the murmurs of all that grows and blossoms.

He contemplates the shoreline, enveloped in a misty light whose shudders are like the sweet rustling of a nest. From the village's interior comes the cheerful ringing of a school bell, and its clear peals dissipate the fog, which flees like a bird. Under dawn's arch of triumph, the mountains rise up, cradling the bay in their lap.

At the far end of the dock, beyond the other spectators, stands a dog with a raised tail and twitching muscles, his ears perked with excitement. Having been thrown out repeatedly from the *Hardy,* he looks at the ship with growing anxiousness. With a yelp, he leaps into the water in a mad attempt to pursue the fleeing furrow.

Gabriel watches the animal's battle in distress, knowing that the dog is not allowed on board. He does not want to see him die, but cannot avert his eyes and he runs along the deck, talking, shouting, and opening his arms with an impulse of fervid compassion.

"Is he yours?" asks the only woman passenger in dismay, pointing to the dog.

"Yes, ma'am," answers the young man in a muffled voice.

In that moment the faithful Bolina emits his saddest lament, and, showing the whites of his frightened eyes, he drowns amidst the floating foam and the algae that search for sunshine.

The woman passenger has turned very pale, and, holding on to the gunwale, she fixes her gaze, as does the sailor, on that fickle spot that has closed up once more and reflects the clouds.

THE HUMAN BIRD

A vessel sails in those clouds, gently rippling the waters and casting a shadow in the form of a cross on the bay.

"An airplane!" everybody shouts.

The young girl with the short hair is being called by her companion:

"Rosario, take a look!"

He offers her a pair of binoculars and she looks at the sky, tossing back her head. Her curls tumble wildly, exposing her forehead, and the breeze blows happily through her black hair that is suddenly illuminated by a reddish light. The sun has appeared, and its fiery wheel sweeps across the open Cantabrian horizon like a bloody tide, dying the sky's pale forehead.

Everything that dawn had painted with vague and cold colors begins to burn in the newborn light and melt into a single flame, which strangely conjures up thoughts—along the coast and aboard ship—about the war. People suddenly realize, as if discovering a novelty, that times are cruel and barbarian, that men's veins are cast in coral-red rivers, that death prowls the world, and that humanity moans as it bleeds to death.

Out on the open sea, the *Hardy* sails close to the wind. The violent keel shines like a brilliant scar on its tragic, dark silhouette. The crewmen's faces, gleaming in the light of the furnaces they stoke, turn toward the splendors of the east, lured by the sun, the universal red chimera.

Up above, the bird with the outstretched wings flies away toward the sun, without rising too high, just like goshawks when they are inebriated with the fresh sea breeze. Suddenly, it gains speed and altitude, and, plunging down again, it imprints the sky with the Christian image of the cross, left suspended on heaven's threshold, as if waiting.

The ship breathes noisily and its crewmen, who live precariously by the law of the wind, have fallen silent. This moment of indefinable solemnity is broken when Rosario, who has followed the plane with her eyes, exclaims in an emotional and melodious voice:

"If only it could pierce the sun's very heart!"

As if in obedience to this request, the plane soars upward, and then, as swiftly as a quivering arrow, it heads eastward to hide in the sun's fire, which glows in all its splendor.

Gabriel stands motionless near the bow. He has watched the flight of the human bird, has heard the wish of the dark-haired girl, and he is tortured by a perturbing emptiness, so vast that

it cannot be filled by the immensity of space. His clear eyes
sparkle with tears in his black face.

SUN AND PEACE

After four days of successful navigation, the *Hardy* approaches Estuaria, staying prudently close to the shore, without thereby relinquishing its hardiness. In the distance it has
sighted many warships from different countries, bristling with
cannons; arrogant submarine periscopes; gunrunners; and
remnants of shipwrecks, all crouched and hidden amidst the
foam. The *Hardy*'s course began in the proud Cantabrian
landscape of mountains and waves, in front of Naranjo de
Bulnes and Peña Labra; it followed the dangerous beauty of
the Costa de la Muerte; and turned the corner by Fin de la
Tierra to contemplate Galicia's delightful estuaries, greet Portugal's fine-grained sand, and conquer the Old World's west-
ern-most point, where Europe's hostilities should come to an
end just like the shore and be engulfed by the sea's eternal
song.

The royal officer is engaged in a farewell conversation with
the passengers, and he is charmed by the young woman's
dark eyes. Casually reclining against the railing, she answers
him in English, somewhat distractedly.

"Yes, I would like to sketch these landscapes, become familiar with the countryside, and help my brother with his research as much as I can."

"Will you be staying a long time?"

"It depends . . . We're free as birds, but we are easily captivated by novelty and emotions; if we like the country and our
work goes well . . . Who knows!"

"Could you give me your address in case I return to Estuaria
soon . . . as I intend to?"

"That's difficult! We wander around without stopping for
long in any one place. But knowing our names and our
profession . . ." The young girl takes a business card from her
pocket and places it in the Englishman's eager hand. "José
Luis and Rosario Garcillán, reporters for *La Evolución*, Madrid," the sailor reads, adding, "Do you live in the capital?"

"We have a winter retreat there in the house of some relatives because our own home was disbanded when our parents died. But we travel quite a bit, usually on assignment for the newspaper or financed by us, if we can afford it. "

"Lucky you," sighed the officer with the wistfulness of someone who feels weighed down by obligation and sees others leading a full life.

"Bah! We can make do with very little," José Luis points out, tearing himself away from the horizon flooded with light.

"You call that little, to be independent and enjoy peace in the land of the sun?"

"You're right, that's quite a lot," Rosario agrees, feeling suddenly more amiably inclined toward the officer.

"Yes, we've managed to work hard and remain poor," mumbles her brother, still smiling.

The two were obviously proud of their fate, brimming with hope and buoyed by intense illusions. Their modest pension, increased by earnings from their writings, allowed them to follow their vocation and maintain their ideal, often thanks to privations and sacrifices. Artists and true believers, with the faith of apostles and the fervor of martyrs, they professed the pure doctrine of Brotherhood in the simple and generous Christian sense of the word as defined by Jesus Christ. The circumstances of their bourgeois origin and predisposition to emotions, the violent turn of events that left them alone in the world, avid for love and beauty, thirsting for truth and goodness, favored their practicing journalism like the priesthood. This was apparent to the editors of the socialist press in Madrid, whose ideals were less lofty and who saw journalism as a job and a means to an end. And thus José Luis and Rosario served as a shield for a rich and modern publication that claimed to defend the proletariat and be the forum for the worker.

The pair was planning to do a detailed study and learn about the working conditions of the miners in the great Andalusian river basin. Before boarding the ship in Torremar, they had done some preliminary observations in various northern mines. This dangerous trip was Rosario's whimsical idea, and as they neared shore she was already eager to see the new places, while the English sailor would have liked to prolong the journey indefinitely to be with the young girl from Madrid. But they were approaching the mysterious and peculiar southern shore, with its straits and inlets, gullets and channels, reefs and turns. Here the waters, in clear and fluid tones, tell the story of how they descend from solitary peaks and flow along hidden paths known only to them.

THE SONG OF THE TORRENTS

When the tide is high and the boats prosper in fair weather, each torrent raises its voice amidst laughter and sobs, and the dunes and shoals vibrate with vivacious songs that spread to the estuaries and marshes along the whole swampy zone from Esuri's sandbars to the tip of Malandar.

The waters from the Val de Judío precipice and from the Miel Brook swell the mouth of the Ana River, which in turn pours its water onto assorted little beaches and edges of sandbanks between two red lighthouses. Spain's sacred vein, which is born in transparent lagoons and then hides secretively only to reappear miraculously in deep, crystalline, bubbling springs, knows how to form arches and flatlands, curves and alluvia. It crashes down over winding canyons, gently kisses the peaceful land of Don Quixote, flows along cheerful river banks, irrigates islands, blocks water conduits, and carries vessels, before hiding the secret of its sap in the sea's briny slack water.

The Piedras River, which descends from the Almendro Mountains and churns in the surrounding cattails, is fed by the channels of the Enramada and the Resuda and offers the ships a broad and shallow riverbed that extends until the mouth of the Terrón.

Farther to the east, the Saquia and Odiel erupt amidst sandbars and slime pools, enabling small boats to navigate near the influx of the tide and giving them access to Lucena and Gibraleón before flowing into Estuaria's gulf, where tall ships can dock near the city. Odiel's arteries are toughened by the untamed rivers that flow into it, all the way from Molino del Infierno in the Sierra de Aguila until the river splits and gives birth to its brother Saquia, the one with the tragic shores, bleeding branches, and dead fish. Both rivers spread their tributaries through villages and islands, undergrowth and small beaches, straits and salt lagoons, overflowing onto an intricate labyrinth of coasts and coves that harbor various vessels: small caravels and registered brigantines, flying a white flag with a blue square; African catboats, cutters from Moguer, and numerous tiny boats from the whole seaboard.

Also toward the east, at the edge of the coastal horizon, flows the deep Circem, whose fountainhead is the mighty Aguilón, a river whose historic shores have seen treasures of Roman culture and whose salt pools have reflected the trembling image of Muslim minarets.

The entire strange and ruddy seaboard, broken up by inlets and entrances, shoals and diversions, is aglow in the morning's golden silence and offers the *Hardy* its summits and capes; the tips of Umbría and Portil; and the channel of Engañabobos, from which Columbus's ships left to sail the Mar de las Tinieblas.

Rosario is still contemplating the landscape and talking with the seaman. She is telling him various Andalusian legends and pious lore about the Discovery, in which the friars from La Rábida's monastery and Our Lady, the Beautiful Virgin of Saltés, always play a role.

Sailing past the island where the hermitage of Saltés used to stand during those heroic Castilian times when the sun never set over Spain, they enter the Odiel along a shallow inlet.

The Spanish Refuge

Aboard, the arrival is being anticipated with an eager and anxious restlessness. The ship sails past vessels that have been detained by war, and, thanks to a hospitable climate that heaps them with fruit, some of them have been converted into hanging gardens. The deck of a German ship, which has been anchored for three years, displays magnificent rows of vegetables, surrounded by flowers. Its scuppers are open to allow the sweet water to flow in without muddying the crops, and over time the saltwater has formed a crust along the hull's side.

Several of the *Hardy*'s crewmen approach the railing to take a look at the shore and Rosario asks the officer about one of the men who has caught her attention.

"Is that tall, husky fellow in the blue jersey the one you refer to as Thor?"

"That's right."

"The Scandinavian god!" the young woman smiles, observing the young man with certain amazement.

"Yes, the son of Odin and the one who wields the hammer."

"But he isn't British, is he?"

"No, he's Galician; he has been sailing with us for a year now."

"He's a splendid example of his race," interjects José Luis.

"Yes, magnificent; that's why I named him after a giant, and now everybody calls him by this nickname."

"Does he like that?"

"Yes, because he knows we're comparing him to a god."

"He must be proud of that!" remarks Rosario.

"Well, he's just a plain and simple man, but he does enjoy being seen as the embodiment of strength and power."

The colossus was walking back from the gunwale, leaning on the shoulder of Gabriel Suárez, towering over him in stature and talking to him confidentially, as to a close friend. Both of them stole glances at the young lady on the sly, admiring her beauty and elegance. She observed them openly with sweet seriousness and proceeded to take a notebook and some pencils from a portfolio—which she wore slung diagonally over her shoulder like a quiver—and began to sketch.

7
Estuaria

NOTES

ABOVE THE WIDE, SILENT, AND LIMPID FLUVIAL LANDSCAPE THAT makes Estuaria a unique lakeside town, monstrous iron piers rise up from the estuary's edge. On the loading platforms supported by a framework of beams and founding columns, stand cranes with jaws or magnets, which, along with the ferries that work the marshes, are part of the equipment that enables the great Nordetanian enterprise to accumulate its millions. The huge bulk etches its somber outline into the transparent blue sky above the hamlet, which slides down red, wooded hills until it reaches the flatlands and the bay serrated by inlets.

The roads to Cinta and Gibraleón and the cliffs of Cruz de La Cuesta and Cabeza de la Huerca form the upper limits of the city, which mirrors itself in the transparent tranquillity of the placid bay, where the rivers Anicoba, Aljarauqe, Saquia, and Odiel mingle with the waters that descend from the mountains and sleep in the seedbeds of whirlpools and drains.

At the same moment as the *Hardy* is trapped by the dock's tentacles, Rosario Garcillán writes under her last sketch, "Thor, the god with the hammer."

The officer, standing next to the skillful artist, tells her enthusiastically:

"Oh, that's a superb sketch, a masterwork of charm and expression."

Visibly flattered by the praise, the young woman flips through the pages of her notebook, revealing the caricatured features of the people that had interested her. Each portrait is highlighted by a comment, in the form of a title. For example, "Man with a Dog" shows Gabriel Suárez, his face smeared with charcoal, watching in pain as Bolina is swallowed up by the sea. The uniform and facial expressions of "The Royal Officer" are drawn to make him look like Walter Penn. Feeling uneasy as he studies his features that have been accentuated with light irony, the officer murmurs, "I didn't realize you were such a clever humorist."

"Why?"

"I thought you were too sensitive for that."

"Are those two qualities mutually incompatible?"

"Certainly."

Rosario regrets having hurt his feelings and says ingratiatingly, "A sense of humor is very British."

"And a quick wit is very Spanish," replies the officer gallantly, while leafing through the album full of profiles and outlines, showing that Rosario draws her caricatures with a fine sensitivity and without trespassing the subtle boundary where exaggeration excludes resemblance. The notebook also contains sketches of interiors and landscapes, drawn in the same critical, energetic, charming, and personal style. These rough drafts, sketched with broad and free strokes, were like notations for the future, a seed to be developed, a promise, a revelation.

"Do you wield the pen as expertly as the pencil?" asks Walter Penn, increasingly charmed.

"I'm not an expert in anything yet," replies Rosario with a sincere smile. "Now you sound like an Andalusian!"

"And why did you write 'Royal Officer' under my picture?"

"Because I'm surprised that in a free country like England, the nation's ships and soldiers are still 'Her Majesty's.'"

The officer looks a little puzzled, having perhaps never associated that phrase with a sense of slavery. And he tells her, without being totally convinced by his own explanation, "Formulas linger; in my country, the laws change, but the names remain the same."

Not convinced either, the girl shrugs her shoulders and puts away her drawings. She lowers her hat's small veil over her face while her brother busies himself with the luggage.

Curious bystanders on the docks are surprised to see such a prim and genteel traveler arrive on a coal ship. With one gloved hand on the outstretched ferry cable, Rosario hears the final words of the officer who, wanting to keep her longer, can only think of saying, "So tomorrow you're going to Dite, Pluto's city?"

"Don't exaggerate: it's just a village, a modest, infernal village."

"I'll try to see you tomorrow before we leave; we sail at midnight."

"Goodbye."

"Goodbye."

Rosario joins her brother on the docks, and Walter Penn's eyes follow the firm and youthful steps of these two travelers, who are like daring conquistadors. They turn around to wave to the seaman and he takes off his hat to wave back; then with the nostalgia associated with farewells, they see the ship growing smaller and darker, bobbing along the loading platform's red boundary.

THE CITY

The afternoon after their arrival, Rosario and José Luis had paid their visits, bearing letters of recommendation with the request that the people of importance in Dite provide them with lodgings in the capital and help them carry out their investigative mission. They were introduced to some pleasant people, among them a professor from Jaén with a dyed beard and lordly airs, who used to travel abroad and spend his summers in "prewar Biarritz" and who was very bored in Estuaria.

Right now the professor was upset because neither the beach of La Sardinera in Santander nor the one in San Sebastián were to his liking. In the fall he was planning to go to Madrid, where he always had a good time. Of course he always stayed at the Ritz, a hotel full of millionaire Yankee widows, some of whom were interesting and beautiful, but he could not make up his mind because he was a lazy egotist . . . And he looks at Rosario with a protective air, walking along beside her.

They are strolling in the quiet and secluded main square, which, true to tradition, has a palm in its center to provide shade for the city's oldest inhabitants. Some of them have sought this canopy's peaceful refuge, while young couples in love are walking around, mingling with a handful of people who look rushed or worried. Some squat, modest, white-washed houses are visible behind the row of trees surrounding the square.

Brother and sister exchange bemused looks as the professor chatters away. He had also been a journalist and an illustrator in his early years; had written articles, composed poems, and dabbled in painting. The typical things one does at that age! Now he edits books in Madrid—works of great cultural value: a Latin grammar, a Spanish-Portuguese dictionary, serious and didactic works. Because one can't just stop being an artist from one day to the next, like changing clothes. Poetry is an infantile amusement, art is vulgar, and love is an exquisite folly. Ah! Winter in Madrid, the American widows! Such delirium! It's much too hot in Estuaria . . .

Dying of laughter, the visitors leave the professor, drenched in perspiration, holding his hat and still holding forth. They walk along the burning white streets in the direction of the port to catch the refreshing sea breeze. The coolness from the sea reaches the coastal gardens, enveloped in the long shadow of dusk, as darkness begins to descend from the clouds, and beacons, lamps, and lanterns are lit in the mysterious inlets. The soothing air reaches high above the shoreline, saving the visitors from having to go down to the docks, and in the distance they can hear the chanty of the sailors who ferry slowly along the dark channels.

Soon they return to their hotel to wait for Aurelio Echea, the district's foremost socialist leader, whom they have not met yet. Persecuted by employers, watched by the police, this outstanding organizer has been in and out of jail many times. At this time he has been banned from setting foot in the mining zone. A native of Bizcay, he is courageous and dangerous and has the fame of being "a man to be reckoned with." He will alert them to any possible risks they may run in their journalistic endeavor to investigate the Nordetanian stronghold. They wait for him with the curiosity and excitement elicited by the arrival of a popular leader with a heroic halo.

When he arrives, Rosario and José Luis look at each other, amazed at their error. They cannot believe their eyes: this individual cannot possibly be the famous paladin. Although the waiter introduces him correctly with his name and surname, José Luis repeats questioningly, "Aurelio Echea?"

"At your service."

He is a badly dressed, pale, blond young man of medium height; his voice is gentle, with a trace of humility, and he has a candid smile. After shaking hands with them somewhat bashfully, he murmurs, "What can I do for you?"

THE CHAMPION

To excuse themselves for a reception that was cooled by their surprise, the journalists intensify their amiability and ask the Champion to tell them about himself. José Luis entreats him with various questions, while Rosario listens with interest in discreet silence. Aurelio answers with sparse words and reticent gestures, as if afraid of overstepping himself. He was born in Biscay, grew up in Asturias; lived in Madrid, Valencia, and Andalusia; traveled in France, Belgium, Germany, and Russia; has been a sales clerk, commercial representative, railroad worker. He speaks a few languages and has read a few books; he feels at home in all of Spain and is a son of the people, a brother to those who suffer, and the hope of those who fight.

At this point, his voice grows stronger and a flame burns in his clear blue eyes; he continues with great eloquence and with a radiant and convinced expression—the sacred right of the oppressed sparkles with a divine light in the apostle's sentences. The idea that the providential hour has arrived permeates his discourse and his prophecies; the eternal battle for noble justice will deliver its greatest triumph. "The final day for kings and the first day for the common people has arrived!" He repeats those words, probably without knowing whose lips first pronounced this terrible sentence. And he is drunk with illusions, announcing the kingdom of justice: "Preferential treatment for the young and old; equality for men and women; two jewels in the crown: work and love; one hierarchy: talent and virtue."

"In other words, there will always be a merit scale," José Luis objects.

"Yes, there will be masters and disciples, but all humanity will be at the same level, differentiated only by moral categories, and hopefully these will become superfluous when everybody has passed through the same sieve of receiving an education and striving for the same goals. Nobody is born lucky or unlucky; we all travel the same dark path to reach life, and society should be generous like the sun and bestow the same privileges on everyone."

"Ah, the same old wish! The romantic idealist's eternal sermon, a promise that will never be fulfilled!"

"Well, I see it being achieved; it is being ripened by the sufferings reaped for centuries, a product of this terrible war that without a similar achievement would have no reason to be. All the countries on this continent that bleed today hope for redemption, and they will not be satisfied until they can shake slavery off their shoulders. In the dawning peace, nations must rise up in freedom and pure justice, with reason and morality triumphant in the world."

"And what can we do to make this dream come true?" asks Rosario, moved and fascinated.

Aurelio Echea looks her in the eyes for the first time, and, noticing their deep luminosity, his answer is delayed by the mysterious tremor of ideas he sees in her shiny pupils. Finally he says, "With faith and good will."

"Where do we start?"

"By carrying out your project and using *La Evolución* as a platform to describe how the miners are treated in Dite."

"We will do that," José Luis assures him.

"If they let you . . . "

"Who's going to stop us?"

"The general manager of the mines or your newspaper editor."

"Our newspaper," says the young man proudly, "is socialism's most progressive medium."

"Ah, socialists! That is a weak and outdated designation for the modern liberators; thanks to their theories, the socialists have discredited the name. But names are not what matters most. We're more interested in gaining strength from practical actions to achieve the maximum good in a positive manner. But I have to tell you again, the general manager of the mines will try with all his means to stop you from carrying out your investigation and the newspaper will object to the radicalism of your chronicles. If you do find out the whole truth . . . they won't let you publish it."

"We'll make the test."

"Believe me, there is nobody who is more interested than I am in your success. You would be invaluable allies."

"And with your advice, experience, and help, we'll succeed, won't we?" asks Rosario, in her clear manner, imbuing her phrase with a charming melancholy.

Echea smiles and bows respectfully to show his collaborator that he appreciates her observations, and he decides to tell his new friends about the complications surrounding the problem of the miners in Dite. The issues are not limited to the breach of contract regarding working conditions or the constant fights between bosses and workers because there is also the question of nationality. The Nordetanian Company is the town's absolute proprietor, owning, without any restrictions or conditions, land, farms, subsoil, mountains, air, laws, and liberty. It is the lord and master of lives and haciendas, and—by virtue of this modern feudalism—it literally owns the streets, the square, church, cemetery, public buildings, means of communication.

Furthermore, the company is the moral owner of almost all the popular organizations, and their representatives enjoy the scandalous privileges of holding office in both the company and the state. Right now in Estuaria, a government secretary has refused to accept his promotion because it would force him to move and thus lose out on the opulent company's lucrative bribes. If one of the authorities would like to bring to justice any of the many cases of complaints against the foreigners, he has to interrogate corrupt subordinates and can therefore never gather enough evidence to condemn the exploiters. The countless law suits involving property are always settled in the company's favor. It decides who should be nominated for administrative positions; it determines the taxes to be collected and the declarations to be made by the only Spanish municipality that has been expropriated and cannot expropriate. At its whim, it changes the region's Catholic schools to Protestant ones.

The company's domain is protected by a squad of armed guards who wield more power than the Spanish military forces. Outside the mining zone, it offers lavish subsidies to the most prestigious lawyers wherever these can serve its purposes best and allow it to carry out its brazen dealings with impunity. And now the company, no longer satisfied with exercising its domain along the Saquia's banks, has fixed its eyes and claws on the open seaboard, acquiring an eighth of the province of Huelva as well as a portion of the Sevillian one. In other words, it has appropriated the heart of Spain's southern Atlantic Coast and the bay next to the estuary, which is one of the world's premier ports.

The bubbling waters of the Circem, Spain's sunniest river, flow into a foreign river in their own country, and sixty miles of the clean and brilliant Andalusian sands belong to these greedy and scowling men, cold-blooded animals of a sad, Nordic race, who, thirsting for sun, search along the ocean shores for a place they can invade with impunity and plant their flag in a favorable heaven. And they unfurled it in the wind here, above the waves' clear laughter, down here by the dunes, and up there by the gouged land of the conquered villages, the tortured peaks.

"It seems incredible!" murmurs José Luis.

Rosario, stunned and silent, listens avidly to the revelations of the accuser, who recites his long list of complaints in a heated and lyrical style, with undertones of propagandistic speeches, but full of endearing sincerity. His eyes often lose themselves in hers as if he saw a profound path in them. In those instances, he hesitates a minute, only to express his ideas more passionately afterward.

He knows by heart and has verified the exact amount the Nordetanian Company paid half a century ago to acquire the perpetual rights to Saquia's mines and the subsoil: ninety-two million pesetas. The true value of this purchase, just in relationship to the capital it produces, is worth millions more, without even taking into consideration the rural dwellings, which have already been turned into villages that contribute to the company.

The numbers spill from Aurelio's lips with bitter rancor. He informs them that the stocks that sold at a hundred and twenty-five pesetas when they were originally issued by the company are now worth two thousand. He enumerates the vast foreign holdings in the very heart of Spain, pointing out that they all lack the most basic services, such as telephones and telegraphs, schools, hygiene, electricity, paved roads, or a railroad. The sole purpose of any existing cultural activity or means of communication is to serve the company, which monopolizes and exploits them. Electricity, which illuminates all civilized countries, shines only for the invaders, walled off in their haciendas and gardens, far from the Spanish masses ... The worker lies at the feet of such bosses, sacrificing his life at every moment to receive wages that are about one-seventh of the wealth he produces.

"All of this has to be said loud and clear," exclaims Rosario, full of indignation, turning her sweet face toward her brother.

"Yes," he mumbles with intense eagerness, and his piercing, golden eyes cry out with the heroic words that are left unsaid.

Echea feels overwhelmed and happy that these intelligent and sensitive young people are offering him their support with the most disinterested generosity. The purity of their spirits has allowed him to catch a glimpse of their hearts, and he feels blessed to have the support of such noble souls. In a battle that consumes his existence, Echea dreams of achieving high moral ideals; a worshipper of a humanitarian and just doctrine, he forgets the tribulations he has suffered in its defense and relishes the joyous hope triggered by this unexpected alliance.

He accepts their dinner invitation but barely touches the food, which is too exquisite compared to his customary fare; with a simple delicacy, he tastes every dish without paying too much attention to any of them. In an unpretentious corner of the hotel, seated at a modest table, they learn not about Aurelio the politician or Aurelio the man, but about Aurelio the apostle, who rises above circumstances and conditions. He initiates them into the secret incantations of the eternal entreaty that is always reborn, with small variations, in every society; he takes them into his confidence, sharing his plans and ambitions with them.

At the end of the meal, the three of them have made a firm and valiant pact, without any flourish, toast, or speech, but sealed with an exchange of exalted glances and mute, calm smiles, imbued with a willingness to suffer.

8
Destiny

SMILES

THE CONSPIRATORS RISE FROM THE TABLE, ENVELOPED IN THE TACIT solemnity of their commitment, and, with a strong and forceful gesture, Echea predicts glorious victory. Rosario feels sweetly confused when he directs his clear and energetic gaze at her. As they say goodbye, he takes her outstretched hand with a gentle tremor, causing her blood to flow faster for an instant.

The three have agreed that José Luis and the Champion would go to Estuaria to see the port's most unusual spectacle: the only dance hall in Europe. Rosario accompanies them along the winding and dimly lit hallway and stops at the threshold of her room to smile at the two young men who have just bid her farewell. In the twilight, the white in her eyes and her ivory teeth gleam wonderfully, and Aurelio Echea, dazzled and shaken, turns around to take another look at her . . .

The air is hot in her room, and, without turning on the light, Rosario sits down on the modest sofa, whose shiny satin cover is the worse for wear. But the young girl is not given to excessive fastidiousness. From where she is seated, next to the open balcony, she has a good view of the silent street that loses itself in a garden, and she catches a glimpse of a slice of sky illuminated by tiny suns. Listening anxiously, she distinguishes some vague noises in the silence and wonders whether they are plaintive sounds made by lost birds or the wind's distant harangue in the swamps or the warm hum of stars in the night sky.

Overcome by a sharp stab of emotion that makes her feel like laughing and crying, she asks herself whether the confused, muffled, and alluring rhythm comes from the hot throb-

66

bing of her own youthful blood. Her memory is flooded by the day's events, inextricably linked to the estuary's fluidity, open arms, and sleeping inlets, and to the softly sighing sea. All her impressions take on the great estuary's ever-changing, fluid contours, and she feels engulfed in life's undulating channels, navigating her boat on uncharted waters, between endless shores.

The chimes of a nearby clock remind her that it is late. Rosario looks at the night sky that is lacerated by a fine line of lightning bolts, as thin as smiles. A new name floats up into her thoughts and consciousness; she leaves the balcony door ajar and goes to bed . . .

El Vaivén

After walking along deserted and peaceful streets, Echea and Garcillán had to pass through streets that were less clean and decent on their way to the city's outskirts. Here, near the port, they see the large and resplendent building with a huge sign proclaiming its name, El Vaivén, a reference to the constant comings and goings at the place.

They enter and find themselves submerged in an immense hall with high ceilings and elegant decorations, and with bay windows thrown open to let in the sea breeze. The hall is graced with a stage way in the back, surrounded by numerous tables, benches, and stools, allowing the clients to drink and play and still leave enough room for the dancers.

A variegated and animated mass of people fills the premises. All the different races and temperaments are represented here in speech and manner. And every interesting individual in this vulgar rogues' gallery sports a flower in his lapel, hair, or hand, given to him by one of the flower vendors. These kind, fragrant, and free offerings add a touch of purity to this cave of folly.

The music has stopped for a moment and the tide of conversations rises up, distorted by the violent clinking of glasses, the drunkards' curses, and the women's screeching. The hall belongs to the young pimps, who are slender and elegant, with a Semitic paleness and dark Mediterranean eyes, slick-haired and clean-shaven, wearing tight-fitting pants and a Córdoba hat with an upturned rim. Idols of the women whom they mistreat and exploit with a strange mixture of passion, vice, and cruelty, they often stand up to the rich and idle young men who frequent prostitutes, and to the scoundrels who take pride in being brawlers and troublemakers. The latter abound in the place, along with the more mature and good-natured Andalusian men, examples of the classical figure who is ridiculed in all the jokes. They typically have a hoarse voice, aspirate their h's too strongly, love hardy drinks, and are terrible chatterboxes. Some more formal gentlemen, seldom guilty of any excesses, have joined a group of oblivious peasants and pale miners, a heap of ordinary and anonymous people, without personality or individuality.

The entire motley crowd is dominated by foreigners. El Vaivén is popular among sailors from Philadelphia, Bremen, Antwerp, and Liverpool, and crewmen of ships that carry minerals from the Odiel to the great industrial centers of Lancaster and Pennsylvania, or to the world's most powerful metallurgic centers. The dance hall attracts sons of the icy north escaping from the Arctic seas, fiery men with blue eyes and blond manes shaped like helmets; impetuous Americans, whose eyes reflect the pride and vision of tough New York; blacks, who shout and sing in English; Frenchmen, Austrians, Hungarians; gentle and melancholic Chinese, who speak their monosyllabic language with harmonious inflections; Greeks, Germans, Italians: they all fraternize. Yet the peace that reigns among them is more terrible than war because, though their bodies are united, their souls flee while ferocious bestiality tosses and turns in its spiritual death throes.

The sad lot that befalls the women at El Vaivén is to unite the planet's different castes in an immense erotic embrace, moving from man to man in a traffic of base instincts, without any notion of good and evil. The majority of these women are uneducated and rough, and they exercise their vile profession with domestic passivity, feeling neither suffering nor enjoyment. All they know is that the visits of these crewmen leave them with money in their pockets. In general, these women are not pretty, and their physical appearance reflects their coarse and indifferent souls, though a few do have a certain dramatic charm. The hysterical and degenerate ones cast an

interesting tragic shadow; these are the women who sometimes fall in love, kill someone, or commit suicide.

The music has started up again and the men and women,
locked in a tight embrace, are driven into an unspeakable turmoil by a gust of frantic delirium. The dance hall's gigantic di-
mensions make it possible for the couples to escape, hide, and
withdraw to one of the faraway rooms in that enormous ba-
zaar of vices, without ever running into their previous companions.

The dance gains momentum and becomes distorted by the
addition of barbaric elements. Over here, an African accompanies his Ethiopian dance with a monstrous, high-pitched song;
there, a lithe and robust Yankee in shirt sleeves starts an athletic exercise, moving his legs like the arms of a windmill, and
executing rapid, muscular motions. He could well be a descen-
dant of the nimble and tough cowboys, those modern centaurs
who hunted buffaloes and rode their wild ponies along the
prairies of the Golden West. A little farther off, a huge and ingenuous German leaps up and down clumsily, besotted by the
generous wines of the land. The women drink, jump around,
and laugh.

Brandy, whiskey, gin, and stout flow abundantly, together
with the sweet and dry sherries of Jerez, raw rum from Valver-
de del Camino, and tart Castilian wine. A pimp, holding a girl
with gypsylike features in a lascivious embrace, twists and un-
winds with feline sensuality, gliding through the crowd of Dio-
nysian celebrants and drunken dancers, adding a lively touch
of raffishness to the languid rhythms of the Habanera.

The dance is interrupted once more when wild shouts announce that the curtain has gone up. Half naked, the Beautiful
Esmeralda starts dancing a lecherous tango and taking off the
rest of her clothes little by little. The crowd roars, and the
noise and confusion reach unspeakable proportions until El
Niño de Estepa and his musical accompanist appear on stage.
The Maestro—who has decorated his guitar with a carnation
and placed a flower in his lapel—sits down, spits, and begins
to moan:

> Oh, the sad quandary I'm in,
> not knowing what to do:
> it's impossible to forget you
> and not possible to love you!

Hot like a breath of African simoon, the voice and the heart-rending accompaniment invade the premises. There is a burst of emotion and beauty in their throbbing and caressing modulations, and of a goodness that rebels against superficiality and cannot be understood by those who cultivate artificiality. This is the sacred drop of emotion in a fertile land where the inebriating juices have a divine fragrance and where the Oriental soul has been fused into Western tradition, transforming Spain into a preeminently diverse and mysterious country.

The verses pour out in an atmosphere of hushed emotions; in an air filled with the mist of tears and the hint of a vague fascination, the flamenco song evokes the unmistakable personality and history of a race. But the miraculous spell is soon broken. El Niño de Estepa, somewhat aloof, takes leave haughtily, and the applause, shouts, and coarse gallantries resume in all languages.

In the midst of the atrocious racket that breaks out again, Garcillán sees Thor, towering above the crowd with his lofty height and smiling down at a roguish-faced and vulgar-looking woman. Next to him, and accompanied by a similar type of girl, stands Gabriel Suárez. At first José Luis does not recognize him because the sailor's face is clean of soot, and before Garcillán has a chance to catch up with the group, they disappear, losing themselves in the waves of that furious tide.

Aurelio Echea has stayed close to his friend's side; he wants to show him the monstrosities of El Vaivén, but he does not want to leave him there. He leads José Luis gently to the exit, thinking that he has had his fill of this incredibly huge and colorful spectacle that nobody would expect to find in Estuaria. Just as they are about to leave, Garcillán is surprised to hear someone call him by his name.

"Ah, Walter Penn!"

The flushed official, slightly nauseated and stammering, looks quickly at the clock, asks for Rosario, and starts to run because the *Hardy* is about to sail.

Once outside, the Englishman feels a little more firm and decisive and thanks his two friends for offering to accompany him to the pier. Yes, even though it is a clear night, he does not know the way. Echea takes him by one arm and Garcillán by the other, encouraging the Englishman to lean on him. The official talks and laughs, but he knows that he has little time. He had spent all afternoon looking for his friends, wanting to say goodbye to them one more time, perhaps for the last time . . . Who knows?

"But duty above all," he mumbles incoherently, "the ship must sail."

A loud and urgent whistle corroborates his prediction, and Walter Penn, helped by his friends, arrives on board just as the *Hardy* loosens its anchor amidst the propellers' crackling reverberations.

From the deck the official keeps talking to his friends on shore, "Oh, those Andalusian liqueurs, the Spanish women . . . Rosario's unforgettable charm!"

The noise of the maneuvers drowns out his words. The ship is already afloat, sailing diligently and adventurously by the light of a single lantern, dimmed by fog. The light dissolves until it is no more than a point and then it disappears in the depth of night. The siren's call is also swallowed up by darkness, and with its light and sound extinguished, the *Hardy* turns into a ghost.

THE WINDROSE OF DESTINY

Gabriel awakens, confused and tired. The moment becomes filled with intangible things, a vast expanse of forgetfulness, a vague sensation of absurdity. Still disoriented, he feels the mysterious breath of another presence. He turns his face and by dawn's soft light he sees Thor, his eyes wide open, hunched in the middle of the room.

"What are you doing there?" he asks him brusquely, in a muffled tone, without knowing what he himself was doing, fully dressed and lying in a sordid bed that was not the customary corner of his bunk bed.

"Waiting for you to calm down."

"What for?"

"To tell you that we got drunk."

"Really?"

"And we missed the boat."

Instantly, Gabriel knows that this is true. Fully awake now, he listens silently to his companion, who has stood up and urges him, "Come on, let's go."

"Where are we going?"

"I don't know. Besides everything else they did, these women have also left us without a cent."

The giant, who can handle drink and depression better than his friend, had already sobered up before dawn, and he realized that the *Hardy* had sailed without them and that they are penniless.

"Let's go," he repeats. "For as long as I've been sailing, I've never missed a boat until today. Ah, they must have been witches!"

Like the majority of Basques, Thor was superstitious, and even though he never knew any of his region's legends firsthand because he became a cabin boy at a tender age, he inherited a belief in spirits and magic spells.

The miserable bedstead trembles as Gabriel, sad and humiliated, gets up and follows his companion along the mazelike halls of the building. The sound of snoring, the stench of drunken breathing, humanity's hot and bitter smell, emerge from the other rooms. The huge dance hall, empty and in disarray, is hazy in the gray light of the early morning.

Outside, the more powerful street lights hurt the sailors' eyes, dissipating the last drop of their drunkenness. They find themselves in a poor and run-down neighborhood, on the lee side of a flowering hill, as they walk past numerous shabby inns, seedy hotels, hovels, and brothels that are the foundations and suppliers of El Vaivén.

These outskirts, too disreputable and too popular for such a peaceful, white city with an innocent air, are fed by Industry and Progress, and by the mountains and sea that need them like a warehouse of vile frivolities for the masses who work in the mines and the docks in this cheerful country of wine and sun.

Mechanically, the young men head for the shore, leaving behind the alleys and shacks of the slums. The echo of their fading footsteps is the only audible sound. The city is still asleep, lazily avoiding dawn's gentle chill, and beyond the port, the air and sea are silent, and a serene stillness reigns along the coast.

The iron-rimmed shores rise up darkly from the flat and motionless sea, which, like a mirror, reflects the emerging light, the solid outline of the great ships, the slender ram of the cara-

vels, the graceful slope of the sailboats, the slimness of the ca-
noes and galleys—in short, the enchantment of marine life
that is reborn in the early dawn.

The sailors of the *Hardy* fix their gaze on the horizon and
look longingly for traces of their ship. Each is weighed down
by a different sorrow, but—contrite and confused—they are
immobilized by the same pain.

Gabriel thinks about Aurora and he sees his hopes fluctuate
and vanish, defeated by destiny. He has the feeling that he will
never be able to find a calm path for his beloved in the vast-
ness of the waters, and that the fatal direction of his karmic
wind-rose will take him to the depths of the earth. Twice he
was tossed ashore, starving and destitute, next to the flayed
mountains, and his fate is pulling him down obstinately
toward the abyss of the mines. The call must be heeded; God
can be found in the stones as well as at sea.

Rocked by the waves of his soul, the young man turns his
eyes toward the route he must follow, and, at the end of the
landscape that is unfolding in the light, he can just barely discern the fleshy softness of a warm and sensual mountain, a
lost outline in the sky, a shadow born of an obsession. But he
says, "It's the grave that is calling me loudly!" And a dark, hidden affliction numbs his thoughts.

"What are you mumbling?" asks Thor, worried. His pupils
reflect fear like those of a persecuted deer, and for a moment
his robustness has been drained of all courage; he is an amor-
phous and insecure hulk. Being left ashore by the coal
freighter has deprived him of his Herculean aplomb . . . Without the grimy and pugnacious ship, he has lost his bearings
because to sustain his vigor, his feet have to be planted on a
mechanical power. Now, like a debilitated force, he relies instinctively on his companion's intelligence to supply him with
spiritual support.

"What are you saying?" he repeats. "Where are we going?"

"Well," answers Gabriel with sorrowful resignation, "I'm
going to work in those mines that rise up there above the river
. . . Do you want to come?"

"I'll go wherever you go," mumbles Thor in blind compliance. With his burly figure, dark complexion, disheveled hair,
and thick lips, he looks like a barbarian next to his friend,
whose noble face is flushed with an expression of deep con-

centration. Both look at the estuary's tremulous current, each troubled by different worries. Thor utters a few hoarse words of goodbye; Gabriel listens to a ship's lament piercing the silence, and the long plaintive sigh of the sea escaping from the dunes penetrates his heart.

9

Shores and Hills

HOPE

As PLANNED, ROSARIO AND JOSÉ LUIS ARE READY TO LEAVE ESTU-
aria early in the morning. They are being seen off by Echea,
whom they hope to meet again soon because in just a few
days, at the end of August, the time period of his banishment
from Dite will be over. Echea plans to return there with more
verve than ever to launch another heroic campaign against the
Nordetanos and in favor of the workers, encouraged by having found such providential and conscientious collaborators.

The Champion is indifferent about his worn-out shoes,
shabby suit, and empty pockets. Standing close to the train
window from which Rosario is leaning out, he murmurs with
a gleam of anxiety in his eyes:

"Fortune is smiling on me for the first time. My destiny has
changed and I feel touched by God's hand."

He acts like a sleepwalker, and Rosario, moved and confused by the mixture of hope and worry in his speech and behavior, hardly knows what to answer as she talks to him,
leaning gently and timidly in his direction. Fascinated, she
raises her brown eyes under the dark arch of her eyebrows
and envelops the young man in the insinuating brilliance of
her smile.

José Luis is engaged in a conversation with one of their con-
tacts in Estuaria, who has also come to see them off. This elegant and mature gentleman, whose mission in life is to bear a
historic surname and be Estuaria's representative in sporting
events, knows Echea and greets him in a jovial and condescending manner, "Hello, my friend. What are you doing
around here?"

75

"Not much," Echea answers evasively and without paying much attention to the asker.

The sportsman turns to José Luis and tells him in a low voice, while flashing a disdainful look in Echea's direction, "Poor guy, he doesn't have a penny to his name."

The train huffs and puffs; the courteous exchanges become briefer and the waving of hands begins. Rosario, wearing a lovely flower pinned to her dress, continues to lean out the window, looking at the platform. Aurelio remains standing there a long time, his back to the sportsman, as he follows the departing train with his eyes and listens to the fading sound in the clear silence of the morning.

THE PATH

The early morning hour and the magnificent weather imbue the plains with a diffuse enchantment, a liquid and vaporous vagueness that is a mixture of sun and water.

The train plunges into the zone of the wetlands, between submerged fields and jungles of reeds, through golden roadsides covered with furze and oak plantations. One by one, the alluvia's thin edges are taken over by salty ponds that reflect the clouds and by brilliant pools, asleep amidst the muddy earth. Surrounded by marshes, the estuary's mirrorlike surface seizes the sky and bounces it back, showering the purity of the landscape with delirious brilliance.

On one side, the train leaves the following sites behind along its journey: the Cicrconfuso Sea, as the Muslims called it; the desert of Arenas Gordas, with its herd of untamed horses and its travelers wandering across the dunes; and the boundary line beyond which lies La Rábida, the forgotten and decaying *mossaláh*, or monastery; the towns of Palos de la Frontera and Moguer; and on the other side are the fertile orchards watered by the Anicoba, as well as the vineyards, orange trees, and olive groves that surround the capital.

Some modest coastal vessels, such as the small three-masted xebecs and catboats—reminiscent of the corsairs' swift galliots—are sailing up the estuary, at a distance from the train's inland route. They glide noiselessly, carried by the current and helped by a sail or the gentle rowing of the oars that shine like gold in the sun and gild the slices of foamy water. And with vagrant airs, the vessels lose themselves on the horizon, amid palm trees and tamarinds, almond trees and rosemary fields that bloom marvelously above the motionless crystal surface, near the corner of town that is exposed to frequent flooding.

The train is the company's property and in its first-class compartments there is a notice, signed by the general manager, Martín Leurc: "Passengers are kindly requested not to put their feet up on the cushions and not to commit any other acts that may affect the cleanliness of the compartment." This sign seems to warn against the North's savage invasion of the sweet southern valley. Rosario tells her brother she is concerned that the exploiters of the mine—almost the only ones who travel along this route—need such shameful and explicit reminders. But José Luis reminds her that the Nordetanos are renowned for their courtesy, and therefore he assumes that Dite must have its share of uneducated and coarse immigrants, a horde of newly rich who made their fortune in the bleak shade of the slag heaps. His theory, which coincides with what the Champion had told them, upsets Rosario because it is like a harsh cry that disrupts the moment's extraordinary harmony.

They are the only passengers in the compartment and they yield to the pleasure of admiring the rare beauty of the waters, which casts a lethal spell on the villages and gardens. Magically, the irrigated valley reflects the furtive image of the surroundings: ships, birds, clouds, and the train are mirrored in the inlet's billowy waters with fragile and mysterious enchantment. The two journalists feel fortunate to find such beauty along the way.

The city of San Juan del Puerto, embayed by the river—which here is as broad as a lake—bathes its whitewashed houses in the waters, and when the tide rises, the vessels and their full-blown sails are visible from its gardens and windows. To the west of the city, the landscape consists of hills covered with aloes, rockroses, and wild olive trees.

The train has stopped and the wind's whisper can be heard coming from the sea. The two men who are sitting silently at the train station seem to be listening to this sound. They notice Rosario at the window, and while they confer with each other, she turns to her brother and exclaims, "Those two are sailors from the *Hardy*."

"Are you sure?"

"Look at them: one is the young man with the dog and the other is Thor."

Recognizing them, José Luis is surprised to see them there. They look tired and worried. Since leaving Estuaria at dawn, they have been walking along the railroad tracks, where the many channels and lakes have made them feel pursued by the currents. They are sweaty in their tightly knit jerseys, but they had to sell their cotton blouses to buy some food.

Garcillán wants to ask them questions and offer his assistance. "Yes," agrees Rosario, "we have to help them because they look very forlorn."

But the whistle blows and the platform disappears slowly; the two men remain there, quiet and alone. The two departing passengers visualize the sailors' desperate situation: it is easy to guess that they are thinking of trying their luck in the mines, replacing one abyss with another.

José Luis remembers that he saw Thor at midnight on the dangerous premises of El Vaivén. He can imagine the mishap that befell the sailors, and he regrets not having been able to help them at the station. And from these conjectures his thoughts move on to other reflections when he suddenly notices that the veins of the Saltés, the river that irrigates these plains, have turned bloody, and the valley's gentle slope— broken up by the shoals whose red sands are illuminated by the water—is becoming increasingly barren and sterile.

Here the railroad tracks separate from the sandy terrain and bogs as they start their climb along an arid road up to the unique and romantic city of Niebla, rising above the river's edge. This former capital of a municipality where a king once held court still proudly displays its bastions, painted in a warm vermilion shade, and the round and square towers of its impressive fortification are an excellent example of an *al-medina*, or Islamic city. Its decaying facade shows vestiges of elegantly arched windows, and the pellitories, a type of climbing plant, are anchored in the classic adornment above the Moorish door, letting their flowers fall through the slender vertical supports of the windows.

The entire walled complex, built on an austere lime foundation, protrudes vibrantly, its stone masonry steeped in sunlight. Wreathed around a subterranean cave, the Saquia laps the legendary rocks and serenades them in an eternal tribute. Here the waters of the so-called Copper River have a violent color, tinting the shores with a tragic hue.

Standing by the train window, the travelers are absorbed in the contemplation of the city that rises straight up from the road like a dolmen, the stony monument of yore used for marking tombs. José Luis and Rosario surmise that much suffering lies hidden behind the village's red, rocky profile and that, in the silence of the forest, history's affliction bleeds and cries out to a humanity that is asleep and dreams.

Yet, although the battlements dodder and the walls have sunk into oblivion, a breath of life is perceptible behind those horseshoe arches, those curtains gilded by time, and those monumental doors without panels, submerged between bastions. Every so often, the graceful figure of a woman appears, dressed in white, walking serenely and calmly along the corridors of what was once the Castle of the "Moorish Queen," later Guzmán's Tower, and finally the Palace of Al Motmid. She is an English lady, a lover of the beautiful and the marvelous, who has converted the ruins into rooms and the surrounding corridors into museums, and who, like a spiritual guardian of the relics, lives amid the shaken stone blocks and the ivy's rebellious tufts.

The sky bathes the ruins in an indigo light as intense as an escutcheon's deep azure, a most appropriate background for remembering the valiant image of the *neblí*, the falcon trained by the Visigoths, which gave the city its name. Niebla made Spanish falcons famous, and today the golden almond trees that grow in the clay pits where seashells once fixed their rampant spirals attest to the country's emergence from poverty.

There is no more fitting place for the presence of this symbol of national pride, the "noble and graceful" falcon, profiling its beak in a burning blue coat of arms, than above the desolate mantelpiece of this Andalusian fortress, which has endured through the centuries and which bears the marks left by its formidable invaders.

THE RIVER OF PAIN

Late in the afternoon, the sailors of the *Hardy* also reach the outskirts of Niebla and begin to comb the historic village in search of a place to stay. All day they had been walking around slowly and languidly as if beset by doubts, and they took their time to say goodbye to the last little boat on the horizon lowering its sail with an air of fatigue, like a bird folding its wings. Scorched by heat, they had climbed the reddish, treeless hills of Al-Xaraf, leaving behind the vast terrain that extends toward Seville, and where what were once the fabulous Gardens of Hercules with their many olive trees have become arid lands, royal hunting grounds, and brushwood where goats romp.

The sun is setting and the walkers long for the peace of the little boat that is probably sailing calmly in the red wake left by the dying orb. Some wheat fields, pale and ripe by now, invade the town's outskirts, where the Roman circus, the synagogue, the hermitage, and the Muslim market once stood, and where the immense olive plantations that yielded their exquisite oils to the Orient were no more.

Gabriel and Thor enter the city through an opening in the wall and head for the so-called Black Quarters, inhabited by Indians who, according to popular legend, are descendants of those that Columbus had brought to Palos and to Moguer. The race is represented by some timid, yellow creatures—still pure and unmixed after all these years—who peer cautiously from their huts. The sailors do not dare ask for refuge in the miserable rubble where these strange people live.

After stilling their hunger somewhat, they keep walking and go back out through the cleft in the fortress. There, in the open fields, always along the side of the railroad tracks, they meet up with the Saquia again, withdrawn in its riverbed, but more solemn and less noisy than during its course through the flatlands, more unique and awe inspiring than any other Spanish river.

Its water volume limited by the estuary, it does not bustle too much or too loudly, but runs along its flat and shallow riverbed with a dull murmur and a dramatic color, acquired in the lodes of copperas where it originates.

The river has a rich and malevolent history: known as Urium in Roman times, it was later called Aceche, the fearful "river of tears," about whose waters it is said that "no fish nor any sort of life can exist, neither may persons, nor animals, drink of it with impunity, nor is it of any use to the inhabitants of the villages. . ." Its treacherous waters mix with those of the Agrio River, which originates in the Salomón Hills, and later it also allows the sinister stream of Pozos Amargos to add its waters. On several occasions, the Saquia plunges like a dagger into the mountain's copper-colored flank, and, as it passes through the gray shale, it becomes tinged with the mines' extraordinary colors.

Now the river is asleep, its percussion silenced. It languishes in exhaustion, waiting for the swellings of winter to inflame the rapids that bring death to the peaceful creatures in the sea. And its repose is heavy with guilt and anxiety; its remorse gnaws at the shores and reddens them with a crimson fringe.

The travelers identify intimately with the fateful influences of this river of pain, which is silent and murky like treason. Though afraid, they follow its course, which lures them like a fatal path.

Nightfall is accompanied by a warm breeze that feels like the earth's exhalation. The lonely and gloomy landscape stretches upward until it reaches the contemplative mountain side. An indefinable sound trembles in the air: maybe Time is sharpening its scythe on the scraggy back of the peaks. Trying to stay on course, the itinerants stretch out on the shore's rough edge to sleep at the mercy of the wind and the moon.

10

The Wings of the Mountain

CLIMBING

AFTER WAKING UP, WITH THE SUN IN THEIR EYES AND OBLIVION IN their consciousness, the young men continue to follow the road, obediently and mechanically, as if fulfilling an obligation. They notice that the fields turn more pleasant and delightful the higher they climb and that, contrary to their first impression, the mountains seem farther than when they saw them beneath the trembling cluster of stars.

Now the peaks flee from them to embroider the horizon and only some white fields abloom with rockroses stretch out before them.

The fertile plains, where olive trees and vines grow, are aglow with the oleander's poisonous purple and carpeted with the healthy blue of the borage. Once the sun reaches its zenith, this joyous orgy of colors, sprinkled with dew in the benign light of the early hours, releases an overwhelming perfume that stifles the atmosphere. Plants burn, trees contract into desperate immobility and the thirsty road pushes toward the Saquia, along whose veins vegetation grows in furious abundance. Here the Moorish myrtle's solitary flowers mingle with the sedge's green sprigs, the fennel's golden parasols, the wheat's gleaming spikes, and the willow's yellow antlers. A medicinal and balsamic fragrance lingers, exuded by the rhizomes hidden in the ground, the resin contained in the bark, and the wild fruits' woody stems.

The air is heavy with an exuberance of aromas that perturbs the travelers. The branches emit a muffled moan and the fresh cloud of lilies swoons on the hilltops and the entire hot landscape is reflected in the limpid waters.

The earth's sap is like a crystal with ever-changing shades

of blue, red, black, golden, violet, and pink; it is a lymph that takes on the color of the different coppers and sulfates saturating it. Mysterious and changeable, it flows along a bed of clean and hard slate devoid of any trace of vegetation: it is Death, mirroring the loveliness of the shores and fleeing to Life's dark side, unfurling its livid splendor along the way.

The slopes have become steeper and more mountainous and yet they still bloom with a wild array of flowers; the road narrows into a sickle; trees and people bend down in fatigue toward the deceptive smoothness of the infernal river.

And suddenly the entire landscape rises up at once, the mountain chains collide and break up into fissures and precipices, pursuing each other as if searching for a westward escape. They appear to have lost their direction and become crazed by a sense of violence that pushes them skyward, and they form a terrible mass of strangely colored and slaty clay.

Here the surroundings are devoid of flowers and shrubs, the last remnants of medicinal herbs have disappeared, and the furrows made by the birds are swept clean by the wind: the devastation caused by the mineral begins to manifest itself.

It is growing late. Thor and Gabriel keep walking glumly and warily, without abandoning the curvy shoreline. After passing Jaramar's railroad station, they continue climbing upstream along the edge of the river as if determined to find its sinister source.

Several long trains pass each other along the railroad tracks. They transport the extracted mining products to the capital and bring needed materials to the mine, such as the age-old vine stocks, which once thrived in the neighboring hills, but—as yet another contribution from the country to the company in a time of scarce combustibles—they had been pulled out to feed the furnaces.

The brakemen riding on these trains, which pass every twenty minutes, day and night, stand on a small footboard, without a handgrip or any other safeguard, and jump from one wagon to another while the trains are moving, maybe even turning or descending. Even though it is against the law, they are forced to work fifteen to eighteen hours because of a shortage in personnel.

The sailors pay scant attention to these red-tinged acrobats who are in constant danger of being crushed under the convoy's wheels, because their worried gaze is fixed on pale and sullen men who are wrapped in bandages and blankets. These sick or wounded employees are hospital fodder, being carried back and forth in an unending procession to Estuaria because there is no room for them in Dite's hospital.

Very few passengers willingly choose to take these restless and speedy trains, which encircle the river with a bloody and noisy ribbon. Uniformed employees, a badge on their hat and a sword hanging from their belt, check the tickets and take care of the station in a fierce militaristic manner: these guards are the company's spies and the administration's lackeys.

This road, with its clear green waters and its air saturated by sulfates, belongs to the Nordetanian Company now, all the way from the mine's easterly ridges to the gigantic extensions abutting in Salomón Hill.

THE OLD MAN AND THE YOUNG GIRL

There is an intimation of the town's intense activity. Beneath the transparent river, an extensive cement foundation discharges blue sulfate from its open torrent flumes and drainpipes, tinting the water in brilliant tones of amethyst and dark shades of turquoise.

The walkers hear a fierce droning noise: horrendous voices blend into a burning and agonizing exhalation that shakes the earth with a fearful tremor and undulates in the skies. The sounds, reminiscent of cannon shots, or artillery being dragged, or horses galloping wildly, suggest the feverish convulsion that precedes an important battle.

Confronted with the water's imposing haughtiness, the sailors step back instinctively and cross the railroad tracks; for the first time in the hundred and eighty-three kilometers of their trip they feel disoriented.

Nearby they sight a railroad station and some modest houses that look inhabited. According to the sign at the paltry platform the station is called "Nay." When a warning signal is needed, a piece of railroad track is struck with a hammer to serve as a makeshift bell. Behind the station a few scattered hovels dot the arid and lumpy lots. Gabriel and Thor are now at the outskirts of the mine, driven by necessity to approach

those vile lodgings. Suddenly a cry as piercing as any Moorish
war-whoop catches their attention.

Perched precariously atop an olive bin, a tall old man with
copper-colored skin waves at them. When they get closer, they
see that he is accompanied by a lovely young woman with a
graceful figure, eyes as golden as honeysuckle, and brilliant
black curls, hidden by the simple cloak she wears to protect
herself a little from the sun.

"Where are you going?" asks the old man in a fatherly tone,
lowering his voice as if afraid of being overheard.

"To look for work," answers Gabriel, summing up their
plight in a few words.

Thor adds, "We're hungry."

"Do you have any money?"

"Just a few worthless coins."

"No luggage and no money," mumbles the old man and,
turning to the girl, he asks, "Aren't you carrying bread and
wine?"

She puts down the basket and, unwrapping a loaf of bread
from a clean cloth, she hands it to them, along with a full, pot-
bellied bottle.

Seated on the clumps of earth thrown ashore by the river,
the travelers eat and drink anxiously. The young girl watches
them with a smile as they listen to the old man:

"My name is Vicente Rubio and I've suffered a lot of injustices during the more than forty years that I've been working
in these mines. I'm considered a rebel because I joined the
Nerva labor union and because I'm not afraid to speak up
when necessary. They're watching me carefully, looking for
any excuse to punish me. Tomorrow it'll be two weeks that I
have not had any work this month. I decided to accompany my
daughter so I could help her carry up the laundry that she and
her mother wash for those people. We saw you coming and
knew you weren't from around here because you walked
around aimlessly. I waved to you from my hide-out because
I'm hoping to help you, if I can . . ."

Chewing on the bread crust, Thor mumbles a few words of
thanks and Gabriel shows his appreciation of Vicente Rubio's
confidence by also telling him about his background and circumstances.

"Ah, you're from the cold region!" says the Andalusian, gesturing vaguely in the general direction of Gabriel's distant northerly homeland. He continues talking, quickly and with visible indignation, about the mine workers, more oppressed every day, without any rights to defend or redeem themselves, and suffering all sorts of injustices and abuses.

"You'll find work," he predicts. "They've fired many workers and are short-handed. But you won't find lodgings in Dite because the police are strict with strangers."

"In that case . . ." says Gabriel disheartened.

"You'll come with us. We live up there on Monte Sorromero, a village where we have permission to house strangers. I know a shortcut that gets us to the mine in a jiffy . . . For nine years, I made that trip with my son until one day I returned by myself . . . He stayed at the mine, crushed under a lode that had caved in."

He rises up, as if prodded by the memory of that terrible catastrophe. The young men get up as well, having finished off all the bread and almost all the wine.

An uncomfortable silence sets in as one of the guards approaches.

"Who are these fellows and what are they doing here?" he questions the old man.

"They're strangers who've come to look for work and I've offered to put them up until they can get settled. They were just having a snack."

"That's good. But don't linger near the station because my orders are to keep everyone out."

"Don't worry, we were just about to leave."

The guard salutes with a slight bow and returns to his lookout post in the rickety shop. He is young and seems bored, judging from the unenthusiastic manner in which he wears his military rifle.

Pointing at him, Vicente whispers, "We're friends. He is not too eager to carry out his duties. Before joining the military, he used to work in the open pit, and he'd rather be working with us than for the company."

Slowly, they pick their way in the pit's torrid atmosphere where the sun burns like a volcano. In empathy, Gabriel inquires about the son whose life was sacrificed.

"He was a lot like you," answers the father, "noble and martial. Twenty months have passed since the accident and next month would have been his twenty-fifth birthday. I have no sons left. One of my two daughters is married to an ill-tempered fellow from Córdoba, who is in charge of tending the furnace at the smeltery. They live in Nerva. This is my other daughter who is a great help to me! Her name is Casilda . . ."

Vicente Rubio wants to tell them everything because talking consoles him. His eyes, often clouded by tears, light up at the prospect of helping others. Even though his robustness would make him seem youthful, life has weighed him down so heavily in body and soul that he looks older than his sixty years.

He walks with a stoop because ever since he was a young man his ribs have suffered from hauling heavy loads of metal. His jobs have included carrying slag, rubbish, and copper bars, and working as a borer and machinist. During his frequent visits to the hospital he has been treated for wounds, fevers, "copper-colic," sprains, "tunnel sickness," and exhaustion. His health was buried in the slag heaps and the wells, and his happiness in the landslide that took his son from him.

The acuteness of his suffering and failures and the irrevocable vanishing of hope has made him mutinous. He has joined the rebels, the protesters and redeemers, playing an influential role in a newly formed organization of liberators to which he brings the authority of old age, his sympathetic personality, and insights gained from long years of slavery.

A supreme sense of justice and brotherhood has awakened in this man with religious and selfless fervor. Neither he nor his son will reap any possible benefits, but he works on behalf of others with touching diligence. Presently, there is something akin to an apostolic mission in his concern for these two strangers and the eagerness with which he receives and cares for them.

LUCIFER'S VALLEY

Walking across the barren highland, they follow the path up to the mountain until they reach the small plateau where the pyrite smeltery is located and from where pipes carry the furnace fumes to the nearest peak. The winding pipes, shiny and black, look like monstrous snakes asleep in the sun; they slither and glisten in the red dryness as they undulate and grope in the dark to find the main pipe that opens at the mountaintop and, like an inextinguishable volcanic eruption, spews smoking sparks.

"If the wind blows from the sea," explains Vicente Rubio, pointing at the smoke being belched by the huge chimney, "nobody can breathe in the surrounding places, much less near the furnaces, where the smelters standing under the hood suffocate on arsenic-filled smoke."

He proceeds to tell them some episodes about the days when the copper pyrite was stacked in small pyramid-shaped mounds to be calcinated out in the open. The layers of smoke produced by the fires that converted more than two hundred thousand tons of sulfur into sulfuric acid every year covered the vegetation like a shroud that extended from this spot to the border with Portugal.

"All the hillside orchards and forests were destroyed!" bemoans the miner, feeling like a farmer.

And everybody looks anxiously in the direction of the narrow valley known as Lucifer's Valley, which shelters the smelteries and feeds the laboratories, sifters, electric plants, and reservoirs.

The dreadful complex of buildings extends along the railroad tracks, amidst platforms, piles of combustibles, creaking and screeching railroad equipment—tools and accessories—all covered by fumes and dust. The glass and zinc roofs, the open sheds and windows, all reveal the disheveled heart of the furnace, voracious and crackling. The moaning and trembling of the dark workshops fills Gabriel with terrible memories of similar noises at the mine he just left.

"How many hours a day do the miners work here?" he asks, pointing at the smeltery that seemed far off because it was hidden behind a huge black cloud of debris.

"Eight hours a shift."

"How much do they earn?"

"Between sixteen and twenty reales."

Frail and stunted, palm trees wither along the bright paths leading to the village. In the valley, dusk casts its first shadow and all the light is gathered on the peaks, skipping along the deserted highlands with fiery splendor.

His hunger stilled, Thor forgets about his fatigue and

catches up with the young girl, taking advantage of the narrow path that forces them to walk in pairs. Hoping to sound refined, he says a few innocent phrases to which Casilda listens with the cool air of a virgin, hiding her eyes shyly under her eyelashes.

Her father is still deploring the terrible devastation of the fields. "In this part of the Sierra Morena, the sulfuric fires have not left a single nest or flower nor one healthy blade of grass."

LAND'S END

The landscape seems to respond to his complaint by unfolding its aching soul. The flames and dust swirl on the distant mountaintops, but no wings ruffle the wind up there. The sun has dropped behind the hill, where the mining activities emit the muffled roar of a waterfall. Now the wilderness is plunged into darkness.

The travelers continue to climb in the encompassing solitude and soon they cease to pay attention to the confused rumblings. Casilda amuses herself by watching the clouds, pierced by lightning, rapidly change shape.

"I guess you're bachelors," says Vicente suddenly.

Thor rushes to reply affirmatively and Gabriel, without thinking, does the same. The girl turns around and, emboldened by the cloak of darkness, looks at him without lowering her lids. He receives her gaze eagerly, hoping to mirror himself in the tranquility of her spirit. While in the heavens a marvelous hand lights the stars, he hears a clear voice: this is the intimate moment that softens a sailor's heart and stirs the rocks at the bottom of the precipice.

Invaded by a strange emotion, the four sojourners fall silent as they leave behind the noise of the mine in their climb to the peak, which rises between the workshop and the open pit. The only reminders of the industrial din are the drills' muffled reverberations and the distant whistling of the trains. As they advance, they begin to lose the notion of life, feeling weighed down by the silence of the road that is covered by rocks and copper. Tharsis, or Land's End, could not be a more appropriate name.

At times a thin line of fire winds through the heap of debris: it is a convoy of burning slag along the dark slope that produces a violent flash of luminosity when it breaks up. The night transforms the smoke emitted from the chimney into a proud reddish crest, giving the mountain the semblance of an erupting volcano.

And high above the billowing gusts, a new moon is born whose pure fire will never be extinguished by any human breath.

11

The Metal of the Dead

EVOCATION

PERHAPS IN THEIR ORIGINAL STATE, THESE AGE-OLD CRYSTALLINE slates burned in the incandescent oceans and then suffered the freezing cold of the Ice Age. Maybe since time immemorial, their grains of sand have been dragged out by an infinitely slow molecular force and replaced by metallic sediments that accumulated in their innards. The mountains evolved into rocks swollen with lode, undergoing polishing and refining over thousands of centuries. Their precious treasures of sulfur, zinc, iron, copper, silver, and gold remained deposited at the bottom of Pluto's domains, and many other riches, such as porphyry, marble, alabaster, and crystal gems, were exposed in the strata or in outcropped veins or in the aftermath of a rare flood of lava.

The mysterious liquids of sulfuric acid ran through the mountains' veins, and its virgin marrow trembled and pulsated with the dark birth of the abyss. The mountains arose in silent turbulence, from east to west, thousands of meters above sea level, in a privileged land, where the air and sun robbed their haughty slopes with jungles and forests. They grew in this pure and virtuous manner, like the mountains on Mercury—a planet whose metal deposits are not exploited amidst mud and blood—and they lived in the serene enjoyment of their privileges and served as an example of God's works.

But humanity, emerging at the dawn of civilization, began to feel the fascination exerted by the outcrop of minerals, and men's souls succumbed to the first temptation of avarice. At the time of the industry's primitive beginnings, the rock's sleeping backbone was attacked with axes, hammers, and chisels, and the troglodytes adorned their caves with jasper and basalt amulets. Full of shallow holes from being punctured with rudimentary tools, the mountains looked like honeycombs.

Over the course of centuries, "a vessel from Samos pushed by the wind" reached the nearby coast. In a friendly exchange with the Iberians of the highlands, the ship's crew traded balsams, purple dye, and rubber for silver, gold, and gray copper. Ever since that time, Tartesius, hidden in the west of the peninsula, became the Spanish Tharsis, extolled in the Bible as the promised land.

The Phoenicians made greedy use of slate, while the ships of Tyrean King Hiram, together with those of King Solomon, tried to quench their voraciousness with the country's treasures. The primitive tools were buried under the rubbish and replaced with more efficient means of mining. The fertile crystal deposits ceased to serve as the peaceful abode of Vulcan, the heavenly blacksmith who decorated Venus's palace with coppery stars. And they made a great pact with Pluto, god of the underworld, denizen of the realm of eternal darkness, impassive ruler of the dead.

The brilliance of the "mountain copper" turned the Great Temple of the Jews into one of the world's marvels; Tyre and Sidon prospered thanks to the excavations made by the Asians at the "mysterious confines," and the Tartesians were no longer content with receiving rhymes, poems, perfumes, or the alphabet in exchange for their minerals. All the human passions that lend their force to greed began to rage on Cerro Salomón, the hill that still bears the name of the wise king whose castle dominated the landscape.

Romans and Carthaginians arrived, lured by the booty, growing more cruel at the sight of the dust that could be converted into coins, and fighting over the manufacturing of those red discs that looked like corollas. They showed no compassion for the rich and deep deposits, nor for the sad and miserable men. Imperial Rome became the owner of those mountaintops and subjugated them under the arch of death. More than twenty thousand slaves were buried in the repulsive darkness of wells and caves. They measured the time of their interminable labor by the candle light, and they dragged themselves like snakes through the narrow passageways, carrying the minerals on their shoulders. They passed the dark earth from hand to hand, like the Greeks passing the torch in the Olympic Games, and only the last man in line ever saw the sunlight.

The mountain's bashful bosom was stripped without mercy, leaving a horrendous bald spot at the bottom of the peak. As if guided by rational feeling and human volition, the powerful rocks rebelled tragically against this attack and defended themselves by unleashing livid lakes and venomous acids, as well as the barbaric roar of faults.

The miners would emerge from the light shafts, aflame from the subterranean fire, in pain and near death; meanwhile, the slag heaps, stacked like monstrous columns, grew more numerous, and the wooden piles and windlasses creaked. In the pits, bold metallurgic progress emerged from a mix of Sagunto's furnaces and ancient Italian water vessels: symbols of a new civilization, links in a chain, the cuffs and screws of shackles.

Slavery's infamous history was further blackened with the thirst for gold. Even if it meant sacrificing innocent lives, the medals, cold as ice and pale yellow like envy, which bore the proud profiles of kings and emperors, had to be minted.

Hundreds of years of industrial activity managed to flay mountaintops and slopes, collapse ravines, dig deep abysses, and cover all the vegetation with a horrendous thick black layer. And for a long time now the pain has been rising up from the depths of the ravines, spreading its mourning over the landscape. As Rodrigo Caro wrote in the seventeenth century:

It is almost impossible to walk for even a league without stepping on dross and coal, and without seeing excavations, or scorched rocks, taken from their places and thrown into the valleys, or great hills that have been completely split or have suffered devastation. I cannot deny that I was moved by this horrendous spectacle and that I reacted with indignant surprise and pity when my eyes beheld this novel sight. Who would not be astonished to see that human boldness could be so daring and that the hunger for gold was more powerful than the hardness of rocks. It seemed to me that it was my obligation as a curious bystander to enter the caves of those hills whose innards had been scraped to rob them of their silver and gold. I had the courage to walk through those dark labyrinths where our avaricious ancestors had looked for the dangerous precious metals, and it amazed me that although they fled from the sunlight, they were blindly enthralled by the yellowness of the metal, and that even at these depths they importuned Pluto, the god they both persecuted and adored. I did not dare take another step forward and my eyes did not help me either, but I perceived some shadows signaling a warning, and as I returned to the cave's entrance, still fearful and amazed, I could not completely tear myself away from them. I considered that at the same site where I now stood, some wretched mortals had looked on as half the mountain was being torn violently from its site and hurled into the valleys with a frightful noise, and that they had rejoiced in seeing Nature's destruction. I was astonished that such ravage was the price paid not for finding gold, but merely for looking for it. Near these former mines there are mounds of coal and slag that rival the natural mountains in elevation, but Nature, intent on preventing any benefit to be reaped from these ashes—reminders of the triumphs of haughty greediness—defamed them with black horror and eternal sterility. No tree would be born and no grass would grow to adorn those relics for whose sake Spain sold its liberty and forged the chains of its servitude.

The Arabs did not covet these metals, except to work them. An artistic and sensual people, they were less interested in Spain's riches than in its beauty, and during their reign they devoted themselves to the embellishment of palaces and gardens, rather than to the brutal excavation of lodes. In those times, the king's mines were used only as prisons for the condemned and cemeteries for the dead.

Much later, in the full splendor of the so-called Age of Reason and Enlightenment, it was not men but children who passed the mineral from hand to hand, slaves of a sinister network of galleries often shaken by shadowy gusts. They, like others before and after them, died by the millions in the mines or rotted in hospitals, victims of the blood-red gold and of greed, the incurable vice that numbs feelings, negates sacrifice, and paralyzes noble human efforts.

And all the coins minted at the expense of that enormous crime against the Divine Sower's commandments have always deserved to be called the metal of the dead.

A New Day

A blue star is still visible through the window pane when Casilda begins to get dressed. Unable to sleep, she has been awake since before dawn, contemplating the sky from her tiny bedroom, which looks out on the craggy and abrupt mountainside that is dissected violently into uneven strips. The abundant layers of mica, spreading wildly in all directions and folded into invisible creases, provide the flooring of this village, perched precariously and fantastically on the bluffs. The lowly and modest hamlet, caulked in typical Andalusian fashion with blinding white lime, rises bravely over the gray granite scales and uses them to form a fierce mountain landscape. It is a village devoid of paths or flower gardens, without colors or sounds, lost in the heavy silence of isolated rocks, at the mercy of winds and clouds.

The young girl watches the dawning of the new day as if seeing it for the first time. There is something new in her heart, which makes the most common and humdrum events seem enchanting and surprising. She marvels at the pale light turning red, at the sun touching the tips of the peaks, and at the quivering rainbow gliding off the mountain's dark profile.

The stranger with the sad eyes worries and thrills her. Why? He is just a poor man who arrived starving and miserable. Doesn't she have enough persistent suitors? Doesn't Pedro Abril himself, whom she reluctantly accepts as her beau, cut a much better figure than the stranger?

A gentle voice, slightly thin and brittle, murmurs close to her, "We have to serve these poor fellows some coffee."

Startled, Casilda turns around and stares at her mother with the same sense of strangeness with which she looks at everything around her. Her mother is a slender and delicate woman with white hair and withered features, whose limpid and clear blue eyes are fixed in a rigid gaze. She is deaf and, having shed so many tears, she is almost blind; her pupils billow like a lake, flooded by a light they cannot perceive. She wraps Casilda in a caressing silence and repeats, "We should give them some coffee." She cannot hear her own words, spoken without inflection and imbued with a mysterious echo from afar.

The girl nods her head and gently smoothes her mother's disheveled hair.

Marta looks old at an age when luckier women are still in the bloom of life. She was born in Val-Aroza, the "Valley of the Betrothed," a garden cultivated by the Arabs—like the orchards in Valencia and Murcia—located between the mountains of Aracena, where the Odiel River originates. When she was still young and pretty, she married Vicente Rubio, a good man from Arunda, a village of forgotten origin, who was already working in Dite, a prisoner of the galleries' dark maze. And they settled valiantly in that infernal town, far from the pomegranate trees and roses, to grow old all too fast, sacrificing their youth to the dangerous work, poverty, and meager means that afflicted their home.

Hortensia, the oldest of their three children, whose beauty made her mature fast like precocious fruit, fell in love at an early age like her mother. But she chose a heartless and brutal man as her companion, who treats her shamefully. Their only son, full of health and vigor, died a horrible death in the mine. He was Marta's darling, and she shed so many disconsolate tears over him that her vision became clouded from crying. Plunged into an even greater isolation by her recent deafness, she wanders aimlessly, touching everything around her like a sleepwalker, carrying out her chores mechanically. But instinctively she still extends her heart and hands to her fellowmen, and it is with this hospitable attitude that she received the strangers.

FRESH HOPE

Casilda is pleased to serve the men a modest breakfast. She fills the cups to the brim with dark black coffee, made from hickory that has already been boiled more than once, and no milk. Without her usual calm, the young girl places the sugar and thin slices of bread on the table. Her movements are unpretentious, harmonious, and graceful, and when she is asked a question, she answers mostly with gestures, accustomed as she is to communication in this manner with her mother.

Thor stares at her in fascination, as if contemplating the personification of fresh hope; Gabriel sighs moodily during the

pauses in his conversation with Vicente. The clean and whitewashed kitchen looks cheerful in the light streaming in
through the door.

The young men accept the humble hospitality, confident
that they can soon repay it; the mine needs workers and they
will ask for a job immediately.

"Will you be back for lunch?" interrupts Casilda, bent over
the stove.

"Today they will," answers the father. "Once they get their
wages, you can prepare them some food to take with them as
I do."

Still smiling, Marta keeps quiet.

The men go out into the hallway that leads to the bedrooms.
The parents and Casilda each have a tiny chamber with a window, while the guests sleep in the interior room that used to
belong to the son.

Like their neighbors in this small village, they do not own
their cottage, although the rent they have paid out would have
allowed them to be the proprietors several times over. Yet they
treat their unassuming abode with intimate reverence, and
thanks to their skillful care it has a clean and honest look.

Vicente comes back in from the hall to talk to Marta. Maybe
there are still some clothes in the old trunk, saved as relics of
their beloved son, whose death they mourned so much when
Earth enveloped him in her unrelenting shroud. The couple
agrees that something has to be done about the young men's
garb, and they confer in the back of the kitchen. The wife answers with a trembling voice, acquiescing to everything her
husband says.

Meanwhile Gabriel waits at the entrance. Standing next to
him on the dusty flagstones, Thor stretches his robust frame;
he looks like a native of that rocky region, or one of those legendary giants who dominate the abyss.

Some men are walking down the slippery slopes that in
many places are the only streets connecting the rustic buildings. Their typical black hats from Córdoba look worn and
shabby, their jackets are threadbare, and their pants are torn.
Although they look exhausted and wretched, a certain natural
refinement sets them apart from the working masses from
other regions. For the most part they are from Andalusia and
Valencia: haulers of a drag-seine from Málaga, mountain men

from Córdoba, fruit growers and farmers from Seville, Alicante, and Jaén. Despite their abject conditions as miners, they have preserved the aristocratic bearing of a people that, in southern and eastern Spain, acquired their purest tinge of Greco-Roman distinction. All other Spanish provinces and even Portugal furnish Estuaria with workers, but those groups do not influence the general attire: the clearly plebeian beret and blue blouse are seldom seen in this extremely seigniorial southern region, and the workers descending the craggy incline on their way to the mine are a representative example of their region's sense of elegance.

Without heeding the workers, Casilda, a fixed smile on her blood-red lips, goes up to Gabriel and gives him these fervent and sincere words: "Don't worry. You'll have a better life with us than at sea. I'll comfort you."

He looks at her avidly and sadly, thirsting for freshness like the hills, and she adds, "Do you have a girlfriend?"

He was about to answer yes, but he doesn't say anything, seduced by the innocent carnality of the love that she is offering him.

"Well, do you or don't you have a girlfriend?"

Trying to evade the question, Gabriel answers, "What about you?"

"Bah! My serenading suitors pursue me, but . . . I would only marry you."

She does not blush or feel embarrassed. The transparent words roll off her tongue with a sweet Andalusian lilt and shower the young man's heart with morning dew.

Hearing these words, Thor is more envious than surprised. He doesn't know much about social mores, and maybe it is customary even for pure women to confess their love in this fashion, yet he cannot understand how Gabriel, receiving such a declaration from Casilda, who exudes a wholesome breath of kindness, does not shout with pride and joy.

The fortunate recipient of these remarks does not have a chance to answer because the young girl, hearing her father's footsteps, changes the subject quickly and, pretending to be looking at the ravines, says, "Behind that embankment there are villages with lakes and roses. A long time ago, one of them had ash trees and the village is still called after them . . . The trees were tall and bushy, and they produced clusters of red flowers."

She points at the invisible place beyond the mountain and ponders the beauty of the trees with fierce fascination.

The workers, arriving along the slat furrows, stop and, as if receiving a message, listen respectfully to the loving evocation of plants, tree trunks, and branches that they know only from memory. The tiny village of Los Fresnos lies on the other side of the mountain, and, quenching its thirst in rivulets, it blooms in the scorched plains as a reminder of the two ash trees that once grew there.

Symbols

The group of miners descending the mountain is led by Pedro Abril, a handsome, slender, athletic, and somewhat boastful young man. He has been looking at Casilda jealously, surprised to find her in intimate conversation with two strangers. He is the only young man in the area who has had reason to believe that he is being favored by Rubio's daughter. He loves her with fierce passion, and, longing to fill his arms with her beauty, he feverishly envelops her in his tenacity and watches her as he would a fickle wife.

She usually eludes him disdainfully, but, wavering and irresolute, she pays attention to him from time to time, allowing him to harbor some hope. Suddenly she knows with certainty that she cannot love him, and she lets him know not with words but with a dark and determined gesture. Then she fixes her luminous and enthusiastic gaze on the chosen one.

Pedro Abril feels hate brewing in his soul as his illusions have turned to ashes in one instant, and the desire for vengeance is visible in his eyes as black as a tempest. Everybody catches the meaning of these looks flying back and forth with the exception of Gabriel, who is too absorbed in his own uncertainties to be aware of the mute tragedy being played out that minute.

The tense silence is broken by Vicente, who approaches calmly to do the formal introductions.

"These men," he says with some pride, pointing at his guests, "are two sailors who will work in the mines and they sympathize with our cause. Our friend Suárez here is a man of much education and he will be of great help to us; he has traveled all over the world and knows a lot about our issues."

Everybody shakes hands with Gabriel except Abril, who pretends to be distracted, but who nevertheless tries to disguise his position of presumed rival.

The group continues on their way slowly under a violent sun that bounces off the window panes and blinds them with its painfully brilliant reflections. They do not seem to be in a hurry. Somebody observes, "There's a little mountain breeze." The others turn in the direction where the wind stirs like the soul of the mountain nestled in the mica flakes.

Vicente, walking next to his new friends, warns them about the narrow downward path. "This is not the same path we took last night," he murmurs. "Since Casilda was with us then, we couldn't take this shortcut because it's a shameful place for young girls." And he adds a few words in a serious tone.

A fine thread of water feeds the rows of shrubs amidst the caverns and juttings. It is in this deplorable place that the women of the night, the poor harlots from the outskirts, come to ply their trade. They are escapees from Estuaria's caves, dregs of that infamous industry that feeds El Vaivén. Here they live in scandalously primitive conditions, sleeping in the open air, eating measly scraps ransacked from the provisions of passers-by. They are injured and insulted in exchange for a few cents and a crust of bread, and during some atrocious carousals some are beaten or stabbed to death. On those occasions, the Civil Guards come and break up the encampment, and the wretched prostitutes are taken either to jail or to the hospital.

They have reached the boundary line where the sinful area begins and, amidst the squalid palm trees, and they catch a glimpse of the provocative insinuations of half-naked women. The picaresque novel of the past is reborn in all its impudent and saucy realism under the Andalusian sun.

Taunting and gesticulating, the miners greet the beastlike women lying on the hard granite, asleep next to the rivulet's blackish film. One woman, whose blouse is ripped in shameless strips, tries to get up.

Pedro Abril insults her as he hurls a rock, "You whore . . . !"

The quartz rock glistens in its bold flight. A shout is heard as the woman touches her forehead and her hand turns red with blood.

The men laugh without a trace of compassion. Vicente says disdainfully, "These are forsaken females who turn the miners' heads and corrupt them. Let them go to hell!"

Three men feel particularly disgusted and repelled by this sterile lewdness: Gabriel, Thor, and Pedro Abril, and each one of them thinks of Casilda with different emotions. Without knowing why, they look up to the peaks where the young girl had evoked the beauty of the fields.

The mountain breeze brings a fresh breath of air from the peaks. Perhaps the saga of the mythological ash tree has reached there and the crown of the sacred Iggdrasel tree is scattering its magic in the wind . . .

12

Desolation

THE OPEN PIT

THE GROUND SEEMS TO HAVE DRUNK BLOOD. FROM THE MOMENT the workers set foot on it, they are afflicted by the "red passion," obsessed by this turbulent color that excites and crazes. Their faces become feverish and their voices sear like a ray of light. The Champion's name is mentioned.

"He'll be here soon," they mumble.

"He should have been here by now."

"It's a shame how they're treating him."

The mountains no longer soothe them with their shade; the calm silence has been torn asunder and the air is filled with tragic murmurs like the ones that precede a hurricane.

From where they are standing, they have a good view of Lucifer's Valley, furrowed by luminous gusts like the plains of Provence. They are still too far to observe the frantic activity, but they can see the eerie passing of the trains loaded with burning dross and the shower of red-hot coal emptied at every ramp.

Descending along the right side of Naya's sad brooklet, they arrive at the station with the same name. There they buy a ticket for the platform wagon that takes them to Dite, the center of the excavation, also referred to as "the Mine." In Dite, they turn into a street that bulges as if shaken by an earthquake, and suddenly they find themselves in front of the open pit called the Glory Hole, an enormous and magnificent amphitheater filled with horror.

It is a gigantic area, tiered into twenty-three stories, each thirty-six feet high and two thousand four hundred feet long, with every platform wider than the preceding one. The train runs along the rims, which are lined with dredgers, borers,

and workers rushing around in a whirlwind. Behind them are
the entrances to the former galleries, the drainage for dirty
water, and the tunnels of communication. The workers' hooks
and ropes hang from the highest junctures, looking like birds
soaring over the precipice.

The barren mountain with its coarse and rough terrain
serves as the backdrop for the pit. All around are gigantic
black heaps, formed by the twenty million cubic feet of slag
discarded in the course of twenty centuries of excavation.
Surely these are the strangest and dreariest hills to have ever
appeared on the horizon in search of the sun's caresses! A
thousand wells, innumerable excavations, and underground
galleries confirm that the world's mightiest metallurgical industry has been functioning here since ancient times.

South of the village is another hill that extends westward
until the Altar de los Bermejales, the watershed between the
Saquia and the Guadalquivir. Aptly called La Sombra Negra,
this hill looms over La Ruina, El Extravío, and Salomón, which
resemble the horrendous limbs of a monster. Their fissures
and outflows spew rocks, small mounds, and trenches onto
the terrain, emphasizing its utter harshness. And in the midst
of this barbaric landscape, the immense pit looks like a gigantic tumor that has split open in the titan's entrails.

Tools and machinery act like scalpels on swollen and feverish abscesses. Cells fester between the cracks of the layers
that resemble thick, conjunctival folds. The affected zones
produce pink, blue, and yellow substances in all the ever-
changing shades of Florentine copper. Lifting up in swellings
and furrows, the land, like diseased organic skin, is covered
by pale splotches, brown moles, and grim scars and leaks
bloody fluids, gangrenous serum, and thin, watery discharges.
The sulfate currents look like the dying body's locks of hair,
while the residues and debris are its scabs. The landslides
have the effect of surgical operations; the red entrances to the
caves resemble human arteries; and the inside of the caves is
as dark as a malignant tumor. On the platforms there are cysts
that ooze a yellowish pap; the gold mines and gullies spill liquids with the foul smell of pus. The folds of the malefic wound
provide food for worms—in this case, the miners, who dig to
survive while letting themselves be devoured . . .

A deep, unmistakable voice rises above the din of mining activities surrounding the circular wound: it is the roar of the poor dying earth, the victim of abuses and pilfering, of ulcers and excisions, torn apart by sobs . . .

SHIPWRECK

By the time Gabriel and Thor return from the office, they have been hired; everything they have seen so far surprises, confuses, and worries them in a most peculiar fashion.

They walked by Mesa de los Pinos, a wide plain that, like Vista Hermosa, is higher and more extended than Lucifer's Valley, which is confined by the two mountain chains that imprison the village. Long ago, the bald spot on Mesa de los Pinos had been covered by forest, and there is still a yearning for the pine trees that bequeathed their name to the land that holds them in eternal remembrance.

Fallow and sterile, the grove where the pines once flourished now serves as the workers' quarters. The houses, built by the company to replace those that are about to collapse near the Glory Hole, are rudimentary and identical to all the others built elsewhere for the same purpose and according to the same master plan. Lined up along the bleak wilderness in an effort to simulate streets, their sad, impersonal monotony recalls rows of beds in a public shelter, jail cells, or train wagons.

The administrative offices and the hospital are at the edge of the village. The sailors, having been examined by two doctors, received a note that had to be signed by the general manager so they could start working in the Bessemer foundry. They were to be paid fourteen reales for carrying out special duties during a twelve-hour shift. This was the only remaining option because all the other positions had been filled.

Gabriel has a strangely indifferent attitude toward everything, and Thor imitates him mechanically, without any will of his own. The unexpected and turbulent life around them mesmerizes them.

From afar, the flat land of Vista Hermosa looks like paradise. As they soon find out, the huge, green park with large buildings is protected by guards and walls like a luxurious hacienda, and at night its fountains and roses are illuminated by the magic of the blue electricity fairy. This is where the Nordetanos live, separated from the common worker and enjoying the privileges and pleasures of their culture. They have high hopes for the future, having bought their happiness with gold.

The young men do not dwell on these thoughts. The reddish paths along the deep valley lead them back to the run-down village that is surrounded by a desolate dryness, where the metallic puffs of wind make everything languish and wilt.

In this atmosphere of martyrdom and menace, they return to Dite in silence to wait for the right moment to see the general manager. They are the only ones left; their companions have been swallowed up by the cancer of the mountain like a rivulet of misery.

A temporary railing protects the edge of the village from the tremendous danger of being leveled by the pit. Only a few feet away, some dwellings are about to split when the floor yields, and, bereft of its support, the entire village threatens to collapse.

Rosario Garcillán, accompanied by her brother, is standing next to the railing, listening intently to a smiling young man, whom they just met at the inn. He is Alejandro Romero, a cheerful and kind doctor from Seville. Drawn to the miners' cause for moral and altruistic reasons, he decided to offer his professional services to the labor unions in Nerva after finishing his studies. He is a poet and a romantic with a deeply religious spirit, aware of life's challenges and given to extreme idealism.

He talks about the Champion, a friend of his and a kindred soul, while José Luis takes a newspaper from his pocket and unfolds it.

"Yes," laments the doctor, worried and sympathetic, "wait until poor Aurelio finds out that his wife is in jail!"

"But is he married?" asks a surprised José Luis, overhearing the conversation. Returning to his newspaper, he suddenly begins to tremble and turn pale.

"Oh, my God!" he shouts, "the *Hardy* has been shipwrecked!" And he immerses himself into the article, trying to find out more.

"How?"

"What are you saying?" ask Gabriel and Thor, who recognize him as they come closer.

"Ah, it's you!" answers José Luis, when he sees the sailors. The three of them exchange anxious and perplexed looks. Gabriel wants to convince himself.

"But is it sure? Is it confirmed?"

"Yes, it's completely confirmed: it was torpedoed off the coast of Portugal yesterday."

"What about the crew?"

"Wait . . ." José Luis doesn't lift his eyes from the newspaper. He keeps reading and stammers finally, "They've all perished."

"Poor Walter Penn," exclaims Rosario with a faint, faltering voice; all the blood has drained from her face and her emotions are afflicted by this heavy blow.

Having heard about the Garcillán's voyage on the English ship, the doctor can understand their painful surprise. José Luis explains that Thor and Gabriel had also been on the ship as crew members but had disembarked in Estuaria yesterday.

"By coincidence," murmurs Gabriel, inwardly distressed. In his fatalism he is convinced that Fate is pushing him irrevocably from the sea to the venomous valleys . . . His companion is in such shock that his mind seems paralyzed.

Rosario's radiant gaze peers into the depths of the caverns and glances up at the proud mountains. The secret disappointment that torments her seems insignificant in comparison with the mine's imperturbable eyes, staring at timeless darkness as if looking beyond the universe.

But suddenly the young girl disregards the mute allusion to eternity and, returning to what is troubling her, she considers, "Why shouldn't he be married? Who ever told me that he wasn't?"

She tries to think about the sinking of the *Hardy*, but it becomes confused with the shipwreck of her own illusions, and only one name floats in her consciousness, only one sad realization survives.

"Are you crying over the gunner? I envy him for that," the doctor whispers gallantly to the young girl, who didn't realize that tears were running down her cheeks.

"Oh, am I crying?" she asks, disconcerted, and then repeats with sincere feeling, "Poor Walter Penn!" She remembers her sketch of the officer and has the pious thought of drawing a cross next to it.

All this time, José Luis has been reproaching himself for the insistence with which he and Aurelio Echea had led the poor officer from the dance back to the ship.

"We sent him to his death," he accuses himself.

THE TERRIBLE ORDEAL

A guard interrupts these painful considerations.

"The mining police do not permit you to stay here."

It is Fabián Delgado, the same guard who had surprised them in Naya while the exhausted travelers were having a snack. When he catches sight of them, he worries about seeing them in the company of people he does not know.

"They're all friends of mine," explains the doctor.

"That doesn't matter, Don Alejandro; everybody has to leave from here."

"Come on, is it that urgent?"

"It is. And what's more, today the general manager is making the rounds and he'll come by here soon . . . Don't get me into trouble."

"Relax, we'll leave."

"Besides," adds the guard persuasively, "they're going to start dynamiting."

"All right, all right . . ."

He is about to leave when a shrill alarm goes off.

"That's the signal," says Rosario.

And the group steps back to seek support from a half-destroyed wall, still keeping their eyes on the cliffs. They can see the drainers pulling themselves up, looking like spiders ascending quivering threads, until they reach the picks to which the ropes are fastened. The climbers at the tail end swing back and forth like a pendulum at the sound of the second alarm.

Every miner scrambles for shelter, and the only ones who remain out in the open, besides the guards and the foremen, are the blasters who ready the fuse's capsule and insert it in the cartridge. They approach the mine's subterranean passage with funereal caution and await the final signal.

An unusually gloomy silence hangs over the Glory Hole, as if a savage and criminal plot were being hatched. In his hiding place, Death is holding his breath.

The doctor covers his mouth and whispers in a mysterious voice, "There are a hundred and fifty pounds of powder in each shot; earlier, they buried sticks of dynamite about two feet into the ground."

With all excavations halted, the blaster's task takes on a strange solemnity. It is high noon. Beneath a scorching sun, the hillside burns red and gray with smoldering ashes. Even the slightest noise sounds anxious and seems to convey the tragic impatience of the moment to the gloriously resplendent sky.

The third martial blare is heard. A line of flame extends along the platform, and the artillery men flee as the charges go off with an incredible roar. Like a pale cloud reaching high up and spreading to the very peaks, the ritual smoke of sacrifice rises to the hilltops from the depths of the excavations. A sinister air dominates the landscape; a desperate lament deafens the morning: all the children begotten by Madness seem to be screaming in unison. The rocks, gnawed by centuries, rise up from their hollows, burning and shouting; purple jets gush from the miraculous copper thicket; the innumerable mouths of the slope bark furiously; the landslides and mudslides moan as the powder reverberates.

Exiting from their fragile and half-collapsed shelter, the bystanders count twenty-three shots. Everything in the surrounding area—the ground, houses, and ruins—has been damaged. And another fearful blare, sounding like the trumpet of Jericho on Judgment Day, announces the end of the terrible ordeal.

Amidst the wisps of smoke, the pallid diggers, resigned to constant danger, emerge from the Earth's warm folds. They will rearrange the broken pieces of the terrain and sink the borer into the rocks once more, inviting Death time and again until he appears and crushes them . . .

The doctor, still whispering, tells his friends, "Here comes Don Martín Leurc."

"Who is he?"

"The general manager."

A tall, robust man with carrot-red hair like Judas's beard and a proud and vulgar bearing can be seen approaching. He is probably around forty years old and seems surrounded by hatred and silence, although a benevolent sparkle from his heart may lie hidden in the depth of his mistrustful eyes. Accompanied by an English engineer and followed by a squad of guards and a group of employees, he walks along the edge of town that rises above the pit. When he reaches the Glory Hole, he passes right next to Gabriel and José Luis, who look at him carefully and in silence, with the foreboding of an impending clash.

Rosario, still overwhelmed by everything that she has just witnessed and learned, detects an echo of her own distress in the unforgettable moan emanating from the mines like an insistent death rattle.

Part II

1

Aurora

THE ANGEL

WHEN AURORA COULD NO LONGER HIDE HER PREGNANCY, SHE found herself in the most abject state of neglect and had to make heroic efforts not to give up. Her mother kicked her out of the house; she would have helped her to prostitute herself to earn money, but she did not forgive her for stumbling upon love as well as poverty.

And Gabriel, who had written diligently during the first months of separation, stopped doing so, discouraged by not receiving any reply from her.

"I'll bring her here," the young man told himself, not knowing what to think of her silence. But he had sent her his measly savings and had to start all over with setting aside money for the trip and the days of the voyage during which he would not receive any wages. He was sick with worry thinking that she might be ill; he considered every sad possibility, except unfaithfulness. The beloved image became surrounded by an ever-increasing number of shadows, until he could only see her darkly in the mirror of his heart.

Her letters, written with eager promptness, never reached their destination, undoubtedly intercepted by the same clumsy and jealous hand that sent distressing notes to the hapless fiancée in Traspeña. These anonymous letters, written in an unruly script, claimed that Gabriel was in love with an honorable and adorable young girl, whom he was going to marry very soon, and that he would never return to his home or to the land of the "vile woman."

Aurora understood that the letter in which she had timidly confessed her secret at the bottom of the page had fallen into the hands of a rival. She controlled her anxieties with impressive willpower and carried her sacred burden without complaint, spurned by the very people who had earlier tried to cause her downfall.

Since she had never harmed anyone, she still encountered some compassion in the village, allowing her to eke out a living, although work became more difficult each day. She derived strength in her struggle from a blessed maternal instinct and from the conviction that Gabriel would not forget her. It was impossible to imagine him an accomplice of this woman, whose existence she could not doubt and who had severed their communication with evil intentions.

Nevertheless, a sense of distance and loneliness befell her. Her eyes were often filled with those tears that shine and tremble without falling, and her face was veiled mysteriously while sadness imbued her blood.

Her rosy-colored baby girl was born: the fragrant and miraculous opening of a bud. Holding this treasure in her arms, the young woman felt a strange and almost divine amazement; she treated the little baby with marvelous tenderness, adoring her mystery. She lulled her with delirious words that arose from her heart, and, her soul aflame, she longed impatiently to bestow kisses upon and share her inebriation with her beloved.

Forgetting the enforced isolation, she wrote him a letter to which she received a one-line answer a few days later, "Your kid can wait to see its father 'til it's blue in the face."

The handwriting, uneducated and deformed, was the same as that of the other anonymous letters, but none of the cruelties expressed in the earlier scribbles wounded Aurora as much as the sharp knife of this last reply. She was beset by doubts about the reasons for Gabriel's silence; she began to believe in the possibility of his betrayal, and the thought of having been abandoned froze the very roots of her being.

Underneath that intolerable pain, an idea began to emerge. Her little girl should never have to be ashamed of her birth; she should not inherit dishonor nor be plunged like her mother into the dark night of oblivion, alone in a world without the warmth of a home, without the comfort of a legitimate name.

To protect the defenseless creature, she had to heed the laws of honor, although in her eyes they were simply social conventions; she would demand the marriage vows that she had rejected earlier. She had to look for Gabriel, carrying the little angel in her arms and a cry in her soul.

THE SORROWFUL MOON

During the slow sunset on a June day, Aurora and her daughter left Traspeña to set out on a trip that reminded her of a similar journey not long ago. Having sent her bundles of provisions ahead, Aurora, filled with yearning and uncertainties, planned to spend the night in Torremar and then catch the first train to Dite the next day. Thanks to the pesetas Gabriel had sent her, she managed to scrape together just enough money for the train tickets, but there was almost nothing left for additional expenses, and this is why she decided to go to the station on foot in the peaceful evening hours.

Aurora has arrived at the edge of the village. Night is falling slowly and with such luminosity that it is difficult to follow its descent; its mantle, spread out along the blue edge of the sky, is suffused with a rosy pink, and it is lighting up the stars without extinguishing the brilliant flame of the sun.

To Aurora, who is looking at the landscape through eyes filled with tears, the horizon appears to be trembling, and huge, humid eyes seem to be staring at her from the green fields. She stands still to look back at her village and to say goodbye to all she holds dear there, sensing that she will not be returning again. Her heart swells with the beauty of the moment, and a transparent box filled with memories floats up in her mind, letting her remember her childhood days, her passion, his absence, and her anxieties. Time seems to be walking beside her with his silent sickle, helping her reap the hours she has spent in those mountains.

Down below, the sea returns to its hiding place behind the reef, rising up and clamoring like a soul calling out from afar to the young girl; the air, as salty and bitter as the water, brushes her lips with a spicy and firm caress. She tastes the kiss sadly, remembering that on the other side of the sea she had once dreamed of a productive life amidst liberty, and the prospect of justice and redemption. And yet after her struggle and anguish, she had only succeeded in increasing universal misery by bringing another being into the world, another drop in the human sea of suffering.

"My poor little girl," she murmurs with infinite anguish. She peers anxiously into her baby's eyes, as pure as heaven, and lulls her with a shower of words, asking her forgiveness for having brought her into the world. In an impulsive gesture of sublime madness, she lifts her up in her arms as if wanting to deposit her on heaven's threshold . . . and the fragile child falls back down into the arms of her mother, who sobs and continues walking somberly.

The fireflies have lit their yellow lanterns; the birds, hidden under the foliage's moveable awning, are chirping sweetly and noisily, maternal wings flutter over every nest. Among the three paths that converge, Aurora takes the mountainous one that leads up to the mine and then, flanking the heights, descends in the direction of Torremar. She pauses again, overcome with emotion, imagining that the destined path is shouting at her. She hopes to calm her thoughts and soak up the beauty of all she is leaving behind. Taking a last look at Traspeña, she can barely distinguish the blurred houses, but the valley is clearly visible in the full moon. The sorrowful moon showers the coast stealthily with her haunting sadness, slightly inclined as if listening to what the wind tells the sea.

Suddenly, a glowing flash appears on the opposite river bank, similar to the shore lights that are lit to warn sailors; the sparkle grows into a blazing fire, reminding Aurora that this is the night of St. John's Feast. The nocturnal dance around a bonfire, a remnant of an ancient cult, still forms part of certain Cantabrian festivities. Part of a Druid ritual, the bonfire under the moon may symbolize the astronomical cycle or it may be a form of worship of life's hidden dynamism. And on this incredibly clear night, the sky invites the cosmogony of all religions; it is an immortal altar for every prayer. A whirlwind of lights fills the blue veins of space, and the Ursa Major, hanging from the heavenly canopy like a supreme votive offering, presides over this northerly fiesta.

Aurora lifts up her imploring eyes to this familiar constellation and to the sorrowful moon, queen of the clouds. Looking around, she is intensely surprised by the fragrance of the fresh fields, the gentle swaying of the forest, and the constant vibration of the ground; in the depth of her soul she is aware of life's strong and divine mystery and of God's touch . . . She wipes away her tears and sinks her footsteps into the red path shaded by the awning of the trees. Teardrops of light, shining through the thick curtain, fall on the mother, who is holding the sleeping child.

AT THE EDGE OF THE STREAM

Exhausted and distressed, Aurora had received the following answer to her question, "Yes, the fellow you're looking for still lives on Monte Sorromero."

"How do I get there?"

"Follow the edge of this stream; keep climbing up along its right side until you reach the hamlet. There you'll find some women who know the way."

Trusting in the honesty of a stranger, Aurora had left her modest luggage in Naya and had started her trek in the hot midday sun, nearly immune to all suffering except that of her soul. She was hungry and thirsty, but she had spent her last cents to buy some milk for her daughter; although she had not eaten in a long time, she was only conscious of her spiritual anxieties.

After a long separation, she was close to Gabriel and would soon be able to tell him, "This is your daughter; give her your name." How would he receive her? Would a new love destroy their sacred bond?

Her footsteps were mechanical, and she felt that this march was occurring in a dream from which she would awaken, free of trouble and with the heavy burden lifted from her heart. Her ears were still abuzz with the carefree winds of the beach, and she could not understand how she had become a prisoner of the wild tangles of these mountains, beneath the terrible howling of the furnaces, and scorched by the drought of the untilled land.

She pushed her child away brusquely, maybe to keep her from suffocating or perhaps to cope with the wild beating of her own heart. Having left behind the strident noise of the smelting and loading, the rubble's black ashes, the curvy slopes tinged with rust, she made her way amidst the shiny quartz, whose brown and flaky crystal needles were scattered everywhere. Then she looked for the wash along whose shore the women of ill-repute roamed. Three half-naked ones were sitting together, and, between long swigs of rum, they devoured the morsels of nougat they had saved inside the folds of a basket. Aurora approached them timidly and asked whether she was going in the right direction. The women didn't budge, and rather than answering her, they asked her who she was and what she wanted. Aurora was forced to mention Gabriel's name.

"Ah," answered the youngest one happily, "I know him. He's entangled with Pedro Abril's former girlfriend. When you get up there ask for Casilda Rubio."

"I don't dare," was Aurora's horrified reply.

"Well, that's dumb, especially if that kid is his!"

"Do they live alone?"

"Not at all! They live with her family: an old woman who doesn't see or hear well when she doesn't want to, and an uncle who likes to preach; he's always praising and sanctifying everything according to his taste."

The speaker had gotten up while her companions kept guzzling and licking the sugar off their fingers. Her face was singed; she was fat, cross-eyed, and of uncertain age, although she had a certain youthful air.

"Look," she said, pulling Aurora off to the side and imbuing her words with a touch of mystery, "I'm a low-life woman and they call me La Corales; in the past I've made good money and I have had friends in high places . . . Even today I can still make men's hearts beat faster. Now I've taken up with a stoker who happens to be the brother-in-law of your ex . . ."

Aurora listens anxiously, gazing at the icy and transparent granite that seems on the verge of melting in the sun. She has difficulty fathoming and believing that she has been wandering in the moorlands of the Sierra Morena in total abandonment. Her instinct searches for a soft, green path to restore her hope, but she only finds a desolate landscape, which, like the planet Venus, is devoid of flowers, birds, and butterflies.

A drowsy atmosphere hangs over the slate; secretly everything vibrates with a throbbing rhythm. The wind is still; the water of the large irrigation canal barely moves, making it difficult to imagine that on the other side of the mountains wild torrents rush freely like blood, leaving deep furrows between the mounds.

"Did you get my drift?" yells La Corales suddenly.

"No!" replies Aurora, startled, looking up sadly into the impatient face of the adventuress.

"Well, I'm telling you, this stoker, Manolo Fanjul, a super tiger, is married to Hortensia, Casilda's sister. Thanks to him, I have plenty of information that you could use to cause a ruckus. You know what I'm saying?"

Aurora continues to stare blankly in mute bewilderment, disconnected from reality. The other woman insists, raising her voice in irritation, "I hate Manolo's wife! It's true he mistreats her worse than me, but it's because he loves her more. And she has a house and clothes and beauty, and what do I have? Just look at me! Even animals have their lairs, but I have no place of my own; not one decent dress, and I never know where my next bite is coming from . . . Do you understand?"

Confronted with this obstinate question, Aurora stammers, barely audibly, "Yes . . . yes . . ."

"Well, it's funny. We get burned to a crisp, but we have to steal the kindling from the oven if we want to eat something warm."

Aurora notices that next to a charred log, the women have built a shelter made of a torn skirt supported with some sticks, and this improvised umbrella wafts in the sparsely populated area like a banner announcing their shameful trade.

La Corales is ablaze; her skin is red-hot, her filthy body gives off a strong acrid stench, and her alcohol-laden breath is aflame. Singed by this fire, Aurora feels parched and yearns for the high plateau to quench her thirst.

"Is this water drinkable?" she asks, her eyes widening anxiously.

"Yes, when it's calm because then its poison stays at the bottom of the cup. But anisette is better! Do you want a swig?"

"Oh, God, no. Water, water!"

"Ok, I'll get you some."

La Corales looks for a gourd sunk in the mud of the stream to keep it cool, and Aurora gulps down the rusty lukewarm water. She thanks the woman and says goodbye, without knowing what to do next. Cradled in her arms, her little girl smiles and observes everything with the curiosity of someone just learning about life.

"When I was still innocent, I also had a son," confesses the sinner, touching the baby with nervous hands.

"Is he still alive?"

"How should I know!"

"What do you mean?"

"I gave him up for adoption."

An infinite desperation roars in her hoarse voice, and the sudden contact with that pain makes Aurora realize the intensity of her own misfortune, and she feels the full weight of the cross on her shoulders. Now she knows why she has come and where she is going; inclining her head, she resumes her march.

2
The Meeting

The Burning Peak

BUT LA CORALES RECOVERS FROM HER BRIEF MOMENT OF WEAK-
ness and runs after the traveler, shouting, "Hey, you! Wait a
minute . . . Did you know there's a celebration up there?"

"No, I didn't know."

"Well, yes, tomorrow Sunday they're going to celebrate the
Day of the Cross with a lot of pomp. The masters of ceremony
will be your *rival* and Pedro Abril. The 'other guy' will have a
fit so you've come at the right time."

"Aren't the men going to the mines?"

"No, in the afternoon everybody from the village will join
in; this is the only pilgrimage of the year."

Being so close to Gabriel troubles Aurora; she thought she
would not see him until the evening, and the immediacy of the
meeting accentuates her frightened and gloomy facial expression. She only half hears the rest of what the strumpet says;
overcome by a feeling of inadequacy and perturbation, she
follows the uphill path, resigned to fatality. All she can hear
with certainty is the sound of her footsteps and the impetuous
beating of her heart, which she fears can be heard from afar.
When she is close to the first houses nestled in the mountain's
lap, she imagines that people will rush out, alarmed by the
noise of that throbbing. But no one runs to the doors, left open
confidently, and no one comes along the convoluted path that
leads her within view of the village.

She seems to have arrived at a strange and deserted world
where summertime has been transformed into a volcano.
Scorched by the air and burning up from the heat given off by
the calcinated hillside, the poor woman is almost overcome by
her cruel pain and close to fainting from fear and exhaustion.

Instinctively, she has stopped in front of a clean and very quiet old house. Creaking with age, the door swings open and a boy comes out into the reflected heat of the desert, half-blinded by the light. The brown-skinned and nimble child, cute and tousled, wears a torn shirt and his pants are unbuttoned. He looks at the stranger in surprise and she trembles as she pronounces a name.

The boy shrugs his shoulders, "I don't know," he mutters, "I'm not from around here. I've come for the fiesta and later I'll put on a clean suit." He feels like talking; it is obvious that he is happy and that he is already aware of being handsome.

The stranger adds another two words, more timidly than ever, and the boy repeats them with a smile, "Casilda Rubio is my mother's sister; this is her house and she is here. Do you want me to call her?"

"No, no!"

As she refuses the offer, Aurora jumps up so violently that she wakes up her daughter, who shudders and starts to cry.

The door creaks again. A young girl appears under the lintel, with flowing hair, a comb in one hand, and a surprised look on her charming face.

The two women, sensing who they are, look at each other avidly; they're aflame, trembling, uncertain. Aurora has whispered a name again and Casilda, without answering, asks her in a domineering tone, "Do you want any alms?"

"No," answers the traveler, with a voice hardened by necessity, "I want Gabriel: he belongs to me; he's mine!"

The baby has stopped crying and seems to be listening. Casilda answers elusively, "He's not here."

"I'll wait for him."

"It'll be a while."

"I don't care . . . I've climbed up to this peak that is on fire and earlier I went down to the deepest roots of the earth . . . "

"In other words, you've been running after him?"

"You don't know what you're talking about!" exclaims Aurora with sharp bitterness.

Attracted by the sound of the dialogue, a youthful man, with an elegant bearing and a peaceful and pleasant look, appears behind Casilda. He is followed almost immediately by Marta, who asks, "Tell me, Estévez, what does this sad young woman want?"

In a few moments Estévez has informed himself about everything, and, as if it were his house, he quickly issues a generous invitation, "Please come in." Turning to the old woman, he tells her the news about the visitor.

But Aurora does not move. Her forces fail her, her face becomes drained of all color like a flame turning to ashes, and feeling faint, she holds out her arms with the child.

Among the people who are watching her worriedly, Casilda is the first one to reach out for the sweet and light burden, while the mother leans against the door hinge and glides down to the floor. Making sure that she does not hurt herself, Estévez lets Aurora stretch out gradually and relax her infinite fatigue. He takes her pulse and mumbles, "She has fainted!"

He orders the young boy standing nearby, feeling sorry and curious, "Joaquín, run to the Casino and tell them to give you some ice wrapped in salt and placed in an earthenware pot."

The Casino is a paltry tavern, nestled in the rocks like the rest of the hamlet. During important festivities, people dance on the dirt floor in the Casino's large back room, by the light of a smelly acetylene lamp. Today there is a pervasive smell of alcohol and fried dishes, and even the ice maker is in operation, enabling Estévez to obtain a remedy against Aurora's sunstroke.

When Joaquín returns with the ice that cools him deliciously as it melts, the sick woman is lying in Casilda's bed. Very pale and motionless, she does not even lift her eyelids, covering the polished crystal of her pupils. Marta undresses her with tender care, and Casilda, her hair disheveled, grabs the sleeping baby and flees into the hallway, afraid of those unforgettable half-closed and brilliant eyes.

Before Aurora's arrival, Casilda had just been getting ready for the fiesta. While waiting for the miners to come home for lunch, they had invited Santiago Estévez, the peaceful and gentle philosopher, who became a schoolteacher out of love for humanity. Compelled by pity and tenderness, he had abandoned the Nordetano Company to dedicate himself to the education of poor children, with no other aspiration than to combat their ignorance. Later, the radius of his goodwill expanded to include the adults who also wanted to benefit from the splendor.

Like a dispenser of bright stars amidst darkness, Estévez

helps everybody by holding out hope and sowing seeds in the parched hearts of those suffering in the depths of spiritual despair. He is satisfied with receiving kind treatment in return, and he lives frugally from the modest inheritance left him by his parents. He seems free of blame or passion, perhaps shielded from worldly greediness by being a philosopher. All that is certain is that his goodness extends throughout the area, offering help to the needy and pouring soothing balsam on rancor.

In this moment, Estévez goes up to Rubio's daughter and tells her, "You have done this woman great harm."

"Yes."

"Out of jealousy, right?"

"Because she's in my way."

"Did you know she had a child?"

"I did."

"And did you forget that this is sacred? A mother has something divine because a child is the continuation of life and it knows God's secret."

"But I love Gabriel."

"He's told me about the doubts and uncertainties he suffered because of Aurora's silence. And having looked into your soul, I thought you might be capable of interrupting their communication."

"And I did," she mutters, cringing from a sharp pang of remorse. "I stole her letters and answered them my way."

"As long as you're sorry now!"

"No," she bursts out, scowling. "I despise her!"

"What about this little angel?"

Trying not to wake the child, the highland girl controls her crying, and, gazing at the baby fiercely with moist eyes, the golden color of amber, she roars desperately, "She looks just like him!"

Marta comes running toward them quickly, all upset and worried, "Is she dead?"

Estévez rushes to the bedroom and Casilda, racked by pity and guilt, follows him, her face ashen from fear. Drained of all color and lying motionless on the bed, Aurora looks dead. But after checking her pulse, observing her closely, and placing some ice wrapped in cloth on her forehead, the young man declares with conviction, "She's asleep."

The Thorns of Sleep

Estévez goes out to meet the miners so he can alert them to what has happened and to prepare Gabriel for the tremendous shock awaiting him. Taking him aside, he tells him Casilda's confession and at the same time asks him to pardon her.

"Don't let her parents find out," he urges, adding under his breath, "Maybe you encouraged her a little in her delinquency."

Gabriel, taking huge strides, blinded by impatience, composes himself, dominating his angry and vengeful impulses. It is true that at times he had felt desire, stirred by the young girl's ruddy loveliness; it is true that his eyes were saturated with her beauty, that he had suffered terrible temptations, and that his beloved's image had been relegated to the periphery . . . Seeing him waver, Casilda had undoubtedly thought that he was her accomplice: he had to forgive her!

"She's a noble and pure girl," whispers Estévez, as if guessing the other's thoughts and trying to reinforce them. "You've poisoned her with the venom of this passion."

"That was never my intention."

"Well, we'll have to cure her."

They walk in silence. Gabriel is tormented by a sudden and painful convergence of emotions. He adores his beloved more than ever and feels remorse for vague sins of omission that would only afflict someone with an honest conscience. Climbing the rocks in leaps, he is ablaze like the air and light, aware of the tragic galloping of his veins.

When Marta places his daughter in his arms, he feels the heat in the very marrow of his bones, and an inebriated clumsiness prevents him from moving. Not the shadow of a doubt interposes itself between him and this angel; he hears the blood's mysterious calling and kisses the baby with bittersweet eagerness. An aura of purity and faith emanates from them, sanctifying their encounter: this embrace has touched only the divine nerve of the flesh.

Wisely, the witnesses to this silent scene hide their emotions, but suddenly a loud sob explodes nearby. Wrapped up in himself, Gabriel does not pay any attention; he returns the baby to Marta and starts to look for Aurora desperately.

Like a corpse, she is inert, quiet, as if pierced by the thorns of sleep. He kisses her cold lips and talks to her with dark vehemence, caressing her full of pain and fury. When she does not move, he asks with a terrified and hoarse voice, "Is she dead?"

"She's asleep," Estévez assures them again, and adds, "She's recovering from an incredible effort and tremendous fatigue; this is why her repose is so deep and quiet."

Everybody stands around her worriedly. Her skin is pale, her aquiline nose has a sharp edge, and her brilliant pupils look forlorn under the eyelids: she is completely in the grips of sleep, a kin of Night and Death.

The icy compresses have been replaced by a hot water bottle for her feet to make her react. Estévez has rubbed some stimulants on her pulse and is listening to her heart.

"We have to wait until she wakes up by herself," he insists.

Those present agree. No one in the region doubts the prestige of this young man, who is considered well versed in human and divine sciences. The fact that he speaks several languages and receives mail from all parts of the world elevates him to enviable heights above the insignificant masses. He seems oblivious to his superiority, bestowing his friendship and kindness with admirable simplicity and empathizing with the sorrows of others, with no other ambition than to improve the life of his fellow men.

With the exception of Gabriel, everyone leaves the bedroom and disperses in the rather dilapidated cottage. The old people are dismayed, Casilda tries to hide her haughty defiance, and Thor pursues her with tawny and tenacious eyes, hoping that his chances have been renewed.

INVINCIBLE

The meal in Vicente's house is silent and brief. The women did not have a chance to show off the modest special dishes they had prepared for their guest; the fish remained half fried, the dessert half done, and only the soup was actually served. Every minute one of the diners gets up from the table, intent as they all are to check up on Aurora.

Although still asleep, Aurora seems calmer; she moves,

sighs, and is covered in a sweat as warm and salty as tears. Gabriel savors the bitter fluid on the flesh that he had feared would harden into the frozen clay of the dead.

Some people are climbing up the slopes from Nerva, Naya, Campillo, Marigenta, and Buitrón, villages located in the district of Zalamea la Real, between the violent peaks and hard jasper of the mountains. Weary men, exhausted from gnawing the earth's innards and from trembling in the heat of the vitriol; ardent women, dressed in their Sunday best; tired and grumpy children; sickly and sad old men, all have come to participate in the pilgrimage of the cross. They had looked at the high peak stoically and started on their way in the unbearable heat when the vapors of siesta time tremble over the valleys. They are not motivated by religious zeal but are convinced that they have to join in the party to drink and dance, an obligation the majority of them is fulfilling with an air of brusque conformity. Only in the younger faces is there a burst of illusion that overshadows the exhaustion of the climb.

Casilda has to get dressed; she was chosen to preside over the procession, and her presence is of utmost importance. Her sister, Hortensia, Joaquín's mother, is here with another little boy, and some of her friends have come to the house, moving around silently, bumping into each other in the kitchen amidst comments and murmurs. Casilda enters her closet as quietly as possible, looking for her dress. Her self-esteem is a source of unexpected strength, enabling her to overcome the defeat of her desires, to hide her sorrows with bitter cunning, and still harbor a flicker of hope. She knows that she is lovely and wants to be more beautiful than ever today. She has succeeded in wiping away the traces of tears and her feminine instinct aspires to greater success. She attempts to smile sweetly and look cheerful; she has to hide her broken heart.

Hearing voices, she stops near the door, which closes partially. She realizes that Aurora has woken up, and she can see Gabriel kneeling by the bed and kissing her hands with fiery abandon. Aurora speaks clearly, and her musical words are endowed with a poignant charm and a perturbing mystery. She is talking about her daughter, whom she refers to as Nena, waiting to give her a real name. As if hypnotized, the father agrees to everything, grateful that she has returned from the feared land of the shadows. He makes promises and assurances while she revives, rediscovers the sleeping fire in his look, and seizes health and love. In her sea-green eyes, a hot, dark liquid full of secrets rises up, and the roses on her tanned skin are reborn with timid sparks. She seems calm and confident, without fears or doubts; her thoughts infuse her memories with peaceful trust. By an inexplicable grace, as soon as she opened her eyes and heard Gabriel, she accepted life as she wished it to be . . . perhaps because she could not support having it be any different.

And she takes hold of life with such dominion, such miraculous fullness, that Casilda flees from her observation post in desperation and cowardice. Realizing that this woman is invincible, she loses her bravura to defend herself and takes refuge in a corner, mad with jealousy. She remembers the words of Estévez; she believes that her rival's weapons have a sacred superiority, and her rustic and fervent heart gives rise to delirious intentions.

In that very moment, Estévez, sensible and concerned, comes to ask her, "Aren't you getting dressed? People are wondering about you."

But she just stares at him, and with a sinuous and honeyed look, she confesses another secret in a dull and muffled voice, "I want to have a baby, you know? Gabriel's baby."

"What are you saying!"

"I want to have his baby!"

"Have you lost your mind?"

Marta walks in on her daughter's distress, and, disconnected from reality, she asks, "What's the matter with her?"

Although Estévez tries to calm her with a gesture, Marta's timid blue eyes keep looking into space, while Casilda, feverish and dazed, repeats clearly with innocent impudence, "I want to have a baby!"

3

Pilgrims of the Cross

The Ritual Plant

Many andalusian villages compete with each other in the celebration of the pilgrimage of the cross that begins in May and extends into the summer months. The bucolic paganism of these festivities manifests itself in the rowdy songs, the barrels of rum, and the noisy ruckus of the revelers.

The cross as a religious symbol of faith is almost unknown in these arid areas where its day is celebrated with fireworks and liquor, music and banners. Along the Sierra Morena's scorched roads, some inhabitants have heard that Jesus the Savior was crucified on the tree, but this somber and otherworldly version is mellowed into legend. Around here the sacred wood is decorated with tassels of twisted flowers, and people fasten signs and streamers to it during the procession.

Customarily, the cross sways high above the pilgrims, who devote songs to it as they pass through the narrow gorge of the mountain on their way to the modest gate of the mistress of ceremonies, who perfumes the wood with rosemary. During three days she displays the decorated cross triumphantly, but then, without a blessing or a prayer, it is returned to its storage place where it remains for the rest of the year.

Unlike in other parts of Spain, in these tragically arid peaks there are few temples and almost no wayside chapels or sanctuaries where one can kneel to praise God amidst the wondrous reddish and dark brown rocks.

This Saturday afternoon belongs to the old people, who, following tradition meekly, form a solemn committee and go to the nearest valley to cut the rosemary. Part of the requirement is to take along a horse adorned with colorful trappings and load it with the branches and foliage to be used as the carpet and canopy for the cross. The villagers see the group off with music and rockets, and then, making a noisy racket, they go to wait for it at the outskirts of the village where the master of ceremonies receives the ritual plant. The mountain is still tinged with the splendid red of dusk when the pilgrims return with their fragrant harvest.

They had descended a hillock near Los Fresnos and searched the fertile grounds of the murmuring arroyo, which embroiders the bleak plateau with oleander and lime trees, providing temporary shade, along with orange and olive trees that grow in a tapestry of wild flowers. This is where the rosemary, with its flowering tips and evergreen branches, grows in generous abundance.

The beast, which in this case is the valiant horse of a foreman, is soon loaded with the foliage, and the committee climbs up bravely amidst the fissures that cut like glass and are slippery and oily from the flaky talc. The plant's tart and harsh aroma envelops them, mixed with the exhalations of their own breath. They walk in silent resignation, their bodies gently inclined in the direction of the slope . . . There is a touching sense of failure in this group of old people, who lead their ephemeral lives against the backdrop of the eternal mountain. The sun shines on them diagonally and casts their elongated shadows on the rocks—striking basaltic masses and splendid granite jutting, writhing like twisted tree roots. The membranes of these stones, as delicate as flower petals, barely scratch the crust of the Earth, radiant in the light of the sunset, and still in its full splendor in contrast to aging humanity.

The villagers, presided over by the masters of ceremonies, meet the caravan and welcome it with music and shrill military salutes. Earlier, Pedro Abril, swaggering, full of bravado, had gone with his retinue to pick up Casilda, who was standing in front of the cross at the entrance, wearing a white dress and a hat. The couple was received with rhymed greetings composed by the villagers, in a contest with neighboring pilgrims. Some verses contain allusions, others are a vibrant and uncouth barb similar to the thirteenth-century picaresque poems of the troubadours. Other lines do not hark back to ancient times and simply say:

> Let's look for a sprig of rosemary,
> let's go with the grace of God;

> keep the branch from withering
> and don't let the flower wilt.

And they proceed jubilantly, amidst shrieks and explosions of firecrackers, bullfight marches and other chants, to welcome the horse bringing the branches of rosemary. Vicente Rubio steps forward to accept the offering. In charge of the most colorful pennant, Casilda twirls its handle skillfully before passing it on to Pedro.

The cheering and chanting resume. With one leap, the master of ceremonies jumps on the fluffy back of the horse, and, whirling the banner, he gives his companion an insinuating look. She can either accept the tacit invitation or accompany the others on foot. She hesitates a moment, looking up with her pale and jealous pupils; suddenly she makes an affirmative gesture, and when the rider comes closer, she uses the ledge of a protruding rock to climb up on the horse's haunches.

The young man feels the caress of an arm next to his heart and he impetuously sinks the flagpole deeply into the rosemary branches until it touches the horse's caparison. The voices turn to howls; sacred flamenco songs, flowery compliments, and chants envelop the couple in a frantic aura.

Now that the sun has set, a light breeze murmurs beguilingly; the rosemary's fuzzy leaves release their fragrance and a lascivious perfume permeates the air. With flared nostrils and foamy lower lips, the horse, a real prancer, trots elegantly, and after it reaches the summit jauntily, its noble profile is silhouetted against the twilight's purplish clouds.

A halo of bonfires encircle the peak where men and women have begun to sing and dance with delirious enthusiasm. Driven by a surge of violent energy, dazed by heat and thirst, they would let themselves be trampled by the rosemary-laden horse, like the masses in India under Vishnu's carriage . . .

THE SUNSET

Rosario and José Luis stand in front of the Casino, slightly removed from the crowd. She had wanted to see the pilgrimage of the cross in its wild setting and had ridden up the mountain on a guided mule, while night was mercifully beginning to fall on the inflamed precipices.

They both watched the rosemary's arrival and witnessed its consecration at the entrance of Casilda's house. People do not know, either in their hearts or minds, the origin of this supposedly religious ritual, but a warm breath of fantasy hovers over the tradition, and thanks to the isolation of the rugged mountains, it is preserved in its rudimentary form.

The sacred wood, illuminated and adorned with flowers, stands abandoned. In the interior of the house some voices mumble about the quarrels of human love, and outside the Casino, still savoring the drinks and sweets they just enjoyed, the young are dancing happily, each pair separated from the others by boulders, while the elderly rest, also each on his own mountain spot.

This terrain, full of uninterrupted and harsh irregularities, fibrous like puff pastry, does not offer an inch of flat land in its surroundings. The houses, people, and roads, either split apart from each other or pressed together randomly to avoid collapsing, are proof of a brave and daring independence. This is why the miners who live here often regain the haughty demeanor of free men, and the bosses know that the soft womb of the shale is a breeding ground for strikes and unrest.

The craggy and impressive landscape is made more formidable by a row of peaks. The Lobo, Carriles, Fuentefría, Alcornocal, and Guijarroso all raise their enormous crests over the ravines, where the residue from the cementation, seepage, and water basins mingles with the torrential and vitriolized waters of the Agrio River that flee without bequeathing more to the mountains than their barbarous roar. The sierra of Padre Caro appears to the south, as majestically sweeping as all the primordial mountain masses.

And the pilgrims of the cross weave their southern dances on these archaic porphyry, showing off their intuitive artistic grace. Andalusians have a mysterious gift for interpreting songs and dances with an inexplicable fervor that comes close to worship. They have a prodigious ability to intuit and assimilate these arts and treasure them as a legacy from long ago, full of sacred vibrations. Rather than transforming the art, they have preserved and transmitted it, converting their very culture into an additional instrument.

The masters of ceremonies dance together to the sound of guitars nearby. Casilda's hat has fallen down onto her shoulders, and her enigmatic eyes shine in the dark shadow of her hair. Pedro Abril wears a fiery red carnation like wine in his lapel.

Everybody is absorbed by the dance, and the burst of madness reigning during the horse ride has died down, along with the setting sun. The shooting, cheering, and recital competitions have ceased. The wind instruments playing the tunes of the pasodoble have been replaced by the rhythmic beauty of the guitars, and the cadences of the popular seguidillas and fandangos fall on the rocks with elegance and harmony. An atavistic mysticism subdues the passions of the uncouth masses, while the chords of the musical instrument that is as old as civilization add a touch of intimacy to the strange poetry of the scene.

Tearing themselves away from the magic of the dance, the drinkers submerge themselves in the tavern's gloom, while the children swarm around the sweets piled on tables outdoors: cakes with pinyon nuts, honey-coated pastry in syrup, fried dough, and other sticky treats.

The occasional notes of the Moorish trumpet, echoing in the hollow of the mountains to announce that some straggling miners have belatedly joined in the festivities, take on an almost warlike sound as they ripple over the bands of gneiss.

They brought a wicker chair for Rosario and she is engaged in a conversation with Estévez, who is sitting on the floor next to her. They discuss the arrival of the grief-stricken young woman who is searching for Gabriel. As Rosario listens with interest, Estévez tells her the sad story of their love, and he also mentions Casilda's suffering and guilt, hoping to enlist Rosario's help.

The hidden wound in Rosario's heart deepens as she remembers the pain of her own impossible love, and, empathizing with the young girl, she agrees to help her.

"Hortensia Rubio is a neighbor of mine," Estévez reflects. "I'll have her invite Casilda to her house and we'll try to help her forget."

"She should take her tonight . . . Since the visitor is sleeping in her bedroom, Casilda will spend the night with some neighbors who don't look too trustworthy to me. There will be alcohol, carousing, and pandemonium . . . and that Pedro Abril pursues her like a beast in heat."

"Let me look for Hortensia. I'll talk to her right now."

Left alone, Rosario fixes her bright and sweet glance on the horizon, watching the sunset through the opening in the cliffs made by a ravine. Her affliction is like a festering wound in the dark prison of her heart. Similarly, at the bottom of the cliffs, dusk is bleeding like a divine wound, oppressed by the shadows of the night.

TEMPESTUOUS GUSTS

Having conferred with Vicente Rubio, José Luis returns to his sister.

"I should stay here tonight; they say that Aurelio has received alarming news from Estuaria."

"A strike?"

"Something like that, and the pilgrimage is the pretext for a meeting."

"Well, then we'll stay."

"But there's no place for you to stay."

"What about you?"

"I can stay anywhere . . . maybe with Aurelio. I would feel better if you went down to Nerva with Vicente's daughter."

"All right."

Casilda and Hortensia appear, engaged in a heated discussion and walking hurriedly.

"You're coming with me," insists the older one.

"No, I'm not leaving the dance. I'll spend the night with Anuncia."

"Wouldn't it be better to stay at my house rather than at somebody else's?"

"Those are Santiago's words."

"That's right," corroborates Estévez himself, catching up with them.

"Well, I want to have fun," she answers with an obstinate frown.

"What do you call having fun?"

"What you're thinking," she mumbles in a trembling and provocative voice, blushing violently.

"Did you know," answers Estévez calmly, "that the first se-
ductive woman was in possession of a hermetically sealed
urn, and that when curiosity made her open it, all the misfortunes were poured out onto the world?"

"I'm not that educated."

"However," continues the teacher, "there was one thing
that remained at the bottom: hope."

Casilda interrupts him, more unapproachable than ever, "I
don't have any hope!"

The three of them have stopped next to José Luis and Rosario; Hortensia is worried about her trip back. Tall, dark, and
mature at twenty-eight, she has a ready smile, a passionate
look, and a heavy Andalusian accent.

"I'm going to pick up the kids at their grandparents' house
and I also want to take this dove with me because she looks all
aflutter."

"I'm not going," groans the "dove," and keeps walking
slowly, following the group.

Estévez and José Luis decide to accompany the women part
of the way until they meet up with the Champion. Along the
way, Hortensia pours her worries out to Rosario.

"I'm so upset!" she tells her. "Manolo has been drinking all
afternoon at the Casino with that tramp."

"Who is it?"

"She's fat, blond, indecent . . . They've probably spent his
week's wages and I'll have to suffer the hardships and the
blows."

"Weren't you going to leave him?"

"Yeah, but that's easier said than done . . . "

"Don't tell me you love him?"

"I can't help it . . . " Her eyes cloud over as if darkened by
love and pain; her words become inflamed with fiery passion.
"I'm crazy about him," she murmurs, "and what really torments me is to surprise him with another woman . . . He didn't
know I was following him and when he saw me there in the
darkness of the café, he made a face!"

"Right now you have to worry about Casilda. You know
she's at risk in this gypsy festivity, far from your mother."

"Poor mother! She lives in another world and is as innocent
as a saint. Santiago told me about the headaches my sister has
caused."

"We have to take her with us."

They reached the doorway, perfumed with rosemary, which has the same acid and pungent aroma as lemon. Entranced and absorbed, Joaquín was sitting on the foliage, holding Nena on his knees. He didn't have any brother or sister as tiny as this little creature, and he had given up going to the fiesta to have the pleasure of taking care of her. He put a finger to his lips, requesting silence.

"Ssh! She has fallen asleep again!"

Behind the children, the coarse and colorful cross lifts its arms in infinite resignation.

While the women busy themselves with Casilda's trip, José Luis goes to look for Gabriel.

"You don't have to explain anything," he tells him gently, "I just came to tell you that there isn't enough room here for everybody and to offer you a place to stay in Nerva."

"Where?"

"You can choose one of the three rooms given to us by the labor union."

The miner thanks him most profusely and explains that he has no belongings or savings to establish a new home; finally, he calms down and accepts the noble offer with gratitude. Santiago whispers fervently, "You're a sailor and you've forgotten that God provides the wind for the sailboats."

Rosario has gone to see Aurora, who is still worn out from fatigue and happiness. The two young women look at each other in amazement, convinced that they have met before: they recognize the flames in their eyes, the lamentation in their voices, and when they say goodbye a minute later, they know that their hearts have been linked by a mysterious bond. Since when? That they don't remember.

They want to make their way down to Nerva before it is completely dark. Suddenly Hortensia, who is still trying to corral her sister, turns pale and her face twitches convulsively. Crouched in the doorway, a man grabs her and shouts, "Who told you to follow me? What are you doing here, in this den of thieves?"

"Manolo, please have mercy."

Her pleas embolden the stoker. Marta, who doesn't hear and barely sees, walks by with outstretched arms and her eternal smile; Joaquín cries in silent panic; and Manolo Fanjul looks in his pocket for a treacherous dagger, and, full of bravura, he tries to swing it above his wife.

But another man intercepts his gesture.

"You cowardly fiend!"

Pedro Abril, who must have been roaming nearby, tries to grab the dagger, and the threat, which could have been just a boastful form of bullying, ends up in a swift and mild blow that wounds Hortensia's arm.

Hearing curses and laments, the three friends, who had been talking in the dark kitchen, come running. Subdued by Pedro's strength, the aggressor is already disarmed when the Civil Guard and the guardians in charge of the fiesta arrive. The house and its surroundings begin to overflow with people, and the children take refuge in Aurora's room. The cross has been knocked down and its pious promise lies on the ground.

4

The Extinguished Star

The Search

LIKE AN EXTINGUISHED STAR, THE EARTH GROWS DARK AT NIGHT until daylight illuminates it once more. In the summer sky, constantly zigzagged by serpentine blue lightning, many new stars unfold, their light contrasting sharply with the surrounding darkness. When the last sunrays die down, some fluttering torches can be seen on Monte Sorromero, coming and going in the furrows between the rocks.

On this moonless night, the flickering lanterns are moving toward the tavern, where the dance is about to begin amidst some unhappy mumbling because the rumors of the latest scandal and the news of a possible strike are now mingled with the feverish desire to have a good time.

Echea has arrived to discuss the labor union agreements with his friends, but they can no longer meet in Vicente Rubio's modest house, which is in the throes of another upheaval. There Hortensia, wounded and afflicted, does not want her husband to be taken away to prison. Delirious from the fever and the heat, she moans, "I'm all right! Let Manolo go!"

But after putting up some resistance, Manolo is taken to the awful place that serves as Nerva's prison and with which the stoker is most familiar.

With great efficiency, Rosario helps a surprised and worried Marta attend to her daughter. The incident and her sense of gratitude enable Aurora to forget her physical exhaustion, and, at the first sounds of alarm, she leaves her bed, ready to lend a hand. Her anxieties have vanished, and she feels so renewed after her long sleep and the talk of love that she doesn't even remember her defeated rival.

In her stupor, Marta also doesn't ask about her daughter be-

cause the shock of touching the tepid blood of her firstborn
has stunned her. Nor is Casilda missed by the neighbors or the
curious bystanders who had crowded into the house and have
left again to take care of their own business and prepare for
the party. Santiago is busy exercising his provident talent for
curing, and only the father and the Garcilláns notice the peculiar absence. Vicente asks Aurora as she passes by, "And
where is Casilda?"

"Casilda? . . . Oh, yes, the mistress of ceremonies," says the
visitor, who suddenly remembers that name darkly as one Gabriel mentioned while he swore her his love. "Yes, where is
she?"

Rosario answers pensively, "We have to look for her."

And when Estévez finds out about her disappearance, he
agrees, "We have to look for her!"

But José Luis and Echea are waiting for him. He turns to Vicente and utters Pedro Abril's name; feverish and determined,
the old man sets out immediately.

Calling to him from the doorway, Echea asks, "Where are
you going? We need you."

Without answering, he disappears among the mounds of the
road. His far-seeing eyes jab the darkness; his feet cling like
claws to the dangerous crystal threads, and with his sunken
chest he looks tragically poised for a leap. Vicente Rubio is a
changed man: he is a tiger clamoring for his cub.

He has no luck in either the Casino or among her friends; he
doesn't want to ask and evades all questions with a disguised
effort.

"Casilda? Yes, she's around here somewhere, maybe on
some errand. She has plenty of problems and the party can go
on perfectly well without the mistress of ceremonies."

"That's true," the others chime in, sympathetically.

Some people suppose that she is at the socialist meeting.
"That's where I'm going," he replies. He returns home, dodg-
ing the weak light of the lanterns. He asks anxiously, "Has she
come?"

"No," answers Rosario at the entrance. She has lifted the
cross and put it atop the rosemary leaves and is fastening the
little bundles of blue flowers and the small pointed and lan-
ceolated leaves to it. There is only enough light to see her face
and hands because with her dark dress she blends in with the

black night. Alone with the women and children, she is also waiting in suspense.

Vicente watches her, piercing the blackness with a gloomy expression, and, uttering a curse, he disappears like a fleeing shadow. He raises his eyes up to the sky for a moment, hoping to see some bright flash . . . The distant stars shine like fiery ashes scattered among the clouds, and as he looks down at the mountains, their dismal profile seems more unrelenting than ever.

At the same time, a tall mass and a deep sigh make him stop. Someone pronounces this accusation with fury: "She's with the master of ceremonies."

"Who?"

"She."

"Who's she?"

"Casilda."

"And what do you care?"

"I care!" Thor cries out, savage and taciturn. "I also love her!"

A festive kettledrum roll fills the air. Feeling lightheaded, the father asks hoarsely, "Where did you see them?"

"In the Gorge of Perdition."

"And have you told anyone?"

"No sir, only you."

"If you really love her . . . don't besmirch her!"

And the father walks off, continuing in the direction that he knows intuitively. He knows each bend of the ravine by heart and he is aware of where the dangerous jasper can be found in each sand bank.

But the place that Thor has just mentioned blinds him and shrouds the night in impenetrable darkness. This June night, so pure and dazzling, pulls down a whirlwind of stars in its wake!

THE GORGE OF PERDITION

When Manolo was being led out of his in-laws' house amidst violent commotion and curious neighbors, Casilda distinguished one voice among the many, that penetrating and mellow voice she could not forget, and she saw the lovely and steadfast stranger by Gabriel's side.

In this painful moment, Pedro Abril whispered a question, as sharp as a stab, in her ear, "Are you coming or aren't you?"

Decked out in his festive attire, with a silk cummerbund and a fiery red carnation in his lapel, the young man looked handsome, and his elegance exuded vigor and lustiness. Except for the missing bridal veil, the mistress of ceremonies, in her modest white dress and quiet pose, resembled a bride on the steps of the altar.

She raised her eyes, so stubbornly hidden before, and gave her companion a darkly enigmatic look. Even more than his masculine spruceness, she adored the slight squint in his pupils, but she did not bat an eyelash when he repeated his question impatiently, "Are you coming or aren't you?"

Earlier she had promised to talk to Pedro that night and he reasoned with her, "You won't go to the dance; you don't feel like it. You'll lock yourself up and won't keep your promise . . . Come, now that nobody sees us; we'll talk and I'll bring you back . . . What do you say?"

She answered in a trembling, hot voice, "Yes."

It is true that nobody saw the fugitives. They left the house, turned at the first bend in the road, and let themselves glide down a slope.

Night was falling. The clouds veiled the majestic peaks, giving them a look of atoning faces amid burial mounds, and shadows filled the silent beds of the valleys, channels of the secret life that had once pushed up the rock from the bottom of the ocean and transformed it into peaks that reach the stars and sun.

The sliver of new moon did not illuminate the precipices along which they descended, and the valley's fruitful aroma attracted the young people with its promise of hidden abundance. They looked at the frightening crests of the peaks and at the serrated silhouettes they projected, and unconsciously they kept searching eagerly for inclines, as if fleeing from death and ritual sacrifice, to let themselves fall in the sustaining lap of life and love.

Their footsteps were accompanied by a flow of strange, almost delirious, words. "You fell for a man who knows a lot of things and looks cross-eyed," said Pedro. "You can see how he repaid you . . . He's from a far-away and cold place . . . He can't love you!"

"I wasn't his girl."

"People said you were."

"Because they thought he was unattached and that so was I."

"They said some other things . . ."

"Like what?"

"I never believed it."

"But what did they say?"

"That you're damaged goods now because of him," says Pedro with bitter honesty.

The young girl thought sadly and angrily about this slander of her honor, and disheartened, she exclaimed with a sigh, "It's so easy to tell lies!"

"And if it were true, you wouldn't be at fault and I wouldn't blame you," added Pedro, his promise mixed with strong desire.

"Do you love me that much?"

"You know I do."

These words warmed the ashes in the poor girl's heart and rekindled a strange fire in the rubble of her illusions. She sighed again and Pedro continued with his tender entreaties, which fell from his lips like glowing coal, assuring her of his immense love and eternal faithfulness.

Thirsting for hope, Casilda let herself be intoxicated by the opium of his cooing, and, innocent and absorbed, she kept walking until she was overcome by fatigue, and her feet, tired from dancing, hurt from the spiked shale. Suddenly, frightened by the enclosing darkness, she wanted to turn back, but Pedro convinced her to sit down and rest.

The dry and barren laps of these hills are familiar with this young virgin girl, having seen her be born amidst these rocks and flourish amid gorges and slopes, never hurt by the amicable crystals, but rather defended and protected by them. She loves these rocks and is convinced they have a soul; she trusts this bed in which she has lain so many times before.

Bewildered and happy, Pedro Abril rests next to her, his heart beating violently. His eyes, accustomed to the darkness of the mines, have no trouble seeing the girl's features and her dress, white like that of a bride.

They are lying in peaceful silence when they hear a hidden and uncertain sound; Casilda thinks it is the voice of the torrents in the gorge, but Pedro, trembling with nervous tension, believes it is the echo of some words of love left unspoken.

Leaning her worried and slightly perspiring face close to the ground, she places her hands on the earth's crust, as if trying to find out the true nature of this noise. The inanimate materials seem to come alive with her touch, and her fingers vibrate with the pulse of all these seeds scattered beneath the surface, which will soon be transformed into ruby, topaz, opal, garnet, amethyst, and sapphire . . . The girl is enveloped by the mysterious chaos, which appears to be telling her the laws of life and the story of creation, all condensed in these rocks that support the world.

She stands up again, on the verge of torrential tears, pierced without realizing it by the mountain's amorous secret, the reef's fervent shout, and the river's sad and bitter turmoil.

Pedro stands up as well; his arms feel weighed down by a delicious emotion, and he credits the dark forces of the night for his good fortune.

THE FESTIVAL

Rosario is still standing where Vicente Rubio left her. She is not simply waiting for Casilda, nor is she motivated merely by charity or pity to listen like a spy to the murmurs of the brown rocks.

Some steps, a shadow, an accent make her shudder but don't surprise her. The person who is approaching knows that he is being awaited because from a distance, and without raising his voice, he calls out, "Are you coming?"

"Yes. And what about José Luis?"

"He has allowed me to accompany you while he looks for his friends."

"But will I have a place to stay?"

"Sort of . . . But first you'll have to sacrifice yourself and have dinner with us and attend the meeting."

"Am I the only guest?"

"Yes, Santiago says we need you . . . I don't dare add anything."

After a moment's silence, Rosario says somewhat perturbed, "Wait a minute. I'll be right back."

Aurelio hears her say goodbye to Marta, reminding her to make sure that Hortensia follows the doctor's orders of "rest and tranquility; no talking and no crying," as prescribed by Don Alejandro after his conscientious visit.

"She's stopped crying because she's worn out from the fever!" observes Aurora, accompanying Rosario outside and lighting the way with an oil lamp. She lifts up the lamp and says, looking at Echea, "Yes, this is the Champion."

"Have you met him before?"

"No, but Gabriel has already told me about the fears and goals of the miners; I knew who they were waiting for and I can see that he's arrived."

"Yes," Aurelio and Rosario agree with her pure and simple statement.

And she adds, "Well, go in peace."

Aurora speaks with a calm openness as if fully aware of all that goes on in this dark and hostile mountain. She continues to hold the lamp firmly in her delicate round arm, like a provident torchbearer.

"Is she a friend of yours?" Aurelio asks Rosario.

"No, we've just met . . . But the truth is that I'm trying to remember where I've seen her before."

She searches the clouds for an answer and her memory gets tangled up in the seven stars of the Ursa Major, trembling vividly in the infinite forest of stars.

"I don't know where it could have been," she mumbles, and, too far now from the light Aurora is holding up, Rosario trips on the slippery leaves on the ground.

"You're going to hurt yourself," warns Echea, guiding her. "Over here."

"I can't see a thing."

"I know this road well; give me your hand."

She obeys and advances with difficulty, more nervous and flustered by his kind gesture.

"Where are we going?" she asks softly.

"To eat dinner at the Casino."

Musical fanfares continue to fill the air; the lanterns bob up and disappear amid the twists and turns, but all are headed for the tavern, the locale for the festival.

Garcillán has made arrangements for the dinner to be served in one of the Casino's private rooms, and when Rosario arrives with Echea, her brother is already seated around the table in the company of Estévez, Doctor Romero, Gabriel Suárez, Enrique Salmerón, and Félix Garcés.

"Well, my friends, Providence has helped us," says the doctor, rubbing his hands together in satisfaction. And he adds ironically, "That is if by any chance you believe in Providence . . . "

"I do," says Rosario, sitting down, tired and a little enervated.

"So do I!" asserts Estévez.

"The fact is," replies the doctor, "that without calling a meeting and by sheer chance, the entire executive committee is gathered here."

"Yes, pure luck!" exclaims Echea. "And you are here thanks to Manolo Fanjul."

"That's right. If nothing else, we have to believe in fate."

"Vicente Rubio hasn't come," notes José Luis.

The schoolmaster asks Rosario guardedly, "Did Casilda ever show up?"

"No."

"Then it's useless to wait for the father," he thinks, and out loud he says, "We'll eat without him; maybe he can't join us."

The only embellishments in the room are a bed, which, aspiring to be elegant, is covered by a bright yellow caparison, and a lamp bracket with a carbide oil lamp. Several pictures from almanacs hang on the walls, as well as a mirror with a scratched surface. The middle of the room is taken up by the table, modestly set, and the circle of crude footstools. The one door, without panels and covered with a percale curtain, leads into the establishment right across from the counter and on to the patio, where misty fennel flowers hang on the walls, and where the dancers go to drink or get some fresh air because the Casino has no ventilation.

It is near midnight and the dance is at its height. In the brief pauses, the guitar strings vibrate with the lament of some popular songs, which, when art was in its infancy, were played on the sistrum—that ancient Egyptian percussion instrument. The clicking of the castanets, the clinking of the glasses, the beat of the clapping and tapping penetrate the improvised din-

ing room, filling it with dizzying noises. With only a sill separating them from the tavern's ballroom, the diners are
deafened and exhausted by the festivities. Yet they dine so-
berly amidst this Andalusian merrymaking, happy with their
banquet where words are more abundant than food; fish, frit-
ters, olives, light rolls of bread are all washed down with table
wine and one or two bottles of a local specialty.

"We can't talk here," laments the doctor.

José Luis remembers El Vaivén and is amazed by the re-
straint in this merriment, without scandals or riots, harmonious and solid like a ritual bonfire.

Everybody seems to have fallen under the dance's spell and
the fiesta's solemn rhythm, and a song full of primitive passion
fills the ballroom:

> If I don't take revenge in life,
> I'll avenge myself in death;
> I'll look for you in your tomb,
> Highlander, until I find you.

The sweet and cloying voice pierces their souls and the quivering of the last cadences remains suspended in the atmosphere.

"We can't talk here," repeats Aurelio, fixing Rosario with a
thirsty and deep look. Evading the plea in those eyes, Rosario
affirms abruptly, "No!"

They get up to leave.

"Let's see if we can hold the meeting in Salmerón's house."

In the patio they run into a girl, out of breath and with a face
as shiny as if polished with cream. She moves her fan in quick
motion, without releasing the castanets, whose Moorish orna-
ment moves and trembles just like the fringes of her shawl.
She smiles, revealing some lovely teeth, and lifts her Moorish
eyes up to Garcillán, "Sir . . . What a surprise to see you here!"

"Hello, Carmen . . . You look tired . . . and very beautiful!
Have you been dancing a lot?"

"Yes! How about you?"

The schoolmaster interrupts her, "Have you seen Casilda?"

"She's lost," answers the girl, still smiling, and when the
group starts to leave, she runs ahead of Gabriel and asks him,
"You've forfeited your girl, haven't you?"

"What are you talking about?"

"Don't worry: the night is also without her companion."

The allusion to the absent moon makes them more aware of the dark landscape, the secret mountains like shadowy islands, and the roads drowned in silence.

Gabriel murmurs indifferently, "That woman is nothing of mine."

Up here the noises have a clear and sonorous echo, and Carmen's crystalline voice floats over the valleys. "Your eyes reflect a dangerous soul," a captivated José Luis tells her. She looks at him delicately and remains standing at the open door, surrounded by a halo of fading splendor, while the group plunges into the darkness.

THE VIGIL

They can barely move in the room. Rosario leans on Enrique's bed and the men are standing up around her. Aurelio spreads the documents out on the deep windowsill and explains, "Yes, in the capital they went on strike last night in response to the company's unfair punishment of a brakeman. They're calling for a work stoppage here and there's a lot of turmoil in Dite. What should we do?"

"Join the strike," answer the three workers without hesitation.

"We haven't had enough time to prepare and I worry about our organization; a failure now would do irreparable harm."

"Can't we postpone it?" mumbles Rosario, wishing to minimize the great risk.

"No," answer various voices. But Aurelio says, "Yes."

"How?"

"By allowing three consecutive days for a vote in the different parts of the valley and alerting the government about a general strike to be held in a week. This ruse will give us enough time with the excuse of trying to get unanimity among the strikers."

"And when would we make the announcement?"

"As early as tomorrow, by calling for a general assembly; we could meet in the bullring after we get off work."

"In Nerva?"

"Of course."

"Sounds good to me," says the doctor. The schoolmaster and José Luis agree and the workers fall in line.

Leaning on the windowsill, Echea has already begun to write in silence. His motionless profile, outlined against the dark window, is illuminated by the brilliant morning star. Everybody looks at him, moved, and Rosario whispers, "Do we have some money?"

Without interrupting his writing, Aurelio smiles and answers, "Some is right!"

"How much?"

"Let the treasurer tell us."

"A hundred thousand pesetas," murmurs Enrique Salmerón.

"Too little," bemoans the choir. And the girl laments, "Oh! More than sixty thousand people will be left without any resources for who knows how long."

Echea has finished the proclamation, a simple speech urging everybody to gather as soon as possible. After reading it to his companions, the Champion says, "This has to be printed and circulated like wildfire among the people."

In his capacity as secretary, José Luis takes the piece of paper and promises, "By noon, we'll have distributed twenty thousand copies."

Echea then turns to Rosario, who looks crushed by a tremendous melancholy. "Don't worry; we'll multiply the pesetas and there will be bread for everybody."

"Quiet," shouts Vicente Rubio from outside, looking in the window, pale and overcome by emotion.

"What's the matter?"

"We're being watched."

When the old man enters, a gust of wind extinguishes the oil lamp's smelly flame, and the worried and agitated group is left in the dim light of the sky's eternal pearls.

"The Civil Guard and the company guards are looking for us; they were planning to arrest Echea," says Vicente hurriedly.

"How did you find out?"

"Because I was also making the rounds," he says bitterly. "I blended in with the darkness and that's how I learned about treacheries . . . "

Enrique Salmerón closes the window carefully and takes out an electric flashlight from his pocket.

"Let's go to the inner room," he suggests.

The figures move tragically, throwing gigantic shadows on the walls; their muffled voices whisper impassioned anxieties.

"We'll defend ourselves," some say.

"No," thunders Echea. "We have to hide ourselves."

Salmerón has devised a safety plan. "First of all, I'm going to talk to my mother," he says. "Get in this bedroom; it leads to the patio with a canal that has room for several people."

"Amid the slime!" exclaims Rosario, dismayed, but the Champion just shrugs his shoulders.

"All right. If there is a search, we'll hide there: Suárez, Garcés, Vicente, Estévez, and I. You," he tells the others, "have come for the festivities and are Enrique's guests."

Enrique takes them to the small bedroom with two beds and runs to the kitchen where his mother, Dolores, is waiting patiently. A highlander from Valdelamusa, she is around fifty years old, bright and sensitive; after listening to her son for a few minutes, she has grasped the importance of the mission.

Holding a lamp up high, she enters the bedroom resolutely. With a strong regional accent, made more pronounced by her fright, she tells them, "I know the whole story. Some of you, follow me to the kitchen because we were just 'having a chat,' and the rest of you, poor fellows, go to the ditch and let's see if those 'fierce bulls' would dare . . . ."

A harsh knock on the door forces them to take their designated places. Dolores opens the window, and, with astonishing aplomb, she carries on a brief and colorful conversation with the authorities. The guards move on, convinced that Aurelio Echea is not there.

"Don't tell me I can't clown around when necessary," she says proudly, joining the conspirators.

Breathing a little easier, they keep talking softly and agree to take extra precautions when they leave before sunrise.

"But you should stay," José Luis tells his sister. "You need a rest."

"I've prepared a bed for you that is as clean as a new pin," Dolores exaggerates flamboyantly.

The girl protests, "I'll sleep in Nerva."

"No, no, you're exhausted," they all persuade her tenderly.

And they take her back to Enrique's room, the best one in the house.

"This is the best there is," says Aurelio apologetically. He runs the bolt across the connecting door that leads to the other bedroom. "The men who usually sleep in there are at the Casino tonight and they go to work before sunrise; no one will bother you."

"And what about you? Aren't you running a risk by returning to Nerva?" asks Rosario anxiously.

"I don't think so. I'll avoid any danger by going down there with the peons, dressed like one of them. Here in these solitary heights the guards pursue me, but they don't dare come near me in the heat of the battle."

"You need some rest!"

"I've conquered sleep and hunger. When I hear the voice of my devotion and obligation, I'm invincible," he says with a mystic expression. And impelled by his noble and pure thoughts, his tranquil figure takes on gigantic proportions.

Behind a veil of painful tears, Rosario's deep eyes contemplate him, and she listens to him, devoured by her heart.

Dolores has turned down the modest cover, revealing the clean bed sheets, yellowish white because of a shortage of water. The colorful quilt covering the patched-up linen diminishes the sordidness of the lodgings. But the air is murky from the fumes of the candle and from cigarette smoke, and a pungent odor is seeping in from the other bedrooms. Aurelio notices it and leans down dejectedly, "Poverty doesn't smell good, does it?"

"No," replies the girl.

More than ever, both of them taste life's bitter flavor; they raise their heads and say goodbye with their eyes.

Watchful and attentive, the men in the kitchen try to make themselves comfortable. Enrique tells his mother, "After the young girl has fallen asleep, you can open the window a little."

The good woman tiptoes into the room to do as she was told, and the young girl, awake but motionless, looks out anxiously at the trembling openness of the skies, suffering and kept awake by pain, while the night dissolves in stars.

5
White Hands

THE TRAIN OF DEATH

"HEY, YOU THERE! DON'T YOU SAY HELLO TO YOUR FRIENDS ANY-more?" La Corales yells out, intoxicated and belligerent, her hands on her hips.

"I told you we shouldn't have come this way," grumbles Dolores, accompanying Rosario and Aurora, as they pass by the arroyo where the harlots camp out.

"We're in a big hurry!"

"These hags are liable to stone us," Dolores worries, and she hastens to cover up the baby she carries in her arms.

The rowdy woman, looking threatening and hostile, starts running and shouting but falls flat on her face, sputtering insults. She keeps yelling but her companions don't wake up, and the other women escape around the bend, looking for the fastest downhill slopes.

Absorbed in her conversation with Rosario, Aurora doesn't pay attention to the uncultivated fields, which she had walked in great pain the night before. They have left behind the shale's dusky trail, escaped from the scandalous arroyo, and are now walking on the golden red path that suffers the torments of incessant excavations.

Already the sun's rays emit considerable heat as they prance around on the grimy hills where the foundries howl like a blazing inferno; some of the workers, with sledgehammers and picks, are headed for the station, their knapsacks draped over their shoulders like quivers.

"I'll be glad to help you with all my heart," promises Aurora, who since the first encounter has used the familiar form of address with Rosario, assuming that any social differences have

151

been leveled by the uniqueness of their situation and their
wonderful mutual sympathy.

"Your arrival has been providential," replies Rosario enthusiastically. "We women can participate in organizing the
strike. Until now the organization could count on only one
woman who knows how to write: Aurelio's wife."

"Oh! Is he married?"

"Yes."

"That surprises me . . . I don't know why. What is she like?"

"She's a sad and sickly girl who does not really understand
him well."

"What a shame!"

The exclamation seems to refer more to the husband than
the wife, and Rosario adds with sweet severity, "Let me tell
you that Natalia is intelligent and kind . . . and at one time she
was also pretty; she has suffered so much that she only wants
to rest."

"But she's married to a great fighter!"

"She can't do more than sacrifice herself for him."

"And that's enough if she loves him," remarks Aurora with
a fiery gesture, but noticing that the remark has perturbed her
friend, she changes the subject.

"It's wonderful," she states, "to find a woman like you, who
is happy to live among the wretched and helps them cheer-
fully."

Now Rosario becomes even more embarrassed. "You have
to give my brother full credit in this campaign. He wanted to
stay in the mines after we wrote our report, and I, who don't
have anyone else besides him in the world, decided to accompany him."

"Only for his sake?"

She poses this question, thinking about the miners' appreciation of Rosario, but there is a different indication, maybe an
actual affirmation, when the young girl inquires, very upset,
"Why else?"

Aurora pursues her original idea and concludes discreetly,
"For the sake of all those miserable people that you help and
console; for all those poor women who don't know how to
read or write and are tired of crying."

"That's true; I love them very much and you'll see how nice
and intelligent they are."

"I know them . . . even without having seen them; we're all part of the same family . . ."

"Yes, you've also suffered unjustly," exclaims Rosario, looking admiringly at the interesting girl from the mountains. "Yesterday you made an incredible trip."

"Pains are soon forgotten if they are rewarded with happiness," smiles Aurora, and Rosario's sigh hovers over this with hopeful emotion.

Both women show signs of their recent vigil: there are traces of sleeplessness and exhaustion, and rings under their eyes moistened by passion. Looking at each other, they can read the other's thoughts, and their conversation turns to Casilda Rubio.

"I feel terribly sorry for those who suffer because of love," alludes Rosario.

"So do I."

"This poor girl is desperate and I'm afraid she's destined for some terrible unhappiness."

"I'm ready to forgive her the harm she wanted to do me."

"And that she did."

"I've already forgotten it!" Aurora turns her attention to the baby, who is being lulled to sleep by Dolores, who is walking a few steps behind them. The mother's face fills with calm, confirming that she has forgotten all nightmares.

They are close to the calcinations; the air, whipped by the flames, whirs above the roar of the ovens and chimneys. The noise of the rails, the machinery's deafening din, the dizzying turmoil of the various jobs, all produce a hurricane of nefarious sounds that frighten the women. They hurry along a road covered with ashes and smoke, amid throngs of overworked and suspicious men.

Naya: the railroad; Aurora picks up her belongings at the station. Many of the workers greet Rosario, whom they know and admire as the village's benefactress. Almost all of them are on their way to Dite to work the second shift in the pit and countermine, and they have a grim and anxious look.

"Before the week is out, right?" some whisper in Rosario's ear.

"Before!" she hints in a serious and fervent tone. "We'll send word secretly . . . you need to be calm and courageous."

She seems a different person: erect and pale, her hair flows like a plume, her eyes sparkle with intimations and light, and her transfigured face looks like a brilliant star with new fire. Standing next to her, a solemn and moved Aurora observes her proudly.

Suddenly a persistent and merciless whistle pierces the noise, crosses the valleys, and echoes in the ravines, paths, and narrow gorges. This scream, which sows terror in the coal fields and splits the air like a lightning bolt, signifies that there has been a victim. The train transporting the injured person to the hospital is urging everyone, brusquely and ominously, to clear the way immediately. In the hustle and bustle of the workshops, a man has been hurt, perhaps fatally wounded, maybe killed. Who is it? The women are in a state of atrocious uncertainty, running to the platform in droves, with hoarse voices, uncontrolled movements. They would like to stop the humming departure of the fatal convoy, which leaves them like reeds swept by the wind as it passes noisily and dizzily, spreading endless pain over the region.

This is what has happened now. The stationmaster hurries to send a telegram, while the furious women and children of the vicinity rush along crossroads and paths, their arms crossed, yelling and cursing.

A little later, with the ceaseless whistle insisting on having free access, the locomotive goes by, exhaling fumes, dragging a flatcar on which some sorrowful workers accompany God knows which unfortunate person. Laments, questions, and tears trail tumultuously in the wake of the ill-fated gallop . . .

Soon the train the women are waiting for arrives and they get on quickly. A miner lies stretched out on one of the benches of the wagon, which is full of flies and dust. His chest and shoulders are bandaged, he is shaking with fever, and he is being looked after by an old woman, who is on her knees in the back of the wagon.

The convoy plunges into Lucifer's Valley. Filled with compassion, they inquire about the latest victim, and when the old woman is about to answer, the company-appointed inspector appears on the runningboard, asking to see their tickets. An uneasy silence reigns until the spy has disappeared again. Then, fixing her eyes strangely on Aurora, the old woman explains, "They cut off his arm because he was injured in the factory, and now he is sick from the infection."

Everybody bends down, horrified to look at the mutilated young man, who opens his eyes, burning with life and maybe also a streak of madness.

"Is he your son?" Rosario asks with infinite compassion for the poor woman who is taking care of him.

"My only one!"

An odor of putrid flesh, mixed with iodine, escapes from the rags that are wrapped around the wounds.

The women take refuge toward one side, afraid of this horrible trip, feeling overcome by all the evils of the world, on the rails of death.

Holding her baby in her arms, Aurora is nursing her and showering her with plaintive tenderness, having suddenly fallen from the height of illusion to the abyss of reality.

"This is the life that's waiting for her," she sobs. "She'll have an adolescence like mine, an old age like the one of this other mother . . . No, no, I don't want this. Let's get out of here," and, shaking inconsolably, she turns to Rosario, "You have to help me."

"Elsewhere you might be even worse off."

"Worse?"

"Yes. In Peñarroya the miners don't have any hospitals; they live in some ferret holes dug into the hills, and they die of lead poisoning. In Sisapó, the infamous village of the fences, they suffer from the shakes and drowsiness, they die in their prime, victims of mercury poisoning, tuberculosis, and consumption."

"Stop it, stop it!"

The young mother closes her eyes, panting, and arches over her child in a heroic attitude of succor and defense. And Dolores, observing the old mother with pious interest, asks her gently, "Aren't you originally from Almonaster la Real? Aren't you the Jesusa who lived in El Campillo?"

"That's me."

"I knew you as a cheerful and pretty young girl, when I was growing up in my village. After that I lost track of you in the bustle of the mine work. I even heard about your son, who is sick now . . . Aren't you a widow?"

"I've been a widow for years!" moans the poor woman in a broken voice.

Through their tears, the two women roam the fields of memory for an instant, recalling the peaceful hamlets of the Moorish garden known as Al Munia and the innocent hours of childhood.

But Dolores returns from her reverie to add with keen sadness, "And you said you have no other family?"

"Nobody besides him! I lost my husband to the dark tunnel's poison . . . All I had left was this son," she says, as if talking about a deceased.

"And where are you going?"

"They sent us to the capital to see if they could cure the gangrene, but he doesn't want to go; he only trusts Don Alejandro."

The patient turns around morosely. Gasping, he is thirsty. The mother keeps talking about current events in the past tense.

"We were on our way back to Nerva . . ."

Speedy and thunderous, the train clanks, arches its back, and plunges in between black hovels and red huts, seemingly fleeing along the dark road to eternity . . .

THE CITY OF THE MINERS

Dry, parched, and withered, the city of the miners looks terribly poor. The sad and modest houses are piled up like in a Bedouin village, and, having run out of room in the prairie, the settlement extends itself, in the form of camps, all along the flanks of the Sierra Morena, reaching as high as Ventoso.

The streets bear ancient and resonant names, vestiges of the Roman Empire, and the road leading to Dite, which is still in good condition, stems from the same time.

Forty thousand souls are forced to live out their miserable existence in this village, which, in typically Andalusian fashion, has whitewashed walls and is incredibly clean, a miracle considering it has no water or sewer.

The carelessly built rooms are divided by low partition walls under an improvised roof, which is actually a curtain. The walls are dirty, the bedrooms, cramped and smelly, and the patio serves as a drying area for clothes and a garbage dump.

Since the majority of houses do not have any real waste disposal, at any time of the day the women can be seen in a fetid procession, carrying buckets of dirty water and excrement. Aside from causing a nauseous stench, the debris of the entire population, from the village and beyond, is mixed with the sources of drinking water—springs and arroyos—often already contaminated or destroyed by the copper deposits and replaced by the stagnant waters found in the company's dikes and its impure veins of cementation.

Drop by drop, some of these filaments seep into the slimy shores, and in the months of low tide they rot away, contributing to the unbearable stench the neighborhood has to suffer in the searing sun, dying of thirst.

There is no originality or peculiarity to change the appearance of this hamlet, as miserable and dull in the prairie as on the hillsides, always garbed in the uniform of slavery. All the streets are alike, things look the same, and the people, in tune with their surroundings, resemble each other and share the same exhaustion and despair.

Rosario and José Luis have known the sadness of many working-class barrios, unhealthy suburbs of the great industries in the world, which, like a dark halo of martyrdom, surround power and pride. But they had no idea that in Spain, and precisely under its bluest and haughtiest sky, there was an unhappy mass subjected to foreign bosses, a tragic kingdom of the poor, whose suffering was a symbol of human injustice.

Thus Nerva was of extraordinary interest to these Spanish journalists. This village was the soul of the mines, the living and painful result of the excavations: fearsome catacombs, gigantic workshops, Dite in shambles, the mountains cracked, the rivers poisoned, the air contaminated, the horizons appalling—all the evils of life were imposed on thousands of innocent creatures in the service of foreign ambitions.

The brother and sister were absorbed by the gloomy drama and regarded their trip as fortuitous. In keeping with their lofty idealism, they began to write energetic and courageous articles for *La Evolución*, accusing the Nordetanos, bosses and colonizers, of being guilty of crimes against Spain and against humanity.

They decided to lodge in Dite because it was the center and capital of the zone, and they worked with exalted fever. Their first reports were published in the great newspaper amid much publicity, but suddenly they ceased to appear.

One day the journalists received a visit from an engineer who represented the company. This envoy, by the name of Jacobo Pmip, was a hypocrite but an astute one, and he did not pursue his plan of offering the Garcilláns money when he saw their reactions at the hint of a bribe. Instead, he hid his shady intentions by adopting an air of superiority and experience, telling them about the follies of youth and the mirages of the imagination. Taking pride in what he saw as his masterful ability, he called the romantics useless, the redeemers mad, and the powerful company invincible, in a speech full of confusion, circumlocution, and vagueness.

The Garcilláns listened to him, smiling with irony and slight amusement, concluding from this lecture that the general manager was asking them to leave his domain because of an "incompatibility of opinions," and that the famous Madrid newspaper was not as immune to gold as certain standoffish journalists.

The envoy affirmed shamelessly, "Yes, you are unusual; some of your colleagues who have studied the social aspect of these mines have given the Company their unconditional support. The same can be said for the government commissions, political entities, public officials, and the most progressive press . . ." He pierced them with his hard and gray little eyes, adding, "We're lucky! Only some foolish or delirious visionaries would dare fight us."

The Garcilláns bowed slightly, as if to express their gratitude for this allusion, without hiding their pride in meriting it, and indifferent to the rancor of Mr. Pmip, who was also bowing but to take his leave.

So this was the diplomat in the service of the mighty Rehtron Company. His bosses thought he was such a lynx and psychologist that he ended up believing in his own virtues, increasing them in size and scope over the years.

Skinny, clean-shaven, and diminutive, he looked younger than his forty years. There were rumors about the scandals in his private life and the dishonor he did his profession, which he did not practice, preferring to occupy himself with dubious efforts of spying and capturing, and with overseeing a vast network of espionage and another equally murky network of catechism. He had even converted from Protestantism to Catholicism so he could devote himself more intensely to his Sunday School activities. At his behest, the schools, which the company had converted to Protestantism, using the workers' monthly wages, reverted to Catholicism—a sham conversion, but which the company wanted to be seen as a friendly gesture toward Spain.

Jacobo Pmip, who was promoted and received an increase in salary, was hailed as a great transformer by his co-workers, and some people tried to beatify him by praising his maneuvers as heroic acts. Others grumbled that he was a fraud who was no engineer and not even a Nordetano, and that all that could be known with certainty is that he was a big scoundrel.

He continued with his comedy of being a convert, which allowed him to pretend that he had saintly intentions when he stormed into homes. Actually, it gave him an advantage in courting the most beautiful girls of the neighborhood and in discovering people's worries. Among the most unwary, he even acquired a reputation for being generous, although he lived like a prince in his Vista Hermosa cottage, surrounded by pretty servant girls.

His mishap with the Castilian journalists did not discourage him in the least. Knowing that he had many means at his disposal, he relied on time and adversity. He even felt a little sorry for that young woman, who had a calm beauty and fiery words, and whom he would like to have impressed as gallant. Turning his back to José Luis, he asked her about her job in a tone that was half kind and half condescending, trying to show that he was well versed in literature and had a good command of Spanish.

That same night the innkeeper apologized profusely for having to tell the Garcilláns that he could no longer lodge them, and upon seeing the young people's protests, he added hesitantly that the inn belonged to the company, and that "he had received strict orders . . ." He also gave them his opinion that they would not find any place to stay in Dite because "the whole village belongs to the bosses."

He was right. Without shelter, but more determined than ever in the face of their persecution, they took refuge in Nerva, an impenetrable shelter, and decided to hide out in the miserable neighborhoods.

Fortunately, Echea had arrived, having completed his time of exile, and he proceeded to guide them through the monotonous labyrinth of the streets, where Rosario's elegant attire caused some noisy curiosity.

But even here it was impossible to find a hut that was quasi-independent; those that took in lodgers—and had pompous names like Hotel, Casino, or Salon, though they were barely more than a tavern or café—belonged to the cowardly company's minions, and rather than expose his friends to another unpleasant experience, Echea decided to take them to the Workers' Center, where he lived. From the very beginning he had wanted to take his friends to the Syndicate, as everyone called the building because it belonged to the union, but a delicate secret had prevented him from doing so; but now he could no longer hesitate.

They returned to the house on Cicerón Street, which was slightly taller and more spacious than the neighboring ones. Entering the gate, which was always open, they passed some shops and offices, a doctor's office, and a pharmacy, before reaching a steep and hazardous staircase without rails that led to the upstairs.

A little girl, about three years old, was crawling down backward on all fours, one step at a time. Rushing forward, Aurelio caught her in his arms, "Where are you going? Are you escaping already?" he asked. Rosario, knowing the answer, asked her genially, "Tell me, who are you?"

"Ero," stammered Anita, surprised by the lady's hat and demeanor.

"She's never seen a lady before," her father remarked.

The upstairs was divided into two apartments, and Aurelio pushed open one of the two adjacent doors, revealing two rooms with ledges, as well as a dark bedroom connected to the kitchen by a balcony, a place the inhabitants of both apartments used to dump their garbage, and where some abandoned junk lay around, gathering dust in the corners.

"This is too shabby for you," he lamented unhappily, "but there's nothing else and at least you'll be safe!"

Garcillán looked at his sister.

"Are you willing?"

"Yes."

They were caught up in a lofty madness of sacrifice, burning with indescribable ambitions, and they looked at each other proudly, with a caressing smile.

Echea turned away to hide his feelings, and he said with a barely noticeable uneasiness, "I'm going to call Natalia."

He had not mentioned his wife before. He left. Anita, who kept clinging to Rosario's dress, could not stop looking at her. The girl bent down to give her a nervous kiss when a calm voice called to them from the corridor, "Please come in here."

Natalia entered and repeated her invitation. She was a sickly and sweet young woman, with clear vestiges of her former beauty, and she soon found some words of ingenuous hospitality. From that moment on, she felt a humble and silent devotion for Rosario, filled with gratitude.

The Garcilláns installed themselves in the modest room, which had stood empty since the death of the secretary of the committee, who had lived there with his family.

At first José Luis paid little attention to the terrible inconveniences they had to endure. More intoxicated than ever with the intensity of his life, he let himself be carried away by his heart and by events, undaunted by privations. Echea's example, his will to win, his strength to support suffering, emboldened him heroically, and he admired Aurelio like a god, following him like a star trailing the moon.

His sad sister, in closer contact with her bitter misery, constantly forced to disguise her passion, felt her soul faltering in the light of these rebellions. But her mute fight to control her sobs and to overcome her disgust with the work sowed virtues in her vehement artistic spirit, and she, an angel in human form, earned her wings. Rosario achieved such victories over instinct and need that she forgave herself for loving the husband of another woman.

They were no longer representatives of the socialist newspaper in Madrid, having been removed from its payroll, supposedly because the party's defenders of humanity and of the working class considered that their vociferous campaign about Dite was too daring and ill timed. Once more the allpowerful metal of the dead had won again in the highest national spheres! Deputies, senators, ministers of the Crown, presidents of everything that was presided over in Spain reacted with indignant abomination against those devastating articles that were published by accident.

When the courageous journalists had to fall back on the meager family pension, José Luis began to feel discouraged. Accustomed to sharing whatever money he had with his friends, he suffered greatly from being short on cash, especially in the company of the poor, whose friend and protector he considered himself to be. Normally only Estévez or the doctor could afford to treat their companions to the traditional sip of rum to go with the frugal afternoon snack at the Casino.

Humiliated and melancholic, the young man felt nostalgic about another way of life that was more in keeping with his habits and upbringing. But Rosario was there, conquering all dejection, driven by a desire to follow the harsh road, and José Luis was deeply influenced by his sister, who, predisposed to revere Good, was persuading him with a profound prayer in her eyes to join her in the homage.

José Luis had accepted the vacant post of secretary of the committee, donating his modest salary to the union's treasury. The stimulus of his own gallantry and of the overwhelming yet novel and exciting tasks he carried out with Rosario and Aurelio enabled him to regain his serenity and high spirits.

Soon, the credit for the accomplishments of Nerva's socialist organization belonged as much to José Luis and Rosario—who were intimately involved and had taken the tasks close to their pure hearts—as to the Andalusian workers. And the region's rough men took pride in knowing that a woman's white hands were working ceaselessly on their behalf.

6
The Roads to Perfection

LIFE'S HURRICANE

THE HEAT AND UPHEAVALS OF THE TRIP ADDED TO THE EXHAUSTION that Aurora and Rosarito felt. When they arrived back in Nerva, totally worn out, the house was in a state of turmoil. José Luis, who had returned with Aurelio before dawn, wanted to move to the bedroom in the back so the ladies could use his room. The neighbors, intent on helping with the furniture for the new bedroom, rigged up a bed on some easels, with burlap and cushions; they even found two chairs, and there was some talk of a wardrobe that Natalia was thinking of emptying . . . Suddenly, José Luis rushed to the printer, returned to the office where Santiago was at work with the president and the doctor, and forgot about everything else.

It was lucky that Dolores had followed her son's suggestion to accompany the girls, "Go down there with them; they'll have a lot to do and will need you. I'll join you when I get off work this afternoon. Whatever happens, we won't come back up here until the strike is over."

Tireless, strong, and determined, the mother had no other desire but to please him. She lived for Enrique and was always ready to agree with his wishes and do everything to satisfy them. Her impetuous nature harbored a guarded hatred for the employers who were squeezing her son's health out of him in exchange for some miserable wages. Even though a strike would have serious consequences for the workers, she was happy and supportive because she saw it as a form of sublime vengeance.

Her sleepless night forgotten, Dolores takes over the abandoned household because Natalia, restless and despondent about her husband's dangerous dealings, can already see her-

163

self in jail again, persecuted by his enemies and accused of being mixed up in crimes. Less than a year ago, she suffered an unjust martyrdom in Nerva's jails, which caused a relapse in her illness. Only her youth helped her survive these vicissitudes, extending her lease on life and giving her some hours of hope.

Now her friends shower her with tenderness.

"Nothing terrible is going to happen, my child," Dolores tries to allay the sick woman's fears. "The bosses will be far worse off than us. They'll have to bite their tongue and put up with it." Singing and sweating, she rushes around, filling all the empty pitchers, preparing the meal, and straightening out the clutter.

Suddenly Aurora appears at the door and makes this timid announcement, "I have to tell you, I'm not married . . ."

"Don't worry, you will be," answers Rosario in a sympathetic and firm tone.

Dolores intervenes unexpectedly, "I was never married and I'm an honorable woman."

But the mother of the little girl who still goes by the generic name of Nena is apprehensive. Her situation oppresses her more than at other times, and her soul is aflame with anxieties and subtleties as she thinks about her friends' generous words. She is about to express her ideas when Aurelio comes upstairs to announce, "They would like to confer with us! The manager's wife sends you a message, Rosario, inviting you and some of the women from the mines to visit Vista Hermosa."

"Really?"

"That's right. She wrote to Estévez because he's a friend of hers. They think of you as the president of the Syndicate."

The girl blushes and asks, "Should I go?"

"No doubt about it."

While Aurelio shows her the polite letter, José Luis appears, carrying a stack of yellow leaflets.

"This is the announcement for the meeting this afternoon," he says, tossing a handful into the air. "They're already being distributed everywhere; probably one of them reached the ladies and they were alarmed." Anita, with her tiny dovelike steps, goes around picking up the sheets.

"Whom should I go with?"

Aurelio turns to Natalia, "With you, of course."

"No, they want to talk to the women of the mines. I'm not from here."

"Are you afraid?"

The unwarranted question, said in a violent and annoyed tone, confuses the girl.

"No, I just don't want to go," whispers Natalia. "What I really want is to die as soon as possible."

They surround her, full of pity. Aurora has already taken this sad and weak creature into her heart, and Rosario looks sternly at the person who is responsible for those bitter tears. "You who are so compassionate with everyone, how can you cause her such pain?" she whispers reproachfully in his ear.

"I don't know myself," he stammers. "It's my curse to torment those I adore the most." His gentle bluish eyes look tenderly at the sick woman and then at Rosario, who is all too familiar with those ardent pupils, where passion and will conflict. Reining in her fleeting thoughts, Rosario says out loud, "Natalia doesn't feel well; she has to lie down. I'll go with Aurora."

"And I'm here as well," says Dolores, hitting her chest, no doubt as further proof of her presence, "I'll accompany you wherever necessary."

"But you'll let Rosario do the talking, right?" Aurelio reminds her.

"You can be sure of that. I'm just going along with the girls as an escort, if you agree."

"Agreed." And to Natalia, still shaking from her crying, he says in front of everyone, "I know how very brave you are. Why do you torment yourself because of some words I said without meaning to?"

Still sorrowful, she doesn't answer.

"Do you forgive me?"

"But you're right: I am afraid," she answers finally.

"Of what?"

"I'm afraid of life . . . more than of death. I'm no good for anything!"

Her husband goes to console her. Standing near her, he notices that her skin is limp, her eyes, blue and humble like cornflowers, look dull.

"You have to lie down right now," he tells her, his heart full of regret and grief. As he helps her undress, she begs him softly in a voice soaked in sadness, "If I die, you have to marry Rosario."

She smiles through her tears. The husband, dazed and confused, interrupts her, "Be quiet! What are you saying?"

"You love each other . . . that's visible. I'm not the companion you need; the two of you are made for each other . . . I have no right to be offended."

"For God's sake, Natalia!"

"You've been more than kind to me . . . and so has she. I'm not the companion you need . . . I want you to find some happiness in your life."

Her smile yields to a lament, and Aurelio, all compassion and gratitude, showers her with caresses and protests.

In a flash he relives the story of his first meeting with this young and naive blond girl who reminded him of a human rose: it was in Oviedo, where she was studying at the Normal School for Teachers, and he was spending a few weeks of vacation with his family. He fell in love with her sweet and docile demeanor, so in contrast with his rebellious and combative temperament. They became friends and were soon engaged. She confided in him, full of illusions and hopes, and he gave her his name and tried to live up to her expectations. Intending to make her happy, he pulled her into the hurricane of his life. She gave birth to their first child while serving a prison term in Madrid, implicated in the accusation brought against her husband of being the instigator in a violent labor movement. The newborn died and the mother contracted an illness from which her weak constitution did not allow her to recover fully. A second birth, more persecutions, more prison sentences—in five years of marriage the candid young girl had become an emaciated woman dying of tuberculosis. She never complained. Her passive character and her physical weakness prevented her from participating in her husband's causes, yet she was always at the periphery of those tempestuous endeavors that nevertheless brought her closer to the shores of her tomb.

These recollections make Aurelio aware of his full responsibility toward the sick woman, and his words to her are imbued with infinite pain. But she hears them listlessly, starved for rest and thirsting for sleep. Smiling weakly again, she assures him that she feels better.

Thousands of people, eager for peace and justice, are waiting for the document of social vindication that is being drafted right now in the downstairs office. The cry of oppressive fetters stirs the young man's conscience; he kisses Natalia on the forehead, and, emerging from the bedroom, he places a finger on his lips, "Don't make any noise; she's going to sleep."

The two apartments, joined by friendship, expand or shrink in size according to circumstances. Right now its inhabitants form a single family, and they exit quietly from the sick woman's bedroom.

There is no time to be wasted; it is noon and they haven't had lunch, but the exhausted girls have no appetite and eat only a few bites. They still have to get dressed, catch the train, and return with a report on the impressions of their visit before the assembly begins.

The sister of Félix Garcés, Obdulia, a serious and diligent girl who lives near the Syndicate and helps Rosarito with the cleaning, has come upstairs to look after Natalia and the little girls.

The envoys go to the office to receive instructions from the president. They find him absorbed in his tremendous obligation, organizing, studying, writing, and mobilizing, with his delicate and expert handwriting, the vast network of communication that puts the Andalusian miners in contact with their European companions.

Rosario and he converse for a few minutes, standing up, without looking at each other, carefully keeping their thoughts from straying. In the meantime, Aurora looks around the barren room and is amazed by the desks piled high with books and papers, and by the tenacious and self-sacrificing men who carry out their activities with religious enthusiasm. The schoolmaster, the doctor, and José Luis help the president, while the other four committee members complete their assigned tasks.

The woman from Valdelamusa asks Aurora in a muffled voice, as if they were in a temple, "Do you see those stacks of letters? They're 'put' in many languages. The secretary understands all the dialects in the world; the others only understand a few of them. Some of these letters are from England and Russia or even India or Paris."

The three women depart, deep in thought. The sound of pens scratching the paper continues; the pulse of universal justice, pierced by God's mysterious spirit, beats loudly in this paltry and suffocating room.

VISTA HERMOSA

The almost deserted city is seared by the hostile sun; all able men are at work; the doors, wrought-iron gates, and windows are half-shut with the fatigue of siesta time.

To avoid calling attention to herself, Rosario is dressed simply and without her usual hat. In one hand she carries a fan, in the other a parasol with which she also shades Aurora, who is wearing the only good dress in her extremely poor wardrobe. The two of them walk impatiently ahead of Dolores.

One of the many trains that extend like tentacles from the mine takes them back to the fateful furrow of victims and tears. Numb from the strain and the stifling atmosphere, they sit in the compartment half-asleep, catching nightmarish glimpses of the landscape.

From Dite it is still a long way to Vista Hermosa, the residence of the Nordetanos, situated in the interior valley of the coal fields, as far away as possible from the masses.

The travelers confront the road with stoic vigor, climbing up the reddish and scorched terraces of Mesa de los Pinos. They leave behind the luxurious and well-tended Protestant cemetery, with tombs covered by the sacred tranquility of marble, so unlike Dite's miserable Catholic burial ground, damaged by nearby cave-ins. Although they are already at a distance, the women still pause, captivated by the placidity of the concealing jasper, the long line of fences, and the open-armed crosses inviting peace. Maybe the women, aching from exhaustion, think that only the voyage into eternity will assure them the rest they long for.

They cross the prairie toward the west, where the mountain chain is lit up along the horizon, and the steep hills surround the valley where the lodes are buried. A green and lush patch, unusual in the arid land, brings them to a halt. Next they see a fence, a guard, and an entrance to the oasis—a miracle of good living and good taste—where an order has been issued to show the visitors in immediately.

To the poor women, out of breath and dying of thirst, the breeze blowing from the trees feels like a caress; they walk as if in a dream amid the murmuring fountains and the delicate aroma of the flowers. The pebbles along the path creak, a benevolent shade spreads out above, life vibrates in the nests, and beauty fills the heart of the buds. The notes of a piano, the strain of a song, children's laughter, and suddenly, near a house, an insistent, angry bark: they have reached the manager's home, and the watchful bulldog cautions against the suspicious poverty of the visitors.

They are only detained there for a minute, entertained with admiring the elegance of the park dotted with light-colored and lovely buildings, the majority in a Spanish colonial style. Many houses are covered by jasmine and ivy, and bordered by gladiolas, oleanders, and yellow wallflowers. Elms, myrtles, acacias, and poplars grow along the avenues and walls. The miraculous growth of these plants in the wasteland is achieved by sparing no expenses in water and special soil.

Near the interior gate, a youngish woman, skinny and blond, receives the visitors with a smile.

"She looks like a scarecrow," mutters Dolores in her Andalusian dialect. The wife of the manager invites them in with a gesture and adds in correct Spanish, "Please come in and follow me."

She guides them along a cool and shady hall and into the living room, which faces the shadowed part of the garden and is perfumed by a bouquet of wallflowers; cretonne decorates the walls, the floor tiles are marble, and a chandelier as delicate as gossamer hangs from the panelled ceiling.

Two of the people sitting on the plush and comfortable sofa and armchairs stand up: Don Martín Leurc and Don Jacobo Pmip. The others, a priest and two young men, sons of the manager, remain seated, and the ladies make a half-hearted attempt at greeting, more so the youngest one, who is Don Martín's daughter. The baby of the family, she is called Berta after her mother, whom she resembles, although she is livelier and not as skinny or as blond. Seated next to her is her governess, Miss Clara Ylevol, an eccentric type of undetermined age, with an intelligent and kind face. Another English woman, Diana Erecnis, the wife of a technician, holds a little four- or five-year-old girl on her knees, who looks slightly mistrustfully at the strangers.

The visitors have taken a seat at Doña Berta's request, and she is talking to them, though addressing her words exclusively to Rosarito. At first the young girl, flushed from the trip and jarred from being observed by so many eyes, feels inhibited. Furthermore, she is fighting the temptation of making a mental sketch for her album of caricatures of the rotund, healthy-looking, and beatific priest; the skeletal manager's wife; the outfit the governess is wearing; Don Jacobo's pedantic gestures. For some time now her humoristic talents have not had any stimulus, and she has to fight off the sudden inspiration so she can concentrate on the serious and sad reasons for her visit.

"You are very active in the labor union," says Doña Berta, "and, out of a sense of solidarity and compassion, we thought it would be wise to invite you. We would like a woman from the mines to listen to us before the strike is organized."

"That's right," interrupts Don Martín. "We know you have called for an assembly today to discuss the general strike, which will be catastrophic for the workers. Although I am not in the habit of negotiating with agitators, I'm making an exception for you."

"I have not requested this audience," answers Rosarito coolly. And suddenly she is again in full control of herself, realizing that by one of those twists of fate, her words and behavior may influence the destiny of thousands of hapless people.

"No, I have taken the liberty of asking you to come," repeats Doña Berta, "disregarding some rumors that I pay no attention to," she emphasizes tolerantly, "because I know you are talented and educated."

"Thank you."

"And I think we'll be able to understand each other."

"What do you have in mind?"

"To spare the region many days of mourning, we ladies would like to join the women of the village, regardless of class differences," states the lady categorically and grandly.

"Yes, yes," the others agree, and the little tables with the coffee dishes tremble, shaken by the commotion.

The Contrast

Huddled together, apart from the other guests, the women from Nerva have the impression of facing a large tribunal. Their hot, sunburnt faces, their dark and simple clothes contrast with the elegant silhouettes of the other ladies; yet the beauty of the two girls acquires a mysterious and distant charm, which works its silent magic.

Aurora cannot take her eyes off a little lace tablecloth on which, amid the fine porcelain, stands a crystal pitcher, misty from the cool water. An irrepressible cry floats to the surface from the depth of her green pupils: *I'm thirsty!*

Diana Erecnis, caressing the little girl in her lap, intercepts that anguished look. "Would you like some water?"

She gulps the cool drink greedily. Her companions, also in need of refreshment, instinctively stretch out their hands, and the three drink avidly from the same glass. Finding this behavior most unusual, the other ladies exchange a slightly scandalized look.

"Days of mourning, you said," repeats Rosarito, picking up the strand of conversation. "I would like to avoid them as well; tell me what I can do."

"It's simple; persuade the executive board, and especially the poor wretch who presides over it, to stop encouraging the revolutionary attempts that would be the consequences of a general strike. You are headed for horrendous failure; you don't have the resources to resist. The management cannot agree to the union's impositions, especially not in today's climate of socialist unrest, which the government represses in no uncertain terms, even if it pretends not to."

"We can count on military forces," adds Don Martín solemnly, "to punish any riots—and even threats of riots—with severity. We have more than enough millions to weather the strike. As you can see, there is a big difference."

"But we also have more than enough compassion," boasts Doña Berta, "to warn you of the danger and extend our hand. We do this precisely because we have all the advantages."

These gallant words are corroborated by Don Martín, who adds condescendingly, "Nowadays social prejudices should yield to moral and regional interests."

Dolores makes a grimace that betrays her doubts; Aurora listens, looking intently at a large window sill with tulle curtains and a downy cushion; the little girl tears herself away from her mother and moves slowly closer to the strangers; and the priest blesses his friends' ideas with mellifluous words, "Remember your responsibilities, my daughters. If you do not heed the advice of these good people as you should, you will bear the consequences of your rebellion; the blood of your brothers will flow . . ."

"Yes, of our brothers," whispers Aurora, still with a distracted look, her thoughts seemingly elsewhere.

"We ladies are the ones who have taken this peace initiative," insists Doña Berta, "following the dictates of our hearts. I speak on behalf of all the women who belong to the company and who have authorized me to do so. Right now we are busy founding another hospital and we will be bringing some Dominican nuns as teachers for the schools."

The governess says a few kind words in English; Berta and Diana chime in with promises of support, and the gentlemen murmur amiably. A benevolent piety envelops the room.

Rosario tries to calm herself before answering, "Let me see: you have the guns, the millions, and the priest's blessings on your side; in other words, all the advantages of this life and all the promises of the next. Very good. Rethron's workers earn three pesetas a day for their backbreaking work, barely enough to buy food or clothing . . . They have slavery and death on their side in this world and perhaps eternal damnation in the next. Tell me, Señora, do we all belong to the same human race?"

"Naturally," replies Doña Berta hesitantly, uncertain about how she can refute the challenge, when Don Martín comes to her rescue with this convincing argument, "The world has always been divided—and will always continue to be divided—into rich and poor!"

"And the poor," affirms Rosario with a slight tremor in her sweet voice, "have always tried to improve their lot."

"Faith and Christian resignation," intones the priest, "help us accept our destiny, and thus achieve happiness in this life and also prepare us for the kingdom of heaven in the next."

"But when the people who call themselves Christians behave pretty much like atheists, and when the ministers of our Lord take the side of the powerful and the unjust . . . then where should the wretched find an example and inspiration for faith and resignation?"

"You sound like a sectarian!" reprimands the priest severely, turning red.

Rosario smiles bitterly, "You should examine, without losing your composure, whether Christ's laws constitute a religion of slaves or of free men."

"For God's sake," intervenes an alarmed Doña Berta, "Don Facundo is a most esteemed person who deserves to be treated respectfully."

The person in question swells up with pride and calms down. Rosarito is about to stand up, but Don Martín, who is interested in resuming the previous topic of conversation, holds her back.

"All right, let's see now: what exactly do the workers hope to achieve with this absurd strike you're organizing?"

"The rehiring of a miner who was fired in Estuaria."

"That's what I call solidarity!"

"And an opportunity to demand . . ."

"To demand?"

"Yes, Señor, to demand that you fulfill their more than justified requests from last year."

"I don't remember."

"Then please read this."

Slowly, the young girl takes her wallet out of her pocket and removes a piece of paper from it. Her dark locks fall on her gentle forehead as she bends her face down to read the contents of the familiar leaflet out loud:

Petitions presented on July 30, 19 . . . .
Rehiring of the fired workers.
An 8-hour work day.
The elimination of contractors.
A 50% increase in salary across the board.
A minimum wage of 6 pesetas a day.
The cessation of payroll deductions for doctors, medicines, and

the schooling of children, giving workers the option of establishing a medical-pharmaceutical cooperative and of selecting the schools of their choice.

Decent treatment of the workers by bosses and foremen.

Additional and improved safety measures to protect workers in high-risk areas.

The reader raises her lovely eyes and focuses them on the manager, who hides his.

"Do you remember these demands?"

He also evades the question by replying, "So you see even our generosity as a bone of contention? You complain about the favors we do you? That's the height of unreasonableness!"

"But this is nothing new; you've known for a long time that they want to govern themselves."

"It would be more accurate to say that somebody wants to govern them; that four freeloaders want to manipulate these uneducated masses like puppets and use their ignorance as a stepping stone for their own greed."

Don Martín looks at the others for support of his indignation, and then he confronts Rosario, who is pale but calm. "Let me repeat what you already know, señorita, that it disgusts me to deal with agitators, so let's not talk any more. Well, ladies, what do you say?"

"I agree with everything Doña Rosarito said," bursts out Dolores, unable to control herself any longer.

Furiously, the manager turns to Mr. Pmip, "Of course, utter servility! They protest against enslavement by their superiors and willingly subject themselves to a worse slavery. They are just like sheep, don't you see?"

Doña Berta tries to pacify her husband.

"Oh, I don't want to sow discord, especially since my new project is planned in the spirit of better understanding and democracy. Miss Garcillán, please allow your companion to speak."

"I would like nothing better."

"And this young lady will tell us whether our message of peace suits the women of the mine."

She turns to Aurora, counting on her lack of guile.

"I don't understand," answers the girl calmly. Like Rosarito's voice, Aurora's has an indescribable charm to which Don

Jacobo succumbs. He intervenes and explains, "We're asking whether you accept our offer to help—an offer consisting of several thousands of pesetas—or whether you continue to let yourselves be fooled by lies about independence and be led into this odious strike. These ladies, out of the goodness of their hearts, want to warn you and save you."

Rosario smiles again. The little English girl is standing between the two friends, and Aurora places her hand gently on those blond curls, and contemplates her own reflection in those innocent, amber-colored eyes. Then she says with much aplomb, "Workers, here or elsewhere, should never ask for alms, but for justice. A worker earns his keep and it would be humiliating to accept as a favor what can be demanded as a right."

The gentlemen are thunderstruck. They have just heard the word "demand" for the second time: the nefarious revolutionary seed was growing roots in the minds of common men and even women.

"They've been corrupted," grumbles Doña Berta, incensed, and starts conversing in English with the other ladies.

Rosario is able to pick up some phrases regarding the cruel disappointment felt by the ladies. Though sad and bitter, they were convinced of their supreme charity in trying to mediate between the company and the workers. They had given their project the resonant name of "Feminine Social Action," and, intent on elevating it to the level of a large enterprise, they devised rules, designated officers, and even published a bimonthly magazine. It was most unfortunate that their magnanimous first attempt had failed because of these poor people's ungrateful stubbornness. But praise God and keep up the good work! The ladies wash their hands of this matter and hope the strike will serve as a warning to these incorrigible people. And even though they could not prevent this punishment, they will always be ready to help and forgive unconditionally, without holding any grudges . . .

SACRED DISQUIET

As Rosario continues to hear some of their conversation, she is surprised, shocked, and sorry to discover the monstrous conceptions they have of Christian ideals.

At this time they are being joined by elegant families of high-ranking foreign employees living in Vista Hermosa. Some of the ladies have brought books and folders so they can carry out their feminine social activity in a dignified manner; other delicate hands hold lovely bags with needlework, lace, and half-finished embroideries. These ladies have come to participate in a meeting called by the manager's wife, and their husbands accompany them, eager to exchange impressions with Don Martín. They arrive in clusters, passing from the open balcony that surrounds the bungalow into the vestibule with the large windows, and then entering with a discrete and cheerful noise from behind a delicate screen.

They had not expected Nerva's delegation to arrive so soon, and when they hear about their reaction, they explode in indignant comments and prophecies.

"We mustn't be discouraged," Doña Berta reminds them in pious exaltation. "God is testing us and we must follow his divine intentions: we will establish the hospital, the school, and the magazine; cost what it may, we will continue to do good, and we'll elevate our charity to heroic heights."

She is sublime. Moved to tears, her friends surround her with faith and devotion. Too enthusiastic and excited to sit down, they stand around, filled with sacred restlessness.

The majority of them come from generations of Catholics; a few are recent converts—having availed themselves of the doctrinal policy adopted by the company as a political measure—but all of them burn with a vocational fever that they regard as religious and devout.

In the heat of this pious fervor, they would have completely forgotten about the women from Nerva, had not Don Jacobo—impressed by Aurora's beauty and decisiveness—taken this opportunity to talk to her.

"You're not from here, are you?" he asks her under his breath, basing his conclusion on information gathered from his daily inquiries.

"I'm from all over," she answers, scowling.

"You've come from far away to look for a man."

"Do I have to justify myself to you?"

"I'm your superior."

"Oh!"

"You arrived sick and with a child."

"Not sick, just exhausted."

"Your lover lives with another woman."

"I will not allow you to speak this way to me."

"That man is under suspicion and is being watched. As for you, it would behoove you to be less rude."

"With you?"

"Yes, with me."

Aurora gives him an infinitely contemptuous sidelong glance and turns her attention to Rosario, who is still amazed at having found out that these ladies have desperate need of the sick and the poor on whom to bestow their thoughtful and heartfelt charity . . .

"Are we ready to go?"

"More than ready."

But Diana Erecnis is talking to Dolores in a hesitant and broken Spanish.

"And where is your son?"

"In the sulfuric acid factory. Because of the fumes, he wears a gas mask and he's tied to a rope in case he faints, and he has a stretcher and a first aid kit by his side . . . He earns three pesetas."

"Oh! Is it possible?"

"Cross my heart and hope to die," says the woman from Valdelamusa, making the sign of the cross. Berta Leurc, whose Spanish is better, translates the answer for her friend.

"That's intolerable!" says Diana in English, addressing her husband, who, hearing the story, agrees with her and repeats softly, "Totally intolerable!"

Leonardo Erecnis, an American, is the head of the chemical laboratory, and has lived in Dite for some time. Young, robust, and cheerful, with a face that radiates understanding and kindness, he matches his wife in spiritual gifts. He just arrived at the house of Leurc to pick up his little girl, but she escapes from his arms to run back to Aurora, fascinated by this woman who looks at her tenderly with eyes as deep and green as the sea. The little girl would like to say something to her, but does not know what, and seizing one of Aurora's hands, she asks sweetly in English, *Will you have a little more water?*

"I don't understand you, sweetie," answers the young girl, leaning over with loving devotion.

And standing next to the little girl, Erecnis tells her in Spanish, "She's asking whether you would like more water?"

"Yes, a little more. What a darling girl," says Aurora, touched and surprised that a gentleman addresses her formally, and does not look at her with too much curiosity or disdain. "What's your name?" she asks the little girl, but the father has to answer, "Alicia; she knows only a few words of Spanish." Then he lets the child lead him, listening to her explain something important while he fills another glass with water.

At this time, order is restored in the living room; the visitors take a seat, the strident tones die down, and suddenly the only ones who remain standing are the women from Nerva, along with Alicia and her father, who is offering them a drink.

"What silence!" whispers Dolores, disconcerted by the sudden muffling of all noise, and Rosario, recalling a popular saying, observes softly, "An angel is passing."

The three of them drink; standing in the middle of the room, they resemble a symbolic sculpture, protected by Innocence. Alicia is bursting with pride that her father paid attention to her advice and that everyone is looking at her admiringly. She smiles joyfully as the women from Nerva express their gratitude and say goodbye, causing a resumption of the nervous noises.

The manager's wife has risen politely, and she leads the visitors along the external balcony surrounding the house, no doubt to prolong the leave-taking; in the living room, there is a renewed choir of predictions.

Doña Berta walks ahead with Rosario and asks her in a confidential tone, "How can you live with these degenerates who know neither decency nor religion: a young woman running after a man; an old one who did the same as long as she could; depraved and obscene people who reject peace because they prefer the turmoil of a revolution?"

Rosario turns her head, attracted by the luxury of the rooms and she looks at the display of soft beds, thick rugs, rich bronze and glass furniture visible from the balcony. She stops in front of the bathroom, surprised and envious to see the shiny and deep bathtub, the mirrors hung with lace, the polished Spanish tiles on the wall, a counter full of toiletries and aromatic substances. From an open faucet comes the sweet sound of water running along marble . . .

Aurora is also looking at the rooms with the same longing, while the lady continues her severe and persuasive interrogation, "Tell me, how can you have anything to do with that insolent jailbird called 'the Champion' by the masses?"

These harsh words bring Rosario back from her reveries, and, referring to the Oriental mysticism of her beliefs, she answers thoughtfully, "I don't judge good and evil as you do, señora, and even if I did, goodness is a form of luck, and no one has the right to be good and happy while others are bad and unhappy. I would like all of humanity to enjoy happiness and the joys of paradise here on Earth."

"You're mad!"

"Maybe . . ."

They have reached the staircase. The lady of the house remains standing beneath the polished gables, enveloped in the sensuous perfume of the balcony, with its armchairs, cushions, flower pots, and incense burners. She lowers her eyes with a peevish pout; a peculiar smile appears on her lips, and the jewel around her neck shines brilliantly: she is basking in her enviable good fortune.

In the meantime, the women from Nerva cross the park, which exudes a warm wave of aromas; they pass fish ponds and fountains where jets of water foam and gurgle with a nostalgic and evocative melody like the echo of beloved voices that are forever extinguished.

And they leave the garden's peaceful atmosphere to step out onto the hostile and seared wasteland . . . A plaintive sigh startles them: it is the generous spirit of the trees wailing in the wind . . .

7

The Cause of Madness

THE BLOODSTONE MANTLE

THE GROUP LOOKS TIMID AND FRAGILE AS IT IS SWALLOWED UP ONCE more by the sunken valley. No one would guess that the three travelers walking silently and humbly in this Andalusian wilderness are playing an important role in the fight for freedom, like the Three Marias who fought for the ideals of redemption.

The plateau of Mesa de los Pinos is dominated by a monstrous cluster of hills whose peaks are transformed when their shale comes in contact with lava; they soften and turn white or yellow like clay, or harden into jasper, or turn black like porphyry, or take on the reddish, at times ash-gray, hue of porcelanite. A rainbow of ever-changing colors spreads over the ravines and cliffs: the silvery shimmer of mica, gray veins of copper, green masses of granite, layers of white quartz, blue plates of gneiss, dark dikes of flint. The mysterious and variegated horizon glimmers and laments, without betraying its origin, keeping its history enveloped in the secrecy of centuries.

These mountains, which emerged from the glowing interior of the earth, have been broken into smithereens, raped by universal greed; victims of the world, they moan as they open themselves to the sun. When the iron pyrite from their caverns and galleries reaches the prairie, it is metamorphosed into a thick red mantle—a violent nightmare that drives people to madness.

Beneath the bloodstone mantle, there is an iron forest with angular grains of crystal beneath the sulfur, but the women keep their eyes firmly fixed on the path as if avoiding the rock's potential attraction. Perhaps they don't want to see the painful contortions of the peaks, the terrible yawn of the tunnels, the coming and going of the men who move around in those caves like worms in an enormous coffin.

The powerful industry's vast ring of work imprisons the valley like an infernal enclosure. The open pits, trains, landslides, excavating machines—all the intense work of exploitation produces a feverish and deafening roar, as if the entire mine was trembling with a nervous vibration.

Against her will, Aurora lifts her eyes up to the tormented hills, listens anxiously to the howling clamor that fills the air incessantly, and longs to explore the depth of those caverns, which exhale darkness. She thinks of Gabriel, whom she has not seen since their sad farewell in the early morning, and she awaits him eagerly, knowing the dangers to which miners are exposed in their fiery graves, threatened by suffocation, eroded by darkness.

The wanderers have arrived in Dite, pushed by a dusty wind that has arisen suddenly and that clouds their way. Dolores calls it the "wind from Lebrija" or the "turbulent wind." Its wings glow as if heated by heaven's eternal flame and it stifles the village with its dry volcanic air. The mute streets, split open and filled with rubble, simmer in the dust storm and the sun. Along the busiest avenues the silence is interrupted by the cries of a cripple who is hawking newspapers from Madrid. He drags himself along on metal braces and seems to be weeping as he calls out, "Ay, *Heraldo*! Ay, *España Nueva*!"

His words have become a lament since the time an explosion threw his mangled body into the ditch outside the mine. His voice, gasping with dust, swallowed by the wind, pursues the travelers until other sounds catch their attention.

Near the train station they hear talk about dangerous tremors in the vicinity of the Glory Hole. Some of the miners, who have finished their work and are waiting for the train, affirm that "the copper is groaning" in the countermine and that the props are sinking. The frightening foreboding of an imminent tragedy spreads all along the tracks.

Naya's platform is full of workers who already completed their first shift but who, in spite of their exhaustion, decide to make the trip to Nerva; they look questioningly at the yellow leaflet in their nervously shaking hands.

From the train window, Aurora spots Gabriel, who stares at her without believing his eyes. Enrique Salmerón, Vicente

Rubio, and Félix Garcés are accompanying him on his trip to the city. All four enter the compartment occupied by the women from Nerva and are surprised to see them there. Since there are no empty seats, the men travel standing up, bending down to talk to the women hastily and propping each other up when the train takes the curves.

The amorous pair look each other in the eyes and lose the drift of the general conversation. They tell each other strange things that gain a new meaning on their lips, but whose only purpose is to convey their hidden emotions. Dressed in his bright red miner's clothes, Gabriel is sweaty, out of breath, and weighed down by his bitter martyrdom; she smiles sweetly with glowing but inert eyes. They relive the story of their love, wounded by absence, tormented by doubts, realizing that they are eternally united by the chains of suffering and hope.

As they cross the fiery region of smelteries and calcinations once more, the air is aglow amid sudden flashes of flames and plumes of smoke; the drill's thundering voice begins to descend from the narrow mountain passes and ravines, rumbling above the train and accompanying it through the fields of poisoned water.

Several times a bright red train crosses paths with theirs, rushing by noisily: it is the pulse of a dizzyingly intense activity. A rush of wind from that madness deposits the passengers in the city. Arriving excited and nervous, they fill the streets and pile into taverns and casinos.

Aurora and Gabriel walk together, drunk with their good fortune. She asks him for one more sacrifice, and the young man, a smile on his lips, acquiesces readily.

"I'll stay with Félix," he decides, looking into the grateful pale green eyes. And they continue talking, wrapping their conversation in cheerful joy.

Rosarito is walking silently next to Dolores, listening to the thousand details with which she tells her friends the story of their recent visit.

"Listen, kids," she says jauntily, "The women were incredibly skinny and not too charming, either! It's a good thing ugliness doesn't hurt or they'd be in constant pain!"

"The manager's daughter is pretty," points out Enrique.

"Yeah, from far away. She's too much like her mother, and

she'd have to put on several pairs of stockings to make her look like she has calves."

Rosario would like to join in the laughter of the workers, but some sudden reflections hold her back. They have reached Nerva, the frightening Andalusian city of pain, where old people crouch like hunted animals; women are lifeless; men deprived of freedom and health; children naked and anemic; and the atmosphere is charged with threats.

The crowd on Cicerón Street makes way respectfully for Rosario; Echea welcomes her at the entrance of the house, and as he starts to go upstairs, she asks him apprehensively, "How is Natalia doing?"

"She's feeling worse."

"What does Romero say?"

"He thinks her condition has become serious."

"Since this morning?"

"No, in the last few days."

"Then . . . she didn't have a relapse because of the upheaval today?"

"I don't know," stammers Aurelio, thoughtful and taciturn, and he musters the courage to look into his friend's gentle deep eyes.

The Speech

A platform has been erected on top of the bleachers for the president's table; an excited throng fills the bullring. The president is explaining the reason for having this assembly, and he is asking for a vote from each sector in the zone to make sure that the miners are in favor of the strike and are ready to maintain it until the company honors their petitions from last year. The people in charge of picking up the votes from the four districts have been designated, and the meeting is about to come to a close, when the crowd clamors for a speech from Echea. It is well known that he is a great orator who can stir the audience's passions with his improvised speeches, but he is seldom afforded an opportunity to show off his abilities.

Two years ago, some leaflets inviting the railroad workers to unionize made their way clandestinely along the winding and deadly paths of the mines. This was the labor union's first cry, and the miners, thirsting for hope and liberty, gave their support to the new-born organization, in whose offices Aurelio Echea signed up three thousand Andalusian workers in one month. This was the birth of Nerva's Syndicate, and soon it needed a life of its own and special nourishment.

At that time the secretary of Madrid's railroad union, who had an outstanding record of fighting for socialist goals, was elected as Dite's Champion. Skillful in recruiting valuable collaborators in the valley, he inspired confidence and enthusiasm and was successful in laying the groundwork for a solid organization. The persecutions, imprisonment in provincial jails, and constant threats that surrounded him added to his prestige but made it more difficult for him to accomplish the lofty goals of his project, which was still in its initial stage. He suspected that the employers, pretending to be merciful, encouraged them to go on strike, knowing that it would end in failure given that their fledgling organization was insufficiently prepared. He was worried about the organization but, yielding to pressure, he exposed it to danger, outdoing himself in bravery and perhaps foolhardiness. Constrained by prohibitions and rejections, he could almost never raise his conquering and outstanding voice during the campaigns. Even today, the assembly had not received authorization to hold speeches even though—thanks to the Syndicate—Nerva had a socialist mayor.

But the shouts grow louder; the impetuous, almost violent crowd, filling the entire bullring, wants their Champion to speak.

Suddenly there is an abrupt silence; with calm words, and in a somewhat cool and mechanical manner, this man—standing dutifully on the platform—expounds the need to oppose capitalism's relentless tyranny with a constitutional and legal power that gives the proletariat the right to organize and defend itself.

"If they restrain us and impose slavery upon us at work, at rest, in the street, at home, and in school, forcing us to increase production—so they can grow even richer—obligating us to obey their laws, rules, and dogmas, and to fight, believe, and die at their whim, how can they forbid us to defend life's dignity?"

An entranced gasp goes through the masses and keeps them from answering this serious and firm question.

The afternoon is fading. The light is dying in the incandescent clouds, the wind has fallen asleep, and the easterly shadow is pulling down the sun.

Echea goes on to say that the capitalists abhor the leaders of the people, accusing them of being the only ones with revolutionary ambitions, as if the masses—generally ignorant and with an inherited sense of submission and obedience—did not have the ability to choose more educated and daring persons and let themselves be motivated and guided by them. Individually, workers can never expect more from employers than philanthropic acts, and these handouts are an insult to those who work.

"All of us together," he assures them, "guided by those whom you yourselves have elevated to leadership positions, can *make demands* . . . and that is the only way that we will receive . . ."

He hesitates a minute, as if afraid to continue. The Civil Guards and the company guards, posted around the arena, listen patiently; the City Hall delegate smiles. Stimulated by the applause and excitement, the orator resumes with more verve, "Another comfortable statement bosses like to make is that revolutions can and should come from above. It is difficult to distinguish these two terms, *above* and *below*, and to avoid making an arbitrary distinction, as happens in cosmography. And besides, the real political renovations have to be grassroots movements, started at the very heart of our social being and born with the trauma and pangs that accompany all births.

"There are some—no doubt motivated by pious intentions— who would like to delete the 'r' from revolution and change it to evolution. This is a delusion advocated by people with a callous soul, who cannot feel the grandeur and depth of pain that is needed for everything seeking liberation in life, from the most humble and hidden seed to man, and beyond man, infinitely beyond . . . Social upheavals are the motor of progress, with change and enterprise acting as an impelling and fortifying tonic. Revolution produces evolution because there is no growth without suffering: every fertile womb pulsates with pain; an eternal peace would be as tragic as a barren woman . . ."

The Champion's words grow more heated. He hears his companions' pleased murmur behind him, and, looking out at the audience, his gaze is attracted by the magnet of a pair of eyes that make him tremble as if he were hallucinating. Rosario Garcillán is standing near one of the barriers, extremely pale and exhausted, her eyes filled with nightfall's violet shadows.

"But we also don't believe that a revolution, however renovating and violent, can work sudden miracles. Perhaps lofty goals such as Liberty transmigrate like souls and abandon an element when it becomes useless or worn out to inhabit another unused and more vigorous one. Thus we inherit the eternal ideal of liberation from antiquated religions, and we imbue it with fresh blood, youth, and vigor, until our impulse is spent as well and we become empty shells. Then new forms will emerge with aspirations that have either evolved or have become reality or have begotten new ones, but always through injustice, hatred, and after many centuries and much sorrow . . ."

A gust of incomprehension wafts over the crowd. Aurelio senses the confusion, searches for Rosario's impenetrable pupils that are turning ever darker, and composes his subtle thoughts into a categorical affirmation.

"But it is our fate to live in productive times. Humanity stands on the bloody edge of war, waiting for the fruit of this tragic seed, and it is inappropriate to talk about world peace while livid Europe is in its birth throes and while we await the incorporation of Liberty into the economic order. As we know, 'Nations must die so nations can be born.'"

Now the amazed crowd, startled by the vehemence of his speech, waits anxiously for happier predictions. Aurelio feels invaded by a passion; a marvelous inspiration flows to his mind and lips, inciting him to daring and arrogance, provoking his brazenness and haughtiness.

"It is our fate to live," he repeats, stretching out his arms in a sweeping gesture, "in times of revelation and compensation. Beneath war's sinister plow, furrows of a more egalitarian and just society are opening up, purified by the sacrifice of those heroes who, fallen on land or at sea, have entered the kingdom of silence. Change does not have to be swift or constant; it is subject to alterations and fickleness, battle and defeat, according to life's rhythm, but the need for change manifests itself with such urgency that no one can ignore or exclude it, and its wild force floods even the most peaceful shore.

"This is why, even though, thanks to our country's geographic location we have been spared these intense invasions, we also feel the ripple effects of their waves, as is evident by the systematic currents of some theories. Socialism, both written and verbal, has become fashionable; writers, politicians, and speakers find nothing easier or more convenient than to espouse the cause and use their pens and voices to join the universal movement on behalf of the proletariat. But all this is done with great caution, reserve, and selfishness, so as not to diminish anyone's extravagant privileges. They unearth Christ's teachings as if they were a novelty, admitting unabashedly that they had completely forgotten them . . . No ruling class is ever ready to give up its supremacy, and each class wants to be the one with unconquerable power, which arises, bloodstained and mysterious, like the Second Coming.

"The same is true for feminism, another salutary movement that exploiters would like to make their own. Following Muslim guidelines, they have always denied women their rights, and suddenly they court women so they can use feminism as a pretense for their maneuvers; they offer women autonomy without having prepared or educated them for it; today they are like merchants flattering them, having previously neglected them as fellow humans!

"Yet these postures are inefficient because they lack sincerity; they are simply another manifestation of fear, one more display of greediness on the part of the insatiable powerful. We should not expect salvation to come from them because it is in their interest to foster the doctrine of resignation for modern slaves. They are opposed to anyone's independence that decreases theirs; they are the tetrarchs of Jerusalem, the high priests, Anas and Caiaphas, who, after twenty centuries, make a pact with today's bourgeoisie—that deplorable middle class, a victim of its own cowardice, a sad parody of the aristocracy rather than a fraternal ally of the people. Like reincarnations of Pontius Pilate, they make sure that the tyrannical hordes can always count on the servitude of the ignorant common people . . ."

The listeners tremble like a forest of quivering reeds. The guards are worried, wondering whether their worry is justified, and they keep their eyes fixed on the delegate, who does not intervene because the orator has not made a reference to the Nordetanos, but only spoken about audacious and brilliant issues, at times too abstractly for some people in the audience.

"Be careful!" Estévez whispers in his ear, and Rosario looks at him, ashen with fear, counting the minutes by the accelerated beating of her heart.

The whiteness of her eloquent face is barely visible, darkened by the night, who has already donned her crown of rubies.

The mumbling and shivering miners, tinted in vermilion, form a dense and dark mass. The stars hang down cautiously from the vaulted sky, as if trying to overhear. The president ignores his friend's warning, and, throwing caution to the wind, he continues with his fiery speech, "A successful end justifies the means: we must win! Murder and petty theft are crimes that are punished with a life sentence; but mowing down mobs with cannons is glorious, and it is a triumph to get rich at the nation's expense. Only the mighty deserve to live."

"Aurelio, for God's sake!"

This clear and vivid plea, heard above the noisy applause, brings the speaker to his senses. Taking advantage of the confusion and darkness, Rosario has approached the table. Her warning pierces Aurelio's soul like a dart, softening its bitterness and dissolving it in feeling.

The authorities confer in the middle of the arena; a sense of alarm floats in the air, and the dark bullring seems filled with rustling leaves. This subdued and incipient agitation quiets down as soon as the Champion takes the floor again. The fire of his words circles the arena like a torch.

"But love consecrates all," he states, expanding enthusiastically on his previous phrases, "We have to love! To suffer shame and martyrdom in life and in death for having loved too much is glorious. To sacrifice oneself for love is to touch the waters of immortality with one's lips; only those who love are worthy of life . . .

"We condemn confusion and quarrels, we hate elitism and

excess, and we want to rise up against despots for the good of the people. Impelled by necessity, we are capable of resorting to force as a means of defense and to fight for survival. We demand that everyone be invited to life's banquet; some should not feast happily while others are being battered by the wheel of fortune. We demand Love and Justice! Privileges should not be inherited, but earned; all children should receive the same education so the most gifted can rise to the top. Let experts govern us, according to their qualifications and without class distinctions. We want work to be a universal obligation, without exceptions, and let the least competent be consoled with a compensation. In short, we want to tear down the old order—entrenched in hatred and selfishness, stained by the desperation of thousands—and build a new world with welcoming horizons and room for all ideals. Why does our yearning have to be a dream?

"Spain, the discoverer of new continents, the mother of free nations, is an ideal land for great longings, a land capable of absorbing the dawning light that shines like a promise on the fields of Europe.

"Love can save us, and its help should come to us from the most intelligent, purest, most talented, and happiest. Let them hear what God is telling them softly: that for a civilization to reach its highest peak, its heart must be enlightened; let them look through the veil of eternity and forgive us our impatience, our lament. Because cruel life afflicts us greatly and even the copper complains in these tormented mountains . . ."

The speaker's voice reaches a sublime intensity, emotional and fearless beneath the sky's breeze, clairvoyant in its sacred inspiration. And surpassing himself in even higher flights, he continues, "Although our brothers deny us their love here on earth, don't despair, my friends. We live in times of transitions and revelations. Even now, the telegraph lines are receiving mysterious messages beyond human control. We catch dim glimpses of past worlds; perhaps, as has been said, mankind's knowledge is simply a premonition. And God is not so distant that he does not answer our anguished cry: look how he sends us his fiery whirlwind. Soon we will receive new messages of his invincible greatness . . . These murmurs that bounce off the planet's watchtowers could be voices of other creatures calling to us from a star . . ."

His speech is over. Hearing a long and resonant drone, people look up to the high peaks where eagles and spirits dwell. But no one knows how to decipher the profound book of the heavens, and the mute crowd disperses, overwhelmed by the stars.

THE CONVERSATION

A restless little man, of elegant appearance and arrogant bearing, spent the entire duration of the speech moving around the arena with obvious displeasure; a taller and more robust man, whose appearance indicates an inferior status, accompanied him, making similar signs of disapproval and protest. They are Jacobo Pmip and his deputy, Isidoro Zabala, a sly and groveling Spaniard, who started as a guard and was promoted first to secretary, then to deputy of the famous convert. The miners, who call him "the traitor," hate him even more than they hate the Nordetano bosses because they have more to fear from him. He uses and abuses his power, confident of his influence with his superiors, thanks to his many years of service as a masterful spy and squealer.

After the crowd has dispersed, Pmip and Zabala stop to talk to Leonardo Erecnis, who is leaving the bullring very thoughtfully and aimlessly, with his hat in his hand and his eyes on the ground.

"That was pretty outrageous, wasn't it?" says Pmip, raising his voice boldly. "It's obvious that the mayor is one of them!"

"It was shameful!" Zabala chimes in equally indignantly.

Erecnis looks at them distractedly, as if he didn't hear them. He wipes his brow with his handkerchief and remarks excitedly, "What a magnificent speech! The light of genius illuminated this young man's face; I'm deeply moved."

"Incoherent quotes from his reading material," is Pmip's scathing opinion. "You're too emotional."

Suddenly two young girls appear and Pmip turns his attention to them. They are Casilda Rubio and her friend Carmen, the lovely dancer at the pilgrimage of the cross, who has a vivid and roguish face, and whose Byzantine eyes are the reflection, as José Luis noticed, of a dangerous soul. Currently, she is the prey that Don Jacobo is most eager to catch.

He moves away from the group and stops her to say, "Why didn't you come to my house?'

"My mother didn't want me to."

"But haven't you been working in Vista Hermosa until recently?"

"Yes, but you're a bachelor."

"So what?"

"You have a bad reputation," she adds, half laughing, half bashful.

"Others who were no worse than you have worked for me; I pay well."

"They won't let me."

"You girls are fools!" declares the catechist furiously. "You'd be better off with gentlemen than with those coarse fellows who mistreat you and then abandon you—as happened to her," he says, turning to Casilda, another booty that is beyond his reach.

She looks down in embarrassment, trying to hide her confused thoughts and the marks of an unforgettable night. Finally, she mutters, "No one has abandoned me."

"What about that squinting anarchist?"

"I don't know who you mean."

"Come on, I mean that sailor."

"He was our lodger and he left with his wife."

"A lovely woman!" the hunter lets slip.

"Do you know her?" Love reawakens violently in Casilda's sad golden eyes.

"You're jealous," observes Pmip, bemused, enjoying the young girl's suffering, and then he adds cunningly, "I don't know her, but she must be beautiful if he left you for her."

He says goodbye, and when the passersby look at the group suspiciously and curiously, Don Jacobo gladly resorts to dissimulation, one of the many weapons in his arsenal.

"I'll talk to your mother," he tells Carmela, and from a little farther away, he reminds them in a dignified tone of voice, "Don't forget that every afternoon on holidays there are catechism classes in Dite . . ."

Erecnis and Zabala are discussing the Champion.

"Sure, I'd like to talk to him," repeats the chemist.

"Close up, you'll see that he's just a poor fellow without the least importance."

"It all depends on your definition of importance . . . Do you think I could meet with him this very evening?"

"If Don Jacobo can arrange it . . ."

"That shouldn't be a problem," remarks Pmip, who has rejoined them, and who adds conceitedly, "I have friends everywhere, and the Syndicate is not as ferocious as its founders make it out to be."

"He seems rather reasonable to me!"

"At times . . . Do you know what he's up to?"

"I think I do."

"Well, you'll know for sure if the fellow receives us."

They walk in the direction of Cicerón Street, bumping into noisy urchins, women sitting on the sidewalks, perplexed workers in the midst of discussions. The entire city has burst its banks, overflowing, convulsed, and baffled by the confusing comments and emotions. The electricity, supplied by a private company, is weak and insufficient, leaving pools of darkness in the squares and side streets.

The news continues to spread that the ground near the pit is groaning; the palpable anxiety in the streets upsets the men, and their faces, covered with mineral dust, turn gloomier and redder as they recall the metallic howls . . .

The two girlfriends, absorbed in their confidential conversation, cut across the groups.

"And you love him in spite of everything!" observes Carmen with pity.

"Yes," answers Casilda bitterly, and an inextinguishable light burns in her eyes.

"I'd hate him if I were you."

"I also hate him."

"That's impossible."

"I'm telling the truth: I love him like crazy and I'd love to kill him."

"She's the one you should kill," smiles Carmen, without being too serious about this plan of extermination. And then she asks with gnawing curiosity, "But did he make you promises?"

"Not with words."

"How then?"

"He let me know that he liked me with his eyes, with other signs . . . If only that woman hadn't shown up!"

"She may leave again."

"She's invincible," mumbles Casilda jealously, piercing unfathomable space with her eyes and poisoning herself with the dark flower of a dangerous thought; she shudders as if she had heard the cry of an extinguishing star.

"What's the matter?"

"Nothing . . . I'm trembling!"

Carmela can't contain her curiosity and dares to ask, "And what about last night? What was that all about?"

"Don't ask me," begs the amorous girl, gripped by terrible fear and unable to hide her misfortune.

"You lost yourself with Pedro Abril among the rocks?"

"Be quiet! It's all that woman's fault."

"Her fault?"

"Ever since she arrived, I can't think straight; I've lost my mind . . . At the pilgrimage's opening ceremony I didn't know what I was doing . . . and later either! *They* were in my house together, loving each other . . . I had to revenge myself."

"But your revenge was against yourself!"

"Because they bewitched me!" affirms Casilda fearfully. And her parched soul yearns, "If only there were a God!"

"And there is."

"That's what my mother says . . . but it's a lie."

"There is one. Haven't you ever gone to church?"

"Not often."

"Well, that's where he is—amid the incense that makes you drowsy and the piano playing," Carmen declares with childish and ingenuous sensuality. "A priest, dressed in petticoats with ironed and starched lace, and a large scapular embroidered with flowers, speaks on his behalf . . . You go there, tell him what's happening to you, he makes the sign of the cross and forgives you . . . and you're the same as before."

"No, I'm not the same! Besides, you have to know Latin for all that," argues Casilda, with primitive fear. "I don't want God to forgive me," she hisses savagely, "but to help me."

"Everything will work out, child: you'll marry Pedro, who's better looking than the other, and you'll be happy."

"I can't love him . . . and I don't want to mislead him . . ."

"After what happened . . ." insinuates Carmen.

But her friend stops timidly, and her troubled and fatal eyes have a hypnotic look in the somber night.

"As long as I'm racked by this pain, I can't do anything but hate and suffer!"

Her words are drowned out by the city's muffled mutter. Nearby, the chords of a song, played masterfully on a guitar, evoke the mysterious and distant enchantment of Persia, like a memento from the desert.

The bitter cup of Casilda Rubio's heart overflows and she bursts into tears.

8

In Prison

As THE CHORDS DIE DOWN IN THE HOT NIGHT AIR, CARMELA TRIES hard to resist the sadness.

"One man or another, what's the difference? Don't make yourself so miserable."

"Haven't you ever been in love?" sobs Casilda without lifting her head, swallowing her tears. And Carmela, wise for her seventeen years, answers, "We can only choose among those who come to look for us and those all seem the same to me: greasy from the machines or red from the mines. They're all uncouth brutes, as Don Jacobo said."

Inconsolable, Casilda looks up in surprise and says, "But there aren't any others!"

"No?"

"Well, who else?" Casilda cannot conceive of a man who doesn't have the earthy smell of the mineral deposits. Just as the Egyptians believed that all animals emerged from the mud in the Nile, for her the hidden mountain lode is the only source of life and of passion.

Carmela laughs and repeats, "Who else? Why, the others!"

"The gentlemen?"

"Sure . . . if they choose us."

"So you'd sell yourself?"

"No, but I'd let myself be loved with delicacy and grace."

"By Don Jacobo?" asks Casilda in consternation, almost forgetting her grief.

"Never! He's old."

"Oh, I know: you like the young gentleman from Madrid."

"I like clean and elegant men who say nice things."

"And has he said those to you?"

195

"Sometimes . . . very few times. He only talks to me if I happen to run into him." Her troubled voice sounds sad and timid; then she continues in a firmer tone with a fatalism that seems painful on such sweet young lips, "But you're right; we're here for the miners. They need us when they come out of the caves or off the ships, when they escape from the mouth of the ovens or lie torn to pieces on the *special train*—like my father."

They hasten their pace, as if driven on by the force of those tragic reasons, walking in silence, each one remembering the grief that had the greatest impact on their family: the brother buried in the mine, the father caught in the teeth of a motor . . . Since they had stopped to talk rather than find their way out of the tangle of streets, they now try to make up for lost time.

Casilda had come down the mountain with her sister because Hortensia could not find peace as long as she was away from Nerva. Even though she was in pain, ran a fever, and could not use her arm, she swore that her wound was not serious and cited maternal duties as an added reason for wanting to return home. The first thing she did was to visit her husband in jail, smile at him despite his frown, take him some food, and hide her bandages under a shawl so her hero would not have a bad conscience. She forgot Casilda's problems over her own and did not realize how unhappy her sister was. For her part, Casilda was glad to escape from her father's accusing eyes, Gabriel's absence, and Pedro Abril's dangerous proximity. She wanted to be giddy, talk, run, and open her poor heart, which was beginning to overflow with the cold and bitter drink of reality.

Carmela tries to reciprocate her friend's trust. Although she is slightly younger, she is less impulsive and more circumspect. Despite her childish and playful appearance, she has a mature and thoughtful character, overshadowed by a melancholy foreboding: she knows what is waiting for her in life, though she resists accepting it; she retreats from the edge of the inevitable, pricked by the temptation to conquer destiny. In her love of cleanliness and refinement, she only consorts with miners at dances and pilgrimages, when they are washed and festively attired. She prefers working for the proud foreigners in the beautiful gardens of Vista Hermosa to toiling in the dirty and wretched village.

She has an older brother who earns his keep and two younger ones. For Carmela's mother, feeble and enervated ever since her husband's death, her daughter's wages would be a welcome boon, but she considers her presence and help even more beneficial. She cannot convince herself to let Carmela go, especially not to the house of a man who has a bad reputation and is despised in the region for his treachery. She does not dare give Pmip a negative answer, and at the same time it pains her to see her daughter's irritation. Casilda, who can choose among the job offers in Vista Hermosa, has decided not to put up with Pmip's advances any longer. Tonight she gave him a definite and firm answer so she could determine her course of action without his interference.

Carmela's yearnings for independence, her rebellious instincts against destiny awaken in this intimate hour. Her friend's bitter lot frightens her and fills her with a deep disquiet. The terrible memories they invoked together and the lessons of the speech they have just heard churn in her troubled heart, and like a reverberation of her anxiety, she also murmurs, "One has to be strong, stronger than the others!"

Speaking softly, she doesn't even know whom she is addressing, imbued by the general discontent that lurks in the city's shadow like a thief; the harsh and hostile words sound infinitely bitter on her innocent lips.

And suddenly Casilda Rubio contradicts herself, justifying her tears with a profound sigh, "More than anything, one has to love . . . Don't you see that we can't live without love?"

"Didn't you just say that you could only hate?"

"Yes, because I'm in love!"

Pale and nervous, they look at each other with a gesture of amazement. They have reached the dark alley where Hortensia lives, near the Syndicate. Supporting each other, they enter, chatting absentmindedly, and feeling their way as if walking blindly among souls.

The Visit

At the entrance of the untidy room, Don Jacobo asks Estévez with a smile, "Are you willing to receive us? My friend, Mr. Erecnis, would like to say hello to you."

"Please, come in. Not you, Zabala."

"Why?"

Santiago gives him a direct and candid look, as he pushes him out coldly and closes the door. For an instant, the fellow's curses and footsteps are audible near the gate, and five minutes later Echea is talking to the foreigners in the corner of the room that is set up as a doctor's office.

Furnished with a rustic table, a wicker chair, and a shelf for the medicine chest, the tiny cubicle looks out on the patio that is illuminated by a light bulb with coal filaments. The dense air is heavy with a mixture of medicinal smells and the stench from a cloaca.

Estévez stays with them during the visit, trying to make sure that Pmip is not offended by the fact that Echea hardly pays attention to him, intent on satisfying the chemist's curiosity, who tells him kindly and respectfully, "Forgive me for disturbing you, but I've just heard your speech and I must confess that I was extremely surprised by it. Suddenly I'm very interested in the project over which you preside, and if you don't mind my asking, I would be grateful to you if you could tell me which goals the Syndicate is pursuing."

Don Jacobo is still smiling, displaying a disdainful indulgence for his friend's enthusiasm and a benevolent contempt for everything that is being discussed.

Aurelio looks at Erecnis with his clear and proud eyes, doubting his sincerity; he is tired, impatient, and exhausted, but this man's face intrigues him. He passes his hand over his high and broad forehead, as if trying to remember, and answers decisively, "This special Syndicate, which tries to serve the extraordinary needs of this region, has various goals. I'll try to sum them up in a few words: to maintain the freedom and right of association, assembly, and thought; to expel the Rehtron Company from the judicial courts and town councils, where it acts to the proletariat's detriment; to eliminate the contractors and their intolerable abuses; to bring the work day in line with physical energies, and adjust the salaries according to the needs of each family; to boycott all institutions, such as schools, hospitals, stores, and any others run by the company so it can multiply its gains at the workers' expense; to revise the 1872 mining contract and declare it illegal because it conflicts with laws currently in effect; to make an inventory

of the company's territorial holdings and expropriate all un-
lawfully acquired land; to apply this process to all the company's assets in Spain and compare them to the tax it now
pays the state; to check whether the fees assessed by customs
match the volume of exports during a given time period; to investigate the criminal occurrences in 1888, and try to have
those who were responsible for that slaughter, and their ac-
complices, brought to justice; to examine the harm caused by
the fumes and exact legal compensation; to demand that an
indictment be issued for damages caused by cave-ins and forbid excavations in hazardous places."

With the Syndicate's projects threatening to go on forever,
Pmip feels a mute rage, while his friend listens thoughtfully,
agitated by swift and burning reflections. Echea proceeds un-
perturbed, "To declare Dite unsafe and ask the demolition
crew to examine other municipalities in the region in search
of terrain that is suitable for building a village where citizens
can organize themselves into a community and enjoy the advantages of progress; to raise the workers' consciousness by
means of a scientific and practical education so that they merit
being mine owners, transforming themselves from workers
into proprietors, managing and being managed, in full possession of their work and its profits . . ."

Jacobo Pmip cannot take this any longer; his steely eyes
flash like sharp spears. He is about to stand up brusquely, but
instead he reaches into his pocket, takes out his cigarette case,
and offers the three men some tobacco; he has managed to
control his strong nervous vibrations. Estévez, rolling a cigarette, tells him in an undertone, half jokingly, in a placating
and amiable tone, "Well, disdain is the virtue of superior
souls," letting him know that he had noticed Pmip's gesture of
fury and protest.

Turning to the chemist, the president tells him, "That's all."

The ensuing moment of silence fills with noises coming
from the office.

"Do you think it's possible to achieve all that?" asks Erecnis
with an alert look, full of lively interest.

"Yes, it's possible."

"And fair?"

"Oh, more than fair."

"But difficult, right?" Pmip suggests ironically with a

slightly shaky voice. Without looking at him, Echea, self-assured and impervious, concurs, "Very difficult!"

"You have to fight!" says the Yankee with a heavy heart, realizing the enormous inequality of this confrontation. "Fight against a multimillion dollar entity, with prestige in various nations, and which in this country alone owns an entire seaboard of the most important mining region and has the blessings of the politicians who, according to you, are subsidized by the company."

The president, with a somber expression on his face and a cryptic gleam in his eyes, agrees with everything, and then states emphatically and with a serene gesture, "All I can offer in opposition to this power and these interests is the right of thousands of workers, representatives of many generations of slaves, who in their search for copper descend to the very bottom of the earth, where atrocious heat grinds the rocks and the vitriol scalds their skin, the realm of the unknown where dynamite's titanic voice reigns . . . These men live shriveled by darkness and drunk with sadness; with every blow they open a wound in the world's structure; and the roads give way beneath their feet, the abyss gapes, the rocks crackle and collapse into the undermined ground: the miners remain alone with night and death! Don't you think it's fair that they should be the owners of the mines?"

"Yes," answers Erecnis, moved, and with a voice steeped in profound compassion.

Aurelio turns to Pmip and, addressing him openly for the first time, he asks gently, "How about you?"

"Yes," replies the engineer hesitantly; he is pale and there is a spark of anxiety in his cold, shrewd eyes.

"Well, these *legitimate owners* of the mines," underlines Echea calmly and firmly, "are those who labor in the acid factory and foundries; they man the doors of the furnaces, amid the whistling flames, under a shower of incandescent ashes, threatened by suffocation and poisoning, corroded by gases and high temperatures; they work out in the open on the trains that move with dizzying speed; they disembowel the mountains in the pit, pursued by a painful and terrible death . . . Don't you think they're entitled to reap the fruits of their labor?"

"Yes," repeats Erecnis quickly and resolutely.

And Don Jacobo, trying to avoid Aurelio's question, tells his friend, "A moral right without any practical basis . . . and it's madness to pretend otherwise."

"But it's sublime!"

"And fruitless."

"But reasonable," argues an unruffled Santiago between puffs of smoke.

Aurelio pursues that line of thought.

"We live in a time of renewal," he exclaims, sensing the flutter of a breeze of liberty. "Life will lose its harsh and bitter taste; Justice will prevail among God's creatures."

"You're a poet," smiles the chemist, who suddenly realizes the impossibility of all he has heard.

"A fanatic," grumbles Pmip under his breath.

There is a knock on the door; the doctor is looking for a tonic.

"For whom?" asks Aurelio in alarm.

"For our friend Vicente Rubio, who doesn't feel too well."

The old man stands on the threshold, out of breath and with gloomy eyes; a cruel sleepless night and a few hours of shame and distress have enveloped him in a trembling twilight. He is a changed person; his shoulders, bent from climbing the mountain, have difficulty carrying this new burden, and he bows his head as if weighed down by the ashes on his hair.

Don Jacobo gives him a sideways glance, and Santiago rises up, eager to help him, "What's the matter, my friend?"

"My heart wants to jump out of its place."

He puts his hand on his chest and vents his bitterness with a painful smile. "I'm no good for anything anymore—I can't even take revenge!"

"But is there something to avenge?"

"Yes, and how . . . The whole village knows about my dishonor."

They go to the back of the room and continue their conversation very quietly.

"Are you sure?"

"Sure! The fellow boasts about it to get even for earlier rejections."

"And is he going to keep his word?"

"I doubt it."

"I think so, don't lose heart. Have you talked with your daughter?"

"I couldn't . . . but her flight and tears are like a confession."

"Does she love this man?" inquires Estévez, talking mostly to himself, trying to understand this enigma.

The amazed father replies, "Why wouldn't she?" And then he adds softly, with a dark voice, "I myself saw the two of them alone together amid the rocky stumps. They were walking home . . . it was late!"

The schoolmaster remembers Casilda's fervent love for the other man, and he tries to comprehend the desperation that made her act out of senseless spite. "That's the punishment," he thinks, without daring to tell that to the father, who is begging him anxiously, "Please help me! You know how to talk and convince; I only know how to suffer . . . If only my son were alive!"

Tears well up in his eyes; his ancient body quivers. Touched by the old man's pain, Estévez promises to help him out in this thorny matter.

The medicine is ready. While Mr. Pmip chats with the doctor, Erecnis asks Echea about the slaughter of 1888, alluded to earlier when he was listing the Syndicate's goals. Wasn't there a dash of imagination in that description? Because now Erecnis thinks that the president is a fantasist, a speaker who rises up and loses himself in flights of fancy beyond logic. As if guessing these doubts, Aurelio looks at him fixedly, and his face darkens as he answers, "Yes, sir, it was a heinous crime that has gone unpunished. Neither you nor I were here then, but that horrible event continues to rankle in the hearts of many, and it is one of the strongest and most enduring motives for revenge against the company."

"How could it have happened?"

"It happened in the easiest and most natural fashion. The miners and villagers were gathered in Dite's main square to protest peacefully against the harm caused by the fumes. Tired of the miners' repeated demonstrations, the company decided to teach them a lesson. The authorities, who were in collusion with the employers, had brought in soldiers from Sevilla—as will happen again now—and without any preamble or other incidents, an entire squadron opened fire on the group . . . The official report listed thirty dead and a dozen wounded, but according to public opinion there were five hundred victims, among whom more than a hundred corpses were incinerated in the burning rubble . . ."

Vicente Rubio has finished drinking his medicine and the doctor returns to his other duties. Pmip, waiting to leave, listens to the Champion's last words with an air of indifference; his entire attitude expresses boredom and a mocking leniency. Estévez joins him, and the chemist, realizing that his visit has been too long, also gets up, ready to depart. Echea, raising his voice, adds this comment to his previous remarks, "The one who started to prosper at that time was Isidro Zabala, who went from being a miserable lackey to becoming an influential person . . . and here he is now—a successful capitalist."

Unfazed, Don Jacobo keeps smiling as he continues his conversation with Estévez. Confused and upset, Erecnis exclaims, "The current management can't be held accountable for what happened thirty years ago!"

"But the Rehtron Company is still the same, even if the names of the managers have changed . . ."

They walk across the living room on their way out.

"Could you receive me tomorrow around this time?" asks the chemist somewhat shyly.

"With great pleasure . . ."

Even before they open the door, the trilling sound of a woman's warm laughter reaches them from the entrance downstairs.

THE BLACK RING

They had agreed to meet after the assembly so they could talk to each other in private like newlyweds.

He does not grow tired of looking at Aurora, to feel the indescribable caress of her soothing voice that subjugates and inflames him. Near Gabriel, the flame of intimacy warms her heart; she forgets the past and her painful memories sleep in her consciousness. She has the feeling that she has lived here for a long time, that she is friends with the people and knows their worries and goals. She has a wonderful intuitive understanding and is not amazed by anything her beloved tells her about the needs of the miners; it is as if she had a foreknowledge of all the suffering in the world. But she wants to save Gabriel from the clutches of this pain.

"I've come to bring you joy," she reminds him. "We have to be happy and overcome our destiny."

"With force or with love?" asks the young man, remembering Aurelio's talk.

"With love!" says Aurora, laughing, tipsy with youth. Feeling his desires whipped up by the music of this laughter, he tries to soak in the enchantment of her sunburnt face, although in the dark entrance he can see only the white of her teeth and her pupils. Drunk with ambition, he dreams of once more riding the furious waves in his boat and of gliding freely over the wide roads of the sea with his beloved, far from the enclosing mountains and the industrial lairs. He is tormented by the feeling that the mountains engulf the coal fields without mercy; he suffers from the dominion of the peaks extending in closed rows beyond the hills, one after the other, without an end in sight: the passes of Rubio and Mármol; the mountain chains of Hinojales, Tudía, and Gandul; and the peaks of Aroche, followed by ravines, cliffs, slopes, bluffs, and torrents. How far away is the open sea! Gabriel remembers his slow and tortuous voyage across marshes and hills, his climb up the wild mountain folds to reach the peak "at the end of the world," and finally his descent from the immense crystal zone to the ashes of the simmering iron in the depths of the mine, where the yoke of brutal work near the furnaces and in the tunnels imprisons like the metallic fetters.

The fleeting vision of his slavery is linked to the memory of another softer and more desirable yoke, which consoles him immediately. He takes a tiny object wrapped in paper from his pocket and in the dimly lit doorway, and under Aurora's eager glance, he offers her a ring.

"This is for you," he says. She places it on her open palm and examines it curiously.

"Black!" she stammers, shocked.

"Don't you like it?"

"Yes, yes. What is it made of?"

"It's vulcanite. That's what all the miners buy as wedding bands; they're made here and are cheap."

"Oh, it's a wedding band?"

"Yes, but a rather poor one as you can see," laments Gabriel as he tries to put the ring on her finger.

"Won't it break?" asks the girl, resisting gently.

"No, it's really strong. It's made of hardened rubber, gum, and sulfur, a mixture used to make machine bearings and supports for the instruments; we make the rings from the shavings."

"It looks like crystal!"

"Your initials and mine are engraved inside, just like in the wedding rings of the rich."

Hiding her insurmountable distress, Aurora lets him put the ring on her finger, and the groom caresses her trembling hand, shaken himself.

"When?" asks the girl insinuatingly, with fervent and smiling eyes, surrendering to happiness once more.

"As soon as possible!" he exclaims, his lips ripe with kisses as he talks and laughs. His ardent and sensitive temperament vibrates with vehement passion for this woman—his woman, his drop of eternal hope in the fountain of humanity.

"We have to ask for the papers in Traspeña," he says, suddenly worried.

He is afraid that it will prove difficult to obtain documents that may not exist because perhaps Aurora's birth and his were not even recorded in either a religious or civil registry. Once more he is tormented by the trauma of their clandestine birth that haunts them like a curse. Vaguely he tries to think of someone in the distant past who was responsible for this injustice, but he doesn't know who. And again he feels oppressed by life's fetters, the ring of mountains enclosing his freedom, gripping his heart like a hard and rigid hoop.

"Like this ring!" he murmurs suddenly, seeing the black band shine on Aurora's finger.

She doesn't hear his anguished cry. The name he just mentioned has conjured up beautiful green fields born of the sea and evoked the comforting coolness of paths and forests. Meanwhile Gabriel, tortured by his obsession, sees the darkness around the valley pushing back the outlines of Andalusian hills. They are the prison wardens of his youth, and he must demolish them blow by blow with his pickax, just as he brought down other strong walls in the pit; he must bore an exit through the tunnel so he can escape with his beloved and regain the beach and his boat.

"What madness!" he bursts out, starting to laugh to calm down his delirious vagaries.

Aurora is not surprised by his exclamation; she lives it and savors it, joining in his laughter without reason. She lets her fiancé hold her hand where the vulcanite shines on her ring finger, black and hard like the chain around a galley slave's neck. Looking into each other's eyes, they talk about Nena; about Rosario and José Luis, whose fate seems tied to Gabriel's with a mysterious bond since the *Hardy*'s accident . . . The remembrance of the boat and its tragic end always appears to be an omen of predestination to the sailor. The land calls to him; the sea does not want to destroy or keep him, but deposits him time and again on the shore with undeniable determination . . . The rebel looks up at the pure and sparkling sky where the heart of the stars sparkles, and he feels the touch of a generous breeze. With a tender gesture, he turns to his companion.

Aurora is still thinking about "la señorita," as Rosario is referred to in the region, and she cannot stop praising her incredible sweetness, her virtues, her modesty; it is as if she had known her for a long time and had already tested her.

"Meeting her here seems so strange to me!" she murmurs.

"But did you know her before?"

"No, not all . . . I don't even know how I could have immediately used the familiar form with her, without thinking about her social position, and I told her the story of our lives, our love . . ."

"You did the right thing."

"She was not surprised that I confided in her, nor by my trip or our situation; she understands and forgives everything. I think of her as a supernatural being."

"On the ship, I thought she was an apparition!"

Anything concerning Rosarito and her brother is of special interest to the couple; but the reason for their gratitude is tied to the thread of another memory, which causes them to fall silent.

"And that girl from the mountain . . . ?" asks Aurora with some concern.

"Casilda Rubio?"

"Yes."

"Are you worried about her?"

"Because she is unhappy . . ."

"It's not that bad! They say that last night she became engaged to a long-time suitor."

"I saw her here today. Didn't you?"

"No, I didn't."

The young man speaks openly and without conceit. Aurora, although a little bitter, doesn't want her love to cause anyone pain. Yet she is convinced that Casilda is a violent and unbridled young girl, moody rather than passionate, who wants to avenge her disillusion. She calms down, and when the time comes to leave Gabriel to go up to her new refuge, she is overcome by exhaustion and bliss.

They take leave of each other happily. Sounds of footsteps come from the offices, but when the door opens, Aurora has already disappeared.

Erecnis and Pmip leave the Syndicate in silence. Gabriel remains standing in the doorway. Overflowing with tenderness, he strains to hear the adored voice one more time; he wants to continue living and loving under the spell of the summer night. And his desires rise up into the clouds, where the seven-armed candelabra of the Pleiades emerges among the constellations in the immense and luminous star-studded sky.

He sighs; everything up above is beautiful and free. A shooting star flies across the blue space like a firebird.

9

Infernal Chants

The Night Before

THREE MORE DAYS HAVE PASSED. IN THE SYNDICATE, PREPARATIONS are being made with incredible perseverance; the members of the executive committee take turns working through the night, assisted by those Syndicate members who are authorized to participate in organizing the strike. For only a few hours and without getting undressed, the president lies down on the bed where his wife hovers between life and death. He watches over her agony, but is ready to be called away in case he is needed for some unexpected consultations downstairs. A sense of restless anxiety pervades the Syndicate's living quarters; only the warbling of the little girls lends it a faint note of cheer.

According to the publicized agreement, the strike was to begin on July 6. This is the date that appears on the leaflets circulating in the mines of the region, and the bosses and authorities have fallen for the ruse because in reality the strike is scheduled for the afternoon of July 2.

Thousands of flyers asking for support have been distributed in Spain and sent abroad, in the hope of catching the attention of Europe's labor unions. And today hundreds of new leaflets have to be distributed in the valley with instructions about the event that will take place July 2. These red flyers, piled up in the Syndicate's office, state categorically that the strike will begin tomorrow at six o'clock in the evening, after the workers have finished part of their tasks. At midnight, the tremendous commotion at the mines will come to a complete standstill; workers are urged to maintain order and follow the legal regulations as stated.

The pertinent paperwork has already been sent to the gov-

ernor's office by the executive committee, which also func-
tions as the commission in charge of organizing the strike,
with deputies in each section. The commission hopes that discipline and moderation will add to the event's extraordinary
solemnity. Right now the red flyers have to be distributed
throughout the sections with extreme caution, and the women
plan to hide them at the bottoms of the lunch boxes.

Aurora is carrying Gabriel's provisions, as well as those of
Enrique Salmerón, whose mother is still living at the Syndicate. Two days ago Enrique started working at the same Bessemer smeltery as Gabriel; this unsolicited transfer, intended
as a form of punishment, also affected Félix Garcés and even
Vicente Rubio himself, in other words, the four miners who
belong to the executive committee. A dismissal would have
been unprecedented, but Pmip's spirit of balance compelled
him to rectify the workers' excesses. He did not realize that
Enrique was now better off than before in the sulfur factory,
where he had been sent a few months ago as punishment for
his hostility toward an overseer. Nor did the snoopy engineer
remember that the smeltery excluded all old people from its
premises because its work required virile energy, youthful
blood, and muscles that crackle like granite in the ravines and
crush like mountainous avalanches.

Aurora walks next to Obdulia, who carries her brother's
provisions, and they hope that this will give them a chance to
smuggle more leaflets into the factories. They have reached
the crimson earth in the factory's vicinity, amidst the reddish
mineral cinders and the water's red gully. It is noon, the hour
when the sun's delirious and cruel light bounces off the black
cavernous mountainside and sizzles in the plains.

Aurora, who is growing more comely and willowy with
every passing day, marches sprightly and impatiently, as if
propelled forward by her thoughts. Obdulia Garcés walks silently by her side, with the solemn and shy manner that sets
her apart from other young girls. She was born in Rosal de la
Frontera, near Portugal, and came to Dite to accompany her
brothers, who were attracted by the mine's maelstrom and
dazzled by the fire in Lucifer's Valley. But the girl lives a sheltered life, far from the industry's tumultuous whirlpool. Her
soul recalls the peaceful hilly corner, shaded by the Aroche

and bathed by the Chanza, and she feels less at home in these fiery plains than Aurora.

Shortly before they arrive at the plant, they are overtaken by another woman. It is Casilda Rubio, who is headed in the same direction and carries a similar basket full of mutinous leaflets. She had stopped at the Syndicate's office to pick up the flyers and is now carrying them proudly to prove that she is privy to the organization's secrets. Curious to see her rival's face, she lifts her shy eyes under their feverish lids and gives Aurora a sideways glance.

Aurora notices the look and cannot help betraying her displeasure. But the next minute she smiles and asks about Casilda's mother, whom she remembers with gratitude. She has a sudden vision of herself, when she arrived exhausted and feverish; she recalls her fainting spell, and her strange dream, so similar to death, which helped her forget and be reborn. And her battered body and restless soul still feel the touch of Marta's trembling hands and the curative effect of her compassion.

"I'll go and see her," she promises.

Casilda answers timidly but does not move away; she is detained and overwhelmed by loathing and admiration. More than ever, she is fascinated by this hated woman, whose mysterious voice seems deeper and purer, and whose green eyes shine with the intense light of a sacred spark. As she follows her, adjusting her pace to Aurora's, she finds a perverse joy in envying her. Aurora's body, marked by motherhood and pain, appears youthful, and the scorned woman is filled with an irresistible and morbid fascination by the gracefulness of her mouth when she speaks and the gentleness that envelops her like a halo.

At the beginning of the encounter, Obdulia said a few soothing phrases, but now all three women have fallen silent. Deafened by the roar and blinded by a curtain of smoke, they walk up the steps of the smeltery, and, entering with determination, they try to find their way in the dark place.

Everything seems to be seething in the gigantic and sinister shed: converters, boilers, dross, and molten metal burn and roar with a thunderous blaze. The steel cables over the deposits and drainage channels rise up red-hot next to the pits where the smelters struggle; the chimneys spew embers; the foul-smelling and fire-belching towers and smokestacks cover the workers with their gases and soot. The liquids pour out of the ovens like volcanic lava, flow down to the trough, and are carried back by cranes to the crucible, whose lips sputter gray flames, brilliant blue and white stripes, green lines, sparks, stars, and small metal globes. The tip of each flame extends its fiery tongue, and the poem recited by the glowing metal is accompanied by fierce explosions and the propulsion of burning material. The rusty ceiling and uneven floor tremble with the unbearable echo of the electrical machinery, sounding like the creaking of hinges in Hades. And the half-naked workers—wasted, grimy, and sweaty—look as if they had been molded from the mud of human ashes.

The noontime siren's strident and peremptory sound erupts in this cacophonous delirium, announcing a lunch break in the twelve-hour workday. Some workers, however, cannot abandon their tasks and have to eat right there, where the air is almost impossible to breathe because of the sulfuric acid emissions. Those who are free to leave follow the women, standing at the entrance of the workshop and waving furtively. The workers gladly make room for the pretty wreath of mostly young girls, who have to rush through the different industrial departments to take the meals to the workers manning the furnaces.

Today Casilda's father cannot leave his post because the molten metal he is pushing into the molds with a rod refuses to coagulate. Like a delicious breeze, the young girl sweeps past the nozzles of the furnaces, past the infernal crucibles, under the clouds emitted by the flumes, and appears at the red edge of the foundry, out of breath and shaken.

Some of the workers want to stop her to warn her about the dangers along her path, but she looks at them without seeing them; she is escaping from Gabriel and Aurora, who are sitting at the edge of the factory, getting ready to eat.

When Vicente Rubio feels his daughter's hand on his shoulder and sees her in front of him unexpectedly, a severe and penetrating cold invades him amidst the throbbing flames as if his bones were made of marble. In helpless dismay he recognizes signs of shame and desperation in the beloved face, and her desire to beg him for help and support.

He lets out a shout, which is drowned out by the surrounding din; his vision clouds and he tumbles to the ground, dragging down the girl, who wanted to catch him; as he falls, the burning rod singes Casilda's skirts.

Some of his companions rush over, gesticulating wildly, and carry Vicente out to the exterior platform, where the rest of them are eating, shaded by the wall. Casilda's sobs can be heard, stifled by the racket of the machines and the curses of the workers, who are shocked by his sudden collapse. The women wail in unison as they attempt to revive the old man's motionless body.

"He has fainted," they say. "He's dead!" they cry.

A few try to breathe life back into him with mouth to mouth respiration as in cases of choking. All is in vain. Pale blue spots begin to appear on the victim's forehead, and his nose looks more pinched; a bloody foam forms in his mouth, and his gray eyes, drawn toward the sun as if by magnetic force, are heavy with an eternal light that shines with absolute lucidity.

Two foremen arrive and order the injured to be taken to the hospital.

"What for? Take him to the graveyard!" shouts one of his companions angrily.

"Yes, into the ground," says another with harsh reproach.

And Felix Garcés mumbles bitterly:

"The regulations forbid having old people work in the foundry."

"This is scandalous," exclaims one of them.

"It's a crime!"

"They've killed him."

"He was sick," a foreman remarks, trying to avoid an argument.

"That's even worse!"

While the protests grow louder and more heated, an iron dump car arrives—still hot from the cinders—pulled by a locomotive, whose whistle insists on the removal of any obstacle in the way of its mournful voyage.

"This wagon is burning hot," Garcés criticizes.

A master electrician, who has joined the crowd, murmurs indifferently, "The dead don't feel the heat."

"But I want to accompany him," says Gabriel, who has remained standing next to the corpse.

"Oh, really?"

"Yes, sir."

"So do I," says Casilda, with sullen eagerness.

"That won't be necessary because it's a case of confirmed death," says the foreman.

A dangerous murmur can be heard. Insults spurt out of the seared jaws of these rugged, mud-covered men, who look sad and ravaged.

"I want to accompany him," Gabriel insists. The women want Casilda to go with her father, and, although Aurora is unhappy about it, even she understands that it must be so.

They are joined by Leonardo Erecnis, who in the past few days had been making the rounds with an air of contrition, visiting the mechanical department's most dangerous areas and those where the heaviest work is done. He could be seen in the heat of the sun, leaving his laboratory and crossing the roads, examining the puddles and cementation channels and exploring the various sections of the factory, stopping by the furnaces, bending over the hearth's immense stone, like the most wretched of the workers. Emerging burnt and blackened, and with a tortured soul and a pained look, he would climb up along the hollowed mountain to the cemetery where the victims of 1888 lie buried . . . Time and again he stared at the monstrous slag heap, nourishing itself, like a vulture, with lifeless things. Standing next to the buckets that bleed burning dross at all hours, he contemplated it, sizing it up with a squint . . . On his way back to Villa Hermosa, he would continue staring at it from the train window and see—as if for the first time—the red confusion of the crimson paths.

During the peaceful gatherings in Villa Hermosa, he would report his new impressions with such impetuous words and reveal the conflict raging in his conscience with such spirit that Don Martín called him a lunatic and Don Jacobo mocked him with condescending laughter. But the chemist did not concern himself too much with these gentlemen; he was intent on gaining a deeper understanding of the thorny question of human rights, which a few days ago had been of only vague and limited importance to him. He was filled with compassion for others, uncertain whether that was a virtue or a duty, and he began to look at life profoundly and religiously, without selfishness or prejudices. Everything appeared to him transformed, and he hardly recognized himself in this process of renewal . . .

The moment Erecnis finds out what has happened, he tries to avert the conflict that is threatening to break out next to the strange convoy on the pier. He quickly succeeds in having the hot dump car replaced by a flat car and orders burlap to be spread out on its floor. This unexpected consideration touches the workers, and they are even more moved by his immediate agreement that Rubio's daughter and friend should be allowed to accompany the deceased.

"Having a woman go along . . . that's a first!" grumbles the foreman under his breath, while his superior himself helps the girl climb up on the train, pressing several coins into her palm, and removing his cap in a show of respect when they load the corpse. He remembers seeing the old man at the Syndicate on the night of the speech, medicating himself in the doctor's office.

"Yes, he wasn't feeling too well a few days ago," admits Enrique Salmerón.

The grumbling has stopped; the tough, uncouth men, covered with mud and sweat, have been softened by a kind man's mere presence, his sympathetic words, wise manner, and pleasant smile.

The noise of the noonday explosions has started up. The remote mountains' vibrations resonate in the valley like the palpitations of the earth's heart.

Casilda is melting with love and anguish, while her father's corpse stiffens and grows cold at her feet, devoured by the darkness of the terrible hour. All aflame, with her singed dress, darkly flushed cheeks, and her sensual lips aglow, the young girl looks like the muse of the foundry. Her golden eyes, having shed all their tears, are fixed on Gabriel in an arid and dark stare.

The young man takes his leave of Aurora with an intense look, and she remains motionless as if suspended in time; everything around her flees and turns cloudy when Gabriel climbs up on the train with Casilda. The locomotive's strident whistle requests a clear path for its funereal journey, and the death train travels speedily beneath a noonday brilliance and amidst the crowd's lament.

METAL SILO

In the course of the pleasant chat that followed their first meeting, Erecnis promised to meet his new friend that night so they could go down to the countermines together. This visit, which had not seemed important to him previously, suddenly took on a pressing urgency. As Aurelio had pointed out, if Erecnis went with a guide he would not see everything, because visitors were only taken to the more accessible sections.

"Do you know your way around?" the chemist asked him.

"I've been down there many times in disguise and with my friends' protection. I also have a map of all the galleries, but I can't claim to be able to manage by myself."

"Do you have some people you can trust?"

"Many."

"I'll take care of getting permission to enter if you don't mind disguising yourself again and going down there with me at night. We don't want anyone to recognize you."

Echea hesitated, worried about endangering himself, but he was carried away by the enthusiasm of his supervisor, who had been transformed into a sensitive investigator of the workers' drama. They agreed to go and take Gabriel Suárez with them.

Erecnis has arrived punctually at the designated place, eager like a man embarking on a hazardous mission for his beloved's sake. He risks suffering serious financial consequences if the company suspects him of being an accomplice of the union members, but he is in such a state of agitation and curiosity that no logical reasoning can interfere with his wishes. He wants to see with his own eyes and feel with his own hands the misery that surrounds him; he longs to saturate himself with his fellowmen's pain, which has been gnawing at him accusingly ever since he learned to recognize it.

His companions have also appeared on time at the mine's entrance, near the Sombra Negra Hill. Dressed in torn clothing with splotches of makeup, their Córdoba hats pulled down to hide their faces, they look like colorful conspirators. One of them says softly and mournfully, "I've come instead of Echea because his wife is dying."

The chemist recognizes Santiago Estévez.

"Oh!" he murmurs, "I've chosen a bad time. You should be with your poor friend; we'll go down some other night."

"That won't be possible . . . we have to go tonight," says the teacher and whispers into his ear, "tomorrow the mine will shut down."

"Tomorrow? Wasn't it planned for the sixth?"

"Yes, officially; please don't betray us."

"Of course not!" promises Erecnis, making it sound like a solemn oath. "But is everybody ready?"

"As much as possible . . ."

They walk cautiously amidst the sheds, trying not to be seen, determined to make their descent before the ten o'clock shift fills the ducts. One of the nearby high-tension electric stations resonates powerfully, adding its whir to the noise made by a variety of drills—among them, steel borers equipped with diamond bits—the swinging, turning, moving of pistons and cylinders; the crashing and smashing of hammers, the rush of water and electricity—the entire powerful pressure leveled at the rock, inside and outside the mountain, exerts its extraordinary strength. Above the hills, beyond Mesa de los Pinos, the flames of Lucifer's Valley outline the horizon in blood red.

Erecnis marvels at the thought that in just a few hours, a handful of poor but strong-willed men from Nerva's humblest quarters will silence this noisy racket, extinguishing the proud industrial valley's fires and commotion with a breath of righteousness. Undoubtedly, they are aided by a sacred right, which allows them to be poor and empowered at the same time. And the boss, who walks in the middle, flanked by the two young men, looks at them with secret admiration, as if they were strange and mysterious creatures.

In the next shed, Erecnis changes from his jacket into a lightweight raincoat that had been readied for him and puts on a stiff leather hat. The men take three miner's lamps, but there is no need to turn them on yet because there is light from the special torches that are reserved for illustrious visitors. The company is pleased that its chemical engineer, an eminent personality and the director of a great laboratory, is interested in visiting the countermine.

They walk toward the entrance of Berta, a pit that is several hundred feet deep and one of the most important ones. After ringing some bells and receiving the signals they had previously agreed on, they enter the huge and deep elevator, which has enough room for nine to ten loaded wagons.

The luminous blue sky is waiting for the new moon, and E-recnis, lifting up his eyes, casts a slightly anxious glance at the peaceful sky above before submerging himself into the earth's entrails.

A nearby light illuminates the rim as the cage begins its descent, at first tinted in gentle splendor, and then timidly revealing the openings in the rocks and the cracks in the walls through which the greenish water swells and flows briskly with the sound of a riptide. The shaking of the cyclone separators, drainers, capstans, and cranes and the deafening sound of the locomotive's whistle are the same as in the valleys.

The descent continues into the unseen, and there is a terrible sensation of emptiness. The three men have lit their lamps as they keep sinking into the bottomless night's intangible darkness. Halfway down the mine's thirty-six floors, they step off onto a dark platform on the nineteenth floor.

"Doesn't the electric current reach down here?" asks Erecnis, who has not said a word up until now.

Gabriel Suárez, generally a man of few words himself, answers, "It does, but it's only used for the machines. Can't you hear their furious sound?"

"Yes, but why isn't there any light?"

"Because seeing the dangers too clearly would hinder us in our work. This little light," he adds ironically, lifting his lamp, "is more convenient; it illuminates only the spot we have to hit with the pickaxe."

They proceed along a gallery shored up with crossbeams, leading to the canals, boilers, and turntables; it is traversed by a wide path with safety niches and gutters. They walk fast along the wide, slightly inclined path; the cold air is drenched in fog and filled with the smell of creosote from the wood. From above and below the tunnel come the sounds of trains; faults intersect the path; the copper veins bleed. Along the sides, dark mouths disgorge mineral avalanches; scores of scarlet-colored men hang like bunches of grapes from the cages.

The visitors look for a sloping alleyway and let themselves glide down a stretch to escape from the racket of the machines. They breathe a heavy and damp air and feel the tem-

perature increase until suddenly a cool breeze wafts toward
them from the shadows. The noises die down in the distance
and an increasingly deep isolation surrounds them.

"Lean toward your right," warns the miner. "We're crossing
a ditch and there's no wall on the other side."

Instinctively, they feel the emptiness over the ditch and they
lean cautiously toward one side, with the lamps barely illuminating their steps. After a few more minutes of descent, Gabriel calls out, "Here are the grottos."

He lets his companions pass through a natural arch, and he
takes a torch from the hallway leading to a network of strange
and inscrutable chambers. These caves, which are linked by
windy paths and metal stairs, have blue marble walls and sta-
lactites that look like satin and crepe; some are green, others
white or rose-colored, and some fuse with stalagmites and
form marvelous crystal columns, or statues and monsters,
rings and flowers. The scarlet-tinted floor seems sprinkled
with pieces of these jewels and leaves from these bouquets.
The ceaselessly falling drops of water cover the fragments
with eternal dew, converting them into beautiful diamond
baubles. The high ceilings, studded with colorful rocks, shine
with prisms and brilliant gems; the air is thin, fresh, vibrant;
the sounds echo, multiply, and repeat themselves with endless
harmonies; the rivulets, bouncing like echoes from one level
to another with melody and rhythm, foam and whirl at the
spot where they are suddenly swallowed up by the earth.

The Yankee is amazed; his companions are quite familiar
with the famous grottos where the Rehtron Company usually
receives the visitors interested in seeing the countermines, but
Estévez is astonished by the sight. He imagines the ceiling
being covered with mysterious words, the curtains moving
gently and smoothly, and the rock beneath this glistening
rainbow filled with seeds like cosmic dust, bestowing life
and—after a long voyage through space—trapped by time in
the mountain's roots.

In these grottos, which are as sonorous as a temple or the
forest primeval, a philosophic mind contemplates growth and
survival, while a scientific mind, like that of the chemist, examines, admires, and studies everything: the nodules and supports in the walls and apexes, the water's corrosive action,
and every mineral's ramifications.

Here there are no organic fossils; this rock, so ancient that it is unclassifiable, exudes the world's primordial substance and illuminates every particle's multicolored grace and nuance. Like a magnificent sampler, it offers varieties of hard, firm, and volcanic rocks: solar and lunar; diamond splinters; cross-shaped and streaked; flintstones, bloodstones, eaglestones; crazy, sensible, and deceitful stones; rocks from the Amazons; luminous and contentious rocks.

Some are curved and brilliant, polished with metallic reflections like tiger's eyes; others are silky, with a diamantine shine; translucid, glistening, and prismatic; with moss green and seagreen tints, crimson, pearly white, red, lavender blue, yellow like gold, lemon, sulfur, or honey . . . Some have a changeable core in the center, others, a smooth surface that reflects the light, and under the artificial light, all of them acquire expressions and aspects that belie the classical phrase of "lifeless earth" used to describe the Silurian era.

Erecnis tracks them by picking up his lantern and casting its light on the fissures in the wall, the moldings and cantilevers, and then lowering it to illuminate the buttresses and hollows, igniting the resin with nervous eagerness. And everywhere he finds lovely clusters of embers and atoms, transforming themselves into corundum, spinel ruby, hematite, onyx, tourmaline . . . He is fascinated by the rocks slashed by precious crystals, and he has a nebulous image of subterranean elves in a mythical village, guarding the mountain's gemstones and enjoying their beauty. Perhaps some legendary Greek gnomes survived, and these lords of the earth continue to inhabit the gneiss from which rubies are born.

Gabriel Suárez tries to flee as much as possible from the glimmering treasure in the company's splendid reception room, because for him its enchantment is overshadowed by the horrors of the mines. He recalls the ones in Cantabria, whose yoke was less cruel to bear than here, where a foreign entity is colonizing a Spanish village's most sacred core, usurping not only the mines and the people, but their moral values of religion, fatherland, and liberty.

The miner feels that his destiny has grown ever harsher since the time he was initially tossed ashore by the sea onto the first red path; it was soft, with trees and a lulling breeze,

near the waves, beneath a gentle sky . . . He smiles bitterly. It
was difficult, he tells himself, but this is much worse!

In this comparison, which he has already made many times,
he imagines Aurora's search in those zinc caves, and he is horrified to think that she had been ready to keep looking in the
Nordetanian copper mines.

"Nature is engaged in a slow process that takes thousands
of centuries," muses the chemist in dreamy amazement.

"Like humanity," adds the schoolmaster, "through suffering and love."

"Yes, rocks and flesh are not immutable; rather, everything
germinates lovingly in crystals and souls."

The words bounce off the hard granite, liberating the glowing seeds of life, which disperse in echoes and roll down into
the depths, where the last beams of the torch are extinguished.

"This way," says Gabriel, guiding them by the light of the
three drops of light that flicker in their candles.

And they inch their way down some craggy inclines that feel
hot to the touch, far below the galleries where the train can be
heard. Down here, along these twisted and difficult roads, not
even the sleds or boxcars on rollers can move, and the metal
has to be transported manually, on shoulders, in troughs and
buckets, carried by men or children; this is the tragic "procession through the earth" to reach the small furnaces or the hole
for dumping ore.

Vestiges of Phoenician and Roman exploitation are still visible in the conduits and copper plating, but modern machinery's shrill and restless din does not reach down here. In these
frighteningly cramped holes, the miners have only a primitive
lathe, some ancient hoses, and rudimentary pulleys to help
them in their work. Here it is always man who strikes the rock,
plunges his needle into the mine's arteries, and—now and always—listens from his dungeon to the lament of the centuries.
The seed of redemption has not yet taken root in the darkness
of these pits!

A hot breeze from a distant fire bellows in the dark like a
furnace's vent; the men fear it because it makes breathing
more difficult and prevents them from hearing the moans of
the metal, the compassionate warnings that sound when an
excessive heat builds up between floors and covers the pillars

with sulfur, causing large crusts to collapse like terrible coffin lids.

With the reappearance of the seam, which had disappeared beneath the grottos in a sterile area, the cuts into the rocks become more numerous once more. The visitors advance with difficulty along these paths, feeling the dripping of water, falling in fiery drops like infernal rain.

Gabriel leads the way, pausing frequently next to the carpenters, the dross carriers, and the children in charge of the troughs, who work naked and emit occasional bestial moans. When the workers recognize the engineer, they take on a calm expression. Erecnis asks Estévez softly, "Is it true that the mine employs a lot of convicts?"

The schoolmaster replies with a sad and skeptical smile, "Even if they aren't already felons, the company increases their chances of ending up fingerprinted by treating them like defiant jailbirds. Working here, they suffer the humiliation of mistrust and the stigma of suspected wrongdoing . . . plus I don't think this darkness helps."

"No," concurs Erecnis, who is groping his way amid the treacherous cavities.

For the past half hour, they have been gliding like acrobats down the excavation's incredibly scraggy slope, catching only vague and veiled glimpses of the crystals' dense magnificence. The walls are full of eyes, alight with the secret of creation, and in the shadows, the colors sing their melodies with a quivering breath of mystery. Next to the mica's black foliage, the quartz displays its glassy pyramids; the copper, its shimmering stones; and the iron, its golden ore. Porphyry inserts its intrusive veins into marble and flint, while in every nook and cranny there are shiny strands of noble opal, blue malachite, and gray cobalt. Pyrite, limestone, and blue lead unfold their shades and mantles, pulsating with life's soundless motion, and there is such a multitude of creatures in the metal silo that each blow of a pickaxe is answered by the echo of a soul.

THE SON OF THE EARTH

They have left behind the fissure through which the burning wind howled; now all the murmurs come from the abundant forms of lower life, which have encrusted themselves into the slate in a spirit of eternal love, and which produce a sense of indescribable anxiety in anyone who catches a glimpse of them in the twilight. The soft sounds are being drowned out by loud and clear ones; the incessant staccato beat of tools is intertwined with strings of words that curl up into a ball in the cavernous tombs.

Gabriel leads the visitors along the edge of the pit where the borers are at work with the pestle. Their naked bodies covered with grey clay, these men resemble wolves, and they accompany every blow with harsh and stubborn howls, which are often no more than a moan, but other times form a woman's name or a verse from a song.

"What sounds do we hear from down below?" asks Erecnis anxiously.

"It's 'the lament,' the musical accompaniment to the work."

Standing on top of the seam, they hear the tortured, savage cries emerging from the depths, reminiscent of Jeremiad's lamentations and Mohammed's chants, the prodigious reverberations of an infernal choir.

Aglow from the heat, exhausted and depressed, Leonardo Erecnis is racked with guilt and a gnawing remorse, and yet a strange curiosity pushes him along the ramps and gutters. Beset by a wild desire, he wants to destroy the wall that separates him from death, reach the limits of other human cultures, and burrow through the Earth's mass until he finds the sky once more. He fears the touch of Lucifer's wings in the darkness or an encounter with Dante Alighieri's pale shadow, asking him in an accusing and pained voice to account for the miners' damnation. Panting and struggling, he follows Gabriel, climbing down the ladder of the windlasses, on vertical rungs barely large enough for one person.

Wishing to oblige, Gabriel leads Erecnis through murky and dangerous passageways, across planks suspended over a deep abyss filled with darkness, and plunges him into the full dread of night by taking him to the most forsaken depths of the world.

"That's enough," repeats Santiago, who has trouble keeping up. His explorations of the countermine had never taken him to such depths, and he feels his strength and courage failing him.

But Gabriel pretends not to hear. Determined and agile like a reptile, he continues in the direction of a certain pit, where he is often tempted to bore through its infernal walls to reach the sea . . .

As they move farther away from the ventilators, the smell of the acid's pernicious gas grows stronger, mixed with the stench of human decay from the detritus of thousands of men abandoned in these dungeons without any hygienic provisions.

Erecnis talks to Santiago about this new danger.

"Yes," agrees the schoolmaster, well aware of this problem, and welcoming the opportunity to catch his breath, "our friend Alejandro gives conferences and publishes articles about the serious oversights in the company's vigilance. Around here we're all familiar with what is known as miners' anemia."

"Is that the famous tunnel sickness?"

"Yes, and another name is Nile chlorosis—it's all the same thing. It's caused by a special parasite, a worm that lodges itself in the human intestine and leads to death by consumption."

"It's also called 'Negro sickness,'" murmurs Gabriel, who has stopped to listen; he adds gloomily, "The nickname comes from the slave era . . . but it's still around for whites as well."

Giant rats race through the rubbish, unafraid of the people. The miner comments, "These beasts may be blind, but we wouldn't have any food left if we didn't hang our lunch high up."

"You mean you eat down here?" asks the chemist in dismay.

"Yes, sir, too much time would be lost with going up and down."

A hint of criticism tinges the young man's words; his resentment grows along with the increasingly horrifying panorama of the mines. Driven by a certain foolish grudge, he wants to show the boss all the dangers and sufferings, without sparing him any inconveniences or risks.

Now he leads him down a steep and narrow incline of a hundred and fifty feet to reach the vein, crisscrossed by a spider's web of passageways. The black air is oppressively thick, as if simmering inside a volcano. The firedamp releases intense miasma; the nitric acid wets the gallery walls, flowing treacherously through the black magnesium and between the layers of gneiss. Here the abyss guards its treasure with fierce fury.

Gabriel declares with a grim smile, "We've reached the end!"

His savage pride makes him impervious to fatigue, despite his full day's work in the smeltery. Panting and out of breath, his two companions, who suffer from bodily pains and conscience pangs, remain quiet, lapping up the shade to quench their endless thirst.

Strong voices, menacing like the howling of wolves, drift through the grooves from neighboring passageways; some acetate lamps hang from the granite ceiling and—like prehistoric clay candles—they shed little light, illuminating only the point where the tools strike the rock's nerve. Accompanying each blow like a whiplash, a name reverberates in the darkness, repeated frantically and sounding like the monstrous pounding of a heart that knows no other word, "Casilda! Casilda! Casilda!"

Leonardo Erecnis doesn't know what he is hearing; horrified and bewildered, he lives outside of time and space. The schoolmaster listens in fright to the hoarse voices from the ravines, which remind him vaguely of Pedro Abril.

Both men instinctively fall back behind Gabriel and move closer to the wall. Their raised lamps reveal a tall, strong man without a stitch of clothing except for the reddish gold covering his gigantic body.

It is Thor, the son of the Earth, who, having drifted ashore like a piece of wood after sinking his soles into the crystalline ocean—which is deeper than the crib where the sun sleeps—is back on these continents that coalesced long ago beneath the waters. He is still a barbarian, reminiscent of the first primitive man who beheld the fall of cascades and heard the roaring of wild beasts. Copper and iron have tinged his body the color of blood, and he swings his hammer like a Nordic god, so forcefully that his knuckles turn white.

He spins around without altering his frightening pose. When he recognizes Gabriel, whom he has not seen in days, he drops his weapons and asks him in a husky voice, ignoring the intruders, "Aren't you supposed to be working in the smeltery?"

"Yes."

"What are you doing here?"

"I'm accompanying these gentlemen."

"Ah!"

He examines the visitors, who look faint. The temperature, according to a thermometer Erecnis takes from his pocket, is over a hundred degrees. The igneous rock discharges its lethal heat from its inner core; the blue vitriolic acid trickles down the grooves of the walls in fiery rivulets of boiling water.

Suddenly a tidal wave of men rushes in from the tubelike passageway, dragging the visitors along. Thor follows, right behind an overseer who is searching the edges of the passageway for one of those ventilation shafts that send occasional wafts of air to the poor men on the verge of suffocating. Every ten minutes, sometimes every five, a guard has to rescue a miner who works in a section where he is exposed to the deadly fumes released by the decomposing pyrite and let him breathe some fresh air.

The procession of naked bodies, shining reddish brown in the dark, charred with burns, and breathing with a death rattle, looks like a parade of disheveled prisoners. Paying no attention to anyone else, the two former sailors chat.

"Did you know that Vicente Rubio has died?" asks Gabriel, his memory kindled by the name embedded in Thor's lament.

"Yes, this morning, and that you were the one who accompanied the dead man and his daughter to the hospital."

"I took her to her mother."

"Don't you love her?"

"No."

"Really?"

"I've never loved her."

They look at each other by the mournful flicker of the candlelight, certain that Gabriel's amorous temptations have evaporated like perfume. The gladiator's eyes shine with satisfaction, and his face breaks into a smile. But still jealous, he persists in his questioning, "Would you marry her, tell me? Would you?"

"I'm married."

"Good. I'm happy to hear that, very happy! That's what I wanted to hear from you because you're my friend . . . and I didn't want to be your rival."

"But you have another: Pedro Abril."

"I can handle him . . ."

As Erecnis listens to Thor in amazement, he wonders with faded lucidity whether this man is made of the same material as other men. But the sounds of wild passion that fall from the lips and hammer of this Hercules bring the engineer back to reality. He thinks of his wife and daughter with fearful uncertainty, feeling feverishly delirious. Racked by thirst, he has an uncontrollable desire to press his lips against the scorching juice of the metal, to drink the poisonous waters of the Agrio and Saquia, while his tormented memory recalls the sonorous water fountain in the park of the Nordetanos.

Gabriel is still conversing with his friend when Estévez interrupts, "Get us out of here before the dynamite explodes; I can't go on."

The young man boasts triumphantly, "Don't worry, we have time; it'll be another hour before these corridors fill with blinding smoke . . ."

The rest period for the martyrs is over and the miners return to their respective dens, while Gabriel leads the visitors back along the underground galleries.

The lament, intertwined with the eternal suffering of love, emerges once more under the motionless clouds, sounding as dark and sinister as the sobs of chaos.

10
Death

EVER SINCE NATALIA HAD TO LIE DOWN SUDDENLY BECAUSE OF HER weak heart, her life has been a slow dying, a somber journey down nebulous paths that lead to the place of no return.

The new moon witnesses the culmination of her agony; her thoughts, held together with shadowy threads, grow dark, and her clear blue eyes are clouded. She talks to her husband from a land of darkness that moves ever farther away from this world, and she asks about Anita without expecting an answer.

For many hours, Rosario Garcillán has been watching tenderly over the dying woman, selflessly and with complete compassion. Rosario and Aurelio try to outdo each other in abnegation and sacrifices for the vanquished creature, as if both of them were seeing the vanishing of their own souls.

In the afternoon, after the doctor said that Natalia would not live to see the dawn, Rosario took the precaution of telling her friend, "We should get a priest."

"There aren't any."

"What do you mean?"

"I don't consider the chaplain you met in Vista Hermosa and his colleagues around here to be ministers of God."

"They're men," said the young girl in a conciliatory tone. "We can't expect them to be saints."

"But they could at least be worthy administrators of divine grace."

This was not the right moment for a discussion. Rosario had some broad religious ideas, which she held firmly, and which transcended worldly pettiness. She pleaded gently, "In Los Fresnos there is a priest who is as humble and pious as the apostles of old. May I call him?"

"As you wish."

His cold indifference changed to gratitude, warmed by the fire in her eyes.

The young girl mobilized her troops, and at dusk—that mysterious hour when wind and sun depart for other realms—a priest performed the last rights for the sick woman, and sanctified the home of the workers with Charity's pure breath. The holy man's fleeting presence was like a consoling breeze; his voice, as he forgave and blessed, was filled with the moan of everything in life that cries without shedding tears.

"You know that I am always here for you," he said simply. He returned to his remote village on the other side of the mines, where the water springs forth melodiously from a rivulet, and to his modest parish, where he lived in wait of the problems that surround him . . .

The heavy silence of great emotional upheaval fell on the Syndicate; the outside noises became respectfully hushed near the bed where Natalia lay dying.

From time to time a man would appear, motion to Aurelio to come closer for a rapid consultation, and then return to the office with a written note or a verbal solution.

The most frequent visitors to come upstairs were the doctor and José Luis, both of them worried and distressed. The president had delegated his authority to them with a promise of assistance, and he was constantly helping them, following the Syndicate's every action, conscious at all moments of their preoccupations. At times, as he looked compassionately at the dying woman, his gaze traveled beyond her to mingle miraculously with the cinders of the factories or to descend into the dark wells, fixing itself with terrible anxiety on the shadow of a thousand agonies. The astounded Champion sank into an abyss, looking without seeing, blinded by ideals, drunk with benevolence . . .

It is midnight; death has arrived, as inevitable and cold as glacial waters. Aurora is resting near the children; fully dressed, Dolores has fallen asleep on a straw mattress. Natalia utters some unintelligible sounds that echo in the infinite void; she opens her eyes one last time and sighs . . . She is liberated to fly into eternity!

Aurelio responds to her sigh with a mute and indescribable murmur. He leans over the corpse, lost in contemplation, then closes her eyes with tender fervor. His pain is imbued with a brotherly feeling, a gentle and compassionate love, which suffers and moans, without plunging everything into despair. He loved Natalia like a pure and dear child, but he knows that now God has given him the strong woman he has always longed for. He hears her walking around watchfully and he inhales the perfume of her resolute youth, aware that fate has struck the hour of hopeful intimacy for him. But he suffers greatly, overcome by sad pity for Natalia's failed life, and he blames himself for dragging her down, making her suffer with him, and allowing her to succumb. He bends over her again with silent affection, fascinated by her firm and frozen sleep, and he discovers a sweet expression of rest on her face: she has surrendered willingly to the unknown.

"She is happy," he tells himself hesitantly, as if seeing her smile at him behind an enigmatic veil; out loud he says, "What am I going to do with Anita?"

"Leave her in my care," begs Rosario with endearing shyness.

He looks at her pensively. Perhaps this woman is more deserving of his compassion than the other because to live is to weep. Indeed, her eyes are misty with tears, her face is altered, and her clothes are wrinkled. Her anxious insistence on a life of poverty has brought her fatigue and deprivations, and her empathy and love have made her anguish more encompassing.

Captivated by her dark eyes that glow with a secret fire, Aurelio's feelings change from pity to admiration. He wants to answer, eager to express the luminous words that his heart can no longer conceal, and he trembles because of what he is about to say. He unnerves Rosario, and with a small timid gesture she invokes silence and oblivion. "I'll take Anita," she says, and, without waiting for an answer, she leaves the bedroom to alert her friends.

A little later, Natalia's body, carefully dressed, with folded hands and smoothed hair, awaits its final journey. Above a frozen smile, the partially closed eyes peer out, as if an uncontrollable curiosity kept them open even in the beyond.

The house does not fill with laments or tears; the women, aching, sighing, and exhausted by their excessive work, go about their new task slowly and noiselessly, trying not to wake those who are asleep.

It is one o'clock in the morning, and the foul stench of dung and waste from the patio below wafts in through the balconies. The silence of the air, dimly lit by the new moon, is broken only by the sound of footsteps from the office workers and the click of doors being opened and closed.

Seated at the foot of the double bed, Aurelio is resting his head on the edge of the mattress, where during the cruel past week he has slept fully dressed; he cannot tear himself away.

Some flies, hatched in the garbage, buzz stubbornly around the corpse. Rosario covers the dead woman's face with a tulle veil, lights some oil lamps, and sits down on the other side of the bed; from the balcony, the clear sky offers its candlelight of stars to illuminate the bedroom.

Later, in the wee hours of the night, Santiago Estévez returns to the Syndicate, goes up to the president's living quarters, and heads straight for the bedroom where he had left a dying Natalia. He finds her rigid, between Aurelio and Rosario, who have fallen asleep. Approaching silently, he lifts the veil to examine the motionless face. He bends his brow down over hers, which is beautiful and smooth like a marble dream; the blue blossoms of her eyes have coalesced in the humid splendor of a last glance.

Drained by physical fatigue and emotional upheaval, the schoolmaster does not shudder at the pathetic brilliance of those eyes that look beyond life with eternal clarity. He has just seen the fire of the planet, which pierces the impossible, and he envies the dead woman's smile, like a question mark between the two young lives beset by uncertainties.

"Death is the dawn of the unending day!" he mumbles, dropping the corners of the veil on top of the corpse, and he walks out quietly, leaving red footprints along the corridor.

Rosario wakes up, startled by the light touch of something; she imagines that it is the veil, moved by Natalia's breath, and half crazed by fear, she stammers, "Aurelio!"

Startled, he jumps up, "What?"

"Nothing . . . We had fallen asleep!"

Confused, she gets up to see the time; it is three o'clock. In her perturbation, she goes out on the balcony and Aurelio follows her, mechanically. The moon is waning, and the two entranced lovers look at each other by its soft light, which—like love—is unique but always changing and transformed in different hearts.

SHIELDS

A memorable day. The morning sky is overcast and a hot, moaning wind pushes the clouds. In the mining zone, life proceeds normally with the usual intense and demanding work, and yet beneath the dark routine, a momentous event is being forged.

Early in the morning, the industrious Jacobo Pmip is already busy spying in the city of the miners, visiting the hovels and distributing sacred shields to children and their mothers. Made of cloth, these "protectors" have an embroidered heart surrounded by a printed verse designed to ward off sins. In the hands of the schemer, this harmless religious propaganda becomes a political tool and a personal asset.

Carrying the presents like a big shield, Don Jacobo enters Carmela's modest home and stays there until noon. As he stands smiling in the doorway to say goodbye, a pointed verse from an Andalusian flamenco song drifts over from a nearby house and pierces the impostor's pose:

> Even if you wear a cross,
> dress like Jesus of Nazarene,
> and fall to the ground three times,
> I have no faith in your words.

The singer, Carmen's charming neighbor, tosses the last verse out the window with fury as she is shaking the dirt out of a machinist's greasy trousers.

Pmip takes no offense. These saucy Spanish girls are incorrigible, he tells himself; we have tried to civilize them, have given them a superb industry where they can earn their daily bread, and have even put the heavenly kingdom within their reach . . . and still they mock us with silly folksongs.

Resigned, he continues on his way; onward in God's name! He is in Spain to serve the company unconditionally, and since he is well paid in the process, he has an obligation to merit his salary. If he needs a housekeeper for his private residence, he should not be looking for her in a noisy and public fashion, but rather in a delicate way, as if doing her a great favor. The fifty-peseta bill he gave Carmela is to pay for her necessary acquisitions if she decides to work in Vista Hermosa. He does not want badly dressed people around him; he loves to appear generous and live as splendidly as possible . . . He has achieved his goal, though it has cost him many a humiliation! But he shouldn't be remembering that—no, not at all! Now he is a person of prominence, a distinguished gentleman . . . who no longer feels any remorse for his incurable ignominy.

He is looking for Santiago Estévez, who is lodged in the outlying district of Ventoso. Spymaster that he is, Pmip wants to discover why Erecnis visited Sombra Negra in the company of Syndicate members. Last night he heard that news and today he hopes to find out more, thanks to the honesty of his friend the philosopher.

Things turn out differently. When Pmip arrives at the house where Santiago is staying, he is informed that the philosopher did not arrive home until the early morning hours and that he left instructions not to be disturbed until late afternoon, when he plans to attend Natalia's funeral.

Don Jacobo responds with, "Good, good." Standing in the hallway, he examines the inside of the house carefully, and after giving away some "protectors," he departs, more convinced than ever that the time for the strike has not come yet. He fails to notice the general restlessness that presages the momentous event; everywhere he is greeted the same as always, with smiles and kind words, couched in light sarcasm.

He descends Ventoso's slopes, satisfied with his investigation. Nothing special is afoot in Nerva; he has explored half the town without finding any alarming sign. He has conquered Carmela. Mourning and confusion reign in the Syndicate . . .

"Good, good," he repeats, passing near the miserable shacks, as he is being swept along the slippery crystalline rocks by the wind. Ventoso's irregular streets are exhausting for its inhabitants because they zigzag up and down, following the folds of the slate. But the catechist is nimble like a mouse; he climbs and slides with admirable ease along the steep hills and banks, surveying every corner to his heart's content. As he is about to emerge from the last crossroad, he runs into the doctor, who is climbing up the hill, deep in thought, carrying his hat in his hand.

"Visiting the sick?" asks Pmip, amiable as usual, to show that he is friends with the whole world.

"And you're competing with me," answers Romero sarcastically. "You cure the soul by conquering the heart . . ."

"Just trying, that's all."

"Well, good luck."

"Thank you."

Obviously, Romero does not want to linger. And Don Jacobo arrives in town, wrapped in the pestilence of the slippery waste that has been thrown down the cliffs; he endures the torment stoically, willing to bear all suffering for the sake of doing good unto his fellowmen! His plan is to go by Morayta Street, where Hortensia Rubio lives, to tell her that, although her father died of natural causes, the Company intends to give the widow a small pension, clear proof of Rehtron's generosity, helping even its detractors. This is true munificence!

Absorbed in his monologue, he finds himself in front of Nerva's only bookstore and decides to stop in. This is a place where intellectuals meet and relax, and where the neighborhood's few literate readers come to supply themselves with books and magazines, and to discuss a book or a poet. The schoolmaster and the doctor, avid readers and subscribers to the Madrid newspapers, are daily visitors. Along with Echea and Garcillán, and the owner of the bookstore himself, a bright native of Huelva, they participate in lively discussions, usually around the time the mail arrives. They talk about Spanish politics in general, discuss recent plays being performed in distant theaters, mention the success of a new writer, or read the latest verses of their favorite poet, which have arrived on special order. A faint air of modernity refreshes these men, who are starved for art and inspiration in their exile from the refinements and elegance of life.

Don Jacobo enjoys alighting at the bookstore whenever his walks through town coincide with the time of these delightful meetings. He savors the exchange of words with the paladins of the enemy camp, considering himself generous for sharing his vast knowledge of world literature; he has read many

French masterpieces in cheap paperback editions and knows little about the great writers of his own country.

This morning his timing is good, but he finds the bookstore silent and empty. The owner is standing by the counter, which also serves as the display case, sorting the subscribers' mail. Next to him are several shelves of neatly stacked works that reflect the taste of Nerva's reading public: popular novels of fleeting fame, leaflets, illustrated magazines, and some books with such titles as *Famous Bandits, Erotic Ballads, The Pug-nose from Benamejí, The Ferrer Case, Socialism's Struggles, The Joys of Love* . . .

Pmip leafs through the slightly dog-eared selection and buys some postcards; he offers the vendor some cigarettes and asks, in what he thinks is an indifferent tone, several questions that the other man can apparently not answer. He is anxious to talk about Echea's grief and the Syndicate's loss of one of its members, Vicente Rubio.

"An ill wind is blowing on Cicerón Street," he remarks.

"Yes, it comes from Africa and it'll probably bring rain," is all the vendor replies, teasing evasively.

Through the entrance, which supplies the small store with air and light, a whirlwind sweeps in dust and a dry steam invades the interior. Busy women pass by, their skirts ballooning in the wind; exhausted workers, having finished their shift at noon, crowd the streets on their way home to eat.

"Good, good," says Don Jacobo, growing increasingly more optimistic, feeling the powerful machine's harmonious pulse. And he leaves, under the sky's stormy brow, to visit the Rubios before taking the train.

RESENTMENT

That night, Pedro Abril worked in the countermine. He slept a few hours and then, after changing into clean clothes, he went to town, worried and determined; he had to talk to Casilda immediately. He has not seen her since the pilgrimage of the cross, and the strangest and most absurd rumors are reaching his ears. This morning, a rough and bold miner by the name of Thor announced that he was going to marry Rubio's daughter.

Even though Pedro smiles with pride and swagger, he has misgivings about the behavior of the young girl, who avoids him steadfastly since the dark event in the Gorge of Perdition. He has spent the last five days looking for her, scanning the evidence of his happiness, crazed by the taste of that desperate love, which he enjoyed unexpectedly. He knows she is in Nerva, and not daring to go to Fanjul's house, he walks along the burning channels of the streets and haunts Morayta's hidden side streets whenever he can get away from work. And down in the depths of the red-hot earth, he engraves the beloved name with every stroke of the sledgehammer, like an avenging whiplash.

But they told him that another miner calls out the same name during his work, and that this quiet giant, who is a guest at Vicente Rubio's house, is talking about marrying Casilda. Pedro knows that she had been in love with Gabriel, and he is not surprised that Thor loves her, only that he has reasons to believe that she feels the same. What about him? Doesn't he have every right to this honor that is his?

If he has gone around boasting about his good fortune it is only because he had every intention of behaving like a man of honor . . . He forgets that since the dark night of the cross he has lived blinded by pride, without worrying about any rivals, more interested in enjoying further favors than in restoring her honor. He wants to believe that he is being most noble by not postponing the proposal he owes Casilda, who no longer has her father's protection.

He enters Hortensia's house hurriedly. In the poorly lit corridor, the kitchen fumes mingle with the smells of miasma from the small patio and unsettling feminine odors; murmurs and sobs can be heard from the bedroom.

Hortensia's recurring fever has forced her to lie down again and her mother is at her bedside, a shrunken figure of absolute misery and helplessness. Ever since she saw her husband lying rigidly in the hospital bed, icy cold despite the hot sun, mute beneath the hardened skin, she has been unsteady on her feet, trembling and moaning. She let her daughters take her back to Nerva and now she sits around, crouched and motionless, like an idiot. Her life hangs by a thread; her memories race through her mind in a hazy gallop, fusing the image of the strapping and arrogant young man from Adunda with the old man whom life mistreated and who is now sleeping the sleep of the longest night. The delicate thread that holds the hours together is torn in Marta's consciousness and she can no longer tell the time. She barely hears, and in her eyes, almost deprived of light, there remains only a faint glow, the remnant of a former splendor; yet she still has her habit of smiling.

Several women are keeping the Rubio girls company, and crowded into the small bedroom, they talk about Vicente's sudden death.

"The heat killed him!"

"The factory killed him!"

"Like so many others!"

"And he won't be the last!"

Dolores from Valdelamusa, all compassion, is holding Nena in her arms; she is fond of her neighbors from the mountains and was dismayed when she heard about the accident last night. In a hushed voice she talks to Carmela about the dead man, moving out of the overflowing room.

"Did you see him?" asks Dolores.

"Yes, they had already performed the autopsy and he was in the morgue. According to the doctors, he died of a hemorrhage."

"Who knows! And when was the funeral?"

"I think at midnight. Hortensia and I returned here with Marta and Casilda at nine o'clock; they didn't let us wait there."

"And he was left alone?"

"Yes."

"What a disaster!"

"My father's death was worse!" says Carmela.

"Yes, but they also killed this poor deaf and blind woman's son."

"That's true!"

"If only Casilda would marry!"

"I think she will," says Carmela encouragingly, but her heart feels heavy as she scans the dark room for her friend's enigmatic face. Casilda's mournful and longing eyes shine in the dark, staring fixedly at Gabriel's baby. Carmen tries to hide her secret discomfort.

Pedro Abril appears, and Casilda goes to receive him or,

rather, to detain him, forcing him to back up toward the door of the hallway.

"Why did you come here?"

"Because I have to talk to you."

"Aren't you enemies with Fanjul?"

"Yes, but I'm your friend . . . and this is an opportunity . . . I wanted to tell you . . ."

"Don't tell me anything!" the young girl interrupts him, pressing her lips together painfully, her eyes flashing with resentment.

He looks at her full of desire, flushed with the pulsation of his heart, aglow like the liquid in the copper veins.

"So you're trying to avoid me?" he stammers. Beset by renewed doubts, he demands an explanation, barely able to control his hot fury.

"Don't shout!" orders Casilda, looking at him arrogantly and denying him all hope with her dark, unyielding eyes. And his eyes flash with livid lightning.

"You're still in love with that 'count,' who is married and who despises you . . . you damn . . . !"

And he pronounces the insulting word; Casilda receives the blow, bends down her pale face, ashen like death, and does not answer.

The clouds resound with the wind's thunderous voice, and visible at the end of the street, the distant mountain's profile looks more somber beneath the sad and overcast afternoon sky, as if expressing its empathy with human tragedy.

Impatiently, Pedro Abril is waiting for a plea, a reproach, anything to confirm his ownership of this wildly desired woman. Suddenly she raises her head, shakes her wild hair, black like ebony, and unveils the flames of her glowing pupils. Savoring the intoxication of her pain, she says, "Well, yes, I love him even if he despises me; I love him and hate you. Get out, you thief!" She grabs him boldly and pushes him, repeating in a hoarse and desperate voice, "Thief!"

The dumbfounded miner lets her pummel him until he recovers from his amazement. Then, cursing like the damned, he lifts his fist, ready to strike the rebel with savage pleasure, as if she were his chattel. In that moment, Jacobo Pmip comes around the corner, searching his pockets for something important. Pedro leaves on the other side, defeated and furious, but intending to return later. Don Jacobo greets the girl amiably and frightens her with a deliberate and lascivious look, holding a shield with the embroidered heart in his hand . . .

THE CORPSE

After conferring with the delegates in Dite, José Luis still had an hour before the departure of his train, so he walked over to the restless sector of the city, eager to witness the first dying gasps of work halting in the pit.

For him the day had a special poignancy, and he was intensely fascinated by the transformation of a vision into reality. Garcillán's poetic soul and his pride as a Spaniard were pleased by the working class's brave provocation of the northern colossus, especially since he was partly responsible for the Andalusian miners' daring challenge of the foreign company.

Deeply moved, he bends down to look at the open pit, gnawed by a monstrous cancer, open to the sky like a giant and wounded mouth pleading for mercy. Stampedelike noises can be heard from every opening and crack; men and machines fill the air with the terrible racket of their fight with the mineral, and the cry of the iron compressors threatens the hills, floats up with angry resonance to the ancient, wrinkled mountaintop, and reaches the masses of clouds gathered by the wind.

Suddenly, amid these hostile sounds, José Luis hears a friendly and soft hiss, "Psst . . . psst!" He turns around and sees Carmen, slightly behind him, gracefully balancing a bundle under her arm.

"What are you doing here all by yourself? Where are you going?" he greets her gallantly.

The young girl's face lights up. "I'm not going anywhere, I'm returning," she answers, smiling.

"To Nerva?"

"Yes, señor; I'm going home."

The air of mystery in her reply intrigues the young man, while his eagerness to find out more amuses Carmen.

"But where are you coming from?"

"From right here."

"With your belongings?"

"As you can see."

"I don't understand you."

"Well, it's a little complicated."

"But I saw you enter Fanjul's house this afternoon."

"Yes, señor . . . but then I left to go on a trip . . . to spend my summer vacation here . . . at least for sixty minutes . . . now as soon as the train whistle blows, it's back to the city."

"Come on, you're making fun of me!"

But there is less mockery than a sweet melancholy in the young girl's expression, which enchants José Luis. He insists, pleading with her to tell him the reason for her trip. She lets herself be persuaded, surrendering to the will of this chivalrous gentleman, who treats her with such delightful delicacy.

"Well, you see," she begins, "this morning I agreed to serve in Don Jacobo's house, or rather, it was my mother who had told him I would. Before I could change my mind, I packed my clothes and left in a rush. He had given us some money in advance, and it wouldn't have been nice not to keep our word. When I got here, one of my brother's friends assured me that the maids who were employed in Vista Hermosa would walk off the job tonight. I didn't want to believe it and decided to wait so I could see for myself what's what, and then I ran into you. I told myself, this gentleman is better informed than anyone . . . and that's why I spoke to you . . ."

Her face turns crimson when she realizes that she has contradicted herself; she didn't have anything to ask him, but she loved talking to him! Her dreamy gaze wanders aimlessly, while her sad and unhappy youth fills the young man with admiration and pity.

"Yes," he tells her, "you did the right thing by waiting. The strike begins tonight, in a few moments, and it includes the women. It would have been too bad if you had kept your promise to Don Jacobo!" He looks at his watch and entreats her, "Don't return to Vista Hermosa again! You don't know what your soul deserves or for that matter what your body is worth! Death is better than selling yourself!"

The lively gleam in the young girl's eyes darkens.

"Yes . . . yes," she stammers, touched by this rare and sincere interest.

And José Luis adds, encouragingly, "If you could only see

yourself! Even your name is lovely. Do you know what it means?"

"No."

"In Arabic, it means vineyards, in Latin, poem, and in Spanish, flower garden . . . Carmen, you're a rose, a palm tree, a glass of wine . . ."

The delicate thread of their conversation is torn asunder by the alarm preceding the dynamiting, and by the sound of the explosions themselves. The valleys and perforated hills, trembling from the tremendous vibrations, are enveloped in the roar of dust, rising skyward. In shock, Carmen and José Luis stand next to a quivering and half-collapsed casement. After the deafening clamor abates, waves of dark rumblings linger in the air—they are Death's terrible footsteps.

Silent and haughty, the workers emerge from the pit's gaping wound; they climb out of the crimson holes unarmed, their soul filled with joyous liberation, and make their way up to the path of life, like red foam rising up from copper clots; the mine is in its death throes.

A deadly silence descends upon the Glory Hole and extends over the landscape; the clouds lower themselves as if trying to hear, giving the impression of lending an attentive ear to the strange peace invading the Earth; even the rain remains suspended in space, without falling . . .

The young man and the girl return to the city, swept along by the avalanche of miners, who fill the train and disperse in orderly fashion along the streets and shortcuts. Carmen's smiling and thoughtful eyes look in amazement at the unusual spectacle: the men making a racket, while the rocks below are steeped in silence. But Death has not emerged out of the pit into the fresh air; it is still present in the countermines, the factories, and the vehicles. The strikers, those who live in the city and the mountain dwellers, are headed for Nerva to attend Natalia's funeral this evening.

After paying their last respects in a show of sympathy for the president, the entire village listens for the siren from Lucifer's Valley, announcing the work stoppage in the trains, smelteries, caves, and pits.

Darkness has spread its mantle of shadows over the horizon; it is ten o'clock. From far away comes the muffled echo of the blasters and the final canon shots, which they have converted into a declaration of war against the company.

Scanning the darkness, the villagers imagine a tidal wave of miners pouring out of dungeons and cages, escaping from their prison, through tunnels whose jaws are opened in a soundless bark. Having fled the netherworld, carpenters, gunners, errand boys, clay cutters, children, old men, and youths rest and draw a deep breath.

The last of the glowing lava trickles down from the dark slag heaps; near the peaks, a few dens, still filled with smoldering cinder, shed drops of burning tears. The chimneys of the factories suck in wisps of fire. Slowly, the golden-bearded god dies down, and the many mouths of the furnaces and smelteries release one final smoky exhalation.

With the strident whistle still vibrating in the air, the trains have come to a halt, suddenly immobilized in violent and unexpected contortions along curves and declines. A tragic paralysis befalls the workplace, freezing everything into silent rigidity.

While the terrible fires extinguish themselves, a multitude of flickering lanterns light up along the horizon, brilliant atoms illuminating the mountain path for the workers as they make their way down into the valley on slabs and steep slopes. In the candlelight the men look as though they are flying, like bees abandoning the beehive—the lowly worms of the mines have sprouted wings!

This new legion of creatures joins the other spectators who are watching the gradual death of all activities. The main electric station is still alive, pulsating weakly, but at one o'clock in the morning it dies down completely, together with the zone's twenty-six substations, obeying an alarm's authoritative blare, whose strong and shrill warning comes across the mountains as clearly as Gialar's trumpet, whose sound can supposedly be heard worldwide.

The industry has breathed its last gasp; its brow still smolders with the ashes from the furnace, which—like the huge eye of a dead Cyclops—looks blankly into the darkness; the gigantic corpse is growing cold beneath the night's black crepe band.

The huge mass of strikers disperses, silent like the valley. The stars no longer shine in the sky; and farther to the east, lightning tears the clouds apart in a gesture of mute fury.

11

Hatred

THE HOUR OF PUNISHMENT

WHEN DON JACOBO GOES TO SEE THE MANAGER TO INFORM HIM about his findings, the two men, smoking cigarettes and sipping whiskey, concur that the strike was bound to fail. It had begun in the pits just that afternoon, with a premature haste that betrayed a dismal lack of organization; furthermore, the other sections did not support the move, which meant that the feared uprising would be greatly reduced and would only serve to discredit the Syndicate.

The gentlemen from Vista Hermosa can go to bed peacefully. Smiling, they say good night and go to sleep, only to be awoken soon after by a most unpleasant surprise: they have been plunged into darkness and a sepulchral silence.

Erecnis, better informed than the other bosses, was standing watch in his garden, listening to the rumors afloat in the wind. He saw the splendor of the smelteries diminish in the distance and, a few minutes later, noticed the vanishing of "the blue fairy," leaving him in the dark. He turned on his flashlight and decided to knock on Pmip's window before alerting the manager. This is how Vista Hermosa heard about the news because the guards—blissfully oblivious—were dozing in their sentry boxes.

As he tries to turn on the light in his bedroom, Don Jacobo breaks the switch; he refuses to accept the reality of the events. Groping in the dark, half-dressed and reminiscent of a ludicrous escapee, he feels embarrassed and upset. The other gentlemen do not look particularly dignified either, and even less so the alarmed and impatient ladies. Amid comments and protests, there is an effort to find candles and matches. The general confusion increases even more when all the service

personnel announce that they are giving notice effective immediately.

"At this hour?" shout several indignant voices.

But all the threats, objections, and pleas prove futile; even
two heartless wet nurses reaffirm their decision to join the
strikers—the height of disregard! The men and women, almost all of them locals, tie up their bundles and say their polite
good-byes. In a jovial mood, they disappear in the dark,
headed for Dite.

Overflowing with suspicions and predictions, an excited and
distraught Doña Berta complains about the hoi polloi's un-
gratefulness.

"This is total chaos," she declares. "It's Bolshevism, red
madness!"

Dejected and sad, the other ladies chime in, while the gentlemen, trying to look calm, talked about attitudes and measures to be adopted.

The very first measure is for the manager to check the
phone in his study. "I wonder whether they cut the cable?"
There is no answer in the mine's offices, but he can always try
to call Madrid directly. The rebels wouldn't dare interfere with
the company's private line! He has to ask Sevilla for military
reinforcement and get in touch with the governor. Luckily, in
case of necessity, he can count on the help of many organizations in the capital and in the region!

The group's confidence grows with the firm show of support
they receive from all sides. The strikers' defeat was bound to
be easy and certain. Poor people, they wouldn't be able to resist for long against the bosses' invincible might!

However, at the first flexing of their muscle, the powerful
realize that they need servants. They are eager to find out as
soon as possible what is happening, but who is willing to go to
Dite on this dark and stormy night, risking a possible enemy
ambush?

They cannot let the guards go because they are the only two
remaining men in their service; all others—the gardeners, sta-
ble boys, lackeys, and kitchen help—took off without wasting
a minute.

"I'll go," offers Pmip, who cannot be accused of cowardice.

Other gentlemen volunteer as well, and Martín Leurc reminds them, "You'll have to saddle your horses yourselves."

First Erecnis suggests postponing the investigation, and finally it is agreed that the group will go on foot. They continue
discussing numerous other perturbing details, and at the end
of the lively conversation, their one fervent wish is to have a
glass of beer. The ladies who have to serve them get their first
taste of the disagreeable chores that await them in the kitchen,
the washhouse, and even more unpleasant places. Since this
late-night meeting is being held at the manager's house, it is
his wife who has to go down to the basement to get the bottles.
This is absurd, scandalous, inconceivable! It seems difficult to
believe that everything in the world is so upside down and
topsy-turvy. Where will all this end? Doña Berta was not born
to carry out menial tasks and neither was her daughter. What
madness!

"That's absolutely right," agree her friends, who share the
poor victim's indignation and have accompanied her down
into the depths of the basement.

Doña Berta is somewhat mollified by their assent, and, on
her way back up, she adds with her customary reasonable-
ness, "It is only fair that as Christians, all of us should do our
share, but only according to our aptitude and education; our
job is to do the fine work, and the ordinary chores fall to the
peasant women."

"That's right," comes the voice of a young girl, who was still
down in the basement.

Miss Clara Yevol, the skinny governess who is waiting upstairs to take the bottles and candles from Doña Berta, asks
timidly, "But what if these women received a good education . . . ?"

"Nonsense! Forget these newfangled ideas! Everybody has
to stay in his place, otherwise who would do the most difficult
jobs?"

"We'd share them," says Bertita Leurc seriously, engaged in
arranging the glasses and cigarettes on the dining room table.
Her mother gives her a shocked look and repeats one of her
favorite quotes, "God Himself has told us, 'The poor will always be with us.'"

"Yes, but one has to know how to interpret these words."

"Child!"

When the men return, Bertita disappears. The group of
women—which does not include the young mothers, who are

busy with the care of their infants at home—is thirsty from the
heat and from talking nonstop. During drinks, the omens and
predictions swirl incessantly like the foam in their glasses.
The dry mountain breeze enters freely from the balcony and
twists the candle wicks; a furious gust upsets the salon's elegance.

When at last Don Jacobo and his friends are ready to explore the valley, a squad of guards arrives, prepared to follow
the manager's orders. The guards regret not having sounded
the alarm sooner; however, they could not abandon their posts
in these hours of uncertainty, nor could they communicate
any details about the events that were taking place. The strike
is a mysterious process, behaving like a human being in its
death throes, and the first organs to stop functioning were the
telephones, which are out of commission in the offices and
workshops.

With a glimmer of hope, the manager inquires about the
smelteries. Not a single employee was left in them; the few
who were faithful to the company among the foremen, the list
keeper, and the contractors were forced to leave, along with
the section leaders.

"Does this mean that the furnaces are being neglected?"

Isidro Zabala, veteran spy, steps forward and answers
gruffly, "Yes, sir, as well as everything else; at this time, the
mine has been completely abandoned."

"And can't you organize an emergency crew?"

"We can, as soon as the military forces arrive."

"Are you that afraid?" asks Don Jacobo, displeased.

The respectable guard lifts his head solemnly, "There are
more than twenty thousand men in the enemy camp."

"Are they armed?" asks Don Martín.

"No, but they're brave and determined."

"Have they committed any act of violence?"

"Not really, nothing besides breaking the telephone boxes,
but they're ordering everyone to stop working and they'll re-
sort to force if necessary to insure compliance."

"You're getting old, Zabala," murmurs Pmip, trying to make
light of his assistant's concerns. Actually, he is greatly bothered by the serious tone with which Zabala spoke about the
strikers and by the visible interest shown by his listeners; the

air of reluctant admiration floating in the air offends Don Jacobo.

"These fellows can tell you," says Zabala, hurt in his pride, and he points in the direction of the squadron, who fill the ample passageway leading to the garden.

Leaning out of the enormous dining room windows, opened wide to let in the refreshing breeze, the gentlemen face the militia—that epitome of loyalty—composed of young men equipped with rifles, sabers, badges, and wide-brimmed hats. Their demeanor isn't exactly proud; some of them hide their faces, as if ashamed of their mission, and they all keep quiet.

"All right, what do you want to tell us?" urges Zabala.

A young man volunteers this answer, "This time there won't be any scabs and the damage to the mine will be beyond repair."

"That's inconceivable!" interrupts a furious Pmip.

The young man making this prediction is Fabián Delgado, a former miner, like practically all his companions. Chewing on his moustache and trying to control his anger, the manager fixes his gaze on him. Without flinching, Delgado adds, "In spite of our weapons, we're laughed at by the masses of workers who support the strike." These words are tinged with bitter envy and accompanied by the blush of humiliation.

"Is this why you gave them free reign?" reprimands one of the other bosses.

"What choice did we have?"

Exasperated and perturbed, Don Jacobo asks, "Didn't any of you defend your position?"

"No. The only existing position now is that of quitter."

The manager jumps up abruptly. "What do you mean?" The color drains from everybody's faces, and the ladies in the room begin a fainthearted retreat.

"He didn't mean anything," intercedes Zabala in a conciliatory tone. "Our young friend didn't express himself well. All the guards have left just like us because they can't do anything. A few are coming this way, together with the bosses and the office personnel currently on duty; others have taken up quarters in Dite's City Hall."

"How are things in the city?"

"The city," confesses the guard, chagrined, "has been taken over by the miners."

"And you don't dare go there?"

"What good would it do?" murmurs Zabala, as pessimistic as Fabián Delgado.

Leurc turns to Don Jacobo and remarks defiantly, "But they're all Spaniards."

"Wolves from the same litter," agrees Pmip, hiding his fury behind an icy smile.

A barely audible voice exclaims gently, "They're declaring their independence!"

The catechist glances over his shoulder and meets Bertita's stern and mocking gaze. At the same time, the manager asks him, "Didn't you assure us that we were the absolute rulers here?"

"Owners . . ." stammers Don Jacobo forlornly.

"Who are not permitted to protect their property!"

Leonardo Erecnis intervenes, "You are in possession of a treasure against the will of its owners, and, paradoxically, the mine is protected by guards who are natives of this land, and you're asking these dispossessed to be the defenders."

This was a most inappropriate observation to be made in front of the troops, and Erecnis is an egotist for excluding himself from the company's guilt. Don Martín looks at him in surprise, but, unwilling to expose himself to further unpleasantness, he only says in an undertone, "Our rules do not allow any Nordetano, regardless of social rank, to be employed as a subordinate."

"Out of pride?"

"Yes, to maintain the prestige of the race. Does this surprise you?"

Himself a native of a young and easy-going nation, the Yankee starts to laugh. "It amazes me. I thought a country's reputation was determined by other factors."

"Different people have different opinions," declares Don Jacobo, thinking he has to say something to keep Don Martín from asking him any more questions, but the manager is concerned only with his own grave responsibility.

"The truth is," he observes bitterly, "that we don't own anything here."

Looking in from the doorway, Leurc's daughter pronounces very softly but firmly, "Spain for the Spaniards!"

A similar phrase had echoed in Bertita's ears and she has

yielded to a vague yearning to voice these words. According to her citizenship she is a foreigner, but she was born in Andalusia, and an invincible love binds her to this land that is being enslaved by her countrymen.

By coincidence, Don Jacobo had been the only one to notice Bertita in her hiding place and to hear her crystalline voice. But when he looks at the doorway again, the young girl who interests him most singularly is no longer there. She represents the peak of his ambitions, and he had hoped that by serving Don Martín and gaining merit points with the company, he could conquer the millionaire heiress. Her peaceful and withdrawn character, her sheltered life in Vista Hermosa—without any opportunities for love affairs—have filled the engineer with sweet hope.

But, as Jacobo Pmip realizes full well with bitterness and irritation, this was not the time for lovely illusions. The manager orders the policemen to leave. They could go home or assemble in the carriage house until further orders; here they were not needed. A pronounced displeasure is audible in his words, and Zabala offers humbly to make the rounds of Vista Hermosa until dawn.

"No, that won't be necessary; *we're* not afraid," emphasizes Don Martín acidly.

Unhappy and downcast, the guards disperse in the dark with rankling resentment. A little later, the gentlemen agree to get some rest so they can face the next day with more energy.

The first rays of dawn are already piercing the night when Don Jacobo finally decides to go home. In the great hallway, he meets Bertita, seated on a small chair amid the extinguished candelabra and in a pensive mood.

"Aren't you going to bed?" asks the engineer, trying to see her face in the half-light.

"It's too late for that," she replies with malicious joy. "I have to start the fire and prepare breakfast."

"Oh, we will find someone to help you!"

"Find someone? All you'll find are disillusions," says the young girl disdainfully, and adds on her way out, "The hour of punishment has struck!"

Most annoyed, Don Jacobo goes out into the garden. The wind is blowing with hurricane force in the trees and advancing brusquely down the avenues, like an enemy on the move.

REVENGE

The wind is still blowing and it has been raining since the early morning; night is falling slowly, with a gloomy moan. The Civil Guards have gathered, but they are still waiting for the military forces, which have to travel to the region on foot.

According to some panicky rumors from Vista Hermosa, the miners—equipped with dynamite, blank weapons, and rifles—intend to assault the shops of any sympathizers, break the dikes, bomb Vista Hermosa, and destroy the machinery. All available militiamen are patrolling Nerva's streets because the Nordetanos are worried about terrible plots being hatched there.

Many shops are closed because their owners are worried about the threats, the doorways are half shut because of the rain, and the men have taken refuge in the casinos. The city, quiet and abandoned, has the air of a great tragedy, though its somber aspect actually masks an underlying serenity.

Aside from each family's private conflicts, the strike could not have a more peaceful manifestation. Many of the men are sleeping soundly, overcome by their tremendous exertion, which overshadows all else; they are drunk with the voluptuous pleasure of resting, submerged in sleep as in a refreshing and invigorating bath; they wake up briefly, rejoicing in their good fortune, and fall asleep again. Others smoke and enjoy themselves in the taverns, relishing their leisure and the unaccustomed assurance of not having to rush to work or worry about a master. In general, the conversations are calm and carefree, unconcerned with the tremendous event taking place that day. The Andalusian character—sentimental, generous, childlike—is not given to material worries, preferring to think about lovely and exquisite matters and to discuss delicate and fragile subjects; at this very moment, the miners assembled in the little café are talking with lively interest about a rosebush.

"It has twenty-four open blossoms and eighteen in bloom," says Enrique Salmerón.

"Did you see it?"

"I sure did; the last time I went to Zalamea la Real, I made a detour so I could see this wonder with my own eyes."

"Is it a rambling rose?"

"It looks like one, but the flowers are bigger and glow like gold, and the thorns are more delicate . . . and what an aroma!"

"That's in Los Fresnos, right?" asks Estévez, paying for some glasses of beer at the counter.

"Yes, in a little garden on a slope."

"I know those flowers, they're primroses; they bloom in clusters, with a full calyx and yellow petals."

All the voices fall silent while Santiago describes these roses. He talks about their characteristics, the care they need, the places where they grow; and the miners imagine roses and buds, breathe their perfume, and delight in their beauty, their imagination shaped by the light and magic of their remembrances. Is there an Andalusian who at some time has not had a flower in his garden or patio? The memories flutter like bees and butterflies over the imaginary rosebuds.

Estévez's words die down as he recalls his gardens in Alájar, covered with orange blossoms. Only the sound of raindrops, falling like tears in the city, punctuates the poignant silence.

Manolo Fanjul, just released from prison, reminisces in a dull voice, "In Córdoba I had some carnations . . ."

He is interrupted by the noise of running and screaming coming from the street, startling the group; the rain-soaked crackling of gunshots is transmitted by the wind. Doors are flung open and everybody rushes out, terrified and anxious to see what is happening.

"They're attacking the workers," say some people coming from Cicerón Street and neighboring areas. The air above the muddy ground trembles and a pallor settles over the city.

The manager had insisted that certain papers, the accounting books, and some fragile containers from the laboratories be picked up. Zabala, along with a group of guards, accompanied the employees who had been designated by Erecnis to carry out this mission. They met with no opposition, and the chemist, trying to prove that he trusted the miners, intended to store everything in Nerva.

They reached the city after nightfall, passing the Syndicate on their way to the company's headquarters in Rómulo Street. As they were about to enter, a detachment of Civil Guards appeared nearby. Thinking that the group consisted of aggres-

sive rebels, they proceeded to shoot at them without any
further inquiries. A few of those under fire ran to take refuge
inside the building, but the guards pursued them relentlessly,
even more convinced that the Rehtron Company was being as-
saulted.

The municipal guards came to the aid of the Civil Guards,
and the company guardians started shooting as well; blind
rashness led the entire neighborhood to join in. Fear, the curtain of rain, and the dark of night further contributed to the
disaster. Shots were fired indiscriminately, and the bullets entered through patios and balconies, wounding and killing. The
echoes of the shots, stench of gunpowder, and laments of the
masses spread over the city like a flood of fear.

The firing zone was situated near the Syndicate, and right
there, in Hortensia Rubio's house, a painful scene is taking
place to the sound of gunfire in the background. Manolo Fanjul has told his wife to throw Marta and Casilda out of his
house; he was very happy about his father-in-law's death, and
he did not want to be bothered by any other family problems.

Thanks to Hortensia's caring efforts, he found himself free
and pardoned, and he came straight to the bedroom where she
lay ailing. With harsh words, he dismisses Casilda and Carmen, who were keeping her company, and then hurries to lock
the door from inside. "He's going to kill her," clamor the worried neighbors.

Hortensia, confused by what is happening, remains motionless; the little children hide in the corner, frightened, and the
oldest, Joaquín, runs out into the patio. But Casilda murmurs
under her breath, with jealous bitterness, "No, he isn't going
to kill her! He loves her!"

"And what about her?" asks Carmen, without lifting her
eyes from the black dress she is sewing.

"You mean, does she love him?"

"Yes."

"And how!"

"It's hard to believe."

"Love is not governed by law or logic," declares Casilda
with such wisdom that Carmen looks inquiringly into her dark
and grieving eyes.

Soon after, Fanjul sets out for the tavern, smiling and proud.
With raw bravura, he places a loaded pistol in a visible spot in

the kitchen, leaving it there as a challenge; from the hallway, he is still admonishing his wife with menacing despotism.

Hortensia, feverish and breathless, calls her sister and asks her to return to the mountains with their mother.

"Right now?"

"Yes, yes, for God's sake, before it gets dark and before Manolo comes back."

Casilda gives her a questioning look. This flight away from the man for whom she lives with unbridled passion had not been part of her plans. She addresses the sick woman roughly, showering her with accusations and reproaches. Marta, entering the bedroom like a ghost, realizes that they are arguing; starting to tremble, she calls Carmen.

"Find out what the matter is and let me know."

The friend intercedes, trying to appease the two sisters, just as Dolores arrives, holding Gabriel's daughter in her arms, as usual. She wants to stay a while until the lights are turned on because she is curious about the rumors afloat in the neighborhood that Fanjul had left jail in an angry mood, looking for revenge and, as always, stirring up trouble in the family.

Hortensia does not care that strangers are aware of the intimate details of her household, as long as she can please her husband and avoid his tantrums. Eager to obey him at all costs, she indulges his whims because of a mysterious and fatal attraction. She wants her mother and sister to start on their trek home to the mountains despite the whipping rain and the dangers lurking in the dark, and she tries to enlist her neighbor women's help to carry out the tyrant's will.

Dolores struggles to explain to Marta the need for this hasty trip, and Carmen is trying to think of a way to offer the poor women lodging, at least for the night. Suddenly shots ring out, but the women confuse them with thunder.

Shadows invade the room, and from the gray background outside only a faint light comes in through the window. Like a snake, the storm coils up in coppery splendor, rising above the gallop of the black clouds; the entire sky seems to be advancing violently, pushed by the hurricane.

"That thunderclap sounded like a shot," murmurs Hortensia.

Dolores smiles, "No, child, you're distraught; it's only thunder."

Hearing no cries other than those of her own affliction, Marta stammers, "My God, where will I go?" in a voice suffused with suffering.

"To my place," decides Carmen, filled with pity.

And since the shadows, stirred by the wind, grow darker by the minute, Dolores agrees, "Yes, we have to put them up until tomorrow."

Casilda is staring at Nena in stubborn silence. Feverish and uneasy, Hortensia pleads and cajoles, "Yes, that's the best; let's find a safe shelter for them."

"Like for animals," exclaims Casilda, swallowing her anger.

Another stormy rumble can be heard, the sort that usually follows lightning. The younger children have emerged from their hiding places and are back in the bedroom; Joaquín comes running in from the street, soaked and frightened to death.

"They're killing people," he shouts, arriving at the same time as Aurora, who enters with extended arms.

"Please give me Nena," she asks, stretching her arms out in the dark.

"What's the matter?"

"They're shooting; people are getting killed. Please give me Nena," she repeats anxiously.

Dolores hands her the girl and Aurora leaves the room in nervous haste, gathering her skirt to wrap it around the child. The other women make the sign of the cross; they break the news to Marta, shouting in her ear, and they detain Hortensia, who wants to get up and get dressed.

Casilda, who left the room during the first moments of confusion, now obeys an unconquerable fascination and follows her rival to the entrance of the house, from where she can see Aurora stopping after a few steps, undecided about where to go.

The fateful clamor of fighting and the smell of blood and death that come from the dark lane agitate Casilda's soul, which is as stormy as the night. Suddenly she disappears in the hallway and returns immediately, holding Fanjul's pistol. Leaping like a tiger, she takes aim and takes a shot at Aurora.

The echo of a tragic scream fills the alley. A man comes around the corner and runs into the mother and child; it is Gabriel, who has been looking for them. He realizes that there has been an attack only when Aurora, feeling the warm trickle of blood along her arms, unwraps the child in frenzied distress. A soft moan escapes from that pure and sweet life, felled down in its bloom. Her parents have no idea where the bullet came from that pierced Nena's throat. Standing in front of the Syndicate's entrance, they cradle the child, who no longer moves or breathes. Then they enter the offices that are deserted because the men stormed out in disarray, seeking vengeance.

Aurora's mind is darkened by gusts of madness. Gabriel, pale and worn out, is carrying the little corpse, trying to catch a glimpse of the divine spark in her clear eyes and mumbling confused words that allude to eternity. He feels endless compassion for this child, who died without name or lineage. Brought into life by blind love, she was hurled into the somber beyond, still weak and innocent, before even having learned to smile!

"They killed her, didn't they?" howls the mother.

"Yes."

LAMENT

That terrible certainty is only one drop in the sea of pain that convulses the city. Other bullets have entered apartments, killing women and children, while the men were roaming the streets, engaged in mortal combat. Right there, on Cicerón Street, Leonardo Erecnis has collapsed with a bullet in his chest, and, a little farther, lies Zabala with a hole in his temple. Along with other friends of the company, they were both killed by their own defenders.

Now the red cloud of projectiles, which had burned like a cruel burst of fire in the darkness, has passed. No one can assess the full extent of the tragedy yet, and the neighborhood, still crazed and quivering with fear, attends to the wounded and dead with compassionate pity, ignoring differences in ideology or homeland.

In the Syndicate not even Gabriel exempts himself from helping his fellowmen. He hides his pain with masculine fortitude, and, as magnanimous as his companions, he makes the rounds in the dark night hours, lending his services. Perhaps he is trying to intoxicate himself with the pain of others and drown his own sorrow at the bottom of this great tragedy. He is also fleeing from Aurora, afraid of the voice with which she keeps asking, "Why did they kill her? Tell me, why?" There is an infinite and heartrending consternation in the mother's obsessive question.

"It was the innocent child's fate," cries out Dolores, remembering an incident from the night before. When one of the strings snapped on a neighbor's guitar, she heard him say that the loud click meant the ascent of an angel to heaven, and Dolores is convinced that Aurora's child was destined to meet its death.

Requests for medication and bandages pour into the Syndicate without stop. Romero distributes the contents of the Syndicate's medicine cabinet with open hands; he empties the shelves and attends all the fallen with the same amicable kindness. Santiago Estévez assists the doctor, and Garcillán, whose right hand was grazed by a bullet, helps his companions as best he can.

At the first signals of alarm, Echea, Salmerón, and Garcillán had gone out into the rain and mud, trying to calm the most excited combatants and hoping to calm the struggle's terrible confusion. Now they take Zabala to the doctor's office and stand by him in his agony, forgetting that a short time earlier they had called him "traitor." He emits peculiar noises, as if every animal in the world were groaning in his insides, and an anxious piety befalls those around him, hearing his moans culminate in a rasping death rattle.

Rosario, who is loath to leave her disconsolate friend's side for long, rushes around trying to do everything that is required by the serious circumstances. She comes and goes like a guardian spirit, helping to bandage and distribute medicine downstairs, while upstairs she works quietly by the stove, preparing chamomile teas and infusions. Several times she goes into Anita's room and kisses her gently on her forehead. Lately the little girl has been crying softly, looking for her mother, and she only calms down after Rosario caresses her and assures her that Natalia will be coming back.

Amid the general grief and sorrow, Leonardo Erecnis is being remembered with deep sadness. Visitors to the Syndicate report that the engineer fell to the ground with a bullet in his heart and died instantaneously. His body, laid to rest in the company's office, is being guarded with the same insurmountable paranoia that led to the killing in the first place.

Dolores and Rosario feel sorry for the sweet girl who had quenched their thirst in Vista Hermosa.

"Poor little thing, now she has no father!" they murmur, and Rosario asks Aurora, "She didn't take her eyes off you. Do you remember?"

"I remember," answers Aurora. The mention of this sad incident kindles her memory and makes her think with intense clarity about all the abandoned children. She stares at the bed where Nena lies, her small and white corpse carefully washed and wrapped in clean clothes.

"Why did they kill her, why?" the mother keeps repeating, overcome by sobs.

"Because we don't have enough compassion in this world," replies Rosario, disconsolate.

"Will I see her again?"

"Yes, in another life, because the soul never loses its ability to see."

"Are you certain?"

"As certain as I am about your pain."

"Who told you?"

Dolores chimes in quickly and with conviction, "The gospel!"

Rosario adds fervently, "The man who was born and lived without sin!"

And Aurora, noting a divine breath in these words, lets her tears flow freely.

Outside, wind and rain whirl with sad resonance, as if retelling the eternal story of sighs and tears.

GUILT

When Casilda hears Aurora's scream and sees her tumble in the darkness, she looks at her hands with an abrupt gesture of surprise, as if afraid to find them stained with blood. They smell of smoke, and her right hand, holding the pistol, feels heavy with an icy weight—a frozen sensation of extreme tiredness. She lets her arm fall into her apron folds and proceeds,

with extreme caution, to return the weapon to where Manolo
had left it.

"What are you hiding there?" asks Carmen worriedly when
she runs into her in the corridor.

"Hiding?"

"Yes."

"Nothing."

She tries to resist her friend's inquiries, but Carmen, overcome by curiosity, finds out, "It's a pistol! And it feels hot!
What did you do?"

"Don't shout!"

"You're trembling all over. What have you done?"

"I fired into the air."

"Why?"

"For fun."

"Liar . . . assassin!"

"For God's sake, be quiet."

"Don't you dare invoke God. You don't believe in him and
that's why you hate and kill."

"I haven't killed . . ."

"How do you know? That horrible scream that pierced the
street probably came from the woman . . ."

"The dead don't shout," stammers Casilda in a rough and
hoarse tone, as she hurriedly puts the pistol back in its place.

"You're rotten . . . and evil," whispers Carmela with a quivering voice, standing behind the guilty one.

"Be quiet, don't betray me!"

"If they ask me for a statement, I'll talk."

"And what if they don't ask you?" insists Casilda, with an
expression that wavers between pleading and threatening.

"I'll keep quiet for your mother's sake!"

Dolores and Hortensia come out of the bedroom, lighting
their way with an oil lamp; they talk excitedly about the shot
and the scream, which could be heard almost simultaneously
a minute ago, below the windows. Hiding her face with bewildered gestures, Casilda flees from the light that is illuminating
the apartment; greatly agitated, she suddenly tells Carmen,
"I'm leaving."

"What?"

"Goodbye!" And without looking back, she bolts into the
street, impetuous and angry.

"Casilda, listen; wait!"

"Where is she going?" asks Hortensia, greatly surprised.

"I don't know," murmurs Carmen incoherently, barely able to hide her profound dismay.

"She's mad at me and she's capable of making Mother go back home by herself."

"Yes, she's upset," Carmela agrees, and, worried and afraid herself, she would like to flee as well. "Just in case she doesn't come back, I'm going to take Señora Marta with me." She takes her gently by the arm and the sad woman lets herself be led, assuming that Casilda is also going with them. Weighed down by indecision, the women walk along, keeping close to the houses in an effort to protect themselves a little from the rain shower.

Dolores follows them with her eyes until they are hidden by the black veil of darkness. "I don't understand," she exclaims.

"What?"

"That your mother is leaving like this."

"Oh, my poor mother," moans Fanjul's wife contritely. "It's not my fault."

"But what about your sister?"

"She's half crazy. I'm sure she'll be back."

"Oh, to have two daughters and to end up abandoned, poor, and ailing in one's old age!"

"That's life."

"Aren't you worried that the same thing may happen to you?"

"To me?"

"Yes."

"There are few men who are as undaunted as mine . . ."

"And so handsome, right?" adds Dolores ironically.

"You're accusing me," complains Hortensia, ashamed of her passion.

They are having this lively conversation on the threshold of the primitive cottage as Dolores is about to depart, eager to find out more about the latest occurrences and worried about Enrique.

Hortensia would like to go out and look for Manolo. She is no longer thinking about her sister, her mother, or her own children, only about Manolo, that ruffian who loves a fight and might be risking his life in some commotion. But she worries that he would not want her to leave and so she stays put, alert and watchful, muddled by love and fever.

In the meantime, Casilda crisscrosses the city, unaware of the rain showers, fleeing from people and lights, seeing a pursuer in every shadow and in every noise. Her instinct and habit lead her to her house in the mountains, and without any goal, only pushed by the need to escape, she heads to the outskirts, crosses the highway, leaves the town behind. The weak municipal lights don't reach that far, and the girl's savage bravery is shaken by the sight of the gigantic ridge rising up in front of her, whipped by the storm.

She regrets the absence of the factory's strident noises, the fires of the furnaces—transmitting messages like carrier pigeons—the cinders falling on the slag heaps like corn kernels, all the industrial kettle's sights and sounds, which used to seethe near the first bend of the road. The valley, hushed and blinded, looks like a fugitive too; she traipses back and forth several times between the slime and the slag without finding any trace of a path in this unaccustomed and frighteningly thick solitude.

The tempest highlights the lurid blue flutter of its exhalation, and that sinister light enables Casilda to find Naya's train station, reach the smelteries, and take refuge in a warehouse shed. Here she stops, afraid of the menacing mass of mountains and of the sky arching over the peaks, illuminated by sparks from the storm clouds.

Casilda feels surrounded by a vast and frightening hostility; never before had the horizon appeared so much like a shroud pressing down on the rocks; never before had she heard the wind tell such sad tales in the terrifying night. It is as if the cave of the hurricanes had burst open and all the startled gusts had joined forces to form a devastating front.

Trembling and dazed, the young girl, trying to escape from the cold raindrops on her sweaty body, presses against a heap of wood scraps she discovered. Many thoughts flitter through her mind, barely grazing her consciousness and moving on, like the rain falling on the arid land and the desperate wind howling in the narrow passes.

And she covers her ears with her hands; everything around her seems to be fleeing from her; she is certain that even the mountains are taking flight . . . She thinks vaguely about her guilt and misfortune. Most probably she wounded her rival but she doesn't care; ancestral instincts have hardened her heart. Her happiness had been stolen by "that woman"; Casilda hates her and feels she has the right to kill her. Then why is she hiding in fear? She doesn't know.

Even the most peaceful and innocent recollections frighten her; she is horrified by the memory of Aurora's eyes, glistening like green stars, as they rest gratefully on Marta. In bewilderment, she recalls Estévez's stern words, "You have to marry Pedro Abril; he asked you honorably, and it was your father's dying wish." She chose not to answer; hiding behind a shy reserve, she ignored her friend's advice, but now, she can't prevent his words from reverberating in the infinite night, transformed into a strong accusation.

Her shame singes her blood violently; her sad eyes, scanning the darkness, find that the terrestrial roads are closed to her, as well as the paths to dreams. Crazed and convulsed, she stands up, shaken by a terrible anxiety, like a bird unable to find its nest. Just as abruptly, she sits down again in exhaustion, blots out all memories, and listens only to the torrential rain. Cupping her face in her hands, she closes her eyes and falls asleep, lulled by the rain, which sounds like an eternal dirge.

THE BEAST

Dawn arrives late on this gray day; with the first light, the city's paltry bells awaken and begin their funereal toll, ringing endlessly.

"They're announcing a death!" says Casilda, waking up drowsily in her corner. Her body aches, her skin burns, and her velvety brown hair hangs down in matted strands. She rises, shakes her heavy dress—soaked by rain like the landscape—and peers darkly at the mud and mountains, the silent plain, and the infinite space. She has the sensation of being alone in the world with the wind and water, tossed around by the storm.

But the bells start tolling again. No, she isn't alone! Behind the fog the city is coming to life again and mourning a death.

"Oh, I know," says Casilda, returning to reality and clinging

to hope with a peculiar logic, "it must be the little boy of Jesusa, the one who lives in Almonaster, who died; he had been
close to death, ravaged by an infection." And she smiles cheer-
fully, as if she had found a solution to the terrible enigma of
her fate.

She emerges from the shed, holding her skirt over her head
to shield herself against the rain. Setting out along the mountain paths, she climbs with all the energy of her impetuous nature, despite the weight of her wet clothes and the pains in her
body; she wants to arrive—she is unsure where—right after
dawn. She has chosen the shortest route, across the lime
channels, overflowing onto the deserted and clean-looking
banks; the swollen streams flow noisily, separating into
opaque and somber rivulets.

Casilda keeps her eyes firmly fixed on the road. By not looking back, she doesn't see the pale, thin smoke coming from
the smelteries and descending, together with the clouds, into
the valley—the only sign of the gigantic fire that had burned
there the night before.

She is sustained and driven by the belief that Monte Sorromero will offer an impregnable refuge; the more she slips
on the slick mica, and the more distant and harsh the peaks
appear, the more convinced she is of finding shelter. But it is
a mystery how her confused conscience can have this illusion
because she cannot think of a single friend's name to justify
her conviction. First she must confess, and then find some
strong and generous arms to embrace and console her . . .
"Anuncia," she finally remembers. This slightly frivolous girl,
well-liked by Casilda, has given her several signs of friendship
behind her parents' back. But Casilda reconsiders and murmurs quietly, "No, not Anuncia either," and adds with childish
desolation, "But then who?"

Despite stumbling and falling on the humid and slippery
slate, she continues climbing up to the hills where the hamlet
is nestled. All the dwellings are shuttered, the surroundings
are silent, and the cliff, like an eternal sphinx, is more mysterious than ever. Casilda tries as much as possible to keep out of
sight of the houses until she reaches her own, closed as well.
She pauses, and confident that she will be welcomed, she lifts
the handle and opens the door.

Casilda enters the hallway, together with the raindrops and

the tempestuous wind—that eternal wanderer who roams the mountains with a roar. She shuts the door immediately and looks around in the semidarkness; she doesn't cry out or feel alarmed when a man approaches her with open arms.

"Thor!" she exclaims, overjoyed, yielding without any resistance to the protection of this Hercules.

"Yes, who else would it be?"

"Of course."

And it becomes evident that here, close to thunderheads and clouds, on the dark stump of Land's End, only this man can help her with her guilt.

"Were you waiting for me?" she asks coquettishly, anxious to hear his answer. The barbarian smiles, and, breathing heavily, he replies with a lascivious look, "I've been living here because I knew you'd return home!"

"But I'm returning alone . . ."

"That's even better."

"I escaped . . ."

"To look for me?"

"To ask you to help me and defend me!"

"From what?"

"From the world."

"Of course, since you're my woman."

"What do you mean?"

"Gabriel doesn't love you."

"I know," howls the young girl.

"And you don't love Pedro."

"No!"

"You have to marry me."

"If you'll hide me and protect me."

"See!" says Thor triumphantly, lifting her up like a feather. "You're wet," he notices with concern. He carries her to the kitchen where he has just lit a fire, and he orders her with a smile, "Change your clothes!"

He himself takes off her clothes and she offers no resistance; guided by only one instinct, that of self-preservation, she submits to the giant's brute force. Warmed by the heat, her muscles relax, and like a little beast, she is aware only of her physical needs. "I'm hungry . . ."

The strapping youth searches the cupboards for food and

offers her his meager provisions; she devours everything and asks, "Did you hear the tolling of Nerva's bells?"

"I only heard the downpour and the north wind."

"Well, shots were fired last night."

"Why do we care?" exclaims the miner with longing and impatience.

"Because I fired one of them."

"And did you kill anyone?"

"I don't know."

Thor is frightened by life's enigma; he shudders at the thought of a woman capable of dispatching a fellow human being to the other world.

Having satisfied her appetite, she goes up to him with drowsy, half-shut eyes, unabashed in her nakedness. They look at each other openly, like two animals. "Do you love me or don't you?" she asks with ferocious sensuality.

"Yes," utters the son of the Earth, who has started to tremble like a leaf . . .

The morning rises out of the night's ashes, and the wind glides over the mountains like an eagle, sweeping away the rain. In the sky's outer limits, a rainbow—the bridge of the gods—arches in shimmery innocence above the peaks.

12

Disaster

THE WORM AND THE STAR

A MONTH HAS PASSED SINCE THE DEATH OF THE MINE. ITS CORPSE
lies rotting in the sun; its guts, which have oozed out and ruptured the dikes, flow along furrows and channels to the river
and, mingling with its contaminated water, reach the sea. And
along Estuaria's pleasant coast, along the straits and harbors
of the Saquia and the Odiel, and along every bay of the broad
salt marshes, there is a wide ribbon of dead fish, poisoned by
the mineral's pernicious salts.

Each year more than eighty thousand tons of iron—the by-
product of cleaning copper with bleach—are deposited in
these fluvial veins. Especially in August, the shores overflow
with this greenish-blue coppery water, the famous copperas,
which in the sixteenth century the inhabitants of these shores
offered in tribute to Seville's archbishop. Anyone who dared
to appropriate copperas was severely punished, and groups of
young people were forced to collect it along the windy coast.
Of no practical use today, it adds an ornamental red trim to
the springs that flow down from the hills of Salomón to Estuaria's salt lake, and from there to the ocean, where it dyes the
foam's tremulous gauze with its lethal color.

But the normal eighty thousand tons have been exceeded
beyond belief during this summer's vacation month; at this
time, the water and slime represent an incalculable wealth
worth millions of pesetas. The huge heap of metal and multitude of minute crystals released daily into the river from broken channels, newly formed pools, and flooded caves swell
the Saquia's riverbed and embellish its shores with extravagant bloom.

And the Rehtron Company is appalled to see its capital

being swept away by the swollen waters of this Andalusian river. Three company consultants, an English lord, an Egyptian viceroy, and a Russian prince—all men of great influence in European commerce—have arrived from Nordetania. They have no intention of giving in to the Spanish workers or of deviating from the proud and despotic goal of double exploitation. It humiliates and infuriates them to be defeated by these miserable and long-suffering people, who have few resources and no rights. Nerva's teeming inhabitants remind them of a band of Gypsies, a stoic and strong people, who laugh and sing while dying of hunger.

The manager is reassured that his tyranny is not threatened by these illustrious visitors, who ride back and forth on military trains between Madrid and Dite, watching the hostile Spanish river wash away their millions. They confer with the miners, hoping that they will grow tired of the strike, and they offer to pay any amount to bribe Nerva's Syndicate.

But a sense of patriotic indignation grips the national press; if there are any traitors among the workers who are willing to sell themselves, it is hushed up. The newspaper *La Evolución*, fawning and servile in the end, has folded, and the new owners do not dare contradict the paper's original ideals.

Although the gold of the Nordetanos succeeds in blocking any outside help from reaching the miners, the journalistic criticism of this clandestine action embarrasses the illustrious visitors. Blinded by the sun and tired of repeated failure, they relinquish their powers to Martín Leurc and leave in a huff, having learned that a single person with faith has the power to warm the heart of the masses and persuade them to rise up against the most powerful industry.

Together with this astonishing certainty, they also take with them the image of the modest and peaceful young man responsible for the terrible losses to the mine. From their train window, Don Martín points at the sad, blond youth, "That's the Champion." The foreign millionaires will never be able to forget this insignificant man with the calm, pale-blue eyes.

The furnaces are inoperable and will have to be dynamited once the smelteries are fired up again. All the expensive industrial material is damaged, rusty, and jagged from a lack of care and maintenance. All the machinery—the cyclone separators, fire extinguishers, cranes, and lathes—as well as the excava-

tion's entire gear assembly are disintegrating, covered with
the red dye from the ore, and decaying in the deadly standstill;
not one blade, not a single wheel, not even a cog of the colos-
sal mine has moved.

More than a hundred locomotives and their attached wagons, all covered with rust, have remained frozen in place for a
month, their silhouette etched violently against the valleys
and mountains. The water has inundated the subterranean
corridors, tumbled the walls of the galleries, and destroyed the
supports. From the Phoenician cave of Salitre, "fifteen stadi-
ums high," down to the countermine's last pothole, there is
not a single firm and safe spot that is not threatening to collapse. Outside, the dry and yellow earth, bursting open with
satanic wounds, drinks up the blood seeping out of the caves
with avid lips.

Gradually, Dite is sinking, the houses and streets yield,
seemingly heeding an internal warning, the same signal that
precedes earthquakes; it is as though the mine, missing the
hum of the iron, were imitating its sound in a dream. In the
end, the prophecy is fulfilled; part of the town crumbles, sliding down blood-red cliffs, while in the ditches, avalanches of
rocks fall with a rumble on top of the collapsing props.

But the hecatomb has granted a cease-fire; the townspeople
flee with their depleted belongings, and pitch their tents out in
the open. The owners who lost their haciendas know that they
will not be compensated by the company. They will be dis-
missed if they protest and are Rehtron employees, as is usually the case; if they are not employed by the company, their
lives will be made so miserable that they will want to leave
town. No complaint against the Nordetanos has ever achieved
its desired effect!

A gigantic rock has detached itself from Salomón Hill and
hangs suspended over the sinister Glory Hole; the Catholic
cemetery and parish, the city's only sanctuary, are sinking together with the threatened hamlet. The priest asks the strikers
for help; the saints and the dead have to be "saved." This
priest, like the ones in Nerva, has been unconcerned about
matters he deems to be beyond his divine mission. Having be-
friended the foreigners, he has been infected with their commercial selfishness and views the drama of his countrymen
and of their land with indifference. The workers have little re-

spect for the local priests, who care little about their souls or their fights, and who don't even share their tears, leaving the fields of their hearts deserted and uncultivated.

Nevertheless, the workers lend the priest a hand, helping him to rescue the endangered paintings; the Virgin, baby Jesus, and St. Joseph leave the church on the arms of some young fellows who do not know God but treat the primitive sculptures with exquisite care. With monstrance in hand, the priest follows the saints in silent procession; even the bells in the swaying tower remain mute. The crowd watches, and, moved by the tragedy, the men bare their heads and the women cry. Like a celestial bird, a pure breath of Christian faith hovers over these rustic souls.

The majority of the inhabitants walk quietly behind the figure of the Lord, dislodged from his humble abode, where he had been close to the people. In their avarice, the new Catholics had built the church without regard for his noble lineage or the soul's immortal rights.

The tiny, tremulous voice of the sacristan's bell calls for devotion along the path of the procession; the entire town seems to be agonizing on its deathbed, joined in a single communion, waiting to receive the final unction of the dying . . . The day also raises high its celestial host, which is the same for all of God's creatures . . .

Santiago Estévez, peace-loving and friendly, participates in the effort of rescuing the sacred objects, and after the priest stops by his house—sanctifying it with his presence—to pick up the monstrance, the philosopher and his friends visit the cemetery behind the church. The collapse of the interior galleries has caused the burial ground to sink. The coffins, protruding from the open niches, resemble black skiffs, and the dead, emerging in amazement from their tombs, crumble when touched by human hands, warm air, or a ray of sun; cold, weightless, and fragile, they seem to be made of snow mixed with dust.

Gabriel Suárez assists Estévez in this charitable mission, and he carries the ice-cold urns filled with ashes on his shoulders. Ever since Nena lay motionless on his chest, he has tried to familiarize himself with death. This painful inclination has led him to explore the frightening mystery, unaware that no one has ever succeeded in catching a glimpse of eternity.

Despite their fatigue, the two friends make an effort to complete their macabre task. "We're the ghosts of the temple," murmurs Estévez, as he reassembles the parts of a corpse that had disintegrated when touched. Gabriel keeps quiet, questioning the stubborn silence of the tombs with invincible curiosity. Only the dull noise of the hoes, used to lift some clumps of earth or a stone slab, interrupts the stillness. The workers proceed gently, careful not to cause a landslide on the shaky incline.

The workers carrying out this beneficent task have a permit from the committee in charge of the strike, stating that they are unpaid volunteers. Even though the job is dangerous, they have made a solemn vow to conclude it because they want to move the churchyard to a better place in Mesa de los Pinos, where a broad flatland, covered with rosemary, awaits their dead, who have found no peace even after death . . . Here they are mere remnants of the poor, embers of the destitute!

And the afternoon, searing the metal hills, makes its painstaking way up the hills. The heat vents its fury on the exhausted and debilitated workers, who are sweating, discouraged, and hungry. Stretched out between the hot ground and the cold tombs, they look at each other, perhaps envying those pale bones that rest beneath the tombstones.

Ignoring the danger, some villagers stand near the broken edge, observing the men.

"They're worn out!" the women exclaim.

"Yes!" agrees Santiago, admitting his exhaustion.

For some days now he has shared his modest possessions with the neediest, and he doesn't eat enough to sustain him and enable him to work. Next to him, a man tries to get up and collapses.

"He can't get any air," says a companion.

"He's drunk with bitterness," affirms Gabriel.

The schoolmaster adds, trying to smile, "You can't look the sun or Death in the face!" And these two inscrutable forces pursue the wretches: the celestial body and the skeleton, the worm and the star . . .

Jacobo Pmip arrives and wants to give some alms to the stricken man, who refuses with all the indignation his weakness allows. But the catechist is neither upset nor offended; he puts the coins away, turns around, and delivers a sermon. It's crazy to be worried about the dead when the living are being threatened. What madness! In his official capacity, he forbids them to continue with this absurd task; the company can't be held responsible for whatever happens.

"The prohibition is superfluous," Santiago cuts him off harshly. "We've run out of energy."

"You too?"

"Yes."

"Don't you eat?"

"Little."

"You probably don't have any appetite because you don't work in the mines."

"But my friends do."

"And you've helped to take away their daily bread!"

"I'd advise you to keep quiet."

Don Jacobo gives the crowd a sidelong glance; although he knows them well and has faith in their goodness, he lives with mistrust and eternal vigilance. He understands that the grave diggers are using Santiago's statement as a convenient excuse to halt their terrible work with dignity. The men, almost all from Dite, are exhausted; their houses are in ruins and their belongings lie scattered in the street. With a heavy gait, they march past the engineer, perhaps grateful for his appearance, which allows them to give up a task that surpasses their resistance.

They were deceived by their willpower; without nourishment they can't live or uphold those lofty thoughts. An immense torment accompanies them as they walk with lowered heads, talking, like so many others, about leaving and looking for work or asking for handouts. They are followed by women and children, who seem hitched to the same miserable yoke.

Paying no attention to Pmip, Santiago looks at the group in distress, and then turns to contemplate the burial ground with overflowing corpses and the mountain's cancer, swallowing up the earth. The mine reminds him of a reef from which the men, like waves, are receding. A few steps away, Gabriel is waiting for him, closemouthed; both are reluctant to abandon the mortal remains scattered in such disarray.

Guessing their thoughts, Don Jacobo says loquaciously, "As soon as the strike's over, we'll build a huge parish in a safe place, surrounded by housing . . . The place that has already been designated as a cemetery will be closed off by a wall, and we'll organize a beautiful festivity for its consecration. Then there'll be a solemn ceremony to transport whatever is left here . . ." and he touches a few bones with the tip of his cane.

"The strike won't be over until you want it to end," Santiago points out acidly.

Don Jacobo interprets these words as a clear sign of weariness; undoubtedly, the committee is about to yield because the workers cannot go on for another day. Precisely tonight was the deadline the company had to either accept or reject the terms proposed by the Syndicate. In a gesture of magnanimity, the Syndicate has made some concessions in its final demands.

He recalls these details, together with the workers' weary expressions and Santiago's spontaneous confession, "We've run out of energy." Well, it is clear: even though the Rehtron Company has suffered great losses, it will end up the triumphant winner; the workers will have to return to work without having gained anything, and they may even be subject to some punitive actions, such as lawsuits and massive dismissals.

Pmip has won and he can barely conceal his delight; after the many humiliations, he is savoring these hours of revenge and retribution. Bertita Leurc's mocking smile has tortured him, as have her mother's cruel little jokes, not to mention the manager's rudeness. His personal credit in Vista Hermosa has plummeted, along with Dite's stocks on the London and Paris stock markets. In his desperation, he tried to mix with the people, feigning grief and generosity, while spying on their changing moods.

The townspeople tolerate him, out of habit, accustomed to see him come and go in their huts, distributing candies and "shields" to the children, and to their mothers, an occasional coin—if they have attractive young daughters. At first when the miners stayed home from work, he diminished his visits. But now that the rebels are fleeing from the zone or are brought low by hunger, Don Jacobo, who is no coward and who has the courage of impunity, has again increased the frequency of his meddling. Once more he is victorious on this wretched field of conquest and exploitation, an arrogant feat that will cause his value to rise again in Vista Hermosa. Bursting with boastfulness, he checks out the wretched hovels every day, assuring them that it's all going well.

For more important diplomatic inquiries, Pmip makes use of Santiago. The poor schoolmaster is too honest to hate or pretend; he doesn't make a good conspirator and Don Jacobo can read his transparent soul like an open book. The polyglot, who prides himself in understanding even mysterious mental languages, proceeds peacefully to light a cigarette and offers the philosopher one.

"Thank you, I don't smoke."

"Are you giving up all vices?"

"Yes, of necessity . . ."

Even though Santiago was not, strictly speaking, one of the strikers, his acute poverty has become more evident with every instance. How would the strikers be faring? Don Jacobo is entertaining several pleasing hypotheses when suddenly both men notice that the earth is swaying. An instinctive precaution had led them away from the most dangerous spot, and now they run to where Gabriel is standing, at a distance from the most severe clefts. From here they gaze at the temple's fractured walls, noting a trembling of the cross on top of the damaged belfry.

Night is falling, and the western sky, where the sun is disappearing behind a hill, turns a deep purple. Gabriel is tired of waiting.

"Are you coming?" he asks his friend.

But the catechist is interested in continuing his conversation with the schoolmaster. "Wait a little," he encourages him, "and I'll accompany you to Nerva." But Estévez, who feels drained, objects vaguely, "It's getting late . . ."

"The moon will guide us. I'll spend the night there; I'm curious to know how you'll react to the manager's reply."

The schoolmaster is undecided; Gabriel, who overheard their conversation, says, "I'm off; see you tomorrow," and leaves, without even looking at Pmip.

"Bye," repeats Santiago mechanically.

Black shadows roll into the valley, and the philosopher has the impression that the night is rising up from the earth, spreading darkness in the souls.

SILENT NIGHT

Yes: it was the night's fault. When Pmip took him furtively to a tavern and invited him to dinner, Santiago's instinct was barely awake. Tumbling from exhaustion, he—so pure and rational—was won over by the smell of food, enticed by a glass of wine and a piece of bread.

When they came out again, the moon was shining in full splendor, surrounded by the constellations, illuming the towering mountains, the somber cliffs, the shattered town, and the philosopher's gloomy heart. He is invaded by sadness.

"You've fed me," he remarks desolately. In his glee, Don Jacobo doesn't notice the painful irony.

"As I would any man."

"But not like a man . . . like an animal!"

"Come on, don't exaggerate, you ate very little."

"I've satisfied my hunger and thirst . . . and feel much stronger."

"Good, good," says the engineer, repeating his favorite expression.

Taking the dangerous shortcut straight across the hilly wilderness, they reach the train station and cross the tracks; there is no traffic except for the daily military convoy, which does not issue tickets to fugitive miners and refuses to deliver any packages for the strikers.

"We have time to spare," says Pmip after looking at his watch. "It's nine o'clock and the edict won't be published until midnight."

"I think you know its contents."

"Don't be so sure."

"I'm convinced."

"I can venture a guess, at most."

"And are the terms favorable for us?"

"Look, don't use the plural. You're an exalted idealist, and I have the feeling that you're close to regretting it . . ."

"Tell me what the manager is going to say."

"I think he isn't going to make any concessions."

"Really?"

"Of course! The Rehtron Company has lost a bundle in this adventure, about two million pesetas a week."

"Yes, but they net more than seventy million a year in gold."

"But they've suffered huge losses, in unusable material, factories sunk into mud, collapsed buildings, and the copper carried away by the river . . ."

"The metal of the dead!"

"Don't be so dramatic!"

"Gold is man's worst enemy."

"But how beautiful it is: blond like the sun; the honey of life!"

They walk slowly, stopping frequently. Comforted by dinner, they have a warm longing to confide in each other, and Don Jacobo honors Santiago by treating him like a friend.

"Convince yourself," he adds cynically, "money is the metal of the living."

"Yes, but you pay three pesetas in daily wages and steal ten million from the Spanish state."

"Steal?" repeats Don Jacobo without losing his composure. "That depends on how you look at things. Great enterprises always enjoy some just and well-deserved advantages."

"Do you believe that?"

"I believe in their merits. Note how these wages that you're criticizing support numerous families who would be dying of hunger without them."

"You're right about that. These poor creatures spend their lives locked in mortal combat with death until a strike comes and finishes them off . . . Every year more than two hundred men die in accidents, more than a hundred are wounded, and at least ten thousand become invalids. Others come to fill their places. The damage is renewed, expands, and knows no end. Impunity is another privilege of the great enterprises!"

"No one lives without suffering," declares Pmip pompously. "Material suffering is not more worthy of compassion than the civilized world's moral afflictions; physical struggle stultifies our feelings."

"You're not making sense. All human suffering is spiritual. Christ gave us the clearest proof of spiritual suffering, bleeding to death on a cross. Pains never stultify, they always purify."

"Then why avoid them?"

"Because in our weakness we already suffer them in excess,

and because we should never seek them as a goal, only as a means to an end."

"You," accuses the spy, including Estévez in his incrimination, "don't want to take advantage of them. You're defending yourselves against them in a misguided and suicidal fashion, thus harming your fellowmen."

"So there can be justice and charity in this world."

"Didn't you say that alms offend you?"

"Yes, but we need love."

"Which you don't obtain with violence."

"There's no violence on our part."

"Ah, yes," bemoans Don Jacobo, smooth and flattering again. "We include you among the rabble because you insist on it, although, aside from this mania, you're reasonable and cultured."

"Yes, and an egotist who just had dinner," bemoans the schoolmaster, looking up apprehensively at the infinite cluster of stars.

"You mean, decent people aren't allowed to eat?"

"When their friends fast, they must share bread and night vigil with them."

"My friend, you're an ascetic!" declares Pmip, slightly mockingly. "But let's see, what have the workers gained from the employers with their endless fasting? Isn't this always the same question, only more bitter and hopeless each time?"

"Yes, more hopeless! Because we've achieved very little since the time the greedy Phoenicians starting gnawing at these mountains in the mythic days of David's son, when the kings needed thrones of rubies, crowned by golden vultures, and an army of birds and angels to build their castles with jewels and metal . . . Look over there," continues Estévez, growing more exalted and pointing at Salomón's peak in the bright moonshine. "Look at the monstrous cave that has been transformed into a tremendous geological hole; it offered its riches to Jerusalem's temple, and in the course of the past centuries and throughout all the different eras, it has continued to poison the waters and lives, destroying the bonds of love that unite humans. To this day, it allows a multitude of men to labor beneath the earth so that others can build their marble and crystal towers."

Saddened by his own words, the philosopher pauses, longing desperately for "the Lord's fertile vineyard."

"So you recognize that humanity doesn't change," concludes Pmip proudly, without understanding his friend's holy
indignation. "Today, like yesterday, the powerful have no
choice but to enslave the wretched masses, and all rebellions
against this social law have proved futile. This is why I recommend patience, resignation, and good sense. Do you understand what I mean?"

Self-satisfied, he awaits a reply, but Santiago answers him
abruptly and roughly, "No! No, I don't understand passive
conformity when children do not have a den, as do the bears,
or a nest, like the birds, and clean water in the hollow of a
rock."

"And whose fault is that? I usually side with the poor, as you
well know; I mingle with them, offering them help and support. Well, I myself advised the manager to cancel the leases
of the strikers and evict them from their homes as just punishment for their intolerable attitude. I also suggested cutting off
their water supply, but that would have had endangered public health, with some serious risks for 'us.'"

"You've certainly chosen some radical means . . . yes, very
modern and most appropriate for the twentieth century,"
smiles the schoolmaster, trying to control his dark and husky
voice. "And don't you think that the Spanish government will
take similar measures to defend its people?"

"Defend from what? We're within our rights: we own the
buildings and also the waters, in addition to the land and the
mines."

A breath of recklessness leads the strollers to walk along the
unsafe river bank, absorbed in an age-old conversation full of
horrors, treasures, and human lives. Don Jacobo bursts with
pride, convinced that his arguments are irrefutable; he doesn't
notice the philosopher's dark tone and overlooks the cold
smile on his lips. Estévez, his eyes buried deep in the heart of
the moon, answers distractedly, "That's true."

"Besides," Don Jacobo adds arrogantly, "it is unlikely that
the Spanish government would take an interest in the hordes
of Andalusian strikers."

"That's true," repeats the schoolmaster.

"They're in pretty bad shape, aren't they?"

"Yes."

"What about the strike organizers?"

"Worse."

"The president gets a salary, right?"

"He is working for free and so are the doctors. Several children have died of hunger, and this morning a woman killed herself."

"I didn't know that . . . But José Luis Garcillán and his sister must have some means."

"They don't."

"Aren't they living from their pension?"

"They used to, though modestly; now they share the money with the needy and make do with practically nothing."

Estévez's statements have an ominous ring. Standing perfectly still, as if rooted to the ground, his face registers no emotions as he recites these pains and deprivations in a monotone. Jacobo Pmip listens to him with diabolic delight.

"I have triumphed in my endeavors on behalf of the company, and I don't even miss Zabala," he confesses, blinded by an aggressive shamelessness. "I supposed and guessed almost everything you've told me. In accordance with the information and advice I provided Leurc, his answer, to be published in two hours, will deny the miners any and all concessions. We've won! The haughty will return to the trough, humbled and having learned their lesson. Good, very good! We . . ."

"You wretch!"

At the same time as he shouts this insult, which echoes harshly in the ravines, Estévez pushes Pmip's chest with clawlike hands and kicks him forcefully in the stomach. Too breathless to scream, Pmip falls backward and rolls down until the edge of the Glory Hole, where he sways back and forth for an instant. Trying desperately to hold on to something, he digs his nails into the earth before dropping into the void.

"He fed me like an animal!" mumbles Santiago in a calm voice, having regained his serenity. Peering over the fearful precipice, he can barely see the vague shape lying lifelessly in the deep cavity, an indistinct patch that blends in with the cancer's reddish pulp. The final thump of the body landing on the cliffs sounded like the smashing of a pot into smithereens.

And the night is so silent that one can hear the flight of a butterfly as it cuts the air and light.

Hunger

Money, credit, and illusions have all been exhausted. No one yields. The unity in their attitude prevails, and their loyalty to the strike is absolute and constant; yet their energies are waning and they have given up hope.

A terrible fatalism has overtaken the mute and passive city, which is dying a slow death. The Syndicate's funds and the help received from other unions have been spent; perhaps a malevolent force has barred the strikers from obtaining other contributions that might have saved them.

Estuaria's rail service, the only communication between the province and the capital, has been partially restored, just enough to guarantee the foreigners the protection of Spanish soldiers; one daily train keeps the military apparatus alive but does not supply the towns with provisions or allow the transport of passengers, unless they are Rehtron employees.

But the company, well taken care of in this manner, never considered bringing in scabs. The bosses realize that this action would entail violence not only because the miners, as long as they have strength to draw breath, would rise up, but also because all of Spain might react with vengeful indignation. They have already brought enough loathing upon themselves; the massacre of 1888 is an undying reproach, and there are signs that the desire for vindication has been revived. A note of Spanish nationalism has crept into the accusations against the Nordetanos of appropriating, deceiving, and coveting, which could turn the soldiers against them. They know that the armed forces have come to protect them from aggression, but not to attack the workers. If the miners don't flee or surrender, they have to be annihilated, which may be accomplished by ignoring all their claims and letting them die of hunger, without the most minimal consideration.

It isn't true that this Andalusian city sings like the swan before dying; they sang as long as they had the energy to stand up. Today the town is perishing, and, like a human being, it pays a final tribute in tears, which are shed by the women and children because the men swallow them in their pride.

And the city throbs with a stronger pulse during the dark moments of farewells, which spread a disturbing shadow over the souls and leave a trail of endless and unabated sobs in their wake. Thousands of men flee in rickety and shabby caravans; the oldest probably intend to beg for alms, while the young men hope to find work in other mines, dragging with them slavery's chains. Couples are separated; children, brothers, and lovers have to say goodbye. The dying take their final leave, unable to resist these difficult times; the children die from weakness, reaped in an early harvest. Weak, frail, and exhausted, some of the expectant mothers lose their minds, and daily one of them commits suicide, either charred on the rocks by the heat of the sun or frozen stiff in the desert's cold night air, with an icy face and open eyes staring at the clouds.

One of the first to leave was Thor, the Galician Hercules, who—shortly after the strike broke out—escaped across the Sierra Morena, together with Casilda Rubio. His final destination is unknown because subsequent tumultuous happenings have erased all traces of these early fugitives. Pedro Abril left as well, and there was some speculation as to which of her suitors Casilda had chosen to accompany; according to one version, Pedro took off after the couple in a belligerent mood.

Not even Marta asks for the girl; she doesn't hear or see, and sits, removed from the world, in the corner of Hortensia's apartment, which stands empty ever since Fanjul disappeared amid the murky masses of emigrants.

Other, even crueler, separations are about to take place. Aurelio Echea has tried to enlist the help of Estuaria's authorities on behalf of the children, and a touch of compassion bodes well for the rescue of these innocent souls from the disastrous shipwreck of their homes. Moved, the capital's inhabitants have responded to the Champion's request; and the starving children will be assigned to different families, even though their departure will mean a heartrending uncertainty for their mothers . . .

Tonight the population is galvanized by an unexpected curiosity as it awaits Leurc's edict. In the Syndicate building, as miserable as the surrounding houses, the three neighbor women sit together on the balcony in hushed silence, waiting for the news. Gabriel, who has just returned from the city, joins them. They speak despondently about the destroyed church and the moving of the burial ground, unable to focus their attention completely on this event, which is the latest in a long list of daily misfortunes. The miner's dejected demeanor betrays his extreme fatigue, and Aurora, herself in low spirits and with rings under her eyes, whispers in his ear, "Are you hungry?"

"What difference does it make?" he answers with a shrug.

"They gave Dolores some leftovers in the barracks, and there's a portion for you."

"Really?" he murmurs, unable to control his avidity. He follows her to the kitchen, eager to receive his ration of cold, salty, and unappetizing soup. 'Wait, I'll heat it up," says Aurora, preparing to light a fire in the stove.

"No, no!"

"My God, you're starving!" laments the girl.

Suddenly Gabriel suppresses his nervous gesture with tremendous willpower, and mumbles, "Have you eaten?"

"Yes."

"Do you swear?"

"Yes, I swear."

"Do you want more?"

"No, I'm full."

Leaning over the dish, he devours the food, and then, bending over the water container next to the stove, he drinks with greedy gulps.

"You're dried out from the trip," remarks Aurora.

"Yes, not to mention exhausted!"

She sighs, looking at him, and then shies away immediately, letting her eyes wander over the room. The fire in the hearth has died, an empty coal basket hangs from the wall, and the larder is depleted.

"If I'm not in the way, I'd like to lie down here on the floor for a little while. Is that all right?" entreats Gabriel.

Aurora looks at him again with tender compassion; he seems sadder and more ravaged than ever. Her sweet and piercing look touches him and awakens love's powerful voice. "Aurora!"

"Come with me, you're exhausted. Lie down in my bed."

She takes his hand and leads him gently, sensing his slight tremor. As she turns the light on in the room, she warns him softly, "Don't crush the baby."

Sleeping on the edge of the bed is a little boy, a few months old, and looking like all infants at his age. His father has not been identified and his mother was killed by a bullet the same night as Nena. At that horrendous moment, no one thought of taking him to the orphanage. He was nameless and helpless, just skin and bones, when Aurora, with angelic generosity and turning her grief into fruitfulness, picked him up and nursed him. The first few times she breast-fed him, every fiber in her body rejected this adoption as an unbearable sacrifice.

She dressed the little intruder in Nena's clothes and spent hours contemplating him as he lay in bed or in her arms; she tried calling him "Nene," in the hope of fooling herself a little, but she was unable to overcome her aversion to a creature that was not her flesh and blood. In the end, a tear, a smile, an indescribable look from the innocent baby opened her charitable heart, enabling her to nurture the child without too much torment, although in the depths of her soul she grieved over the substitution.

As for Gabriel, he saw her as the holiest of all mothers and loved her with lofty adoration; eager for a grain of infinity, he sought to elevate the source of his tenderness above mortal passion. Despite all material deprivations—pain, fatigue, fasting—the spell she cast on him grew purer and more sublime than ever, exalting his being.

But that night, Aurora's look awakens in him a tempestuous restlessness, and temptation returns like a bird carried by the wind.

"Don't crush the baby," she repeats, invoking pious duty to fend off the agitation they both feel.

"Aurora!"

His arms are extended in such ardent need for hope and consolation that she goes up to him, poses her cheek near his lips, and says with heartfelt emotion, "We have to keep on suffering, just like the others." Despite their simplicity, these words have a great impact; "the others" are the masses of raggedy and squalid people, hardened by every misfortune.

"Yes, you're right!" whispers Gabriel, his willpower restored by the gentle lilt of his beloved's voice. Glimpsing his still unsettled reflection in her big eyes, he affirms with unexpected emphasis, "I will become worthy of you." She releases him quietly and sees him leave the room; then she undresses and lies down carefully, trying not to wake the child.

Two hours later, near midnight, the city—bathed in moonlight and caressed by stars and a tremulous breeze—is enveloped, gripped, and shaken by a persistent and frightening hum; a mysterious celestial empathy accompanies the turmoil.

Echea and Garcillán are walking arm in arm down Cicerón Street, followed closely by Romero, Estévez, Garcés, and other important union members; they feel oppressed by the dark and menacing masses now that Misery's soft clay has hardened.

No shouts or outcries or discussions are heard; the crowd maintains strict order, repeating the same words over and over. The strikers intend to storm Vista Hermosa, drag Leurc out, and plunder the company's warehouses.

Even before the populace formulated this plan, all sorts of rumors had reached the members of the Syndicate. They knew that in his published proclamations, the manager stated his categorical and forceful refusal to negotiate with the miners, and that this provocative blow exacerbated the victims' bitterness.

It soon becomes evident that not even the sharp tips of the bayonets will prevent the strikers from carrying out their intentions, since their destiny is more cruel than any threat. Yet they are reluctant to break the discipline that binds them in the same pain; the uniformity of their common misery strengthens their fraternal bonds. They want the president to sign the resolution like a general granting a booty.

The clamorous groups surround the Syndicate building, where the committee members are assembled. The doors have been thrown wide open so the other representatives and members can enter; the house belongs to all of them. "Please come in," shouts Salmerón from the threshold.

Rosario appears on top of the landing and implores Aurelio Echea, "For God's sake, don't give in to them!"

"No, I won't; I'll go upstairs to talk to them from the balcony."

He goes up the stairs quickly and decisively. Pale, bareheaded, and worn out by hardship, which has taken its toll on him as much as on the poorest miner, he tells them that he could never give his consent to any personal aggression except in case of self-defense. He adds that furthermore, as the Syndicate's president, he wholeheartedly forbids and condemns any act of violence. As for plundering the warehouses, he fears that such action would occasion very dangerous conflicts and advises them to save that measure as a last desperate recourse. He assures them that Spain will not abandon them. He announces that the first transport of children to the capital is scheduled for the next day; he tells them that help will be forthcoming, that the manager will be replaced, and that they will win the strike. "I swear to you," he closes in a firm and festive tone, "that the company will suffer one more punishment: its terrible greed will be an unforgettable public embarrassment." He kisses the crossed fingers of his right hand, and this fervent and serene gesture adds a religious touch, which works its magic on the crowd.

Those who could hear the Champion's promises and interdictions clearly communicate them to the others. The earlier silence, in which all mumbling had been suffocated, is torn asunder with exclamations and comments. Oscillating along the street, the line of people stops and then keeps flowing along the city's dirty, cavernous paths, illumined by the clear night.

A wave of gratitude suffuses the magnificent cloudscape; a luminous force radiates from the stars, floats to the horizon, and extends generously over the earth.

FATALISM

Moonlight streaming in through the open balcony doors fills the house. Rosarito has extinguished the sad yellowish lights, preferring to enjoy the natural shimmer, and she sits next to Aurora at the back of the room, not knowing what to say. She feels in her own flesh the population's weariness and distress; sorrow overwhelms her spirit and lethargy immobilizes her body.

No one would recognize in Rosarito the elegant traveler of the *Hardy*. Debilitated and fragile, wearing large, ill-fitting clothes that are obviously not her own, she looks like a little girl playing dress-up. In her extreme zeal for sacrifice, she often goes hungry, giving her food to the old, the young, and the sick in the neighborhood. By fibbing and pretending, she manages to make Aurora eat a little more than she does herself and to sneak extra food to Anita.

Only the most indispensable items are left from the belongings she and her brother had brought along; not a single object of value, not even a childish piece of jewelry, has survived the dire shortage. The meager support they received from some distant family members—who did not look fondly upon their atrocious adventure—they distributed like charitable seeds in the vicinity.

But neither they nor their closest friends, who form the moral backbone of the Syndicate and the strike, feel the misfortune as much as the ignorant and desperate masses, who lack their lofty goals or aspirations. The cultured souls suffer, but they also derive pleasure—in varying measure—from vying with each other in effort and virtue, surprising each other with the renewed enthusiasm with which they face every new tribulation; they live in an exalted state, engaged in a constant and intrepid struggle.

These are the creatures who are attracted to Love as butterflies are drawn to light; they have passions and weaknesses, they stumble and rise up again, but they are always illuminated by a spark of immortal grace, which enables them to surpass themselves and elevate their thoughts, refined and purified through pain.

In this difficult hour of responsibilities, Rosario approaches her friend inquiringly, uncertain about how she can be of help to him. Aurelio, absentminded and silent, is still standing near the balcony.

"Yes," he mumbles after a while, "they have to retaliate, at least a little; revenge would nourish and sustain them. It's only fair! Yes, it's necessary!" He uses the impersonal form, deeming it proper to exclude himself.

"Revenge?" the two girls stutter, almost in unison.

"One man should avenge them all; a courageous man."

"Could I be of use?" asks Santiago Estévez in a clear voice, standing in the doorway.

"No, it should be a miner."

"Why a miner?"

"Because we need someone who's familiar with the countermine's passageways."

"Oh!"

"Then I guess I'm of no use either!" regrets the president.

"Don't you know that twenty-two stories collapsed down there?"

"Yes, I know. Now it's harder than ever to find one's way around amid all the rubble; whoever is brave enough must be ready to give up his life."

"Don't talk so loud, for God's sake!" begs Aurora, who hears a noise in the bedroom. A strong and unequivocal foreboding makes her turn around; there is Gabriel, barefooted, his arms hanging by his side, listening attentively with wide-open eyes. The young girl stifles a scream, but Gabriel proves that he has overheard the conversation by saying in a manly voice, "I'm the miner you need!"

They all understand that this is true, and their faces turn as ashen as the moon. The silence is fraught with emotions. Aurora takes a few steps in the room but doesn't know where to go. She seems to be pushed by a mysterious force, like the saints who consecrate themselves at the altar, destined to go in search of pain.

Gabriel looks at her intensely; like her, he takes a few mechanical steps, and asks with a deep and husky voice, "What other choice is there?"

While Echea looks at Aurora in speechless pity, Rosarito goes up to her friend and entreats her with pious devotion, "Come with me!"

After the women leave the room, Aurelio, still unable to speak, embraces Gabriel, and Santiago tells him with calm determination, "I want to go with you wherever you may go."

Beset by doubts, the miner stops and asks hesitantly, "Did Jacobo Pmip invite you tonight?"

"He did; we had dinner together."

"Then . . ."

"You're not hungry!" Aurelio concludes dolefully, proud of his own gnawing hunger.

"That's true, but my shameful satiety has rid us of a reptile; I hope you'll forgive me."

Calm and composed, Aurelio recounts in a soft and steady voice his horrendous adventure near the Glory Hole. He is received with outstretched arms, and their constantly suppressed hatred of Pmip erupts for an instant, filling the noble and sublime souls with a perverse joy.

"Nobody else will be harmed," asserts the president, blushing over his wild glee.

"Nobody," echo his companions.

Standing in a group, the men confer in a reasonable and determined tone; Santiago keeps insisting, "I want to go with you." "No!" repeats Gabriel in a low voice, and his words resound with an invincible fatalism. "It's to me that the Earth is calling out, not to you." And when Garcillán walks up the stairs to tell the president that they are waiting for him in the office down below, Gabriel passes him by in torn clothes, barefooted, bareheaded, livid, but with a firm step, holding his head high.

The tragedy of the miner's silent departure must be accepted with restrained grief. Full of pity, Rosario reassures Aurora, "He'll come back!" but Rosario turns around abruptly, listens for a noise from the outside, and adds in a somber and distressed voice, "I'm going with him." But her words have awoken the little boy, who cries with hunger. Rosario hands her the baby, "You can't abandon him!" Seeing him so puny and feeble, Aurora thinks, despite herself, of the miserable short life he has left to live; she also becomes aware of her own emaciation and weakness.

"It's only a question of a few more days," she estimates. "We'll meet again beyond death and oblivion," and in a loud voice she adds, resigning herself, "I'll wait." She bends over mechanically to pick up the child and nurse it, thinking that her daughter is well off, beyond tears and pains. And she smiles with grim happiness, noting that her forces are being sucked out of her by the baby's thirsty lips.

Saddened by the wasting away of these two creatures, Rosario suddenly feels the pain of all these deprivations. Noticing that she too, as if by contagion, has lost weight and energy, she recalls the radiant expression of well-being exuded by corpses. She longs for the sweet comfort of a bath, the fragrant crispness of linen, the enchantment of clean clothes. For many days now, no one has done any laundry in Nerva, and the city has an unsavory look.

Close to fainting, Rosario is revived unexpectedly by Anita, who is standing next to her without any clothes. When the little girl woke up alone in her bed, she came to the adjoining bedroom to look for her friend. Cradled in Rosario's arms,

Anita sighs, too sad and weak to cry. Rosario hugs and kisses her, rocking her gently, and the two look at each other with fervent woe, swaying like rocking chairs, like stars . . .

The pestilent smell rising up from the filthy streets is accompanied by the perturbing and uneasy sounds of the neighborhood, which is sleepless at night and shuns the sun's curative powers by day. The town has made the same promise as Aurora, "I'll wait," and the echo of its anguish resembles a harsh sylvan sigh.

Tonight most of the people wandering around aimlessly at other times go to the mountains to pick up the sweet fruit of the dwarf palm, an Andalusian plant that grows wild in this area. By some miracle of fertility, it succeeds in spreading its roots in the Sierra Morena, despite the harm done to these mountains by the fumes. But the local examples of this prodigious little palm are stunted; the fruit, which ripens in October, resembles stringy almonds, and the stems are often too tough to eat, yet necessity has converted both into edibles.

To avoid the heat, the women go in nightly caravans, and amidst the thorns and mica, they look for leaves and stalks with which to dupe their empty stomachs. Monte Sorromero, Ventoso, and the surrounding heights and hills provide this perishable nourishment that mothers crave for their children, and they consider themselves fortunate if they can bring back the green, dry, and sour surrogate dates or palmettos.

Tonight the hardy women return from their harvest with the news that Dite's church and cemetery have collapsed. One of them reports hearing a mysterious crash, which may have been the sound of half the town falling into the dark pit; this rumor sweeps through the still-sizzling streets like an early morning shudder.

Dawn is breaking, the hour when the waters ripple on the ocean's surface. Making his pilgrimage across the scarred Sombra Negra, Gabriel feels his heart flutter with life's surprises. From the rugged road, he can see the menacing block hanging over the pit and the full moon shining on the worm-eaten burial ground, and he muses that the mine devours its workers even after death.

"At least," he smiles bitterly, "the stain Pmip left on the rock has been erased."

He observes the waning moon being blotted out by westerly

clouds as he reaches the mouth of the corridors destined to swallow him. Here he is stopped abruptly by Nature's musical sounds, more audible in the profound silence of the country-side. He looks around avidly and listens. In the distance, he hears a crystalline waterfall, the murmur of recent springs, which live and die in the same cliff, the sighing wind in the precipices, and the grinding of rocks in the hollow caves. Slowly, the auroral lights unfold, reminding him of his be-loved. He remembers her with inconsolable sorrow and ponders that he lives among souls that are asleep, and that hers is the only one that watches and suffers for all humanity.

He approaches the excavation's opening as if stepping up to a window to infinity; the earth's dark voice is calling him obstinately. After lighting his lantern, he wraps a protective cover around it and, with a brave look, takes leave of life. Warm and vibrant rays of sun bounce off the peaks; Gabriel faces his destiny and lets himself be devoured by darkness.

THE INNOCENT

The children are departing, and today the train is obligated to provide passenger service to these official representatives of misery. They are being seen off amid tears and hugs by a sad crowd at Nerva's train station; taking them carefully from the maternal arms, the soldiers make them feel comfortable in the wagons.

It is touching to see the kindness with which these young men treat the starving children. The harshness associated with army life is negated by their patient generosity; these military men see a son or a brother in these gaunt Andalusian children, exiled by a foreign power from one of their home-land's most fertile valleys.

This dual insult kindles the regiment's humanitarian impulses; the martial troupe is made up of common Spanish folk, who have been wounded treacherously in body and soul. The armies of a civilized country are no longer formed by the ignorant and uneducated, and today the soldiers of King Alfonso XIII are men with heart and dignity. The haughty Nordetanian Company is making a mistake by relying on Spanish rifles, and, knowing this, the miners trust the forces with which they are being threatened.

The leader in charge of this first transport is a pleasant officer, who, together with his friend José Luis, organized this convoy, which in Naya will link up with one from Dite. All in all, there are two hundred children from these two towns who are being saved from poverty by the noble city of Estuaria. The other provincial towns insist on exercising their charitable rights, and the mothers barely have enough energy to extend their arms with their malnourished young.

Perturbed, Santiago Estévez examines the rows of travelers; many of his long-suffering students form part of the famished group, which has been martyred with impunity. It was for the sake of these poor wretches that he had changed his life to become a teacher, asking for nothing but a room and some notebooks in return. Every week he used to visit a different section of town, trying—with abnegation and devotion—to stimulate the minds of these sufferers, whose huge, sad eyes look at him now with the distant and confused gaze of strangers.

During the past month, the strike has taken him away from his pupils, and he also has trouble recognizing them in their tattered clothes and frightful squalor; it is difficult to tell them apart, melted as they are into a single tortured expression. Trying to smile when Santiago addresses them, they bare their bloodless gums in a ghostly grimace. These unforgettable grins break the philosopher's heart, and he implores silently, "Oh, my Lord! You who by touching the mountains made them exhale smoke, carry these little ones on your wings and nourish them." And with benevolent fervor he goes from student to student.

The women, in whose eyes Estévez is a sage and a saint, cherish and venerate him. Knowing that he is tormented and surmising that he is praying, they are grateful to him for this hint of hope amid the bitter farewells. They even recall Jacobo Pmip, who was so successful in his pretense of being a friend to the poor that the mothers believe they are indebted to him for this transport. In its ingenuous optimism, this town is often won over with kind looks and smiles, unsuspecting of hypocrisy. But there is no sign anywhere of the con artist, and Santiago doesn't let the mention of his name perturb him or interrupt his soliloquy . . .

José Luis Garcillán looks taller and considerably thinner.
Dressed like a worker, he is everywhere, organizing the
groups and promising those who remain behind all they are
asking for in these last anxious moments. He will accompany
the children on behalf of the Syndicate and oversee their
placement with families. His youth and devotion edify the
miners, who admire and trust him.

As José Luis listens patiently to the mothers' thousand requests, he is being observed by the officer, who can hardly believe the incredible change his friend has undergone since
they first met in Madrid just a year ago, when José Luis was a
lighthearted and freewheeling journalist.

The president and the doctor also want to talk to José Luis
to instruct him about the procedures he should follow in the
capital to ensure the future transport of pregnant women and
nursing mothers; this generous offer, supported by all of Andalusia, must be carried out immediately.

"How can we save the rest of the children?" inquires Santiago anxiously. "These are only a few."

"Yes. The day after tomorrow, there will be another train-
load," Echea reassures him.

Putting his arm gently on Echea's shoulder, Garcillán promises him, "I'll pick up Anita to take her along." The father
shudders, "She shouldn't be among the first to be saved," and
then these words escape him against his will, "but I hope to
God she won't be the last."

Deep in thought, Echea seems gnawed by a secret restlessness. His friends assume that he is impatient to know about
Gabriel's heroic efforts, tortured, like them, by uncertainty.
And they talk about other happenings, commenting on the latest event: the decision of all Spanish office employees in the
region to respond to Leurc's unacceptable edict by joining in
the strike, siding with the miners, for the first time ever in this
social struggle. Cheered by this news, Aurelio notes, "This is
a magnificent triumph for us."

"And a good sign for the spirit now prevailing in Spain,"
adds Estévez.

"This calls for a celebration," proposes the doctor. "Today
I've earned a few pesetas; let's have a good dinner."

He looks around worriedly, like someone who has unveiled
a crime, and, feeling everyone's voracious eyes fixed on him

accusingly, he regrets his words as soon as he says them, "We'll eat a little better," he suggests innocently, "and, as always, I'll donate the rest to the Syndicate."

Alejandro Romero comes from a well-to-do family, who supports him loyally even though they think he is crazy. He accepts whatever they offer him, while continuing to dedicate himself to the workers' cause as a volunteer, and suffering together with them misfortune's rigorous penalties. Many of his colleagues—not courageous enough to work without pay—have emigrated, leaving this dreamer to his fasting. Even though his medicine cabinet is empty, and he cannot possibly attend to all the Syndicate's clients, he is bound to the organization by strong emotional ties. And he is also taken with Rosarito Garcillán, revering the admirable young girl with a silent and romantic love, which must remain unanswered. Because of this certainty, his devotion is angelic and Platonic, with a touch of fraternal affection. He was hoping that, amidst the terrible penury, Rosario could benefit directly from his money, but the funds allocated for the strikers are administered with impeccable honesty, and all donations are transformed into morsels for the Syndicate's sixty thousand needy members.

Unwilling to disrupt the harmony of that devout custom, Alejandro Romero feels the banknotes rustle in his pocket and decides proudly, like a knight of the ideal, to join his friends in fasting.

Half the afternoon has already disappeared beneath the luminescent clouds. A heavy pall weighs down the air; arching above the high slate peaks, the horizon is aflame, and the nearby red hills and black pits are plunged in timid silence. Stripped bare by rust and mold, the valley lies motionless, its open trenches resembling slash marks made by a gigantic sword.

Now that the minerals no longer tint the locomotive's ribbon, it has turned black from the slag that is used as gravel. Today it is the focus of nervous attention as the convoy sets out, carrying those children who were deemed the most at risk.

José Luis, standing next to the officer on the running board, cries out, "Long live Estuaria!" An enormous sigh answers him, drowning his cheerful voice; tears flow freely, and, in an instinctive farewell gesture, all arms are raised up to God.

Paying a spontaneous tribute, some of the soldiers salute the emigrants from the platform. Los Fresnos's priest, who has had to minister to so many dying in these last weeks, emerges from a corner, bares his head, and, approaching the tracks with solemn steps, blesses the train.

The Feudal Tower

Night is falling, and the western sky is steeped in liquid light and blood. No one knows who started the rumor that smoke is coming out of the pit called Berta. The news is received with skepticism, but people running to the inner valley and crossing Mesa de los Pinos to reach Vista Hermosa can see that the top of the pit is indeed enveloped in a mist that does not seem to be caused just by ground heat. Suddenly, a blue flame flickers briefly in that transparent and delicate cloud, surges, and turns as red as the sunset.

The evidence of fire is received with a prolonged and piercing shriek. Whirling tongues of fire engulf the surrounding space; the "red hero" is reborn and rises up rebelliously against the masters; set in motion by the avenging hand of a sphinxlike worker, the fire breathes, menaces, and mocks.

Don Martín Leurc's fury knows no bounds. Surrounded by a cortege of Nordetanos, the manager has been enjoying the early evening hours in the shady garden, when the proud spark flashes in front of his eyes as if ignited by lightning.

These days, neither children's laughter nor the silvery peal of feminine voices are heard in Vista Hermosa; the only women who are left in the elegant residential area have little to laugh about, having had to assume, like Miss Clara Ylevol and other governesses, the duties of housekeepers, maids, and cooks.

The rich ladies and their children have departed for fashionable beaches, escaping from the strike's insufferable inconveniences. They have not given up on their humanitarian projects or sociological campaigns, but these plans must be postponed for the fall, when the heat and the rabble's fever have subsided.

Only a sad and sorrowful lady and a blond girl, both dressed in black and sighing softly, stroll hand in hand through the gardens in the afternoon; Erecnis's widow and her little girl are waiting for the arrival of the ship that will take them from Estuaria to New York.

The gentlemen are spending their summer alone, involuntarily idle but well nourished thanks to the train, which also supplies them with some strike breakers, smuggled secretly into Vista Hermosa to carry out the most menial chores. These services do not extend beyond the seigniorial confines, and the other tasks fall to lower-ranking employees, who are forced to cart provisions, packages, trunks, and other luggage from the railroad station, a task they do quite well; the strikers watch them in amusement and conclude that Vista Hermosa's refined gentlemen must have been porters in their own country . . .

The manager, beside himself, orders categorically that the fire be extinguished immediately. Blinded by ire, he shouts and rages, and issues absurd commands that cannot be followed; he keeps asking angrily for Jacobo Pmip, eager to call him to account for this sinister event, so different from the spy's prophecies.

This pit, which cost three million pesetas and needed three years of work, is the Rehtron Company's great triumph amid Spain's rich mines and a source of gold for the invaders. Its foreign name provocatively emblazoned on the banner, Berta is the ornamental entryway to the mine and the Nordetanos' feudal tower in the Sierra Morena . . . It cannot be allowed to burn, no, absolutely not! But where in the world is Jacobo Pmip?

They summon him, but he does not appear; they search for him, but he cannot be found. "The earth must have swallowed him!" mutter the guards, while his kinsmen suspect that an act of treason on his part led him to flee.

Don Martín is already in the saddle of his white steed, spurring it on vehemently; fused into a single beast, horse and rider gallop furiously, unsure of their destination. In this moment, the manager, maddened by the excruciating brightness shining over his dark house in shameless defiance, would gladly give his life to be able to turn off that light. No other damage caused by the strike has wounded him so deeply or infuriated him so much. Leaping over fences like a madman, he crushes the flowers, already wilted from heat; in his wild race he brushes against the leaves, scorched by the August sun, which, instead of dropping, remain trembling on the hedges and rosebushes, the tamarinds, trees of heaven, and Judas trees.

On terraces and footpaths and in doorways, Vista Hermosa's other gentlemen come into view, to listen and wait, perturbed about this turn of events. The galloping hoofs reverberate through the kermes oaks, and after their echo dies down, utter stillness reigns again in the musty and muted park, asleep in the hot silence. Since the expensive mechanism that activates the park's fountains and lights was disconnected at the beginning of the strike, the waters' sweet musicality and the fountains' graceful babble have ceased. The thirsty roses fade before their buds open; whipped by the sun, the trees droop; and the manager's residence looks neglected and uninviting.

At last, the other bosses decide to follow Leurc's example; guards and soldiers are mobilized. The rescue equipment, however, does not function properly, and the technicians worry about not being able to prevent a catastrophe. Hastily, the capital is called for help.

Leurc's desperation increases with the advancing night hours. Debilitated and fatigued, he has returned on foot, without his hat or tie, looking as if he had been locked in combat with his horse, trailing behind him, bathed in sweat and missing its saddle.

And Vista Hermosa continues to face the harsh and wild Sombra Negra, whose devastated landscape is ablaze with a lurid fire and with the moon's yellow light. Comments drone like bees along the edges of the paths where groups of strikers are making their way. The president's promise has been fulfilled; there is a force that is more powerful than the enemy's arrogance: it is a miraculous will at the heart of the organization. Their premonition unveils the mysterious secret and converts it into a certainty: Gabriel Suárez! A thousand lips form his name with awe and devotion.

Anointed by sacred sacrifice, the miner's melancholy figure grows, reaching from the abyss to the peaks, filling hills and dales. They talk about him with the reverence reserved for the dead, remembering that he was a stranger to the mines, that he loved and suffered, and that he arrived after wandering all over Spain and beyond its frontiers. His image is surrounded by enigmas and mysteries, which increase the admiration he inspires. This hero had always lived among them like a worshipper of sadness, with a longing for the faraway and a yearning for love and liberty.

Although the people don't know his soul's secrets, they try to guess and understand them. And today Gabriel's name burns with passion in thousands of hearts, like another inextinguishable fire rising up over the masses, while night hammers the Rock of Ages.

THE PYRE

All that is known with certainty about the silent avenger is that his daughter was killed and that he has a wife; it is to her that all thoughts turn like incense, and all murmurs like prayers. Intuiting this heartfelt homage, Aurora asks and inquires; driven by anxiety and love, she makes a superhuman effort to climb the road blazed by the fire.

The midday luminosity flooding the landscape highlights Berta, enveloped in a cloud of smoke; the sun kindles the flames in the Sombra Negra's volcano. Burning like the sunlight, Aurora's feverish eyes reflect the mountain's ferocious tragedy. She doesn't know how long she has stood there, impervious to the heat, intractable, mute, and oblivious of the friends accompanying her.

"Let's leave!" pleads Dolores, lowering her pained voice.

And Estévez, gnawed by remorse, insists, "Let's leave."

She doesn't answer; with dreadful delectation, she watches the martyrdom of the rocks—naked, wounded, and burning—and the almost motionless smoke cloud, pierced by light, rising slowly skyward from the sacrificial pyre to dissolve in the sun.

Aurora gazes at the mountain's dark tunnels, which look like eyes, and for some time the young girl and the mountains stare at each other in horror. In the depths of her eyes, green like hope, there is only one question, "Will he return?" She knows that the countermine's floors are collapsing, that the loose earth, softened by water, keeps burying the connecting passageways, and that only a divine miracle can save Gabriel.

But she lets herself be swayed by the schoolmaster. "If he found his way in, he'll also be able to find his way out."

"Yes . . ."

The poor girl wants to be brave and have confidence; she smoothes her expression, takes heart, and leans gratefully on Dolores. With her tough constitution and sunny disposition, Dolores can withstand the fasting, and she has been a great support for Aurora in their shared household. Now she caresses Aurora's numb fingers with her maternal hands, while the three of them take the shortcut of a craggy Roman route to return to the city.

The town is quiet; the tents have been dismantled, most houses are empty, and others are asleep in the harsh midday heat and the prevailing lethargy. Aurora sighs, "What a sad sight! It is as if many nations had passed through here!"

"That's probably true," agrees Estévez, forcing a smile. "Yes, many nations have exploited us. Supposedly, in its early days this was once a verdant town called Our Lady of Río Tinto."

Aurora is afraid that she will start crying if she says anything; her senses are clouded with the smoke rising up from the pyre in the distance. And Dolores does her utmost to lessen her friend's affliction. With her sweetest Andalusian accent, she asks "Would you like us to start reciting the Lord's five-day prayer today?"

The girl shrugs her shoulders, then she nods affirmatively. She would like to drink from the fountain of immortal consolation, but she has never prayed! Santiago guesses this and is amazed by her angelic qualities; he knows her story, senses her aura of benevolence, and feels obligated to quench the desperate thirst of such a heart.

THE CHAIN

The realization that Gabriel was giving signs of life and vengeance in the depths of the trenches filled Aurelio with both joy and incredible misgivings; he was happy over the fulfillment of his just and equitable promise to the starving but afraid of losing a friend who was already being venerated as a martyr. But Aurelio's qualms were mitigated by the inkling that he would be held responsible for the fire in the pit, and would thus have the satisfaction of sacrificing himself as well. He went to see the sacred fire, imposing amid the mountains' majestic silence, and its rapturous glow infused his blood with renewed vigor. More convinced of his mission than ever, he returned to Nerva.

Overcoming the pain of human torments, he spends the night working on his daily report to Madrid's press and taking care of other urgent matters. Romero helps him until dawn, and seeing his friend so wakeful and pressed, he wonders on his way out, "From the way you're packing your things, it seems you're getting ready to emigrate."

"Perhaps," smiles the president with cheerful unaffectedness. And the doctor, taking it as a joke, goes to bed carefree.

Until the early morning, Echea continues writing in his office with the help of Enrique Salmerón, who, though less experienced than some of the other members, is very helpful and diligent. Echea informs Salmerón about some details known only to him concerning the administration of funds and hands him some important papers that he has just finished putting in order; then he tells him to get some rest.

Somewhat surprised, Salmerón stares at him and remarks, "You look like someone who has just written his last will!"

Again the president smiles. "No, it's just that during Garcillán's absence, you should be in charge of some things."

Dolores comes downstairs, thoughtfully bringing an infusion made from mountain herbs gathered in the high sierra together with an impressive stack of toasted bread. The drink is unsweetened, but the two men declare that it tastes very good as they sip it enthusiastically before Enrique retires.

Hearing footsteps upstairs, Aurelio asks to talk to Rosarito. She arrives with eager haste, worried about Aurora, who, hearing about the fire, wants to go to Dite. A little later, Santiago arrives from Ventoso, where both he and Felix Garcés had been able to get some sleep on their night off.

While upstairs plans are being made for the difficult excursion to Dite, Echea tells Rosarito, "We have to talk about the fire."

"We?"

"Yes, I expect they will come to arrest me."

"Oh!"

"I made a public oath, which is being fulfilled, and I want to vouch for it."

"With your freedom?"

"Probably."

They look at each other calmly, trying to conceal their inner desolation from each other. Hiding behind this forced feigning, Aurelio forecasts, "You'll be brave and your valor will encourage me; I need your help." It is not quite true because he is serene, almost glad, but he wants to comfort her. And the tone with which she responds is as harmonious and vibrant as the chords of a harp, "I'll be the way you'd like me to be!"

Their lips have never spoken of love, but a blithe tranquillity reigns in their hearts now that nothing stands in the way of their thoughts or prevents their eyes from telling each other the words they cannot speak. This good fortune is a balm in the bitter struggle of their lives, just as the certainty of their mutual passion is a boundless source of hope. To merit these blessings, Rosarito suffers her share of daily tribulations, just as Aurelio feels he has to pay for them with woes.

And in this hour, in which they feel at once grandiose and sad, strong and compassionate, they look at each other, gripped by the gloomy disquiet of separation. "Maybe they won't dare arrest you here among the strikers," hopes Rosarito, clinging to an optimistic possibility.

"They consider us completely powerless; you can see how they're defying us . . . they'll take the next opportunity."

"When?"

"Today."

"Are you sure?"

"I have a feeling."

"What if you fled?"

"No, they'd arrest someone else in my place, and I want to be responsible for my promise."

"Then, there is no hope?" asks Rosarito, trembling and ashen-faced, in a voice that is about to break with indescribable anguish.

Aurelio, deeply moved by this almost childish bereavement, tells his beloved many fervent and idealistic things: he'll be released soon; they'll win the horrendous battle against the employers' selfishness, using reason as their only weapon; they'll be able to take pride in defeating the invaders, and of raising the Spanish flag on the ruins of the feudal tower, on the peak of Salomón Hill, and over all the land in their dominion again, from Estuaria's canals to the rock jutting out at Land's End.

They are standing in the middle of the empty and resonant main office. Forgetting her chores, Rosarito lets herself be soothed by the Champion's warm and sonorous tones; to be part of such an undertaking and carry out those lofty goals in the company of the man she loves seems to her the height of sublime happiness. Noticing that he has her confidence, Aurelio turns to more mundane concerns. He mentions Anita tenderly, and Rosarito says mournfully, "They'll take her away from me. José Luis wants her to leave as soon as possible."

"Maybe that won't be necessary; I have some other solutions in mind, but if necessary . . ."

"Then I'll let her go," promises Rosarito, calming his paternal fears, and she adds with exemplary fortitude, "My brother and I will stay here, representing you and keeping the organization going with our remaining friends."

"Thank you, thank you! I knew I could count on you. The universal fire of the spirit must be kept alive in those hearts, and you're the ideal person to make sure that the flame isn't extinguished."

Rosarito looks more desirable than ever to him. He adores her like this, in the throes of a divine sacrifice for love's sake, for him, and for all those who suffer persecution in the name of justice. Yet his manly egotism is bruised by his holy madness of self-destruction. He would like to spare her any suffering, console her, and comfort her with worldly goods. She submerges her splendid eyes in his and, guessing his melancholy thoughts, reassures him firmly, "I'm very resilient."

"In spirit."

"And also in body. Nothing can happen to me, because hardship doesn't kill if it's sweetened by precious promises."

"That's true," he mumbles aggrieved, remembering Anita's mother. Convincing himself that Rosario has the will to survive, he regains his calm. He gives her some advice concerning the correspondence with foreign labor unions, which she should maintain. They are discussing Aurora with brotherly concern when Dolores comes for Rosarito. The young girl goes to take care of the children, while Aurelio writes some more letters, listening to Rosario's comings and goings and to his daughter's tiny footsteps upstairs.

The city is hot and silent, and the Champion, sleepy and exhausted, is resting his head on the desk. Suddenly, some loud footsteps are heard in the street, followed by urgent knocks on the door.

"It's the Civil Guard," Aurelio thinks to himself, alert and assured. He opens the door and faces the two policemen, who are asking for him. One of them says deliberately, "We've come to arrest you."

"I know. Don't make any noise and give me a moment."

"If you want to pick up something . . ."

"No, I have to say goodbye."

He goes upstairs and finds Rosario waiting anxiously in the hall, "So soon?"

"Yes!"

"Aurelio!"

He stretches his hands out to her with a vigorous gesture and bends down to kiss his daughter, who has walked over to them slowly.

"Can't you wait even one minute?"

"For what?"

"You're right!"

With solemn and silent devotion, they exchange a profound gaze.

"Goodbye!"

"Goodbye!"

From the threshold, Aurelio turns back several times to look at Rosario and the little girl, still standing on the landing.

Outside, the policemen tell him, with visible unease, that they have orders to handcuff him. Pale and glum, he wants to protest, but controlling himself, he remarks, "So you're honoring me with a military decoration," as he offers them his wrists haughtily.

Then he inquires where they are going. "To the train station." He is being taken on a special train, like the one carrying the wounded, and, to avoid any turmoil, they have chosen the lunch hour, when the city is quiet and deserted.

As usual, Aurelio is bareheaded, and he walks with a springy step. Standing on her balcony, her arms around Anita,

Rosarito observes him with a frozen and impenetrable stare. He senses her gaze, and, filled with gratitude, he looks up from the street before turning the corner. His solitary silhouette is etched against the sky, and his forehead seems to touch the sun . . .

When Aurora and her friends return from town, an unexpected and mysterious train pulls out of Nerva, headed for Estuaria. Rosarito Garcillán is still gazing at the blue background where the prisoner left his imprint. The expression of her shiny, deep-set eyes is veiled; she is the divine keeper of the eternal hearth's sacred flame. But this modern maiden, who, like the vestal virgins of antiquity, wears her hair short, is holding a little girl lovingly in her arms.

DEATH WATCH

The city of the miners is almost deserted. After Aurelio Echea's arrest, as swift and surprising as an abduction, the miners continue to flee in orderly and peaceful fashion, some to Portugal, many to Estuaria or Cádiz, to immigrate to the Americas. Numerous women and children have been rescued, diminishing the swarm of needy among whom the few remaining inhabitants have to divide misery's harvest.

There is no word about Gabriel, and Aurora continues to wait for him. Smoke still rises from the mouth of the main pit, glowing in the night with hidden and stubborn cinders. The young girl regards the glimmer of ashes as the promise of a heart's palpitations; she spends her days in silence, straining to hear, and, like a listening post, her window waits for some news or a sign.

Did Gabriel die a terrible and lonely death in the collapsed mine, or did he manage to escape into the light, break through the mountain chain, and save himself at sea? During her less cruel hours, Aurora harbors this hope, having learned by rote like a schoolgirl Santiago's oracle of divine faith. Estévez would like nothing better than to ignite her belief in immortality and alleviate her suffering with the certainty of a transcendent destiny.

"We have to live in order to become worthy," he tells her, and in an attempt to prepare her for a confirmation of her misfortune, he adds, "Death is a ford between two worlds, but we are immortal in God, who never dies." Stirred, Aurora absorbs these lessons, which soothe her soul. Rosarito helps her to trust and have faith, enabling her to endure her nightmarish days with less agonizing exasperation.

Not long ago, along a penitential path, one of the innumerable ones she has had to walk, she held up her daughter, eager for her to cross heaven's threshold. Today she feels that, thanks to a superhuman effort, she has achieved much, but her body is so weary that she can barely lift up this baby who is not her own.

But she doesn't want to abandon the little stranger. With a sweet and wan smile, she lets her friends take care of her; though inconsolable, she agrees to go on living and does not refuse the humble sustenance left by the émigrés for the hungry who stay behind. The committee distributes the donations, which keep trickling into the organization's coffers, with relative efficiency among the inhabitants. Private charity is no longer as imperative, and the strains of sharing have been eased. Now that fewer people are left, Alejandro Romero, Santiago Estévez, and José Luis and Rosario Garcillán can enjoy a respite from hunger, and Anita does not have to chew the palmetto dates, fooled with the fib that they taste like candy . . .

Today Santiago and José Luis are setting out for Estuaria; they will go to Niebla on foot and there take the early morning train from Sevilla. After talking to Aurelio, they may continue to Madrid, because the devastation of the towns hit by the strike is so complete that national attention and support are required, which must be organized on the other side of these mountains.

Mid-afternoon, the travelers depart, intending to walk all night and prepared to exercise however much patience is necessary. Rosario is pleased because they are taking greetings from her to the prisoner, and Aurora is affected by their departure, as she is by any event. Her happiness in shambles, she lives in a state of agitation, and with a keen sense of desperation and abandonment, which Estévez strives to conquer.

He urges her to trust and believe, and his empathy for her is mixed with an exalted admiration. Aurora's black vulcanite ring upsets him, making him think, "She's married to Death."

A mysterious fascination with the funereal band on her white hand haunts him; never has he seen such a sad bride, nor has he ever worried so much about any woman . . .

Following the black edge of the railroad tracks, the pilgrims reach the mine's limits amid the melted furnaces and corroded puddles of the cementation, whose ruptured irrigation ditch is letting its veins bleed their red poison along the paths. Walking along narrow ravines and glens, they leave behind the countryside's grim ruins, the deserted towns and gaping cemeteries, as well as death, loneliness, and perdition . . .

The heavy granite masses blend in with the sun-scorched lands. The landscape seems to frighten itself with its ferocious stillness, like the silence of the tombs; a flapping of wings would be audible here.

But suddenly, near the precipice, a powerful voice rises up, sputtering and hissing: the river, blinded by metals, is rushing down from the mountains. Emerging from the abyss of wealth and destruction, the Saquia carries grey silver, blue copper, reddish sulfur, and iron, whose sparks glitter amidst the pale foam.

Some women are sitting on the riverbank, above the venomous red rust. "There's a group of emigrants," Estévez points out to his friend. One of the women stands up and greets them politely.

"Carmen!" José Luis calls out, overjoyed. "Carmelita! I always meet you near dangerous shores. Where are you going?"

"To Estuaria, with my friends."

Santiago recognizes the other young women, some of them married, others single, but all marked by the same hardship. Carmen says with a touch of pride, "We're going to work, packing fruit that is to be transported far from Spain on trains and boats." She accompanies her words with a sweeping gesture, as if trying to encompass the whole wide world.

José Luis is surprised to see her less gaunt and haggard than the other poor women; a luminous magic protects her incredible beauty, barely affected by adversity. And the poet imagines her surrounded by the colors and perfumes of the exquisite merchandise, wrapping the delicate fruit in silky paper and placing it in containers.

In the west, the sun gazes at the night with a bloodshot eye. The caravan moves slowly along the banks, bending down to see the fleeting river. Carmen falls back to be close to José Luis. "I haven't seen you in a long time," he says pleasantly.

"Yes, I've stayed at home; I had no energy and things weren't going well for me." She doesn't want to admit that she is trying to avoid Aurora, feeling burdened by the terrible secret of Nena's assassination.

"Well, you look really lovely for someone who's had such a difficult time."

"Because I've eaten," confesses Carmen, and, lowering her voice, she adds darkly, "I think my mother stole food for me."

The young man looks at her with lively interest, seeing her become more animated and eager to talk. Her crystalline voice mingles with the current's rumble, joining other murmurs. Each mountain stream has a different sound; the rivulets and brooks sigh distinctly, carried along the rocky beds by maternal waters and bubbling with their impure treasure, which eats away at the shores and taints the sea.

José Luis listens with delight to Carmen's confidences, and noting that she is growing weary, he asks her, "Are you tired?"

"No."

"Would you like to give me your hand?"

"Yes."

"Lean on me."

Her eyes light up with hope. "Is there a place somewhere," she thinks to herself, "where it's possible to work and love with joy, and to live without hate or pain?"

Estévez smiles at the lovely pair, contemplating them with satisfaction. Then the philosopher turns his pristine thoughts to the distant mine's dark shadow, where Love, sublime in its immortality, remains poised on the rock of the world, watching Death . . .

Selected Bibliography

EDITIONS OF *EL METAL DE LOS MUERTOS*

El metal de los muertos. Madrid: Gil-Blas, 1920.

El metal de los muertos. Madrid: Renacimiento, 1920.

El metal de los muertos. Madrid: Compañía Ibero-Americana de Publicaciones, S.A., 1930.

El metal de los muertos. Madrid: Ediciones Afrodisio Aguado, 1941.

El metal de los muertos. Buenos Aires: Editorial Juventud Argentina, 1945.

El metal de los muertos. In *Obras completas de Concha Espina*, 1. Madrid: Ediciones Fax, 1955 [reprinted 1970 and 1972].

El metal de los muertos. Madrid: Novelas y Cuentos, 1969.

El metal de los muertos. Madrid: Editorial Magisterio Español, 1969 [reprinted 1978].

El metal de los muertos. Edited by Antonio Garnica and Antonio Rioja Bolaños. Huelva: Fundación Rio Tinto y Universidad de Huelva, 1996.

TRANSLATIONS OF *EL METAL DE LOS MUERTOS*

German

Das Metall der Toten. Translated by Felicia Pauselius. Berlin: W. I. Mörlin, 1922.

Russian

Metall miertoef. Translated by T. N. Guierssienchtien. Leningrad: Meslin, [?].

Swedish

De dödas metall. Translated by Reigin Fridholm. Stockholm: Albert Bonniers Forlag, 1925.

OTHER WORKS BY CONCHA ESPINA

First published: 1904–1919

Mis flores [poems]. Valladolid: La Libertad, 1904.
Mujeres del Quijote. Madrid, A. López Del Arco, 1905.
La niña de Luzmela. Madrid: Renacimiento, 1916.
La ronda de los galanes. Sevilla: Imp. Editorial Católica Española, S.A., 1939.
Despertar para morir. Madrid: Renacimiento, 1910.
Agua de nieve. Madrid: Renacimiento, 1911.
Al amor de las estrellas. Madrid: Renacimiento, 1916.
La esfinge maragata. Madrid: Imprenta de M. Albero, 1920.
La rosa de los vientos. Madrid: Renacimiento, 1923.
Ruecas de marfil. Madrid: Editorial Pueyo, 1919.
Talín y otros cuentos. Edited by S. L. Millard Rosenberg and M. A. Zeitlin. New York: A. A. Knopf, 1927.
El jayón: drama en tres actos. Madrid, Renacimiento, 1919.
El príncipe del cantar. Toulouse: Editorial Figarola Maurin, 1928.

First published: 1920–1929

Pastorelas. Madrid: Gil-Blas, 1920.
Dulce nombre. Madrid: Ediciones Afrodisio Aguado, 1941.
Cumbres al sol. Madrid: Prensa Gráfica, 1922.
Cuentos. Madrid: Renacimiento, 1922.
Simientes. Madrid: V. H. Sanz Calleja, 1922.
El cáliz rojo. Madrid: Renacimiento, 1923.
El secreto de un disfraz. Madrid: Prensa Gráfica, 1924.
Tierras del aquilón. Madrid: Renacimiento, 1924.
Cura del amor. [?]
Altar mayor. Madrid, Renacimiento, 1926.
Las niñas desaparecidas. Madrid: Renacimiento, 1927.
Llama de cera. Madrid: Renacimiento, 1931.
La virgen prudente. Madrid: Renacimiento, 1929.
Aurora de España. Madrid: Biblioteca Nueva, 1955.
El goce de robar. Madrid: Prensa Moderna, 1928.
Concha Espina. De su vida. De su obra literaria al través de la crítica universal. Madrid: Renacimiento, 1928.
Huerto de rosas. Madrid: Editorial Atlántida, 1929.
Marcha nupcial. Madrid: Editorial Atlántida, 1929.

First published: 1930–1939

Copa de horizontes. Madrid: Compañía Ibero-Americana de Publicaciones, S.A., 1930.

Siete rayos de sol. Madrid: Renacimiento, 1930.

El hermano Caín. Madrid: Editorial Atlántida, 1931.

Singladuras. Madrid: Compañía Ibero-Americana de Publicaciones, S.A., 1932.

Candelabro. Madrid: Hernando, 1933.

Entre la noche y el mar. Madrid: Hernando, 1933.

Flor de ayer. Madrid: Espasa-Calpe, 1934.

Retaguardia. Madrid: Renacimiento, 1939.

Casilda de Toledo. Madrid: Biblioteca Nueva, 1940.

Esclavitud y libertad: Diario de una prisionera. Valladolid: Ediciones Reconquista, 1938.

Luna roja. Valladolid: Librería Santarén, 1939.

El desierto rubio. [?] 1938.

Alas invencibles. Burgos: Imprenta Aldecoa, S.A., 1938.

La ronda de los galanes. Sevilla, Imp. Editorial Católica Española, S. A., 1939.

Princesas del martirio. Barcelona: Gustavo Gili, 1940.

First published: 1940–1955

La tiniebla encendida. [?]

El fraile menor. Madrid: Ediciones Afrodisio Aguado, 1942.

Moneda blanca. Madrid: Afrodisio Aguado, 1942.

La otra. [play] [?]

La segunda mies. Madrid: Afrodisio Aguado, 1943.

Victoria en América. Madrid: Editora Nacional, 1944.

El más fuerte. Madrid: M. Aguilar, 1947.

Un valle en el mar. Barcelona: Editorial Exito, 1952.

De Antonio Machado a su grande y secreto amor. Madrid: Distribución Exclusiva Lifesa, 1950.

Una novela de amor. Madrid: 1953.

Obras completas de Concha Espina. 2 volumes. Madrid: Ediciones Fax, 1955 [reprinted 1970 and 1972].

OTHER WORKS BY CONCHA ESPINA IN TRANSLATION

Czech

Cekala psem na tebe. Prague: Katolinky Literátny Klub, [?].

Dutch

El Jayón. Translated by J. Chabot. The Hague: [?].

English

Mariflor. Translated by Frances Douglas. New York: Macmillan, 1924.
The Red Beacon. Translated by Frances Douglas. New York, London: D. Appleton and Company, 1924.
The Woman and the Sea. Translated by Terrell Louise Tatum. London: Jarrolds, 1935.

French

La rose des vents. Translated by L. Varende. Paris: Plon, 1949.
Le donjon de Luzmela. Translated by Noël Domenge. Paris: Hachette, 1932.
Mariflor. Translated by Théophile Barrère. Paris: [?].

German

Die Sphinx der Maragatos. Translated by Felicia Pauselius. Berlin: W. I. Mörlin, 1924.
Sechs Novellen. Translated by Paula Saatman. Berlin: Otto Müller, 1942.

Italian

Altar maggiore. Translated by Maria Bartolomi. Rome: Instituto Cristóforo Colombo, 1927.
Donne del Don Chisciotte. Translated by Gilberto Beccari. Florence: Fratelli Carabba, [?].
Il trovatello. Translated by Giovanni Calabritto. Florence: Fratelli Carabba, 1920.
Le fanciulle scomparse. Translated by Gasparetti. Rome: Instituto Cristóforo Colombo, 1928.
La sfinge maragata. Translated by Gerolamo Bottoni. Milan: Garzanti, 1943.

Polish

Dulce nombre. Translated by Tadeus Jaknbovicz. Warsaw: [?].

Portuguese

La llama de cera. Translated by Eduardo Malta. Lisbon, [?].

Russian

Sfinks maragataski. Translated by T. N. Guierssienchtien. Leningrad: Meslin, [?].

Swedish

Mariflor, en bok om maragata folket. Translated by Reigin Fridholm. Stockholm: Wahlström-Widstrand, 1929.

WORKS ABOUT CONCHA ESPINA

Agawu Kabkraba, Yaw. "Reinventing Identity: Class, Gender, and Nationalism in Concha Espina's *Retaguardia.*" *Romance Notes* 36: 2 (1996): 167–79.

Ambía, Isabel de. "Concha Espina." *Cuadernos de Literatura Contemporánea* 1 (1942): 7–8.

Andrade Coello, Alejandro. *Mujeres de España: La condesa Emilia Pardo Bazán, doña Concepción Arenal, doña Concha Espina.* Quito: Imprenta Ecuador, 1937.

Bazán de Cámara, Rosa. *Tragedias y almas.* Buenos Aires: Editorial El Inca, 1929.

Behn, Irene. "La obra de Concha Espina." *Cuadernos de Literatura Contemporánea* 1 (1942): 9–17.

Benaim Lasry, Anita. *El judío como héroe de la novela: Humanización del personaje judío en algunas novelas españolas de los siglos XIX y XX.* Madrid: Centro de Estudios Judeo-Cristianos, 1980.

Berges, Consuelo. "El 'caso' Concha Espina." *Insula* 115 (1955): 1, 8.

———. *Escalas.* Buenos Aires: Talleres Gráficos, 1930.

Bernáldez, José María. "Concha Espina." *Razón y Fe* 7–8 (1955): 71–8.

Boussagol, G. "*El cáliz rojo y Tierras del aquilón.*" *Bulletin Hispanique* 11 (1925): 190–92.

———. "Madame Concha Espina." *Bulletin Hispanique* (1923): 149–67.

Boyd, Ernest. *Studies from Ten Literatures.* New York: Charles Scribner and Sons, 1927.

Bretz, Mary Lee. *Concha Espina.* Boston: Twayne Publishers, 1980.

———. "The Theater of Emilia Pardo Bazán and Concha Espina." *Estreno* 10: 2 (1984): 43–5.

Brunet, Domingo. *Testas hispanas: Estudios literarios.* Buenos Aires: Talleres Gráficos Argentinos L. J. Rosso y Cía., 1926.

Canales, Alicia. *Concha Espina.* Madrid: E.P.E.S.A., 1974.

Cano, Juan. "La mujer en la novela de Concha Espina." *Hispania* 22 (1939): 51–60.

Cansinos Assens, Rafael. *Literaturas del Norte: La obra de Concha Espina.* Madrid: G. Hernández y G. Sáez, 1924.

———. "La obsesión del Nobel." *Insula* 38: 444–5 (1983): 27–8.

Cantabria 70 (1929). [Special issue devoted to Concha Espina.]

Clarke, Anthony H. "Naturaleza sin paisaje: Un aspecto desatendido del arte descriptivo de las primeras novelas de Concha Espina." *Boletín de la Biblioteca de Menéndez Pelayo* 45 (1969): 35–46.

Cuadernos de Literatura Contemporánea 1 (1942). [Special issue devoted to Concha Espina.]

Dendle, Brian John. "Aportación a la bibliografía de Concha Espina: Su obra periodística en ABC de Sevilla, 1937–39." *Boletín de la Biblioteca de Menéndez Pelayo* 67 (1991): 367–71.

———. "La novela española de tesis religiosa: De Unamuno a Miró." *Anales de Filología Hispánica* 4 (1988–89): 15–26.

———. La novela española de tesis religiosa: De Unamuno a Miró. Ph.D. diss. University of Michigan, 1993.

———. "Solar Imagery in Three Novels of Concha Espina," *Anales de la Literatura Española Contemporánea* 22: 2 (1997): 199–209.

Diego, Gerardo. *Centenario de Concha Espina.* Santander: Instituto Cultural de Cantabria, 1970.

———. "Homenaje a Concha Espina." *Boletín de la Biblioteca de Menéndez Pelayo* 45 (1969): 15–33.

———. "Poesía y novela de Concha Espina." *Insula* 7 (1955): 1–8.

Domínguez, María Alicia. "Concha Espina y la mujer novelista." *Nosotros* 10 (1929): 323–41.

Douglas, Frances. "Concha Espina: A New Star Ascendant." *Hispania* 7 (1924): 111–20.

———. "Fresh Laurels for Concha Espina." *Hispania* 8 (1925): 192–93.

———. "Recent Works by Concha Espina." *Hispania* 5 (1923): 185–87.

Entrambasaguas, Joaquín de, editor. "Concha Espina." *Las mejores novelas contemporáneas*, 4: 1195–259. Barcelona: Planeta, 1959.

Fría Lagoni, Mauro. *Concha Espina y sus críticos.* Toulouse: Editorial Figarola Maurin, 1929.

Fucelli, Antonietta. *Alla ricerca di una idendità letteraria: vita e romanzi di Concha Espina.* Naples: Edizioni Scientifiche Italiane, 1986.

Garbini, Carla María. "Concha Espina." *Convivium: Filosofía, Psicología, Humanidades* 35 (1967): 354–63.

García de Enterría, María Cruz. "Unas cartas de Concha Espina." *Boletín de la Biblioteca de Menéndez Pelayo* 43 (1967): 283–306.

García Nieto, José. "Una novela de Concha Espina." *Cuadernos de Literatura* 5–6 (1947): 499.

Hierro, José. "Concha Espina." *Revista de Literatura* 7–9 (1955): 100–03.

Jato, Monica. "*Retaguardia* y *Diario de una prisionera*, de Concha Espina: Novela autobiográfica o diario novelado?" *Letras Peninsulares*, 12: 2–3 (Fall–Winter 1999–2000), 437–54.

Johnson, Roberta. "Don Quixote, Gender, and Early Twentieth Century Spanish Narrative." *Letras Peninsulares* 9: 1 (1996): 33–47.

Kirkpatrick, Judith. "Concha Espina: Giros ideológicos y la novela de la mujer." *Hispanic Journal* 17: 1 (1996): 129–39.

———. "From Male Text to Female Community: Concha Espina's *La esfinge maragata*." *Hispania* 78: 3 (1995): 262–71.

———. Redefining Male Tradition: Novels by Early Twentieth-Century Spanish Women Writers. Ph.D. diss. University of Michigan, 1993.

Lavergne, Gérard. "Concha Espina et le monde noir: A propos d'un texte oublié." *Annales de la Faculté des Lettres et Sciences Humaines* 2 (1972), 67–78.

———. *Vida y obra de Concha Espina*. Translated by Irene Gambra. Madrid: Fundación Universitaria Española, 1986.

Lumen 5 (1930). [Special issue dedicated to Concha Espina.]

Marquina, Eduardo. *Biografía literaria de Concha Espina*. Madrid: Gráfica Informaciones, 1940.

Martínez, Graciano. "La labor literaria de Concha Espina." *España y América* 4: 6 (1921): 161–73, 251–65, 411–9.

Martínez Cachero, José M. "Cuatro novelas españolas 'de' y 'en' la guerra civil." *Bulletin Hispanique* 85: 3–4 (1983): 281–98.

Maza, Josefina de la. *Vida de mi madre, Concha Espina*. Alcoy: Editorial Marfil, 1957.

Menéndez Pelayo, Enrique. "Prólogo a *Mis Flores*, de Concha Espina." Valladolid: La Libertad, 1904.

Moore, Roger. "The Role of the Netigua in *La niña de Luzmela*." *International Fiction Review* 7 (1980): 24–8.

Mullor Heymann, Montserrat. "'General y Señor: Yo te bendigo:' Concha Espina y las escritoras partidarias de Franco." In *Vencer no es convencer: Literatura e ideología del fascismo español*, edited by Albert Mechthild. Frankfurt: Vervuert, 1998.

Nora, Eugenio de. *La novela social contemporánea*. Madrid: Gredos, 1958.

Puente, A. "Concha Espina y Matilde de la Torre." *El Cantábrico* (27 March 1930): 4.

Rojas Auda, Elizabeth. *Visión y ceguera de Concha Espina: Su obra comprometida*. Madrid: Editorial Pliegos, 1998.

Rosenberg, Millard S. L. "Concha Espina." *Hispania* 11 (1927): 321–29.

———. "Concha Espina: Poet-Novelist of the Montaña." *Modern Language Forum* 4 (1933): 76–81.

Sainz de la Maza y de la Serna, Paloma. "El tono menor." *Boletín de la Biblioteca de Menéndez Pelayo* 45 (1969): 3–33.

Smith, Charles Wesley. Concha Espina and her Women Characters. Ph.D. diss. George Peabody College for Teachers, 1933.

Swain, James. "A Visit to Concha Espina at Luzmela." *Hispania* 12 (1934): 335–40.

Tejerina, Belén, ed. "Correspondencia entre Concha Espina y Santiago Ramón y Cajal." *Quaderni del Dipartamento di Linguistica* 3: 2 (1986): 139–51.

Ugarte, Michael. "The Fascist Narrative of Concha Espina." *Arizona Journal of Hispanic Cultural Studies* 1 (1997): 97–114.

Valle, A. "Concha Espina, *Retaguardia*." *Razón y Fe* 6 (1938): 222–24.

Vega, Daniel. *Costumbres nuevas y pecados viejos: dintel de Concha Espina.* Madrid: Paulinas, 1958.

Vega Pico, Juan. "Viaje a Concha Espina." *Blanco y Negro* (7 June 1979): 19–28.